The Heights of Zervos

Colin Forbes served with the British Army during the war, mostly in the Mediterranean zone. After 1946 he had various occupations before writing his first book in 1965, and within two years of its publication he left the business world to become a full-time writer. His books have been translated into ten languages and all have been published in the United States as well as in Britain.

His main interest apart from writing is foreign travel and this has taken him to most West European countries. Married to a Scots-Canadian, he has one daughter.

Also by
Colin Forbes in Pan Books

Colin Forbes
The Heights of Zervos

revised edition
Pan Books in association with Collins

First published 1970 by William Collins Sons & Co Ltd
This revised edition published 1972 by Pan Books Ltd,
Cavaye Place, London SW10 9PG
in association with William Collins Sons & Co Ltd
19 18
© Colin Forbes 1970, 1972
ISBN 0 330 23324 6
Printed in Great Britain by
Richard Clay (The Chaucer Press) Ltd, Bungay, Suffolk

Author's Note

I wish to record my thanks to Mr Michael Willis of the
Imperial War Museum for his invaluable technical
assistance.

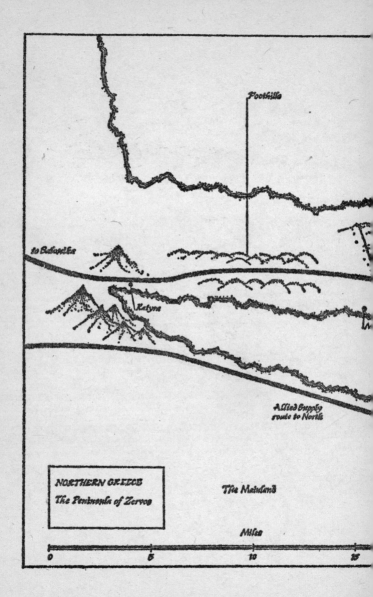

Foothills

to Salonika

Katyra

Allied Supply
route to North

NORTHERN GREECE
The Peninsula of Zervos

The Mainland

Miles

0   5   10   15

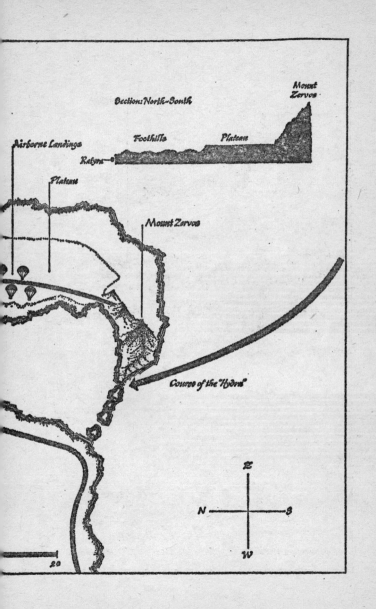

Section: North-South

Mount
Zervos

Foothills

Plateau

Ralyra

Airborne Landings

Plateau

Mount Zervos

Course of the "Hydra"

N — S

Z

W

20

CHAPTER ONE

Thursday, April 3, 1941

Less than ten minutes to zero, to detonation point, Macomber, lying on his stomach along the top of the oil tanker wagon, listened to the German patrol closing in round the Bucharest railyard. His escape route was blocked, his body chilled to the bone by the snow which drifted down through the night, and the frightening barks of the Alsatian dogs assaulted his ears, a sound punctuated by orders rapped out in German. 'Watch the wire ... At the first sign of movement open fire ... Gunther, take the signal-box – you can see what's happening from up there ...'

It was the third night of April and Rumania was still gripped by winter, still showed no inkling of spring on the way, still lay numbed under the icy wind which flowed from the east, from the Russian steppes and Siberia beyond. The insidious cold of 2 AM was penetrating Macomber's leather coat as he remained sprawled over the curve of the tanker, not daring to flex even a gloved finger as a German soldier walked beside the track below, and the crunch of boots breaking the crusted snow came up to the trapped Scot like the sound of twigs snapping.

The sub-zero temperature, the realization that arms, legs, feet were gradually losing all feeling, the trudge of marching troops below the wagon – these were the least of his worries when he remembered what was supporting his precariously poised body. He was lying on top of several thousand gallons of refined aviation spirit, petrol already bound for the Luftwaffe even though the Wehrmacht had occupied Rumania only recently, and a ten-kilogram composite demolition charge was attached under the belly of this huge tanker. The time fuse he had set was ticking down to zero, synchronized with other charges spaced out along the petrol train. And now the patrol had arrived and was checking for an intruder, searching for a saboteur – although perhaps sabotage had not yet entered their minds as they systematically surrounded the petrol train.

The snow, damp and paralysingly cold, was building up over his exposed neck, forming an icy collar where his woollen scarf parted company with his bare skin, but he remained perfectly motionless, thankful that his head at least was protected by the soft hat squashed over his brow. There's too damned much of me for this concealment game, he was thinking. Over six feet tall, over fourteen stone in weight, there was far too much of him, but he dismissed the thought as he stared at the illuminated hands of his watch, a watch strapped to the inside of his wrist as a precaution against the phosphorescent face betraying his position. Eight minutes to zero. Eight minutes before the charges detonated – and the tankers detonated seconds later – turning the railyard into a flaming furnace, a furnace which would cremate Ian Macomber. And there was yet a further hazard which made it impossible for him to protect himself against the elements which were slowly embalming him with a covering of freezing snow – as though to prepare his body for the imminent cremation. Ice had formed over the metal surface of the cylindrical tanker, ice which would send him slithering down into the path of the searching patrol if he altered his position by so much as a centimetre. So he lay still as a dead man while he watched a field-grey figure pass under a lamp close to the wire, mount the steps to the signal-box and enter the stilt-legged structure which overlooked the petrol train.

The lamp was hooded against direct observation from aircraft flying overhead, as were all the lamps inside the yard – hooded to avoid giving guidance to Allied planes which might appear on their way to bomb the vital oil-fields at Ploesti. Not that Macomber was expecting an RAF raid – the chronic shortage of bombers, the lack even of a machine which could fly the distance, guaranteed the Germans the safety of their newly acquired oil reserves – which made the sabotaging of oil for Germany vital. More footsteps crunched in the snow and then stopped immediately below where Macomber lay. His muscles tensed involuntarily and then relaxed. The metal ladder attached to the tanker's side ended a few inches beyond his head where the final rung rested close to the huge cap concealing him. Was someone coming up the ladder to investigate? His brain was still wrestling with this contingency when it received a further shock: something metallic clanged against a wheel. The demolition charge was hidden behind the front wheel. Christ, they'd found it!

'Get under the wagon – cross to the other side and wait there!' The voice spoke in German, a language Macomber understood and spoke fluently. An NCO issuing an order to a soldier – so there were two of them standing not fifteen feet below him. The voice continued, harsh and keyed up by the sub-zero temperature. 'If he runs for it, he'll run for the wire. I'm posting men the whole length of the train...' So they knew someone was inside the railyard. Macomber blinked as a snow flurry percolated under his hat and clouded his eyes; fearful lest the snow should begin to freeze his eyelids, he blinked several times while he waited for the soldier to crawl under the tanker. He would, of course, find the demolition charge. At least there was little sign of activity from the signal-box where he could see two shadowed figures under a blue light behind the windows – Gunther was checking with the signalman presumably. Feet crunched through the snow again, were swallowed up quickly as the NCO continued his march to post more men along the train – men who would inevitably close the door to escape. Not that he had a chance in hell of covering the hundred yards which would take him to the hole in the wire where he had cut his way through, and the wire-cutters in his pocket were now so much dead weight; with the place so well covered he could never hope to cut a fresh hole before they spotted him. He heard a fresh sound from below, the rasp of metal against the tanker as the soldier began clambering under the wagon. A clumsy Jerry, this one. Perhaps a stupid one, too, but not stupid enough to miss seeing the charge...

More scrabbling noises, hurrying noises from under the tanker. The German didn't like passing over the track in case the train started moving. An illogical fear since the wagons would never be moved during the search, but Macomber understood the reaction and had experienced it himself. Wondering whether he would ever be able to stir again, Macomber lay motionless and waited for the noises to stop suddenly, which would warn him that the charge had been found. And then he would wait again, but only briefly before the soldier's shout announced his lethal discovery. The scrabbling sounds ceased and Macomber held his breath, waiting for the shout, but he heard only a wheezing cough and a shuffle of frozen feet. The damned fool had missed seeing it, thank God. He was now standing on the other side of the tanker, the side nearest the signal-box – which put him between Macomber and the wire. The Scot checked his watch. Five minutes to zero.

The uncanny silence of winter's darkness descended on the railyard once more. The dogs had been taken farther up the line, the sound of feet crunching through the snow had ceased, and the wind was dropping. The stage was set, the Wehrmacht were in position, and now it only remained for Macomber's nerve to break, for him to be apprehended when he climbed down the small ladder and ended his career by the tracks of a desolate junction few people had ever heard of. As the snow fell more slowly the silence was so complete he heard in the distance coals going down the iron hopper in the eastern railyard. The silence was broken by the sound of a window opening in the signal-box, opening with a fracturing crack as ice on the ledge shattered. Gunther leaned out of the window and stared directly at the snow-shrouded hump on top of the last petrol wagon.

Macomber stared back at Gunther's silhouette, moving only his eyes to take in this new source of danger. He was boxed in: observed from a distance and trapped by the soldier below. His eyes swivelled back to his watch. Four minutes to zero and still no way out, not even the ghost of a diversion he could take advantage of. It was his swansong as a British saboteur, the end of his dangerous passage down through the Balkans, a trail not only blazed by the series of devastating explosions which had destroyed vast quantities of strategic war materials – but also a trail which the German Abwehr Intelligence service had followed, often only one step behind him. He weighed up his chances.

With a great deal of luck the Luger in his coat pocket would eliminate the soldier below the wagon, but then there was the German in the signal-box who had apparently noticed nothing amiss, who had left the window while he talked to the signal-man again; there was the wire fence he could never hope to climb; and there was the line of Wehrmacht troops posted along the train with instructions to watch that wire, to shoot on sight. His mind raced, estimating possibilities, and his watch raced faster. Three minutes and thirty seconds to go. He had calculated the odds and decided they were loaded impossibly against him. The sound of the car starting up so startled him he almost lost his balance; he hadn't even realized it was there, but now the driver switched on a light inside the vehicle and he saw it parked close to the signal-box on the far side of the wire. A Mercedes. The driver was having trouble firing the motor. A chance in a thousand – but the repeating rattle of the car's engine struggling to fire revived his hopes enormously, stirring the blood inside his half-congealed body as he worked out how to exploit this heaven-sent diversion.

Between the misfires of the numbed engine he heard feet clumping below the wagon as the unseen soldier stamped the ground to bring back the circulation into his frozen system, then the wheezing cough again. The feet began tramping through the snow, moving away from the wagon and over the empty neighbouring track, and Macomber guessed that he was improvising his own sentry-go to neutralize the appalling cold. The open window in the signal-box was still unoccupied as the marching German moved farther away; if only that bloody engine would start, would begin shifting the Mercedes – because stationary the car was useless. His nerves prickled with desperate impatience as the driver tried again and again to wake up the dead motor, and Macomber's prayers were with the driver as he went on struggling to spark life from the sullen engine. The motor caught, ticked over unenthusiastically, died again. God, he'd really thought it was going. He gritted his teeth to prevent them chattering with the cold, stared at the empty window in the signal-box, watched the marching German cross a second track close to the lamp. Another laboured spasm when the car seemed to be going, another false start which faded away – and Macomber suddenly realized that the wheezing German was growing curious about the car because he was marching towards the wire now. Then the engine caught, ticked over, continued ticking as the Scot moved for the first time in ten minutes, breaking the stiffened rigidity of his posture to reach inside his coat pocket and haul out the Luger.

He aimed the Luger, fired once. The car was moving slowly, and he had aimed at the rear window – away from the driver who must remain in control of his vehicle, who must be panicked if the plan was to have any chance of working. The bullet shattered the rear window and its report echoed in the darkness as a voice roared out across the railyard in German. 'He's in that car ... on the other side of the wire ... Don't let him get away!' The darkness, the falling snow, distorted the direction from which the voice came, but Macomber's bellowed command carried a long distance. Someone opened fire, a burst from a machine-pistol which sprayed the rear of the accelerating Mercedes. A fusillade of shots crackled in the darkness and men ran forward, leaving the train. A German, finding the wire barring his way, shouted a warning, retreated behind the signal-box, threw a grenade, then another. The explosions were bright flashes, muffled assaults on the eardrums, the men were pouring through the hole in the shattered wire, a muddle of field-grey figures rushing past the hooded lamp as men already beyond the wire fired long bursts at the retreating vehicle. The Mercedes was still moving, turning a sharp corner and accelerating afresh when the patrol left behind the wire and vanished into the night.

Macomber wasted no time on the ladder. Levering himself over the side farthest away from the signal-box, he fell heavily in the snow, cushioning his fall by rolling away from the wagon. The shock of the impact was still with him as he forced himself to his feet, glanced quickly in both directions and scrambled under the tanker between its wheels. He emerged from underneath gripping the Luger, and his gaze was fixed on the point of maximum danger – the signal-box. Gunther had taken up position, was leaning out of the window with his rifle, unaffected by the headlong rush away from the railyard.

There's always one who uses his head, Macomber thought grimly as the German leaned out farther, raised his rifle and took swift aim at the blurred shadow moving away from the last petrol wagon. Macomber jerked the Luger high, hoped the damned barrel wasn't blocked with ice from his fall, steadied the gun and fired. The sound of his shot was drowned in the rattle of firearms beyond the wire as the German flopped over the window ledge, lost his rifle and hung in mid-air, face downwards. Macomber ran towards the wire, ran awkwardly because his legs were still stiff and unwieldy from the long wait, and as he ran he hoped to God the signalman wasn't the courageous type who raised alarms, but from a brief glance at the window he saw no sign of him – he was crouched on the floor between his levers.

He slowed down to pass through the tangle of wire and then began running in earnest, running to the left – away from the signal-box and away from the road where the Mercedes had driven off. Behind him, some distance up the yard, dogs were barking excitedly; the other section of the patrol had gone to the front of the train to start a systematic search. He ran slowly but steadily, his eyes growing accustomed to the unlit darkness as he threaded his way between man-high piles of wooden sleepers, ran with his Luger held well forward so he could aim it quickly in case of emergency, but this fringe area of the railyard was deserted and he reached the parked Volkswagen safely. Now to start his own engine. At the sixth attempt the car fired and he paused only to haul off the German army blanket he had draped over bonnet and radiator, stuffing it on the passenger seat before driving away across the snow. The blanket had frozen into a natural canopy and it retained its strange shape as he left the field and drove onto a road which would take him the long way back into Bucharest. Remembering what he had deposited under the petrol train, he pressed his foot down as soon as he reached the road, building up speed dangerously as the wheels whipped over the ice-coated surface. His watch registered thirty seconds beyond zero.

He swore in German, the language he had accustomed himself to speak always, to think in, even to dream in as part of his

German cover. Surely all the bloody time fuses couldn't be defective? Or had he gone through all this for nothing? He shivered uncontrollably as he accelerated to even greater speed, gripping the wheel tightly to overcome the tremor. Reaction? Probably. Beyond his headlight beams the flat countryside was a mystery, a realm of darkness which might have contained anything, but from frequent reconnaissance in daylight hours he knew there were only bleak, endless fields stretching away to the Danube. A paling fence rushed towards him, disappeared as he lost speed and started to take a bend, then the skid began. He reacted instinctively, guiding rather than forcing the steering, following the spin while the headlights swept a crazy arc over the snowbound landscape. When he pulled up, by some miracle still on the road, the Volkswagen had swung through one hundred and eighty degrees, so he faced the way he had come at the moment of detonation.

The first sound was a dull boom, like the firing of a sixteen-inch naval gun, followed by a series of repeating booms which thundered out across the plain. A tremendous flash illuminated the snow with a searing light, then the flash died and was succeeded by an appalling roar, a deafening, blasting sound as the petrol went up, wagon after wagon in such swift succession that the night seemed to break apart, to open up with volcanic force, to burst and boil with fire. During all his sabotage missions Macomber had never seen anything like it – the moonless night was suddenly lit with a vast orange conflagration which showed the huddled rooftops of Bucharest to his left, rooftops white with snow and then palely coloured by the glow of the seething fire enveloping the railyard from end to end. He was turning the car when the smoke came, a billowing cloud of blackness which temporarily smothered the orange glow and rolled towards the city. Reversing cautiously, he edged the rear of the Volkswagen into the paling fence, which cracked like glass in its frozen state, pitching an intact section into the field beyond. He changed gear, turned a cautious semi-circle, straightened up, accelerated and headed for Bucharest.

The sabotaging of the petrol train was Macomber's last assignment in the Balkans, since the taking over of Rumania by the

Wehrmacht would soon make any further explosive excursions well-nigh impossible, and while he drove into the outer suburbs of Bucharest his attention was concentrated on the hazards which lay ahead – the hazard of escaping from Rumania, of crossing German-occupied Bulgaria and entering neutral Turkey where he could catch a boat for Greece. The Greek mainland – where Allied troops had recenly landed to meet the threat of German invasion – meant safety, but reaching the haven was quite a different matter. He could only hope to pass through the intervening control points by preserving his impersonation of a German up to the last moment, but it was the Abwehr he feared most. It was the Abwehr who had sent men into the Balkans to end the wave of sabotage and Macomber knew the Abwehr were closing in on him, might even be within twenty-four hours of discovering his true identity. So it was back to his flat to pick up the already packed bag, then on the road again, south for Bulgaria and Istanbul beyond.

Lord, he was tired! Macomber rubbed the back of his hand over his eyes as he drove slowly through the deserted streets – driving at speed inside a built-up area might attract attention. The old stone buildings, five storeys tall, were in darkness, except where here and there a high window showed a light – some family woken by the unnerving explosions which had broken over the city – but the lights were going out again as he drove along a devious route which avoided the main highway, feeling the tension rising as he drew closer to the flat. Returning late at night it was always like this – because you never knew who might be waiting for you on the darkened staircase. Reversing the Volkswagen into the garage which had once served as a stable, he parked it facing the double doors, ready for a speedy departure in case of emergency; then, lighting one of the foul-tasting German cigars he had come to like, he began the five minute-walk to the apartment block.

As he walked steadily through the crusted snow he found his thoughts wandering back over the years to when he had walked through other cities without fear. Through New York as a boy when they had lived there with his American mother, and later, as a youth, through the streets of Edinburgh when his father, a Scot, had decided he should be educated in his home country. He thrust the memories out of his mind quickly, reminding himself that sentiment blunted the edge of alertness. He was nearly there. It would have been more convenient to rent a garage opposite where he lived, but the stopping of a car in the small hours could signal his arrival to anyone who might be waiting for him.

At the entrance to the narrow street, hardly wider than an alley, he dropped the cigar in the snow where it sputtered and extinguished itself. No point in illuminating your approach. He had deliberately chosen this apartment block because its entrance led off from a side street, which made it more difficult for anyone following to be sure which doorway you vanished inside. As he walked along the twisting, canyon-like street, his head bowed with fatigue, he automatically noted the footprints in the snow which preceded him, but people in this district worked a late shift in the factories and so far the footprints did not disturb him. Providing the doorstep to his own entrance was virgin snow – no one in the apartment block worked at night. The footprints went on past his entrance and the doorstep was hidden beneath unspoilt snow. Now for the worst part, the trip up the staircase. Inside his coat pocket his right hand gripped the Luger he had reloaded in the garage; he used his left hand to insert the key gently, turn it quietly and push the door open until it was backed against the wall. Stepping inside, he shut the door with equal care. Then he listened before switching on his pocket torch and aiming it up the staircase. Dry steps. The oppressive silence of three in the morning which always hinted at menace in the shadows.

He went up slowly, pausing at each landing to swivel his torch up the next flight, looking for the shadow which shouldn't be there. When he arrived on the fifth floor outside his own door he paused again, in no hurry to unlock it. A sixth flight led up to the caretaker's cramped quarters in the roof and a brief swing of his torch showed dry steps to where the staircase turned up the last flight. In any case Josef was away in Constanta. Taking out his key, he was about to insert it when he changed his mind. He should never have come back here; this was pushing his luck a shade too far. It must have

18

been the sapping fatigue, the temptation of a few hours in bed which had made him take this needless risk. The place where you stayed was always the most dangerous – they'd taken Forester in his Budapest flat. I'll damned well hold out a few hours longer, let sleep wait until I'm well clear of the city. He had the torch still in his hand when a hard, pipe-like object was rammed into the small of his back and a voice spoke in German.

'Be very careful, Herr Wolff. This is a gun, so why die so early in life? Put on the landing light, please, but do not turn round.'

Macomber's hand, which should have been gripping the Luger, now gripped the torch – another sign of the dreadful weariness which had made him overlook his normal precautions. He raised the hand still holding the torch, wondered briefly whether he could utilize the weapon, whether he could swing round and wield the torch as a club, and dismissed the idea as soon as it entered his head. The man on the landing knew exactly what he was doing, had the gun muzzle pressed firmly into his back, so firmly he would have plenty of time to squeeze the trigger and blow his victim's spine in half at the first hint of a wrong movement. Macomber fumbled for the switch, pressed it down. Light from the low-powered bulb percolated dismally across the landing.

'We will go inside,' the voice continued, a mature experienced voice. 'Use your key to open the door – and be careful!'

Thirty seconds later the pistol in the German's hand was aimed at a point a fraction above Macomber's stomach as he backed through the doorway into his small bedroom. As requested, he pressed down the switch and only the far bedside light came on. 'What is the matter with the overhead light?' the German demanded.

'It's defective – the same switch operates both lights.'

The German, having flashed his own torch into each room, had chosen this one because it was the smallest. Macomber continued backing inside the room where the space for manoeuvre was precisely nil, which presumably was why the German had preferred it, and the watchful look on his adversary's face produced the same reaction in the Scot as the steadiness of the pistol: this was a man who wouldn't be taken by surprise, who wouldn't make a single mistake, a man who would squeeze the trigger instantly if he considered such drastic action necessary. Thin-faced, a shorter man than Macomber, he was in his early forties and he wore a similar leather coat and a similar soft hat. Behind rimless glasses his eyes were unblinking as he gestured for the Scot to sit at the far side of the bed.

'If we're going to talk in here may I take off my coat,' Macomber began, 'and then you can start telling me what the hell this is all about.'

The thin German nodded and issued no further warning about being careful; he simply held his pistol levelled and watched the slow careful movements of taking off the coat. Macomber had noted the rubber overshoes peeping out of his visitor's own coat pocket, which explained his mode of entry – he must have used a skeleton key to open the street door, must then have taken off his overshoes and stepped over the door-step without disturbing the snow. A man who thought of everything – or almost everything. The Scot hung his coat on a hook at the end of the huge wardrobe which was the other main item of furniture in the room, taking up so much space with the double bed that he had to squeeze his way round in the morning when dressing. He hung the coat carefully to conceal the instability of the wardrobe, the fact that it wobbled easily on its rotting plinth, and he hung the coat with one pocket outwards, the pocket containing the Luger. When he turned round the German reacted instantly. 'You have a gun inside your jacket – take it out very carefully and drop it on the bed, Herr Wolff.'

Macomber used his fingertips to extract the second Luger by the butt, keeping his index finger well away from the trigger as he eased the weapon out of the shoulder holster and let it fall on the bed. The shock had gone, his brain was working again, and at least this manoeuvre had succeeded – by drawing the German's attention to the second gun he had distracted his attention from the coat. The German used his left hand to pick up the Luger and slip it into his pocket. 'Now sit on your side of the bed, Herr Wolff. Incidentally, your

German is quite flawless. I congratulate you. My name is Dietrich. Of the Abwehr, of course.'

'Then why the devil do you want to see me?'

Dietrich said nothing while he closed and locked the bedroom door to guard against the arrival of an associate of Macomber's. The precaution taken, the Abwehr man leaned against the door as he began his interrogation.

'It has been a long time to this moment, Herr Wolff – I will call you that until you decide to tell me your real name.'

'My real name?' Macomber stared at Dietrich as though he must be mad. 'I am Hermann Wolff...'

'It has been a long time since January 1940,' the Abwehr man continued as though he hadn't heard the Scot. 'A long way, too, from Budapest to this apartment. I almost caught up with you once in Györ, but I made the mistake of letting my assistant come for you. What happened to him? We never saw him again.'

'As a citizen of the Reich...'

'You demand to be taken to police headquarters?' Dietrich was amused and smiled unpleasantly. 'Do you really think you would enjoy that experience – particularly if I take you to Gestapo headquarters instead?'

'I shall complain direct to Berlin – I know people there,' Macomber growled. 'I am a German businessman sent here by my firm in Munich and I have correspondence with me to prove this...'

'I'm sure you have,' Dietrich replied sarcastically. 'I'm also sure that it would stand up to superficial examination – until we checked back with your so-called employers. You nearly had me killed tonight, Herr Wolff – and by my own people. I was inside that Mercedes the Wehrmacht opened fire on and I had to drive like a maniac to stay alive, so I decided it might be interesting to come straight here – in case you escaped. I have been following you for some time but I lost you this evening on your way to the railyard.'

'I still haven't the least idea what the hell you're talking about,' Macomber told him coolly. He re-crossed his legs and put his hands together in his lap where Dietrich could see them, and at the same time he hooked his right foot round the electric cord attached to the table-lamp plug. Dietrich smiled without humour.

'I was at the railyard tonight, Wolff – when the shooting started. Now do you understand?'

'Which railyard? What am I supposed to understand about this rubbish?'

'That there is no way out, that you have come to the end of the line. That railyard was the end of the line for you – literally.'

'I don't understand one damned thing,' Macomber rasped, 'but if you open the drawer in that other bedside table over there you may grasp what a bloody fool you're making of yourself.' Then the Scot waited.

It was a chance, no more, and Macomber knew that within a few minutes he would be dead or free. He scratched at his knee as though it tickled and this covered the slight movement of his leg testing the cord. The cable felt to be looped firmly round his ankle, but he could only test it by feel; if he dropped his eyes for even a second Dietrich would guess that something was wrong. Macomber waited, saying not a word while the Abwehr man wondered about the closed drawer. Everything depended on whether Macomber's offhand tone of voice, his arrogant manner, had half-convinced the German there might be something important in the bedside table. The Scot's expression had changed during the past minute, had become a mixture of boredom and contempt, as though the pistol had no existence, as though he thought the Abwehr man an idiot and had proof of the fact – inside the closed drawer.

The bait was tempting. The little table was close enough for Dietrich to lean forward, to reach out with one hand and open it, to see what was there. And he still had Macomber safely on the far side of the bed, his hands pacifically clasped in his lap, unable to come anywhere near the Abwehr man without standing up and running down the narrow space between wardrobe and bed – with Dietrich holding his pistol.

'What is in this drawer?' the Abwehr man asked waspishly.

Macomber said nothing and the battle of nerves continued as the Scot used the only weapon available – silence. The German watched him a few moments longer and then he

22

nodded again, as much as to say very well, we will have a look at this great revelation. He stood up from the door, took a step towards the table, his pistol aimed point-blank at Macomber's chest, but his prisoner was looking at the door with a bored expression. Dietrich used his left hand to reach down for the handle, the hand closest to Macomber, who had foreseen his dilemma. With his gun in his right hand while the other reached for the drawer it was physically impossible for him to keep the pistol muzzle trained on the Scot. Macomber was sitting with his hands limply at rest when the telephone beyond the locked door began to ring.

'Who will that be at this hour?' Dietrich demanded.

Macomber shrugged his shoulders, made no reply. The Abwehr man was becoming rattled – the Scot's refusal to speak was getting on his nerves and the muffled ringing of the phone irritated him. And he wanted to see what was inside the drawer before he found out who was calling Wolff, so everything became urgent. He grabbed at the handle, jerked open the drawer, saw a leather-bound book which might have been a diary, and while he stared at the book he wasn't watching the Scot. Still sitting on the bed, Macomber gave his right foot a tremendous jerk. The plug came out of the wall socket, the room went dark, the table lamp fell onto the bed. Macomber lay sprawled on the floor, waiting for the first shot. But the German didn't fire, which showed extraordinary self-control and quick thinking – a shot would reveal his position. To avoid his boots making a sound, Macomber swivelled on his knees, felt up to the coat, scooped the Luger out of the pocket, then pressed his shoulder against the wardrobe and waited for endless seconds. Had he heard the quietest of noises, a swift slither? He was certain the Abwehr man had changed position, that he had moved along the wall and was now standing with his back to the locked door, facing the other end of the unstable wardrobe. Still on his knees, Macomber heaved massively. The wardrobe toppled, left him, over a hundredweight of solid wood moving through an angle of ninety degrees. It struck something brutally and Macomber heard a muffled cry which cut off suddenly as the wardrobe completed its turn and landed on its side. He used his left hand to locate the coat still attached to the hook, fumbled inside the other pocket and pulled out the torch. The beam showed Dietrich lying under the great weight, the upper half of his body turned to one side, crumpled and motionless, although he still wore his glasses. The left side of his head was oddly misshapen where the wardrobe had crushed his skull.

The phone bell had stopped ringing in the outer room but from its limited duration and the lateness of the hour Macomber guessed who had called him. He had difficulty easing open the door past Dietrich's sprawled body and then he went across the living-room and opened the front door. No sound from below. Locking the door, he went back into the bedroom, turned off the light switch, rescued the table lamp, fixed in the plug and then switched on again. The identity cards were inside the dead man's wallet which he levered from his breast pocket. Two of them, and Dietrich was who he claimed to be. One card – the card tucked away inside a secret pocket – identified him as a high-ranking officer of the Abwehr, but it was the other card which interested Macomber. *Dr Richard Dietrich, archaeologist.* He had heard of this practice – the carrying of a civilian card for use when the Abwehr wished to conceal its true identity. Amid the shambles of the room, with the body lying under the wardrobe he couldn't move without help, Macomber sat on the edge of the bed and lit a cigar while he studied the card for several minutes. Then he went back to the living-room and called a number, puffing at his cigar while he waited for the operator to put him through. Baxter answered sleepily, became alert within a few seconds. 'Hermann here . . .' Macomber began.

'I tried to call you a few minutes ago.'

'I know. Get over to Marie's – she's had some news from Munich.'

He slammed down the receiver, hoping the line wasn't tapped, but they had spoken in German and 'Marie's' identified no address; only the mention of Munich warned Baxter that a grave emergency had arisen. While he waited, Macomber sat calmly smoking because there was nothing more to do; the flat held not a single piece of incriminating evidence and the only papers concerned the fictitious Wolff, papers prepared by the ingenious Baxter. Ten minutes after their brief call had ended, the Englishman who was posing as a Spanish mineralogist with Fascist sympathies arrived and he listened without speaking while Macomber explained what had happened, then looked at the two cards the Scot gave him. 'Roy, I want to use that card to take me out of Europe – the civilian version. Can you fix it up for me damned fast – you've still got some of my pictures, haven't you?'

'Should be able to.' Baxter, a wiry, sallow-faced individual in his late thirties stared up from his chair in the living-room, 'You really think you can get away with it – using the card of a man you've just killed? I'd say you were carrying it a bit far this time. The risk is colossal.'

Baxter studied the huge Scot who stood smoking his cigar without replying immediately. An impressive figure, Mac, he was thinking, but the last man he would personally have chosen to lead a sabotage team: he was too prominent, stood out too much in a crowd. It was characteristic of Macomber that he should have turned this seeming disadvantage into a major asset, always taking up an aggressive role when he was in the company of Germans, which in itself made his impersonation so much more convincing in Nazi-occupied Europe. The brutal thrust was absent from his personality now as, for a brief period only, he was able to be himself, to let the natural, dry-humoured smile show at the corners of his mouth. But to impersonate a senior officer of the Abwehr! The idea alone made Baxter want to shudder. Macomber smiled easily as he spoke.

'Look, Roy, as a cover Hermann Wolff is blown sky-high – the presence of Dietrich in there proves that. So I need a fresh identity. Audacity always pays – it's paid me all the way down through the Balkans and it will get me safely home to Greece.'

'Sometimes, Mac, I think you like the big bluff. You play it that way because it suits your temperament as much as for any other reason...'

'I play it that way because it works. And I need that card fixed during the next few hours, so you're going to have to break all records. As soon as you've gone I'm clearing out of Bucharest and I'd like you to deliver the card to me in

Giurgiu. I'll wait at that inn where we once spent a weekend. Can you manage it by noon? Today.'

'I might manage it.' Which was Baxter's way of saying he would be in Giurgiu by noon. 'There's the description to change as well as the photo, but the new quick-drying inks should help. I might even fix up the other one too,' he grinned quickly, 'just in case you want to go the whole hog.' He gestured towards the bedroom. 'Leaving the late Herr Dietrich in there?'

'No, he's got to disappear for several days, but if you'll help me shift that wardrobe I'll cope with the rest. And this, by the way, is your last job. Get that card to me and then make your own way home.' Macomber paused, a gleam of humour in his brown eyes. 'That is, unless you'd sooner come out with me?'

'Thanks, but no thanks. The sort of tricks you go in for would leave me a nervous wreck before we were halfway to the Turkish border.' Baxter grinned wryly. 'If it's all the same to you I'll creep out all by myself.' He looked towards the bedroom again. 'You really think it's wise trying to move him? The city is stiff with German army trucks swarming out to the railyard. Seems someone left a few bombs lying around the place earlier tonight.'

'Then I'll avoid the trucks. But if I'm using Herr Dietrich's card he has to disappear for a while. So long as they don't find him his local people won't know for sure what's happened – don't forget the Abwehr operate on their own a good deal.'

'Better you than me.' Baxter stood up, hoping he wasn't showing too great an eagerness to get away from the flat. 'What do I do with the store of demolition charges? Smash the time fuses and leave them there?'

'Don't bother.' Macomber checked his watch and moved impatiently. 'The Germans have a few more of them, so it's pointless and takes time. Now, I've got to get that body out of here.'

'I'll help you to shift that evidence if you like ...'

'Just help me to shift the wardrobe and then push off. I'd sooner deal with this on my own.' A typical reaction, Baxter thought, and he marvelled at the Scot's steady nerves. Forester, Dyce, Lemaitre – all the rest of the sabotage team were dead and Mac was the sole survivor, possibly because of his habit of working alone. And he can have it, he told himself as he followed Macomber inside the bedroom.

Macomber felt a little more relaxed as he drove the Volkswagen through the still-dark streets of Bucharest, a reaction which would have astounded the less phlegmatic Baxter. Down side roads which led to the main highway the Scot had already seen several army trucks trundling through the snow and for a short distance he must travel along that highway himself. The army blanket, thawed out by the heat of the car on his journey from the railyard, was thrown over the back seat, but it still assumed an odd shape – it had proved impossible to disguise completely the hump of Dietrich's body underneath. So relaxation was perhaps not a correct description of the Scot's present frame of mind. Even so he was relieved, relieved to have accomplished the mind-numbing trip he had made down the apartment block's fire-escape with the Abwehr man looped over his shoulder. The iron treads of the fire-escape had been coated with ice, he had heard a window open in the darkness during his grim journey down the staircase, and there had been no cover to hide his progress across the walled yard to the back street where he had parked his Volkswagen. But for Macomber the worst phase of this problem was over – providing he could avoid those army trucks.

He drove very slowly as he approached the exit to the main highway, then pulled up with his engine still ticking over. He waited half a minute and when nothing passed the exit he drove out and turned left, north towards the railway, the direction which would take him into open country most quickly. He drove steadily at a medium speed and his headlights showed up sombre buildings, their iron balconies laced with snow; later a desolate square, the trees naked and frosted with a bowed statue in the centre; later still shabby tenements forming a continuous wall of poverty. Lord, he'd be glad to leave this place. He was close to the outskirts when the emergency began. Driving at a sober speed along the empty highway, although the fog of fatigue was settling on his weary mind, he still watched the road keenly as he glanced at his watch. 4.15

AM. A little over two hours ago he had been lying on top of that petrol wagon with the sounds of the dogs in his ears. He turned a bend, saw an army truck emerging from a side street ahead, and then he was driving behind it as the vehicle rattled forward over the uneven road. Headlights glared in his rear mirror, roared up behind him, only slowing when he thought he was going to be run down by the second army truck. He was boxed in by the Wehrmacht.

There was no side turning he could take now except the turning a mile ahead he intended using, so he had to put up with the unwelcome escort as they drove on into the country-side. He glanced back quickly, saw the truck behind within twenty feet of the Volkswagen, and when he looked back again where the road curved he saw a stream of headlights coming up. He had slotted himself inside a whole convoy of German trucks. Clenching the cigar more tightly, he concentrated on holding the same speed as the vehicle ahead, his eyes fixed on the red light, the closed canvas covers, while in his rear mirror the oncoming headlights behind remained a constant glare. Even leaving this damned convoy was going to be tricky. He timed it carefully, drawing nearer to the vehicle in front as the vital side turning approached, and he was on the verge of signalling when he saw the pole barricading the side road, the German military policeman behind it. They had blocked it off to prevent civilian traffic entering this route. He drove past his escape exit without a glance while he searched for a solution, tried to foresee the next move. A mile farther on the road forked; the left fork leading to the railyard, the right one across the plain. But logically they would have blocked this off, too, so he would be forced to continue with the convoy until it reached the railyard he had half-destroyed, an area which must be swarming with troops. Perhaps, after all, Baxter had had a point.

As they drove on through the night the fatigue grew worse, encouraged by the monotonous rumble of the truck engines, increased by the necessity to go on staring at the red light ahead, and when the German vehicle's canvas covers parted briefly his headlights picked up the silhouette of a helmet: the trucks were packed with German troops. Wiping sweat away from his forehead, Macomber began to conduct the only possible manoeuvre which might extricate him from the trap, gradually reducing speed so that the truck in front moved farther away. But there was a limit to the loss of speed the driver behind would tolerate, and Macomber was gambling on the lack of enthusiasm for his job which might be expected in the middle of the night. He drove on until there was a gap of twenty yards between the Volkswagen and the truck ahead and then held it at that distance, expecting at any moment a furious burst of hooting from his rear. He had decided to try and use a very minor road turning off to the right, a road which was a dead end, leading over the fields and across the railway to a large farm, but he wanted to conceal the fact that he had turned off up this dangerous dead end. If the driver behind reported the presence of the lone Volkswagen when he reached the railyard they mustn't know where to look for him. The next bend was the crucial point and it needed split-second timing.

A copse of trees flashed into the lights of the vehicle in front and then vanished as the truck turned the corner. Macomber glanced in the mirror, saw the headlights locked onto him, suddenly speeded up. The car raced forward over the wheel-gutted snow, left well behind the truck in his rear as he accelerated, praying he wouldn't go into another skid. As he reduced speed to go round the curve his lights shone on the trees, then he was momentarily out of sight of the truck behind. The wooden gate was set back from the road and he almost missed it, but he saw it just in time, swung his wheel, crashed through the obstacle, turned behind a stone wall and felt the Volkswagen wobble from side to side as it passed over iron-hard ruts. Leaving the engine running, he switched off the lights and waited.

He was chewing at his cigar-end when a glow of lights appeared beyond the wall, silhouetting the naked tree-trunks like a natural palisade. The truck's engine was losing speed as the driver saw the bend, and too much loss of speed enormously increased the danger of his seeing the smashed gate, the tracks left by the Volkswagen in the snow when it plunged into the field. Macomber sat motionless while the truck lost even more speed and lumbered ponderously round the bend, then it sounded as though it were stopping. He had been spotted – the smashed gate, the tyre tracks had been seen! He grabbed the door handle, ready for a futile flight into the wasteland, knowing that the truck had only to follow him once the headlights picked up the fugitive, doubtful whether his legs had the strength to carry him far, when the engine ticked over more strongly and the truck rumbled past the gateway towards the railyard.

He left the car at once, stumbled his way over the ruts in the darkness, found a buttress which he used to haul himself up to where he could see over the wall and back along the road. Between the pole-shapes of the trees he observed the headlights moving towards him, saw a gap between the fourth and fifth set of lights. There would be orders about maintaining an even distance in convoy but there was always a laggard – if only he would continue to lag behind! Macomber ran back towards the Volkswagen, sprawling headlong in the snow when his foot caught in a rut, clambering swiftly to his feet again and reaching the car as the first set of headlights lit the top of the wall. The second vehicle followed closely, then the third and the fourth. Now! The Volkswagen rocked unsteadily as he drove towards the gateway and when he arrived at the exit the road was clear. Turning out of the field, he pressed his foot down and sped after the retreating rear light of the truck in the distance.

The turning onto the farm track came sooner than he expected and he swung the wheel automatically, glancing back the way he had come. No headlights behind: the fifth truck had not yet arrived at the bend. Within a hundred yards the track dropped into a bowl and his own lights were hidden from the main road. As he drove along the track, his headlight beams showing up clumps of frosted glass on either side, he concentrated on the immediate problem – the disposal of Dietrich. In summer, with the grasses grown tall, he could have dumped him in a dozen places, but with the ground frozen to the consistency of iron, the grasses ankle-high and the fields a white sheet against which the body would show up clearly, any unlucky chance might disclose the evidence in daylight. He would have to do better than that.

Five minutes later he was driving up a slope as he approached the bridge which crossed the railway; even in the daytime it was a lonely spot but at this hour there was an atmosphere of eerie desolation about the place and spiked reeds caught in the headlights reminded him he was driving across marshland. He slowed down to take a dangerous turn beyond the bridge and heard the clanking of goods wagons moving up from the south. On the spur of the moment he pulled up, left the engine running and got out to look over the bridge. A hooded lamp a short distance away shone down on a steam engine which passed under him hauling a train of empty coal trucks bound for the eastern section of the railyard, a section unaffected by the explosions. The trucks were on their way to the coal hopper where they would be filled and sent on their long journey to Germany. Macomber felt a sudden lightening of the dreadful fatigue which was steadily wearing him out, making even thought difficult. There could be a ready-made solution to his problem twenty feet below him.

Long weeks of observation had made the Scot an expert on the workings of that railyard, and he knew the coal would be loaded into the trucks as soon as the train arrived. The first trucks were already passing under him as he gauged their speed and the moment when the centre of a truck was exactly below where he stood. Without further calculation he switched off the car lights, opened the rear door and wrestled out the blanketed bundle. Hoisting the German on his shoulders, a major effort in itself, he staggered to the parapet and waited, gauging the right moment afresh, knowing he couldn't afford to misjudge his timing by so much as a second. He waited until one truck was centred under the bridge and flopped the bundle across the wall; as the rear of the truck rolled out of sight he heaved and held his breath. The body dropped, landed in the centre of the next coal truck, vanished under the bridge. Dr Richard Dietrich, archaeologist, was on his way home to Germany.

CHAPTER TWO

Saturday, April 5

Dietrich.

The name on the identity card immediately caught the attention of the Turkish passport control officer. *Dr Richard Dietrich, German national, born Flensburg. Profession: archaeologist. Age: thirty-two.* Officer Sarajoglu buttoned up his collar against the cold and studied the card thoughtfully as though he found it suspect. Behind him in the harbour of the Golden Horn a tugboat siren shrieked non-stop, a piercing sound which the raw, early morning wind from the Black Sea carried clear across Istanbul. Sarajoglu, a man sensitive to atmospheres, was unable to define the feeling of suspense which hung over the waterfront. At half past six on a morning when winter still gripped the straits, the worst always seemed likely to happen.

'You are travelling on business?' the Turk inquired.

'I am leaving Turkey.' Dietrich took a small cigar out of his mouth and flicked ash which fell on the counter separating them. He was a very large man, dressed in a belted leather coat and a dark, soft hat. His reply had been arrogant in manner and wording, implying that since he was leaving the country his activities were of no concern to this bureaucrat. Sarajoglu concealed his annoyance but proceeded to make a gesture of independence, conveying that although German troops had recently marched into Rumania and Bulgaria, his country was still neutral territory: using a gloved finger, he poked the German's ash off the counter. It fell off the edge and landed on Dietrich's highly polished boot. Sarajoglu, who had watched the fall of the ash, looked up and stared at the German. No reaction. Dietrich had clasped his hands behind his back and was staring through a frost-coated window at the harbour.

He was a man whose sheer physical presence was formidable – a man over six feet tall who must weigh at least fourteen stone, Sarajoglu estimated. Even so, the head seemed a little large for the body, a squarish head with a short nose, the mouth wide and firm-lipped, the jaw-line suggesting great energy and enormous determination. But it was the eyes which the Turk found most arresting, large brown eyes which moved slowly and deliberately as though assessing everything. He might be on the list of known German agents, Sarajoglu was thinking. Without much hope, he held onto the card and asked Dietrich to wait a moment.

'I have to catch that boat, the *Hydra*,' Dietrich informed him roughly, 'so hurry it up,' he rumbled as the Turk moved away into a small room behind the counter. Pretending not to have heard, Sarajoglu closed the door, opened a filing cabinet, took out the confidential list of German agents and ran his eye down it. No, his memory had not deceived him: Dietrich was not on the list. He turned to a youth who was typing at a desk close to the wall.

'The *Hydra* – she hasn't changed her sailing schedule so far as you know?'

'No, she's sailing at 7.30 AM and making the normal ferry run – Istanbul to Zervos. Why, sir?'

'Nothing really. But there are three Germans aboard the vessel already and now I've got a fourth outside. It's just unusual – Germans travelling to Greece at this stage of the war.'

'Greece isn't at war with Germany – only with Italy.'

'Yes, and that's a curious situation.' Sarajoglu bit the edge of the identity card between his teeth and failed to notice that some of the ink had flaked off. 'Curious,' he repeated. 'The Greeks have been fighting Germany's ally, Italy, for over six months but the Germans still remain neutral. I heard yesterday that British forces are landing in Greece – one of our captains saw their transports in the Piraeus. They must anticipate a German attack.'

'They probably hope to prevent one.' The typist peered through the window towards the counter beyond. 'Is that him – the big brute out there?

Ah, so you don't like the look of him either, Sarajoglu thought. He stared through the window where he could see the German standing passive and immobile, and this total lack of nervousness impressed him. When a passenger's papers were taken away even the innocent ones displayed a certain perturbation, as though they feared an inadvertent mistake in their documentation. Dietrich, however, stood so still that he might have been carved from wood except for the curl of cigar smoke rising towards the roof of the shed. 'Yes,' Sarajoglu replied, 'that is Dr Richard Dietrich. He is thirty-two years old – so why is he not in the German army, I wonder?'

'Better ask him.' As the typist resumed work Sarajoglu's lips tightened. He flicked the cutting edge of the card sharply across the youth's ear, noted with satisfaction that he had flinched, then went outside to the counter. The German was standing in exactly the same position as when he had left him, hands behind his back, staring out at the harbour, his manner outwardly unruffled by this deliberate delay. Sarajoglu felt even more irked as he laid the card on the counter and spoke with exaggerated courtesy. 'You may go now, Dr Dietrich. A pleasant trip.'

The German picked up the card without haste, put it away inside his wallet, his eyes on Sarajoglu all the time. He stood with that typically German stance, his legs splayed well apart, his body like a human tree-trunk. The Turk began to feel uncomfortable: there had been precise instructions from above as to how to deal with German tourists – don't offend them and treat them with every courtesy so there can be no cause for complaint from Berlin. He felt relieved when Dietrich turned away, nodding curtly to the porter who hastily picked up the single bag and followed him out of the shed and up the ice-sheathed gangway. Inside his cabin Dietrich was feeling in his pocket for the tip when the porter, still nervous of his German passenger, clumsily knocked over the water carafe. Dietrich shook his head brusquely as the porter stooped to pick up the remnants, told him he'd done enough damage already and handed over the modest tip, a sum which normally would have provoked a sarcastic response. But as the German went on staring at him, clearly inviting his immediate departure, the porter thought better of it and left the cabin with a polite mumble.

As soon as the porter had gone, Macomber locked the door, picked up the two largest pieces of broken carafe and deposited them in the wastepaper basket. God, it was a relief to be inside neutral Turkey, to be on board, to be alone in his cabin. And within thirty hours he would be able to revert to his real identity, to be known once more as Ian Macomber, to talk in English all day long if he wished. He went over to the washbasin and looked in the mirror above it, gazing into the glass like a man seeing the result when surgical bandages have been removed.

For the first time since he had left the flat in Bucharest his features relaxed, the crinkles of humour appeared at the corners of his mouth, and even though still wearing the German hat and leather coat the Teutonic image was gone. It was going to be irksome – keeping up his German impersonation until he landed safely on Greek soil – but it was necessary. He was travelling with German papers and the Greek captain might not appreciate his sudden conversion to another nationality. So for one more day and one more night he must go on playing the part of Dr Richard Dietrich, German archaeologist. The knock on the door startled him, reminded him of the extreme fatigue he was labouring under – and also that the danger might not be past yet. He unlocked the door, his hand clutching the Luger inside his coat pocket, opened it cautiously. It was the chief steward and he showed surprise when Macomber addressed him in fluent Greek.

'What do you want?'

'You speak our language – it is most unusual for a German...'

'I said what do you want?'

'Is everything to your satisfaction, sir? Good. If you need something you have only to call me...' The voluble steward chattered on while Macomber stared at him bleakly, then he said something which again startled the Scot. 'I'm sure you'll be interested to know we have three of your fellow-countrymen also on board...'

For a muddled moment Macomber thought he was referring to three Englishmen, then he recovered his tired wits. 'Are they together?' he enquired in a bored tone which concealed his anxiety about the reply.

'No, sir, they are all travelling separately.' The steward paused and there was a malicious gleam in his quick-moving eyes. 'There are also two British passengers.'

'You find that amusing?'

'No, sir.' The steward replied hastily, taken aback by the grimness of this overbearing German. He tried to correct his blunder. 'I shall be in the dining-room where breakfast is being prepared, so if you require anything...'

'Then I shall ask you! And take this – I want a comfortable trip, so do your duty.' Macomber had handed the flabbergasted man a generous tip before turning his back and closing the cabin door, but it had suddenly occurred to him that the steward could be a valuable source of information and he had already decided to question him further about the other passengers. But not now – it would arouse too much interest. Alone again, Macomber stripped off the hat and coat and doused himself in ice-cold water. Three Germans aboard, he was thinking as he dried himself slowly; perhaps it wasn't all over yet. When he had reached Istanbul he had avoided going anywhere near the British Legation -- because the Legation was the very place the Abwehr might be watching for his arrival. It was too late to arrest him but it certainly wasn't too late to have him killed. Not that he feared the Abwehr's revenge – they had a far more powerful motive for ensuring that he never reached Allied territory alive, and they were perfectly capable of putting an assassin aboard the *Hydra*, an assassin not necessarily of German nationality. It's what I'm carrying in my head they'd like to destroy, he reminded himself. Information gathered over months of patient observation in the Balkans – data about assembly points, storage depots, the routes along which supplies were being sent to the Reich ...

He finished drying himself, glanced at the inviting bunk and looked away quickly. Lord, it had been a swine of a trip from Bucharest. Four hours' sleep in forty-eight, his reflexes shot to hell, but he'd better check this damned ship – and forget any ideas about sleep until he was actually on Greek soil. He put on the leather coat and the hat, tested the action of his Luger, glanced in the mirror. He was back in business again. The arrogant, uncompromising image of Dr Richard Dietrich stared back at him. Replacing the gun inside his coat, he left the cabin to carry out his inspection of the 5,000-ton Greek ferry.

The bitter wind raked his face as soon as he reached the deck, a wind unpleasant enough, he soon found, to keep the handful of fellow-passengers below decks. Half an hour later, his tour of the vessel completed, he stood near the stern where he could keep an eye on the gangway for late arrivals. It was just possible that the Abwehr might send someone on board at the last moment. Standing by the rail, Macomber seemed impervious to the weather as he quietly smoked his cigar. The lifeboat covers were still crusted with last night's snowfall, the masthead rigging still encased with glassy ice, but the battered yellow funnel was dripping moisture as the ship began to get up steam. To all outward appearances Macomber had wandered round the vessel with the idle curiosity of the newly arrived passenger who is interested in his temporary home, but now as he smoked his cigar he was cataloguing his discoveries in his mind.

From the chief steward he had learned that the *Hydra* carried a crew of six, that the captain's name was Nopagos, and that he had plied this regular passage between Istanbul and Zervos for the past fourteen years. Macomber stirred at the rail as the chief steward reappeared at his elbow, chattering amiably.

'Looks as though we've got our full complement of passengers aboard, sir.'

Macomber nodded, wondering whether he had overdone the tip: the steward was becoming his shadow. He checked his watch. 'There's still time for last-minute arrivals.' Again he was subtly probing for information.

'Doubt that, sir. I was talking to the ticket office manager a few minutes ago on the phone – he sold seven tickets for this trip, so it looks as though that's the lot.'

Macomber nodded again and the steward, sensing that he was no longer in a talkative mood, excused himself. Left alone once more, the Scot continued his mental inventory. Two British civilians he hadn't yet seen, one man in his late twenties while his companion was probably a few years beyond thirty. Which was interesting, since both men were of military age. One Greek civilian who lived on Zervos and apparently had something to do with the monastic order which owned the ferry – again a man of military age, but Macomber presumed that his slight limp had kept him out of the Greek Army. And, finally, the three Germans. He had seen two of them briefly, both civilians in their early forties who had the appearance of businessmen, but the third, a man called Schnell, had apparently come aboard very early in the morning and locked himself away in his cabin. 'With his cabin trunk,' as the voluble steward had explained earlier. On this point the Scot had detected an uncertain note in the steward's voice and he had asked a question.

'You find that odd – that he should keep a trunk in his cabin?'

'Well, sir, it takes up a lot of space and I offered to have it put in the hold when he came aboard. After all, we shall be docking at Zervos in twenty-four hours. He was quite abrupt with me, the way some...' He had paused and Macomber, knowing he had been about to say 'the way some Germans are', had smiled grimly to himself. But the steward had changed his wording in time. '...the way some people are when they arrive early. He insisted it stayed with him in the cabin so he must be carrying something valuable.'

Something valuable? Macomber frowned as he recalled the steward's words – it was this cabin trunk and its unknown contents which occupied his thoughts as he gazed out over the muddle of decrepit-looking tramps and coasters which congested the Golden Horn harbour. He heard a sound behind him and remained staring out across the water, one large boot resting on the lower rail. Was it likely that an attempt would be made to assassinate him at this late hour – a few minutes before putting to sea? Out of the corner of his eye he watched the Greek approaching, heard the faint slur of his limping step.

The man's name was Grapos and even with that slight limp Macomber thought he would be an asset to any army: of only medium height there was, nevertheless, a suggestion of tremendous physical strength in those broad shoulders and that powerful chest which swelled the coloured shirt. Not a prosperous individual, Macomber decided: his grey jacket and trousers were of poor quality, the red tie round his neck was faded and his boots were shabby. The steward had told him of an unexpected facility Grapos possessed – the monks had taught him to speak English. The Greek was very close now, stopping almost behind the Scot, and his eyes were shrewd and alert.

'Always it seems so long before the boat sails,' he began. 'You have been to Zervos before?'

'Once.' Macomber replied in Greek and turned his head away to study the harbour. Grapos might have been surprised had he known how much Macomber had registered in that brief glance. The Greek's face was strong-featured, the jaw-line formidable, and the long straggle of dark moustache which curved round the corners of his wide mouth gave him the look of a bandit or guerrilla. He was one of the most villainous-looking characters Macomber had encountered since entering the Balkans. But the point which had alerted the Scot was the fact that Grapos had spoken to him in Greek. Which could only mean that he had eavesdropped while Macomber was conversing in that language with the steward, unless that talkative individual had informed Grapos that they had a Greek-speaking German aboard.

'There is bad weather on the way,' Grapos remarked and looked upwards.

'Why do you say that?' Macomber's tone was brusque and unencouraging, but the Greek seemed not to notice.

'Because of the birds.' Grapos lifted a hand and pointed to where a cloud of seagulls wheeled and floated in erratic circles high above the white-coated domes and minarets onshore.

'Don't you always get birds over a harbour?' Macomber sounded bored with the company which had thrust itself upon him, but now he was observing the large, hairy-backed hands which gripped the rail as though they might pull a section loose bodily.

'Yes, but not so many, and they are uneasy – you can tell by the way they fly. I have seen them fly like that over Zervos before the great storms. This will be a bad voyage,' he went on cheerfully. 'We shall run into a storm before we land at Katyra. Let us hope it does not strike us off Cape Zervos. You see,' he continued with relish, 'the entrance to the gulf is very narrow and the cape has been the graveyard of a hundred ships or more...' He broke off, grinning savagely as he displayed a row of perfect white teeth. 'But, of course, you know – you have been there before.'

Macomber said nothing as he hunched his broad shoulders and threw the smoked cigar butt into the water. Two ships away along the wharf another vessel was preparing to leave, her white funnel belching out clouds of murky smoke which the wind dispersed in chaotic trails. Behind him he heard footsteps retreating, one of them out of step. Grapos had taken the hint and was on his way to find someone else who would listen to his chatter. Extracting a Zeiss Monokular glass, a single-lens field-glass, from his pocket, Macomber focused it on the other vessel getting up a head of steam. The Rumanian flag whipped in the wind from her masthead and she was, he knew, the *Rupescu*. Her decks were strangely deserted for a ship on the point of departure and at the head of the gang-plank two seamen stood as though on guard. It was quite clear that shortly she would follow the *Hydra* across the Sea of Marmara and into the Dardanelles, which he found interesting.

From the steward he had learned that the *Rupescu*, a fast motor vessel, was twelve hours out of the Bulgarian port of Varna and the situation could be a little tricky since she was bound for the Aegean. German troops now controlled Bulgaria so technically the Allies might regard the *Rupescu* as an enemy vessel, a prize to be sought out by the Royal Navy. Certainly the British Legation at Istanbul would already have wirelessed Egypt of her presence in the straits, but Macomber doubted whether she would be seized – the British Government had broken off diplomatic relations with Rumania

40

but had not yet declared war on that unhappy country. Satisfied with what he had seen – nothing out of the ordinary –
Macomber put away his glass and then stiffened as a shabbily
dressed man dashed up the gangway. Under his arm he carried
a batch of newspapers and he flourished one in the Scot's face
when he came along the desk. Macomber bought a copy, glancing at the banner headline before he went below. *German
Army Poised To Attack?*

The engines were throbbing steadily as he made his way
along a narrow companionway and walked calmly into the
saloon, a small cramped room with panelled walls which was
already reeking of acrid cigar smoke. Pulling out his copy of the
Frankfurter Zeitung, Macomber sank heavily into an ancient
arm-chair in a corner which allowed him to see the whole
room while he pretended to read. Hahnemann, a thin-faced
German in his early forties and dressed like a travelling sales-
man in a cheap suit, sat in the diagonally opposite corner smoking one of the cigars responsible for the bad air. In another
corner, a heavily built German of medium height, his clothes
well-cut and dark, sat reading some typed sheets and also
smoking a cigar. That would be Volber. The fourth corner was
occupied by a small bar where a man in white uniform was
polishing a glass. Thank God, Macomber was thinking, those
two don't exactly look like sociable types. I could do without
useless conversation in German at the moment. The thought
had hardly passed through his head when two men opened the
doors and stood hesitating as though not sure whether to come
in. Their first words warned Macomber. They were British.

'Go on in, for God's sake,' Prentice said impatiently to Ford,
who was standing in the doorway. 'Don't just stand gawping.
We've paid our fares just like the rest of these johnnies.'

Ford's face was expressionless as he carefully made his way
through the smoke to a table close to the bar. As they settled
behind a low table the steward took Macomber's order and a
minute later placed a glass of beer in front of him. Ford kept
his voice low as he made the remark. 'That chap who's just got
his beer looks like another bleedin' Jerry.'

'I think they all are,' Prentice murmured nonchalantly.

'This is a funny, funny war at times.' Unlike Ford, who sat stiffly and kept an eye on the other three men without appearing to do so, Prentice was outwardly the soul of relaxation. When the steward arrived for their order he deliberately raised his voice so the whole room could hear. 'A beer and a glass of *ouzo*, laddie.'

'Beg, please?' The steward looked at a loss. Prentice leaned round him and stabbed a finger in the direction of Macomber's table, his voice louder still. 'One *ouzo* and a beer – beer – like that chap over there ordered.' The other two Germans glanced in his direction and then looked away, but the Scot, who had lowered his paper, stared hard across the room with an unpleasantly inquiring expression.

'Tough-looking basket, that big one,' Ford remarked, keeping his own voice quiet. 'If I met him in Libya I'd let him have two in the pump. Yes, two – just to be sure.'

The drinks were served and Ford sipped at his palely coloured beer cautiously, then grimaced. 'They've got the washing-up water mixed in with the beer.' He eyed Prentice's glass with even more distaste. 'You're not really drinking that, are you?' But his question was purely rhetorical – Prentice would drink anything, smoke anything, eat anything. Some of the dishes he'd consumed during their brief stay in Turkey had astounded and appalled the conservative Ford. Prentice pushed the glass of yellowish liquid towards him.

'Go on, it tastes just like whisky.' He watched with amusement while his companion took a gulp and then almost dropped the glass, looking round suddenly to make sure his experience hadn't been observed. Macomber was still watching him over his paper.

'Lovely!' Ford choked. 'A delicate mixture of nail varnish and turpentine. If that's the Greek national drink no wonder the Romans licked them. It still seems odd travelling with a bunch of Jerries for company.' He looked round the saloon as he heard a distant rattle. The gangway being hauled up probably. In one corner the thin-faced German was absorbed in a book while the man crouched over some typed sheets made notes with a pencil. They might have been aboard a normal peacetime boat and the war seemed a long way from Istanbul.

'It really is damned funny,' Prentice began, his lean, humorous face serious for a change. 'Here we are on a Greek ferry just leaving for Zervos – in the middle of a life-and-death war with Adolf Hitler's Reich – and because the Greeks are fighting the Italians but not the Germans, we can travel with three Jerries we mustn't even bump into if we meet them in the corridor. I must remember this trip when I write me memoirs, Ford.'

'Yes, sir,' said Ford automatically, and received a sharp dig in the ribs for his pains. He understood the hint and swore inwardly. He'd be glad when this ferry trip was over and they could get back to normal service life, to being Lieutenant Prentice and Staff-Sergeant Ford. Before they had boarded the *Hydra* Prentice had given him a stern lecture in their Istanbul hotel bedroom and he had tripped up already.

'Ford,' Prentice had begun, 'for the purposes of this sea trip back to Greece and while we're on board the ferry, I want you to forget I'm a lieutenant and, what's more important still, forget that you're a staff-sergeant. We're sporting civvies, but if you keep on calling me "sir" it's a dead giveaway. There may even be a German tourist on that broken-down old Greek ferry.' Prentice hadn't really believed that this would happen but he was dramatizing the situation to try and make Ford forget his years of professional training for a few hours.

'I'll watch it, sir,' Ford had replied and had then watched Prentice throw his trilby on the bed with a despairing cry.

'Ford!' he had bellowed. 'You've just done it again! Look, I know we're at the fag-end of our trip with the military mission to carry out liaison with the Turks in case Jerry attacks them, but we really have got to watch it . . .'

The trouble really had been the Turks themselves. Anxious to keep out of the war if they could – and who could blame them for that? – they had invited the British to send a military mission to discuss possible defence measures if the worst happened. But to avoid provoking the attack they feared, or rather, to avoid giving Berlin an excuse for launching that attack, they had insisted that the mission should travel in civilian clothes. A Signal Corps man, Prentice had found plenty to discuss with his Turkish opposite numbers in the way of a plan for setting up communications, and Staff-Sergeant Ford, ex-Royal Artillery, was now one of that rare breed, an ammunition examiner, an expert on explosives, both British and foreign. In this role he had also finished his work late when he had been taken to see a Turkish dam it was proposed to blow up in the event of a German invasion. So both of them had returned to Istanbul to find the plane with the military mission aboard had already left for Athens.

'When's the next one?' Prentice had light-heartedly asked the chap at the Legation.

'There isn't one,' the Legation official had informed him coldly. 'You'll have to catch a boat out of here. The very first available boat,' he had added. 'I've already looked it up for you – it's a ship called the *Hydra*. Sailing for Greece tomorrow morning. Just after dawn,' he had concluded with a twinge of waspish humour which Prentice, who hated rising early, had not fully appreciated.

Later, Prentice had discovered that normally there was a regular service operating between Istanbul and Athens, but the Turks had just cancelled this because of rumours of German troop movements along their northern borders. So, that left the ferry to the peninsula of Zervos, which was in northern Greece, much closer to Salonika than Athens, but at least it would land them on Greek soil. The Legation, of course, had been in the devil of a hurry to see the last of them. Prentice had a shrewd idea that the Ambassador was having kittens at the thought of British soldiers disguised as civilians wandering the streets of Istanbul. As he expressed it quietly to Ford in the saloon of the *Hydra* while he swallowed the *ouzo* in two gulps: 'I really think if there'd been a boat leaving for Russia they'd have pushed us on that.'

'Maybe. I still think it's queer there should be three Jerries all on the same trip on this leaky old tub,' Ford persisted. He could hear the rattle of a chain somewhere. They'd be off any minute now.

Prentice grinned. 'They may be embassy staff transferred from Istanbul to their place in Salonika.' He studied Ford, noted again the stocky build, the neatly cut black hair and the

44

alert eyes which watched the room constantly. Always wanting to have a go, was Ford. An aggressive, controlled chap who carried an air of competence and energetic ability. As for Prentice, he never went out of his way to have a go, but if the necessity arose he was more than able to cope with his leisured, laconic manner. The difference was that for Ford, the army was a way of life, whereas for Prentice it was a necessary but time-wasting interval which kept him from his advertising job in the West End of London.

'But if they're embassy staff,' Ford went on obstinately, his hands cupped to hide his mouth, 'why are they travelling separately? They don't know each other, that's obvious enough.'

Prentice felt the ship moving away from the quayside and checked his watch. 7.30 AM. Ford had a point there, he was thinking. And if they were embassy staff going to Salonika why the devil hadn't they taken the train from Istanbul along that line through Macedonia? By all accounts it was a nightmare trip, stopping at every little out-of-the-way village and taking anything up to a couple of days, but at least it would have got them there direct. So why were they in such a rush to reach Greece by the earliest possible hour? Why, Prentice kept asking himself? Why?

Field-Marshal von List stood up from behind the desk at his GHQ in southern Bulgaria and walked to the window, still holding the meteorological report. Beside the desk his staff officer, Colonel Wilhelm Genke, waited patiently. The field-marshal was worried and from long experience Genke knew that this was not the moment to speak. The clock on the desk registered 7.30 AM.

His face seasoned and grim, List gazed out at the view, and this didn't please him either because it was a reminder of the piece of paper he held in his hands. It was an hour after dawn and beyond the stone houses of the village he could make out where the mountains rose to meet the clouds which hung low over Bulgaria, clouds which promised more snow on the way. Which the Met report also promised. He could vaguely see the

45

snow from where he stood – great drifts of it piled up on the lower slopes under the cloud ceiling. His voice was harsh when he spoke.

'It's foul, unspeakably foul weather. They could be wrong, I suppose. They're wrong half the time, these so-called weather experts. Look at what happened in Norway.'

Genke coughed, timing his intervention carefully. 'Spring is late all over Europe, sir. There is still deep snow across the Russian steppes and no sign of a thaw...'

'Don't let's talk about Russia yet. We have to settle this business first.' List turned round, a tinge of sarcasm in his voice. 'Berlin, of course, is quite confident.'

'Berlin is always confident when other people have to do the work, sir. But you have exceptionally powerful forces under your command.'

On that point, at least, the field-marshal agreed. The Twelfth Army comprised two motorized, three mountain Alpenkorps and light infantry divisions, three regiments of the Liebstandarte Adolf Hitler Division – and five Panzer divisions, the spearhead of the coming onslaught on Greece and Yugoslavia. A force of enormous strength and great mobility – theoretically powerful enough to overwhelm everything which stood in their path. But there was deep snow on the Greek mountains, deep snow on Olympus and Zervos. Could the machines overcome the hazards of this damnably prolonged winter? The question was never far from his mind – and zero hour was almost here.

Gazing out of the window, he thought that Bulgaria was the most Godforsaken spot he had encountered in his life, and even as he watched, white flakes drifted down outside the window, several clinging to the glass and beginning to build up opaque areas. Would spring never come? Yes, zero hour was very close indeed. Beyond the window he heard a familiar sound – the grind and clatter of tank tracks moving over cobbled streets. The supporting Panzers were rolling towards the border and would be in position before nightfall. The time-table had been set in motion and the operation was under way. Now no power on earth except Berlin could stop it. And within hours even Berlin would have forfeited that prerogative.

46

From outside the house came the sound of a vehicle stopping, its engine still left running. Genke shuffled his feet.

'The car has arrived, sir.'

List buttoned up his coat to the neck, put the peaked cap on his head and started for the door. But on the way he paused to glance at the wall map which an orderly would take down as soon as they had left, a map of the southern Balkans and eastern Mediterranean zones. Then Genke opened the door and Field-Marshal von List strode out with his assistant following. Genke had noted that pause to glance at the map and he knew which area had attracted List's attention. He had looked first at Istanbul, then his eye had followed the sea route through the Dardanelles and across the Aegean where it had finally alighted on a certain peninsula.

Zervos.

'The *Rupescu*?' The Senior Naval Intelligence Officer at Alexandria looked up at his assistant, Lieutenant-Commander Browne. 'Is that the Rumanian ship the Legation people at Istanbul sent the message about?'

'Yes, sir. It left the Bulgarian port of Varna yesterday and arrived at the Golden Horn a few hours ago. There's some mystery as to her ultimate destination.'

'What mystery?'

'It's a bit vague, sir. Apparently she's bound for Beirut – but it's her first trip out of the Black Sea for months and I suppose the Legation's bothered because the Germans control Rumania now.'

'I see. That's rather delicate – we still haven't declared war on Rumania. You're suggesting we keep an eye on her? To make sure she is heading for the Lebanon?'

Browne looked out of the window where a white jetty sparkled in the early morning sunshine, its arm enclosing a basin of brilliant blue water where warships lay at anchor. A transport bound for Greece was just beyond the jetty wall, sailing north-west and leaving behind a clear wake of white on the blue. 'It's the only vessel in the area which has the remotest connexion with the Axis powers – and so far we have no idea what she's carrying.'

47

'Probably collecting rather than carrying – trying to pick up a cargo before war is eventually declared and we can pounce on her. We're very stretched, you know that, Browne.'

'I was thinking of the *Daring*, sir. She's patrolling off the Turkish coast and could intercept the *Rupescu* soon after dark. I'm not thinking of boarding her – but it might be interesting to get her reaction when a British destroyer comes in close.'

'Send Willoughby a message, then. And radio another one to Istanbul. We've had two requests already from those querulous diplomats.' The senior officer looked at the wall clock. 7.30 AM. Yes, it would be after nightfall before Willoughby arrived.

CHAPTER THREE

Saturday, 10 PM

The tension had slowly risen aboard the *Hydra*, a tension which seemed reproduced by the steady beat of her throbbing engines as she left the Dardanelles and proceeded far out into the open Aegean. By nightfall she was midway between the Turkish and Greek coasts, steaming through seas which were beginning to curdle. The tension rose from small, meaningless incidents. The meeting at a doorway between Prentice and the squat, dark-haired German, Volber, when the latter had started to push his way through first and had then changed his mind, offering prior entry to Prentice. The episode at dinner when a cork came out of a bottle like a pistol shot and for several seconds the company had frozen. The careful way in which passengers of different nationalities turned to go in another direction when they saw someone coming towards them.

'It's not frightfully funny any more,' Prentice had remarked over dinner irritably. 'Look at the way they're sitting – like pallbearers at a funeral.'

'They'd have more fun at a funeral – afterwards, anyway,' Ford had pointed out. 'It's almost as though they're waiting for something to happen.' All the others occupied a table to themselves. Macomber, Hahnemann, Volber and Grapos – all sitting in splendid isolation with empty tables between them while each ate and drank as though he were the only person in the room, taking care to make no sound except for the occasional clink of cutlery. Even the captain, Nopagos, who came in later, was unable to help. He had explained this briefly to Prentice in his careful English while visiting each table in turn before taking a table of his own.

'It is difficult, Mr Prentice – British and Germans on board, you understand.'

'Frightened there'll be a rumpus?' Prentice had inquired genially.

'Rum . . . pus?'

'A battle, a fight.' Prentice had play-acted with his fists, glad of the chance to pull someone's leg, then had relented when he saw the Greek's doleful expression. 'Don't worry, we'll be good. But I bet you'll be damned glad to drop this lot off at Katyra in the morning.'

'The safe arrival in port is always the happy time,' Nopagos replied ambiguously and went away to his solitary table.

When dinner was over one passenger, Macomber, lingered in the room long after the others had left, smoking his cigar and drinking coffee from the pot the steward had provided after clearing his table. Like the saloon, the dining-room was panelled and small gold curtains were still drawn back from the porthole windows. Occasionally, he glanced out of the nearest window which gave him a view across the moonlit sea to the north-east, a sea which had now ceased to tremble with small waves and was already developing massive undulations which heaved towards the vessel with foam-topped crests. The dining-room was beginning to sway ponderously and the Scot shifted his feet wider apart to counter the movement as the woodwork creaked ominously, the horizon beyond the porthole dipping out of sight and then clambering into view again. The fourth German, Schnell, had still not appeared, and Macomber had mentioned this to the steward when he had brought the extra pot of coffee. 'Perhaps he's dead,' he had said with rough humour, 'he could be for all we've seen of him.'

'He had dinner served in his cabin,' the steward had remarked, 'and he wanted a Thermos of coffee made up for the night. Probably he doesn't sleep well at sea.'

'He won't if he drinks a whole Thermos of this,' Macomber had replied. The coffee was Turkish and the prospect of consuming it in such quantities suggested a steel-plated stomach and an inability to sleep at all.

'We get passengers like that occasionally,' the steward had prattled on. 'They just don't seem to like mixing with strangers. This man is like that – he was in the toilet when the dinner was taken in, as though he didn't even wish to see the steward. He's Austrian, I think,' he had added.

'Indeed? Why do you say that?'

'His big cabin trunk has labels on it from the Hotel Sacher in Vienna. The steward thinks he spends a lot of time sitting by his porthole gazing out to sea – there was a pair of field-glasses opened by the table next to his wrist-watch. Call me if you want anything else, sir.' Left alone by himself Macomber had drunk two cups of the strong-tasting liquid while he thought about the invisible Herr Schnell. It was ten o'clock when he walked out of the deserted dining-room to take a final tour of the vessel, and at this hour the *Hydra* had the feel of a ghost ship, one of those phantom vessels which drift round the seaways of the world and are only seen as a mirage in the night. There was no one about as he descended a creaking staircase and began to walk along the empty companionway on the deck containing the passenger cabins. He had chosen this staircase deliberately and his rubber-soled boots made no sound as he paused by the first cabin which the Austrian occupied. Cabin One was silent but there were narrow streaks of light in the louvred upper half of the closed door. He made no attempt to see through the louvres – he had tested that possibility with his own cabin door earlier in the evening – but clearly the mysterious Schnell was still secreted inside his own quarters. He might not be awake, Macomber was thinking as he stood quite still, since a man who spends hours inside one small room is likely to get drowsy and fall asleep with the lights still on.

The next cabin was the wireless-room. Here, instead of pausing, Macomber walked past slowly, seeing through the half-open door the Greek wireless operator reading a news-paper as one hand reached out for a sandwich. So far every-thing seemed normal, perfectly normal, but the Scot could not rid himself of a feeling of growing unease. The next cabin was in darkness. Volber's. The German who looked like the owner of a small business – or a member of the Gestapo. Often the two types could easily be confused. Cabin Three still had the lights on and from behind the closed door came the faint sounds of dance music. Herr Hahnemann was tuned in to Radio Deutschland, perhaps feeling a little homesick aboard

51

this swaying ferry in the middle of the Aegean. There were lights in the next cabin, too, the temporary home of the two Britishers. Macomber paused outside and then walked steadily on as the mumble of voices died suddenly. When a cabin door opened behind him he was careful not to turn round. An interesting thought had struck him: was Volber really asleep inside that darkened cabin or was he somewhere else, having deliberately given the impression that he had gone down for the night? Silently he passed his own darkened cabin and began to mount the staircase at the other end of the companionway. The vessel was steaming steadily westward and as he opened the door at the top he faced the stern, consciously bracing himself and squaring his shoulders as the moan of the wind took on a higher note, rasping his face with its icy blast. Macomber had experienced the wind from the plains of Hungary, a wind which swept straight in from the depths of faraway Siberia, but as he slammed the door shut he thought he had never felt a more penetrating chill.

The deck was deserted. No sign of Volber. But the boat was still there, the vessel he had seen through the porthole from his dining-room table. She was moving along a course parallel to the *Hydra*'s, ploughing through the rising seas perhaps three kilometres to starboard. The deck was lifting sufficiently for him to hold onto the rail as he made his way to the stern, his face muscles drawn tight and not from the bitter wind which froze his skin. Taking out his Monokular glass, which was small enough to conceal inside the palm of one hand, he looked back along the deck. Lifeboats, the snow melted and gone during the day, swung slowly on their davits, reproducing the movement of the sea. A thin trail of smoke floated from the *Hydra*'s funnel, was caught up by the wind and thrown into a spiral. There was no sign of life anywhere. He aimed his glass, saw the other ship as a blur which merged in one long glowworm of light, focused, brought the lights forward as separate portholes, noted the white funnel and the unidentifiable flag which whipped from the masthead. For perhaps a minute he stood motionless, one part of his mind on the lens, the other part alert for the slightest sound which might warn him that he was no longer alone on that empty deck, a sound which might warn him of the attempt on his life he had feared ever since coming aboard. Then he closed the glass, pocketed it and checked his watch once more. 10.10 PM. Yes, it was the *Rupescu*, the vessel which had got up steam as soon as the *Hydra* had made preparations to leave the Golden Horn. Shoulders hunched against the wind, he made his way back along the unstable deck and went down into the warmth which met him as soon as he opened the door. Inside his own cabin he took off his hat and coat, lit a fresh cigar, put the Luger within easy reach and settled down to wait. Assassins often preferred to operate at night.

'It was the big German,' Ford said as he closed the cabin door and re-locked it. 'I caught him on the staircase at the far end – he still had his coat and hat on and he was going up on deck. I don't like it.'

'Don't like what?' Prentice withdrew his hand from where it had rested near the pillow which concealed his Webley ·455 revolver and began studying the patience cards spread out over his bunk.

'The feel of this old tub – those Jerries being aboard and not talking to each other. They come from the same country and they haven't said a blasted word to each other from what I've seen.'

'Perhaps they're English in disguise – that would explain the non-fraternization.' He picked up a card, placed it over another. 'Not been formally introduced, you see.'

Ford lit the last of his army issue cigarettes, the ones he could only smoke when they were alone, and started thudding a heel against the woodwork as he sat down on his bunk. Prentice looked up and stared pointedly at the thudding heel until Ford stopped the noise, then went back to his game. 'You could always get some kip,' he suggested hopefully.

'Couldn't sleep a wink,' the staff-sergeant told him emphatically. 'Not with those Jerries aboard creeping all over the shop when it's long past their bedtime.' He got up and went over to the porthole, pulling the curtain aside with a jerk. 'That ship's still there, too. Wonder why it's keeping so close to us?'

Prentice slammed down a card and lit a Turkish cigarette quickly while he watched the sergeant who continued staring out of the porthole in his shirt-sleeves. 'Ford, there are things called sea-lanes. Ships are liable to follow them. If you've ever crossed the Channel you'll see quite a few ships not far from each other the whole way across. I really think that Turkish food must have done you a power of harm – you're not normally as jittery as this.'

Ford turned away from the porthole, closing the curtain again. 'And I'm not normally travelling on a boat with a load of Jerries for company. There's something strange going on – I can feel it.'

'Three Jerries . . .' Prentice started to point out.

'Four! There's that other one the captain mentioned to us earlier in the day – the one that never comes out of his cabin at the end of the companionway.'

'All right, four! But hardly a load of Jerries – you make it sound as though there's a division of them aboard. What can four of them do aboard a Greek ferry in the middle of the Aegean which – when I last heard of it – is controlled by the Royal Navy? If you go on like this, Ford,' he continued with a mischievous grin, 'you'll end up in sick bay with some MO asking you what scared you in your cradle! Now, how do you expect me to get this game out if you persist in banging your foot and peering through portholes as though you anticipated a whole German army arriving at any moment?'

'Sorry. It's probably that last meal we had in Istanbul. What was that dish again?'

'Fried octrangel,' said Prentice absent-mindedly as he turned his attention to the cards. 'It's a baby octopus. A great delicacy.' He didn't look up to see Ford's face, but a few minutes later he became aware again of the restless sergeant's movements and glanced up to see him putting on his coat over his jacket.

'Feel like a breath of fresh air,' Ford explained. 'Don't mind, do you?'

'Yes, I think I do.' The lieutenant spoke sharply. 'Going out on your own isn't really a very good idea.'

Ford's eyes gleamed as he dropped the coat onto his

bunk. 'You don't much like it either, then?'

'I just don't think it's too clever for us to separate at this time of night. There!' He dropped a card on a small pile. 'You see, it's coming out.' Prentice smiled grimly to himself as he went on playing: Ford had smoked him out there. No, he wasn't entirely happy about the situation aboard this ferry, but he saw no point in alarming the staff-sergeant at this stage. Prentice was a man who, despite his outwardly extrovert air, preferred to keep his fears to himself. Those Germans who were worrying Ford could, of course, be spies, and if they were they had chosen the right place to come – the strategically important peninsula of Zervos. As he played out his game Prentice was thinking of a military conference he had attended in Athens just before departing for Turkey, a conference he had attended because a question of communications had been involved. He could hear Colonel Wilson's clipped voice speaking now as he automatically placed a fresh card.

'It's the very devil,' Wilson had said, 'getting permission to send some of our chaps to Mount Zervos. The official in the Greek War Ministry who's responsible says Zervos is seventy miles from the Bulgarian frontier and in any case the peninsula comes under the command of the Greek army in Macedonia. He just won't have us there.'

'Not even to send a small unit to set up an observation post?' Prentice had ventured. 'From what I gather the monastery under the summit looks clear across the gulf to the coast road taking our supplies up to the Alkiamon Line.'

'You gather correctly,' Wilson had told him crisply. 'But the monastery seems to be the stumbling-block. Apparently for many years the whole peninsula has been a monastic sanctuary and you need a government permit even to land there. They won't grant one of those to a woman – the only women allowed in the area are the wives and relatives of fishermen who live there . . .' He had paused, his expression icy until the ripple of laughter had died. Perhaps he had sounded unnecessarily indignant on that score. 'The guts of the thing is that this Greek official practically suggests we'd be violating something sacred by sending in a few troops . . .'

'You believe him?' Prentice had interjected quietly, never

backward in speaking up when his interest was aroused. There had been an awkward pause before Wilson had answered that one. Only a tiny fraction of the Greek population was believed to hold secret Nazi sympathies, but it was feared that one or two of these undesirable gentry might occupy key positions inside the Greek government.

'We can only take his word,' Wilson had replied eventually. 'But the thing that sends shivers up the spines of our planning staff is the idea of German troops capturing that monastery. It's perched nearly three thousand feet up at the southern tip of the peninsula and has a clear view across to that vital coast road. And that's not all. There's some freak in the weather up there which means the summit of Mount Zervos is nearly always cloud-free – so you get an uninterrupted view of that road even when visibility's nil a few miles away. A Jerry observation post stuck up there would put us in a proper pickle.'

Afterwards, a Royal Artillery major had further enlightened Prentice: beyond the head of the gulf a range of hills formed a natural defence line, but if the Wehrmacht attacked and were able to emplace heavy guns on the lower slopes they could bring down an annihilating fire on the coast road from behind these hill crests – *providing they had an observation post on Mount Zervos which could guide the fall of the bombardment.* The major ended up by saying that if the Germans ever did get the Allies in such a position it would be little short of a massacre.*

Prentice dropped another card in place and sighed as the *Hydra* tilted again, a slow, deliberate roll as though revolving on an axis. While in Turkey he'd almost forgotten that conference, never believing for one instant that he would ever set eyes on Zervos, and here he was less than eight hours' sailing time from that benighted peninsula. And why the hell did ships always have to leave almost at dawn and arrive somewhere else at that Godforsaken hour? Finishing the game, he started shuffling the cards, uncertain whether to play again.

* Later in the war the same threat materialized at Monte Cassino where a German observation post reported to the gunners every movement of Allied troops.

Then he stopped shuffling. Ford was again standing by the porthole, the curtain drawn back, and there was something in his manner which caught Prentice's attention. 'What's up?' he asked.

'It's this ship – she's coming in damned close, whatever you say about sea-lanes.'

Prentice stood up quickly and went over to the porthole. The unknown vessel was now sailing on a parallel course less than a quarter of a mile from the *Hydra*'s hull and even as he watched the gap seemed to be narrowing. 'She is damned close,' he agreed, and felt a faint prickling of the short hairs at the back of his neck. He watched for a little while longer to be sure the ship wasn't simply passing them, then took a decision. 'I think we'd better pay our friend, Captain Nopagos, a little visit . . .' He broke off in mid-sentence. 'What was that?'

'Sounded like someone falling over in the passage – I think he hit our door . . .'

'Better see – and watch it!' Prentice dropped the pack of cards on his bunk, sat down and idly let his hand rest on the bunk close to the pillow which hid the Webley. He looked half-asleep as he watched Ford, who had now reached the locked door. Ford hesitated, listened for a moment, then heard a groan and a shuffling sound. He unlocked the door, opening it cautiously.

The Greek steward who looked after the cabins was lying face down in the companionway, his body wriggling as a slight moan escaped him. Ford looked both ways along the passage and saw that it was deserted. The *Hydra* was moving in a heavy swell, rocking slowly as the sea lifted and lowered it. He bent down quickly and noted that the man's hands were underneath him as though clasped to his stomach. There was no sign of injury so far as he could see – the poor devil must have been taken sick while walking down the companionway. He looked back inside the cabin and called out to Prentice.

'It's the steward. I think he's had an attack or something. I'd better go along and find someone . . .'

'Hold it a minute!' Prentice's nerves were on edge and his mind raced as he took in the implications of this unexpected incident. Ford going off to seek help would mean they were separated, a situation which could be dangerous. There was something queer going on, very queer indeed. 'No, don't do that,' he told Ford quickly. 'Can we get him in here? Let's have a look at him first.' He stepped into the companionway to give Ford a hand, stooping down to hoist the steward by the shoulders while the sergeant took the legs. They were standing in this position, still in the companionway with their hands encumbered, when the cabin door next to them was thrown open and Hahnemann came out. At waist-height he held a German machine-pistol, the weapon aimed at Ford's chest as he spoke in English.

'Put the Greek down and lift your hands. Be careful! If I shoot, the Greek dies, too.'

They put the steward down gently and as he reached the floor his hands and feet began to scrabble about in a more life-like fashion. His face turned and Prentice saw that he was scared stiff, his complexion whiter than the jacket he wore. With Ford, he raised his hands, turning slowly as he stood up so that he could look down the passage where he caught a glimpse through the half-closed door of the wireless-room. The radio operator still sat in front of his seat but now his hands were tied behind the back of his neck and then the view closed off as Volber came out holding a Luger pistol.

'Look at the wall!' snapped Hahnemann. 'And keep still.'

They faced the wall and Prentice felt Volber's quick hands pat his clothes and explore his body for hidden weapons. The shock of the hold-up was going now and Prentice's mind coldly searched for a way of upsetting the enemy who had decided to continue the war on neutral territory. The Greek steward was standing up and faced the wall when Hahnemann gave the order. The German issued his instructions in a crisp, controlled manner which warned Prentice that any counter-action would have to be swift, unexpected and totally effective.

'And now you go inside the cabin. Quickly!'

Prentice obeyed the order without hesitation. In fact, he went inside so quickly that Hahnemann was caught off-balance as the lieutenant tore through the open doorway, hooked his right heel behind the panel and slammed it in the German's face. His instinct was to dive for the revolver under the pillow, but knowing he hadn't the time, he jumped close to the wall as the door was thrown open again. Hahnemann jumped into the room, literally leapt through the doorway, turning as he saw Prentice a fraction of a second too late. The lieutenant grasped the machine-pistol by the barrel and swung the muzzle viciously to one side, still holding on, then jerked it backwards beyond the German who had expected him to pull it away from him. The muzzle was still aimed futilely at the outer wall. Continuing the rearward jerk, Prentice felt the weapon come free and in the same second felt his feet slip under him. He went over on the back of his head, still gripping the weapon as clouds of dizziness addled his brain and he saw only shadows through a mist. He was still struggling through the mists, seeing them clear gradually, when something hard and heavy hit him in the side. Hahnemann had just kicked him. When he recovered a grip on himself the German was standing over him with the machine-pistol aimed at the centre of his chest. In the doorway Ford stood grimly silent with Volber's Luger pointed at his stomach.

'Get up!' said Hahnemann savagely, backing away as Prentice, wondering why the hell he was still alive, clambered painfully to his feet. That hadn't been too clever. The back of his head felt to be split in two and an iron hammer was banging down the split. He gulped in several breaths of air, trying to hear what Hahnemann was saying. 'Over by the wall. Quick!' Tottering a little, Prentice went over to the outer wall and leant against it where Ford joined him a moment later. Volber went out of the cabin, closing the door behind him. It had all happened so swiftly that he was still wondering what the hell they hoped to achieve, was still suffering from a partial sense of shock. Alongside him Ford stared at the German with an intent look, waiting for him to make just one small mistake. The trouble was he didn't look like a man who repeated his mistakes – letting Prentice break loose had put him in a state of total alertness, and although he was guarding two men on his own he stood back far enough to give his gun a good field of fire. One brief burst would kill both of them: Ford, as a weapons and explosives expert, was under no illusions on this point.

'Why are you aboard this ship, Lieutenant Prentice?' demanded Hahnemann.

Prentice glanced at the table where Volber had left the papers and paybook he had extracted from their pockets while searching them for weapons. Hahnemann must have looked at these while he was coming up out of the mists. He wasn't in any hurry to reply – time was a factor the German clearly valued, as though he were following a carefully worked out timetable, and Prentice had detected a note of anxiety behind the question, so his reply was deliberately non-informative. 'To travel from Istanbul to Zervos,' he said. For a horrible second he thought he had made a fatal mistake. Hahnemann's finger tightened on the trigger and Prentice braced himself for the lacerating burst of bullets, but the German regained control and smiled unpleasantly.

'That I understood! Now, Lieutenant Prentice, before I shoot Sergeant Ford in the stomach I will ask the question again. Why are you travelling on this particular ship on this particular night? You understand? Good.'

Prentice found he was sweating badly on the palms of his hands and under his armpits. He hadn't the least idea of what Hahnemann was talking about but he doubted whether he could convince the German of this. His brain reeled as he sought desperately for words which might half-satisfy their interrogator, and with a tremendous effort he managed a ghastly smile in an endeavour to lower the temperature before it was too late. 'I take it you're in the German army?' For the first time Hahnemann showed a trace of uncertainty and Prentice followed up his tiny advantage quickly. 'Then you'll know that according to the Geneva Convention all we have to give you is name, rank and number. You've got those there on that table already.'

It was a hair-line gamble, switching the conversation to this topic, but Prentice was counting on the German's training to make him pause, to cool his anger, to gain control again. To his great relief he saw the machine-pistol muzzle swing to a point between himself and Ford where it could fire in either direction. The German had, at least temporarily, recovered his balance. Prentice had now assessed Hahnemann as a highly trained individual who normally kept an ice-cold grip on his emotions, but who also, occasionally, in a state of fury, lost that grip and went berserk. They had just witnessed such an occasion when their lives had trembled on the brink.

'What were you doing in Turkey?' Hahnemann asked suddenly.

'Trying to get a berth home to Athens.' Prentice's quick tongue rattled on. 'And the civilian clothes were loaned to us by the Turks. Our ship struck a mine off the Turkish coast two days ago and we were dragged out of the sea more dead than alive. We were the only survivors – and don't ask me the name of the ship or how many she was carrying because you wouldn't answer that either if I were holding the gun. And don't ask me why the Turks didn't intern us because I don't know – except that they seemed damned glad to get rid of us at the earliest possible moment. They'd have put us on the normal Istanbul–Athens service, but that was cancelled at the last minute so we were hustled aboard this ferry. The first available ship out, they said – and this was it.'

It had been a long speech and he hoped to God that it had satisfied Hahnemann on the one question which seemed to bother him – why were they aboard the *Hydra*? There was a hint of respect in the German's eyes now and Prentice decided to press a point home, forgetting that it's always a mistake to overdo a good thing.

'So we're your prisoners-of-war at the moment,' Prentice continued, 'but don't forget that the Royal Navy controls the Aegean. If there's a British destroyer in the area you may find me holding that gun within a few hours, so let's drop the threats.'

'There is a British destroyer near here?' The gun muzzle was aimed straight at Prentice's chest and the note of cold fury had come back into the German's voice. 'You know this?' The words were an accusation and Hahnemann's jaw muscles were rigid with tension, a tension which instantly communicated itself to the two men with their backs to the wall. The tip of the gun muzzle quivered, the outward sign of the nervous vibration bottled up inside the man holding the weapon. Christ! Prentice was thinking, we're a nervous twitch away from a fusillade. Where the devil did I go wrong? He spoke carefully but quickly, his eyes fixed on Hahnemann's as he struggled to gauge the effect of his words while he was talking. 'I'm not thinking of any particular destroyer – I'm in the army, not the navy – you know that. But these seas are constantly patrolled so it's just a matter of luck – yours or ours.' He shut up, hoping for the best, determined not to overdo it a second time. His shirt was clinging to his wet back and he daren't look at Ford in case Hahnemann thought he was passing a signal. It was becoming a nightmare and he had a grisly feeling they might not live through it.

'Turn round and lie on the floor – stretch out your hands to the fullest extent.'

The unexpected order threw Prentice off balance; it was impossible to keep up with this German through his swift changes of mood, but at least there weren't going to be any more of those trigger-loaded questions. He was on his knees when he grasped the meaning of the order, saw out of the corner of his eye the vicious arc of the machine-pistol butt descending on poor Ford's head, and as the sergeant slumped unconscious over the floor he swung round to swear at the German. The muzzle was aimed point-blank at his chest. Prentice was obeying the fresh order to look at the wall when a ton-weight landed on his tender scalp. A brilliant burst of light flashed before his eyes and then vanished in the flood of darkness which overwhelmed him.

The rifle muzzle was pressed into Macomber's face when he opened the cabin door in response to the urgent knocking, and the threat was accompanied by an apology in German. 'You must remain in your cabin until further orders, Herr Dietrich. I am sorry . . .'

'Whose orders?' Macomber stood with his hand behind his back, his manner harsh and unimpressed by the sight of the weapon. For a moment it seemed as though he would push Volber out of the way by walking straight into him. The German had paused, uncertain how to handle this aggressive reaction, but Hahnemann, who stood close behind with a machine-pistol in his hands, was not taken aback.

'By order of the Wehrmacht!'

Macomber stared past Volber, ignoring the squat man as he gazed bleakly at Hahnemann. Again it seemed as though he would push the rifle barrel aside and Hahnemann instinctively raised his own weapon. 'That is not enough,' Macomber rumbled Teutonically. 'The officer's name, if you please.' He might have been a colonel addressing a subordinate.

'Lieutenant Hahnemann, Alpenkorps.' The German had replied automatically and had felt the reflex of snapping his heels to attention, but he desisted just in time. Now he was furious with his own reply, but there was something about the passenger which he found intimidating, an air of authority which was disturbing. 'You will stay in your cabin,' he barked. 'Do you understand? Anyone found outside their cabin without permission will be shot!' Immediately he had spoken he had doubts, and the steely look in Macomber's eye was anything but reassuring. Who the hell could he be? 'Lieutenant Hahnemann?' Macomber repeated slowly, and there was an uncomfortable, mocking note in his voice. 'I think I can remember that for later!'

Hahnemann persisted, but more quietly. 'Please give my sergeant the key of your cabin so it can be locked from the outside.'

Macomber gazed thoughtfully at Hahnemann a moment longer, then turning on his heel so that the cabin door hid part of his body, he slipped the Luger back inside his coat pocket and re-entered the cabin, ignoring the request for the key. Volber he could have dealt with, but the lieutenant's machine-pistol was quite another matter. With a muttered expression of annoyance Hahnemann walked forward, extracted the key himself and locked the door on the outside. The Scot straightened up from the newspaper spread over the table, his expression grim. This was even worse than he had imagined: they were taking over the whole ship.

His initial reaction on opening the door was that the assassins had come for him. This fleeting impression had been succeeded by the revelation that they were not interested in him at all, that a major Wehrmacht operation was under way, a stroke as audacious as the Norwegian campaign*. He stood listening, his head cocked to one side. Yes, he was right – the *Hydra*'s engines were slowing. For the mid-sea rendezvous, of course. They must have taken control of the engine-room at an earlier stage and by now they would command the bridge. An efficient operation planned with the usual meticulous care and attention to detail – including the bringing aboard of Herr Schnell and his outsize cabin trunk containing the weapons. Retrieving his smoking cigar from the ash-tray, he switched off the light and used his torch to find his way across the cabin to the porthole.

The *Hydra*'s engines had almost stopped and the *Rupescu* was so close that a collision seemed likely. Standing by the porthole without any attempt at concealment, his cigar glowing for anyone who cared to see it, he watched the transfer of the German troops from the Rumanian vessel to the Greek ferry. The soldiers, wearing life-jackets, were coping with a heavy swell – had they arrived later or had the weather worsened earlier the operation might have proved impossible. German luck again, Macomber thought bitterly – like the luck of the marvellous weather over France in 1940. You can't get far without luck, he was thinking as he watched a boatload of troops being lowered to the sea. There must have been almost twenty men aboard and he was praying for an accident as the craft almost capsized when the waves heaved up to meet it, but at the last moment someone released the ropes and the boat followed the natural curvature of the sea. The uniformed troops wore soft, large-peaked caps and were heavily laden with equipment. Alpenkorps. A unit of the élite mountain troops who had conquered Norway, men trained to fight in appalling terrain such as the peninsula of Zervos.

He remained standing there for some time, his body now fully accustomed to the sway of the ship under his widespread feet, and during that time he counted the transfer of over two hundred men to the Greek ferry. More than enough to take

* Norway was seized by apparently innocent merchant ships full of German troops which sailed up the Norwegian coast within gun range of the unsuspecting Royal Navy.

Zervos, providing they received heavy reinforcements in the near future. After all, unless the Allies had put their own troops ashore on the peninsula the only people who stood in their way were a handful of monks at the monastery and a few fishermen at Katyra. Even when the transfer had been completed, when a boat containing, so far as Macomber could make out, the crew of the *Rupescu*, had accomplished the narrow crossing, he still waited at the porthole as the *Hydra*'s engines began to throb with power.

The ferry had resumed its interrupted voyage, was moving away and leaving the Rumanian vessel behind like an empty carcass, when Macomber opened the porthole and thrust his head out into the elements. The rising force of the knife-edged wind chilled his face as he watched the *Rupescu* slowly settling in the growing turbulence of the sea. They had switched off all the lights before they left her but by the light of the moon he saw her bows awash, the curling waves submerging her decks, the water-logged wallow of the doomed vessel. The sea-cocks had been opened, of course. He was still leaning out of the porthole when her superstructure disappeared under the billowing waves, leaving for a brief moment only the white funnel thrust up like some strange lighthouse in mid-Aegean. Then that, too, sank and there was no trace left that the *Rupescu* had ever existed.

Macomber withdrew his head, rammed the porthole shut, switched on the cabin light and began slapping his hands across his body to warm up. Sitting down on the bunk, he resisted the fatal temptation to sprawl his legs along it, and lit a fresh cigar. Still no chance to sleep, and it looked as though it might be a long while yet before he dared close his eyes. The period of standing by the porthole had tired his limbs horribly but his growing fury and the night sea air had made him steadily more alert, and now as he smoked the anger helped him to think. All his eager anticipations of returning to a haven of peace had temporarily left him, had left him at the first sight of those uniforms he knew so well. He had to do something to upset the timetable, the careful plan they would be working to, because they were bad improvisers and when things went wrong they reacted badly. His main hope was to persist in his impersonation, to throw them off-balance at the outset, to gain the freedom to move around the ship freely. He stood up to fight down the sleepiness he felt again, shoved the hat on his head, the hat which made him look even more Germanic, and glanced in the washbasin mirror. No need to assume an expression of grimness: that was already only too evident. You're *Dietrich*, he said softly, so from now on forget a chap called Macomber ever existed. And they'll have to maintain radio silence so they can't check anything. It's the first encounter that matters. You're Dietrich, Dr Richard Dietrich. He sat down again in the chair, impatient for the first confrontation, and when they came for him it was close to midnight.

CHAPTER FOUR

Saturday, Midnight

With his machine-pistol cradled under his arm, Lieutenant Hahnemann, now dressed in Alpenkorps uniform, unlocked the door, turned the handle and kicked it open with his foot. Dietrich was sitting at the little table, still wearing his coat and hat with his legs stretched out before him and crossed at the ankles. He was smoking a fresh cigar and the rude entry had no effect on him, caused no change in his relaxed stance; rather it seemed as though he went out of his way to demonstrate his bored unconcern. Dietrich folded his arms. He was regarding Hahnemann as he might have regarded a piece of badly cooked meat, then he transferred his attention to the tall, beak-nosed man who walked briskly in behind the lieutenant. A striking-looking German in his early forties, he held himself very erect as his cold blue eyes studied the seated passenger, and under his civilian coat, which he wore open at the front, Dietrich saw the boots and uniform of the Alpenkorps.

'This is Colonel Burckhardt,' Hahnemann informed him harshly. He paused as though expecting some reaction. 'People normally stand in the colonel's presence,' he went on bleakly.

'Tell this man to go away so we can talk.' Dietrich addressed the suggestion to Burckhardt who was looking down at him with interest. The passenger hadn't moved since he had entered the cabin.

'You can talk with both of us,' Burckhardt began tersely. 'Unless you have a very good reason for wishing to speak to me alone.' Like Hahnemann earlier, Burckhardt was wondering why he had reacted in a way he had hardly intended. And yet...

'What I have to say is not for junior officers.' Dietrich's brief mood of amiability was vanishing rapidly and he looked at the colonel grimly. 'I should have thought you hadn't a great deal of time to waste, so shall we get on with it?'

Burckhardt's expression showed no reaction, but inwardly he felt a trifle off-balance – he had been going to say almost precisely the same thing and now this aggressive-looking brute had forestalled him. He had the odd feeling that he was losing ground so he spoke decisively to the lieutenant. 'Hahnemann, you have duties to attend to. Leave me with this man until I call you.'

'He may be armed,' Hahnemann protested.

'Of course I am armed,' Dietrich replied swiftly, anticipating Burckhardt's next question. A lesser man than Colonel Heinz Burckhardt might have felt annoyance, but the colonel had risen to command an élite arm of the Wehrmacht and he had a grudging appreciation of an independent attitude. 'I am going to take out a Luger pistol,' Dietrich explained, staring at Hahnemann as though he doubted his ability to grasp plain German, 'so kindly keep a hold on yourself – and your weapon.' Producing the pistol from his coat pocket, he laid it on the table. 'It is fully loaded, incidentally – I never bluff when I have to use a weapon, which, fortunately, is a rare occasion.' The sight of the regulation pistol, a minor point, subtly reinforced Burckhardt's growing interest in the huge German passenger. For a moment Hahnemann hesitated whether to pick up the gun, but Dietrich's attention was so clearly concentrated on the colonel, was so obviously no longer aware of his presence, that he felt at a loss and glanced at Burckhardt for instructions.

'Leave us,' the colonel told him brusquely. 'I shall be on the bridge in a few minutes.'

Dietrich waited until the cabin door had closed and then stood up slowly. The action startled Burckhardt, who was six feet tall; he had realized that Dietrich also was a tall man but now he was able to see that the German civilian stood two to three inches above him. Rarely impressed by another man's physique, Burckhardt found himself a little overawed by the formidable figure who stood before him with his shoulders hunched and his hands clasped behind his broad back. Dietrich waited a moment, then put a hand inside his coat, extracted something and dropped it on the table. 'My papers, Colonel Burckhardt.'

With a mounting sense of irritation Burckhardt looked at the card carefully, glancing up to find Dietrich watching him without any particular expression. 'You're an archaeologist, I see, Dr Dietrich?' He couldn't keep the flatness out of his voice: he had suspected that this passenger was someone important from Berlin; it was the only explanation for his arrogant manner.

'Look at them carefully,' Dietrich urged him gruffly. 'See anything unusual about them?'

'No!' Burckhardt replied after a second perusal and there was a snap in his voice now.

'Good!' Dietrich lifted his shoulders and towered over the colonel as he went on with withering sarcasm. 'I was travelling aboard a Greek ferry which might at any time have been stopped and searched by a British destroyer. Under those conditions would you really expect me to present them with papers showing I am a senior officer of the Abwehr?'

Burckhardt stood quite still and his heart sank. Here was the explanation for Dietrich's overbearing attitude since he had entered the cabin. God, the Abwehr! That damned Intelligence organization of the incredibly influential Admiral Canaris. They never told anyone what they were going to do – not until they had done it. And they never told anyone where they were going until they had been there and arrived back in Berlin. They were responsible to no one except the wily old admiral who had started his career with naval Intelligence, and who was now answerable only to the Führer himself. The Abwehr was disliked – feared might be a better word – by all the regular Intelligence services because it lived a life of its own, but even more because of its legendary record of coups. In some uncanny way the admiral managed to be right every time in his forecast of enemy intentions. Oh yes, Burckhardt had heard of the Abwehr, but this was the first time he had met one of them. That is, assuming Dietrich was who he claimed to be ... He looked up suspiciously as something else landed on the table.

'Now you can see what I would have dropped through the

nearest porthole if we had been stopped – along with the Luger, of course.'

Dietrich's tone was ironic, close to sneering, and Burckhardt caught the tone and felt the blood rush to his head, so for a short time while he examined the second card Baxter had doctored and handed over in Giurgiu, his normally ice-cold judgement deserted him. Dietrich walked across the cabin to look out through the porthole, still talking over his shoulder.

'You will require absolute proof of my identity, so you had better send a wireless message to Berlin. I can give you the signal code.'

'Not while we are at sea,' Burckhardt rapped out. 'We must preserve radio silence at all costs.'

'I had assumed that,' Dietrich retorted brusquely. 'I meant after you had gone ashore. You have dealt with the two Englanders, I hope?'

'Yes, Hahnemann dealt with the whole operation most efficiently. They are only a lieutenant and a sergeant travelling home from Turkey.'

'You knew then beforehand that these two men were being put on board?'

Burckhardt paused, staring at the back of the Abwehr man who continued gazing out to sea. There was something in the way the question had been phrased which disturbed him, which made him delay his departure for the bridge. Had there been some awful slip-up somewhere? 'Knew?' he repeated warily.

'Yes, "knew", I said. Did you know?' Dietrich had swung round and was talking with his cigar in his mouth, his legs splayed as he continued to dominate the conversation.

'No,' the colonel admitted reluctantly. 'I was worried when I first heard about them but they are of very junior rank...'

'Are you certain of that? Papers can be easily forged or doctored – including army pay-books. These two men could be far more important for all we know.' He paused to give his insidious suggestion maximum impact. 'They could be on board because some hint of your operation has reached the Allies. You may be lucky they never reached the wireless-room.' He leaned forward grimly. 'I take it they did not reach the wireless-room?'

70

'Of course not! That was part of Hahnemann's job ...'

'Any idea which arm of the service they're attached to?'

Burckhardt felt himself go very cold. Until this unnerving interview he had assumed that the two Englanders were only on board by chance, but now the Abwehr man was raising diabolical possibilities. 'Ford, the staff-sergeant, is an ammunition examiner,' he said slowly.

Had Dietrich detected the note of reluctance in his voice? He pressed the colonel for further information instantly. 'And the other man, the so-called lieutenant – Prentice?'

'He is with the Signals Corps.'

'Ah! So undoubtedly an expert wireless operator ...' Dietrich shrugged his shoulders, his devastating point made. He puffed at his cigar for several seconds and then said something equally disturbing. 'Since we know they have been in Turkey for several weeks it seems an even stranger coincidence that they should choose this particular trip for returning to Greece. Don't you agree?'

'Several weeks? You know this? Is this why you are on board?' Burckhardt took a step towards Dietrich who regarded him without replying. 'They were supposed to have been saved from a ship which sank off the Turkish coast a few days ago ...'

'What ship?' Dietrich pounced on the statement. 'Is this the story they have told you?'

'Yes, when Lieutenant Hahnemann was questioning them ...'

'He has Intelligence training, this Hahnemann?' The ironic note was back in Dietrich's voice.

'No, but he is clever and he said their story rang true. The lieutenant – Prentice – told him this ...'

'I have seen this British lieutenant,' the Abwehr man replied slowly and deliberately, 'and I would say he not only has his wits about him – he is also capable of making up a convincing story on the spur of the moment. I don't like the way the situation is developing, Colonel Burckhardt. You should have the two Englanders questioned again.'

Burckhardt's expression was remote. Under other circumstances, without the enormous responsibility of the expedition

71

resting on his shoulders, he might have thought differently, and he had no way of knowing that he was confronted by a master of the art of psychological aggression. Without realizing it, he had been subjected to a kaleidoscope of changing impressions and anxieties from the moment he had entered the cabin, and during this ordeal he had subconsciously accepted the Abwehr man's credentials at face value. In fact, the subject of the identity of Dietrich had subtly been turned into questioning the identity of the British prisoners. He was also becoming a little worried about his own position. Had this devil been put aboard the *Hydra* to check up on the operation because it involved a naval phase – the seizure of the *Hydra* and its subsequent voyage to their objective! 'I'll get Hahnemann to have another word with the prisoners,' he said crisply.

'This Prentice, he speaks German, then?' Dietrich was staring through the porthole again as he asked the question.

'Not so far as I know – but Hahnemann speaks excellent English. I must leave for the bridge now.' He was talking again to Dietrich's back as the Abwehr man used his hand to smear a hole in the steamed-up glass. The temperature was probably at least thirty degrees higher inside the cabin than on the high seas.

'Did Hahnemann find out anything else when he was interrogating the prisoners?' Dietrich went on peering intently through the porthole and something in his attitude made the colonel wait a few seconds longer.

'I believe there was some mention of a British destroyer being in the area, but I'm convinced he was bluffing.'

'Bluffing!' Dietrich straightened up, swung round abruptly. 'First you talk about it being a coincidence that those men are aboard and now you hope he was bluffing! I'm afraid a very serious situation has arisen – a strange vessel is coming in fast from the north-east and unless I'm very much mistaken it is a British destroyer.'

Burckhardt turned to go quickly, and when Dietrich was left to his own devices he had, by default, been granted the privilege to roam round the vessel as freely as he wished.

Burckhardt was leaving the cabin when he very nearly collided with Hahnemann who was rushing down the companionway. Halting abruptly, the soldier saluted and spoke breathlessly. 'There's an emergency, sir. Lieutenant Schnell would like to see you on the bridge – it's very urgent . . .'

'I know!' Burckhardt was already pushing past him, heading for the staircase. Hard-faced young men of the Alpenkorps, fully uniformed, pressed themselves against the companionway wall with their rifles at their sides to let him pass. One man hastily extinguished a cigarette under his boot. The doorways to the three cabins recently occupied by the German passengers were open and inside more men of the Alpenkorps sat on the floors and leaned against the walls, their faces tense as they watched their colonel pass. The grapevine had worked already, reporting the rumour that a British destroyer was approaching fast. The whole atmosphere of the Greek ferry had changed, had become more akin to that of a troopship. Dodging round kit piled in the passage, Burckhardt made a mental note to get that shifted and then leapt up the staircase. Pushing open the door at the top he received a blast of cold wind and a douche of icy spray full in the face. Without even bothering to wipe himself he glanced quickly along the deserted, wave-washed deck. All the troops were under strict instructions to remain below decks and he was satisfied with the outward appearance of normality. Strange how the sea seemed far worse up here than down below. The thought flashed through his mind as he went into the wheelhouse.

Inside the enclosed area everything was quiet and there was a feeling of disciplined control, but under the silence Burckhardt sensed an atmosphere of nerves tautly strained as the *Hydra* ploughed on through mounting seas. Lieutenant Schnell of the German Navy, wearing inconspicuous dark trousers and a dark woollen sweater, was holding the wheel while the ferry's captain, Nopagos, stood a few feet away with a signalling lamp in his hands. Behind him, crouched on his knees out of sight, an Alpenkorps soldier held a machine-pistol trained on the captain's back.

'Over there. To starboard.' It was the helmsman who had spoken, nodding his head towards the north-east. Schnell was a typical German naval officer, round-faced, his dark hair neatly trimmed, a man of thirty with watchful eyes and a steady manner. Taking in the situation at a glance, Burckhardt accepted a pair of field-glasses from another soldier whose uniform was covered with a civilian raincoat. To starboard a slim grey silhouette was bearing down on the *Hydra*, a silhouette with lights at her masthead. Burckhardt focused the glasses on the ship and his lips tightened. Yes, it was a British destroyer sailing on an oblique course which would take her across the bows of the ferry within a mile or two. He handed back the glasses and moved into the shadows in case other glasses were aimed in his direction from that distant bridge. They wouldn't be able to pick out individuals yet, but within a few minutes they'd pick up all the detail they wanted if the destroyer maintained its present course. He spoke quickly to Schnell. 'What is Nopagos doing with that signalling lamp in his hands?'

'He will have to use it in a minute . . .'

'I don't like that.'

'We have no alternative.' Schnell had half-turned round to stare at the oncoming warship. 'She is bound to signal us, so tell the Greek I understand the use of signals at sea.'

Burckhardt thought quickly. It was a damnable situation: the very existence of the expedition now depended on the signal-lamp in the hands of a Greek whose ship had just been shanghaied from under him. He saw the knuckles of Schnell's hands whitened under the overhead light as he gripped the wheel and steadily kept to his course. Still crouched on the floor, the Alpenkorps soldier with the machine-pistol moved gently with the sway of the ship, his face drawn with tension as he watched Burckhardt and then transferred his gaze to Nopagos' back. Burckhardt maintained his outward appearance of calm confidence, his hands thrust into his coat pockets, although inwardly his nerves were screwed up to fever pitch. He began speaking to Nopagos in his careful, Teutonic-sounding Greek.

'The British destroyer may start signalling. If that happens you only use your lamp when I give the order. I want you to understand this clearly – the man at the wheel is a German naval officer thoroughly conversant with signalling procedures. He will be watching. If you make any attempt to send a distress signal, we shall know. If there is an emergency we shall engage the British destroyer and we shall undoubtedly be sunk. I hope you realize that it is unlikely anyone will be saved in seas like this...' Without putting it in so many words he managed to convey that Nopagos' crew were hostages. He had just finished speaking when the moonlit wake of the oncoming destroyer became clearly visible. A few seconds later the door to the bridge opened and Dietrich came inside. Burckhardt swung round and turned away again when he saw who it was. Completely unruffled by his reception, the Abwehr man walked across to join the colonel after glancing at the approaching destroyer.

'It's probably just a routine check,' he remarked, 'but let's hope they are not expecting a signal from their friends locked up below.'

A nerve jumped by the side of Burckhardt's neck underneath his collar. Dietrich had hardly arrived before voicing the most alarming suggestion at this critical moment. He had just quietened his mind after the Abwehr man's remark when the door burst open again and Hahnemann strode onto the bridge with a furious expression. He had hesitated to stop Dietrich following Burckhardt up to the bridge but now felt he should keep an eye on him. Burckhardt turned on him instantly. 'Hide that gun you bloody fool – they may be watching the bridge. And while you're here – had either of those British soldiers any means of signalling in their possession?'

'No signalling lamp,' Hahnemann reassured him quickly. 'They definitely had no signalling equipment of any kind. The lieutenant, Prentice, had a revolver under his pillow. But nothing to send a message with.'

Burckhardt glanced at Dietrich with an expressionless face, but the Abwehr man was still studying Hahnemann, who glared back at him defiantly. 'And no torch?' Dietrich queried in a deceptively mild tone. 'Not even a pocket torch?'

Hahnemann looked confused. He started to answer Dietrich, then his face stiffened and he addressed Burckhardt. 'One of them had a torch, yes, sir. It was inside the pocket of his coat hanging up behind the door.'

Dietrich caught Burckhardt's glance and he lifted his eyebrows in an expression of foreboding, then frowned at Schnell who had turned to say something. 'Here it comes, sir. They've started.' Across the swelling Aegean where the waves were growing higher a light began to wink on and off from the destroyer. Schnell had half-turned to starboard, his eyes fixed on the flashing lamp which went on with its brief explosions. On the bridge no one moved or spoke as all eyes were fixed hypnotically on the signalling light and Burckhardt could feel the stillness of men suspended in a state of horrible anticipation. So much depended on the next few minutes but Burckhardt had no intention of surrendering, whatever happened. He had had some experience of the devastating fire a British destroyer could lay down; in Norway he had seen a German troop transport reduced to a burning hulk by only a few salvoes. What those four-inch guns might do to the hull of the *Hydra* was something he preferred not to contemplate. The lamp stopped flashing and Schnell spoke.

'We are asked to identify ourselves.'

Burckhardt stood up a little straighter and gave Nopagos his instructions in Greek. 'Signal that we are the Greek ship *Hydra*. Nothing more. And remember that Lieutenant Schnell is a naval officer.'

The tension on the bridge was becoming almost unbearable, like a physical affliction. Nopagos wiped his lips and glanced behind to where the Alpenkorps man gazed straight at him, the muzzle of the machine-pistol aimed at the small of his back. Burckhardt nodded confidently without speaking, as much as to say get on with it. The captain adjusted his cap and started to flash the lamp while Schnell watched him coldly, his hands still on the wheel. To the colonel it seemed to take an age to send the short message. Was marine signalling really so complicated? Was Nopagos managing to trick Schnell while he inserted a desperate SOS among the jumble of flashes? A dozen appalling possibilities ran through his mind but he could do nothing but wait, hoping that his threat had struck home to the Greek. The lamp stopped flashing. Nopagos mopped the back of his neck with a coloured handkerchief as Schnell addressed Burckhardt over his shoulder.

'He has identified us simply as the *Hydra*, ownership Greek. Nothing more.'

With a supreme effort Burckhardt resisted the impulse to let his shoulders relax; both the Alpenkorps soldiers kept glancing towards him for reassurance. German soldiers, Burckhardt had noticed before, were never entirely happy at sea – the existence of the British Navy probably had something to do with their lack of enthusiasm for water-borne expeditions. He watched the destroyer still moving on her oblique course. Would her captain be satisfied with that signal? Just a routine check, Dietrich had suggested. But a moment later he had raised the unnerving suggestion that the two British soldiers might have been put on board deliberately – that the destroyer out there was expecting another flashing signal from a porthole confirming that all was well aboard the *Hydra*. Blast the Abwehr!

'They're signalling again!' Schnell spoke quietly, his eyes on the distant flashing light which was now less than a quarter of a mile away. Burckhardt stood quite still, resisting the impulse to pace up and down the bridge: it was vital at this moment to preserve an absolute outward calm. He felt that his feet had been glued to the deck for hours and God knew there were enough signs of tension on the bridge already. The signal lamp in Nopagos' hands wobbled slightly – if he had to carry on answering these bloody questions much longer he was going to crack. The soldier crouched behind the Greek captain was sweating profusely, his forehead gleaming from the light over the bridge. Hahnemann was lightly tapping a nervous fingernail on the butt of his machine-pistol and Burckhardt wanted to roar at him for God's sake stop it! Schnell, a highly experienced naval officer, was still holding the wheel tightly. All these little details Burckhardt took in automatically while the lamp on the British destroyer blandly went on flashing its message. Only Dietrich seemed undisturbed, almost at ease as he stared at the ceiling with the unlit cigar motionless in the centre of his mouth. He dropped his eyes and caught the colonel watching him.

'There is a Greek called Grapos aboard,' Dietrich com-

77

mented. 'I think he could be dangerous if he isn't watched carefully.'

'I dealt with him myself,' said Hahnemann in a flat tone. 'He was sleeping in the saloon -- he had no cabin – and I was able to knock him out before he knew I was there. He's tied up in one of the holds.' The endless strain of waiting had neutralized his natural dislike of the Abwehr man and he looked at Dietrich without resentment.

'I do have this ship under control,' Burckhardt added icily.

'Perhaps it might be better if I went below,' Dietrich said almost amiably. He glanced to his left and saw that Hahnemann was leaving the bridge as a cloud of spray broke over the bows of the *Hydra*. When the lieutenant had gone there was a loaded silence as the light from the destroyer continued flashing, the ferry's engines went on throbbing heavily, and the sea heaved endlessly under them. After the winking light had stopped, Schnell cleared his throat twice before speaking. 'They wish us to report where we're from, our ultimate destination and the time of arrival.'

Without hesitation Burckhardt rapped out more instructions in Greek. 'Tell them we're bound from Istanbul, that our destination is Katyra, Zervos, and our estimated time of arrival 05·30 hours.' Nopagos blinked, glanced again at the sweating soldier behind him, took a firmer grip on the lamp and began signalling. The gun muzzles of the destroyer could be clearly seen in the moonlight as the vessel remorselessly continued on course without altering direction by as much as a single degree. Burckhardt found it unnerving – why was all this interest being shown in an ancient Greek ferry which spent its life plying between Istanbul and the remote peninsula of Zervos? He kept a tight grip on himself as Dietrich's rumbling voice spoke again behind his back. 'I'm wondering now whether this signalling isn't a smoke-screen put out until they get close to us. If they were expecting their own private signal from the prisoners below the course they are maintaining would make sense – they would keep on that course until they fired the first shot across our bows. Ten minutes should tell us the worst.' And having fired this last shot across the colonel's bows he quietly left the bridge and went out on deck.

Tight-lipped, Burckhardt heard him go, relieved that at long last the Abwehr man was leaving the bridge. But secretly Burckhardt agreed that Dietrich's estimate was just about right. In the next ten minutes they should know the worst.

CHAPTER FIVE

Sunday, April 6

As he struggled in the darkness with the ropes which bound his wrists, Prentice was bathed in sweat from his exertions. He lay in his bunk sprawled on his side, his ankles also tightly bound together while a further length of rope joined his wrists to his ankles, a rope drawn up so tautly that his knees were permanently bent. The fact that they had thought of turning out the cabin lights didn't help him either; it meant he had to work blindly by feel and this made ten times more difficult a task which already seemed insuperable. And because his hands were tied behind his back he had soon given up the attempt to fiddle with the knots he couldn't see, and a little later, when it struck him that they had probably used Alpenkorps climbing rope, he gave up his efforts to break the cords by stretching his wrists against them – a rope which could support a man dangling from a cliff face was hardly likely to weaken under the mere pressure of two straining wrists. So it seemed hopeless: a rope which couldn't be broken and which couldn't be untied. There was, however, one other alternative. Prentice was thin-boned and he had unusually slim wrists, so now he was concentrating all his strength on compressing his hands into the smallest possible area and then trying to pull them upwards through the loops which imprisoned him. His success to date had fallen rather short of the milder achievements of Houdini and for a few minutes he stopped struggling while he rested.

He was turned on his left side, facing inwards to the cabin, and while he rested he contented himself with straining to see the time by the light of the phosphorescent numerals of his watch on the table. Almost 12.10 AM so far as he could make out. In that case the guard would be looking in on them shortly – he checked the cabin every quarter-hour. With typical

Teutonic punctuality he had, so far, arrived at precisely the quarter-hour. He lay listening for the sound of footsteps and heard only the distant murmur of voices. Twisting his head round, he called out in a loud whisper. 'All right, Ford?'

The sergeant, similarly bound in the next bunk, was just recovering from the pounding headache which had assailed him when he regained consciousness after the blow from Hahnemann's machine-pistol. From the sound of Prentice's voice he guessed that the lieutenant had enjoyed a less painful return to the land of the living, something which didn't entirely surprise him when he recalled Prentice's speedy recovery from a hangover after a night of Turkish hospitality. He wet his lips before replying. 'Fine and dandy, sir. We'll have to sue the *Hydra*'s owners for damages when we arrive back.'

Prentice grinned in the darkness. 'We might just do that, laddie. Now, the guard'll be looking in any minute, so pretend you're still out cold.'

'Got it, sir.' The faint hammering inside his brain was sending waves of dizziness through Ford, a sensation which wasn't improved by the Aegean waves outside which regularly lifted the ship and tilted the cabin with an unpleasant rolling motion. Combined with his dizziness, Ford had the feeling that he was turning over and over and over. It cost him a certain effort to make his enquiry. 'Making any progress, sir?'

'A bit,' Prentice lied cheerfully, 'but not enough yet. I think they used steel hawser cable to truss us up.' He checked his watch again. Nearly a quarter past twelve. Was the guard going to be late this time? The curtains were closed over the port-hole so the cabin was in almost total darkness except for the light seeping in from the door which was not quite closed. He found that slightly ajar door tantalizing – for all the use that unlocked door was to Prentice at the moment it might have been locked and bolted on the outside. But it did give him warning of the guard's approach as he proceeded with his unvarying patrol. After he had entered the cabin to make his quick check on the prisoners he continued his slow tread along the companionway and Prentice, who had exceptional hearing, found previously that he was able to follow the tramp of the retreating boots and their progress up the distant staircase

81

which ended with the thud of a door closing. So his sentry-go also took in the open deck aloft, God help him. But for Prentice this made sense – the German commander, knowing there was little risk of an emergency while they were on board, was conserving his manpower, letting his troops rest as best they could before morning. Prentice lifted his head, then called out quickly. 'Here he comes!'

The Alpenkorps guard reached the door and reacted with his normal caution, switching on the light and entering the cabin with his rifle levelled. He stood there for a moment, watching the two inert bodies, then peered round the cabin to make sure that it was empty. As he left he switched off the light and closed the door firmly. Lying on his bunk, Prentice used a little army language wordlessly – now he couldn't hear the basket marching away and, more to the point, he wouldn't be able to hear him coming back again. Gritting his teeth, he renewed the struggle to free himself, pushing down his left hand to hold the rope taut while he compressed his right hand and pulled upwards, wriggling a wrist which was now moist with sweat. The moisture might help, might eventually make it a little easier to slip his wrist upwards out of that biting rope. To give himself extra leverage he pressed his bound feet against the side of the bunk, breathing heavily as he strained desperately at the rope. Five minutes later he lay limp and exhausted by his exertions, taking in great breaths of muggy air as he summoned up his strength for a renewed onslaught. The cabin seemed to be tilting more steeply now and the woodwork was groaning as though the timbers might give under the enormous pressure of the sea. The effort to free himself had been so great that his head was beginning to ache badly and he felt that he had a steel band drawn round his temples. A light flashed briefly and he bit his lips. God, this was no time to black-out. A second later he lay still as a dead man, his heart pounding with excitement. That flash of light hadn't been his eyes playing him tricks. The light had flashed from the companionway as someone opened and closed the door soundlessly. *Someone had come inside the cabin!*

Fear. Uncertainty. Growing alarm. The emotions darted across his fatigued brain as he continued to lie quite still, straining his ears, trying to accustom his eyes to the darkness quickly. The trouble was that damned sentry lighting up the cabin had taken away his night sight for a few minutes and he wished he hadn't watched him through half-closed eyes. Had Ford also realized what had happened – that some unknown person had crept inside their cabin with uncanny silence? He had no idea. His ears had still provided no evidence that there was someone else present but instinctively Prentice knew that they were no longer alone. He found the stillness unnerving, the creaking of the ship ominous, and the thought that someone who moved like a ghost was approaching him terrifying. His mind was strained, his nerves strung up to fever pitch with their recent experiences, and now a nightmare idea flooded over him – someone had been sent in to kill them quietly. A knife in the chest, then a swift despatch overboard into the Aegean. Feverishly his imagination worked it out: the German commander might not want his unit to know about an episode like this, or perhaps there was an SS section aboard. Lying helpless in the darkness, his nerves close to breaking-point, he foresaw the next step – the hand coming out of the darkness to feel over his chest, finding the right place, the upheld hand striking downwards with one savage thrust. Keep a grip on yourself, for Christ's sake, Prentice... His heart jumped, his throat went dry, he felt he was choking – now he could see something, a shadow which had interposed itself between the bunk and the phosphorescent hands of his watch on the table. The intruder was feet away, standing beside his bunk, looking down at him. He tried to call out, but croaked instead, a sound like a bullfrog. A hand touched his cheek and he jerked involuntarily.

'Keep quiet! Listen!'

Prentice was stunned, lay absolutely still with sheer shock. The voice had spoken in English with a distinct Scots burr. He swallowed quickly and kept his voice down to little more than a whisper.

'Who is it?'

The voice ignored the question, speaking in an urgent Morse-code fashion. 'Keep still! I have a knife ... I'll cut the ropes on your hands ... a British destroyer is close...' Prentice felt cold steel between his wrists, stiffening the rope as the knife began to saw the fibres apart. '... at the back of the ship is a raft ... use the knife to cut it free ... when the raft is on the sea and you are away from the ship...' The knife sawed steadily, one of the ropes snapped. '... you send up a distress light ... they're on the raft...' Another rope snapped as Prentice pulled his hands away from each other to increase the tension on the remaining rope. He spoke quickly.

'I ought to know who you are – I may be able to help you later...'

'Shut up!' The knife was sawing more slowly now and Prentice realized that the man who was freeing him was taking care the knife didn't jab into him as the last rope snapped. The voice went on speaking. 'The distress light will be seen ... by the destroyer ... but Burckhardt won't dare shoot at you since that will warn the destroyer something's wrong...' Prentice felt the last rope part, freeing his hands, then heard the measured tramp of an Alpenkorps guard approaching along the companionway, the boots clumping dully on the wood.

He froze, his feet still tied. It wasn't time, not nearly time, for the guard to check on them. The intruder had entered the cabin soon after the guard had left – deliberately so. Prentice had already grasped that. So had the guard changed his routine? He was going to enter the cabin and catch him with his hands free – and catch this unknown helper in the act. The guard's tread was closer now, was slowing down prior to switching on the light and coming inside. Another thought struck Prentice and he felt a shiver run through his body – since he could hear the guard coming the door must be slightly open. Yes, it was! A thin line of light showed round the door frame. The intruder hadn't closed the door properly and the swaying of the ship had opened it wider. Lying quite still in the darkness, Prentice realized that they were finished. The guard had closed the door last time, so when he noticed that it was open, and even if he hadn't intended coming in this time ... He wondered what the feelings of the unknown Scot were who was waiting with them in the unlit cabin without making a sound. He still had the knife – would he use it on one of his own men? Would he even get the chance? That partly opened door would alert the guard and he'd come inside prepared for anything. Lying back on the bunk, he turned himself sideways and hid his hands, hoping they would still look to be roped up. Another huge wave caught the vessel, thudding against the hull with such force that he felt it was coming through. A second later he heard a further thud outside in the companionway and a muttered oath in German. The wave had caught the guard off-balance. Bathed in sweat, his heart pounding solidly, he waited and listened. For a moment there was a drawn-out silence, followed by a metallic click. The guard cocking his weapon? Prentice had a fierce impulse to call out a warning, but he kept his mouth closed, then heard the tread of the guard's footsteps again just beyond the cabin door. He had turned his head sideways now, his eyes almost closed as he watched the entrance for the first shaft of light which would tell him the door was being opened. Then he heard more footsteps coming along the companionway, brisk footsteps which hurried. He could imagine the scene clearly – the guard noticing the door which should have been closed, his beckoning to a comrade who was hurrying along the passage to join him. Then the two of them would burst inside the cabin and it would be all over. The hurrying footsteps stopped outside the door and voices were raised in German. Prentice knew a little German, but not enough to speak it, and they were talking too rapidly for him to grasp what they were saying. Perhaps the new arrival was the sentry who normally checked their cabin? His mind was still grappling with possibilities when he heard feet hurrying away along the passage, followed by the deliberate tread of the sentry's footsteps as he also proceeded into the distance and up the staircase. A door thudded shut. Both men had gone.

'You must cut the ropes on your feet yourself...' The voice of the unknown man spoke quickly again. 'There's a coat and cap on the floor ... you turn left when you leave the cabin ... hurry!'

The knife had already been placed on Prentice's leg and he was working on the ropes round his ankles when light flooded briefly into the cabin and then the door closed again. Prentice looked up quickly but he was too late – he saw no more than the departure of a shadow as the intruder disappeared. While he was sawing at the ropes the ship began to roll more violently, the angle of the cabin's tilt increasing steadily. They were moving into dirty weather. Behind him he heard a creak inside Ford's bunk and the sergeant's voice was a careful whisper. 'Who the devil was that?'

'God knows, but the Scots accent was unmistakable. He must be a stowaway.' Prentice was free now and he nearly stumbled full length as the vessel rose abruptly while he was feeling his way across the darkened cabin. He'd have to risk a light -- there had been a fierce urgency in the intruder's final words and in less than fifteen minutes the sentry would be back. And this time he would come inside their cabin. Switching on the light, he noted that the door was firmly closed, then ran across to Ford's bunk. He used his knife to cut the ropes as he talked. 'We've got to get on that raft and away from this ship pdq. Then we can loose off a signal to that destroyer...' Ford was rubbing the circulation back into his wrists when Prentice tried on the coat which had been dropped on the floor. An Alpenkorps greatcoat, it was a little too long and fitted loosely across the shoulders, but he thought it might serve. The soft, large-peaked cap was also ill-fitting but he settled it on his head as the sergeant looked at him.

'You're the spitting image of a Jerry,' Ford informed him. 'And your face fits, too.'

'Thanks very much...' Prentice was moving towards the door, the knife concealed inside his pocket. 'I'll walk on the left - you keep to my right. That way I'll try and cover you if any cabin doors are open.' Switching off the light, he paused while he listened with his ear pressed to the inner side of the door. He thought he understood now the restless wakefulness of those murmuring voices he had heard earlier - if the Alpenkorps men below decks knew of the destroyer's presence that would be more than enough to spoil their beauty sleep. It also meant that they were likely to be alert, which would make their walk along that companionway a hundred times more dangerous. He whispered to Ford quickly. 'Here we go. If anyone calls out to us we just keep moving as though we haven't heard. Now!' Opening the door quietly, he peered out.

The passage was deserted in both directions. He walked straight out, closed the door behind them, and began walking down the companionway with Ford at his side.

The first cabin door was half-open and before he had reached it he heard voices speaking in German. He walked at a steady pace, not too quickly, not too slowly, staring ahead as they drew level with the doorway. Out of the corner of his eye he had a glimpse of a smoke-filled cabin, a blur of uniformed bodies, and then they had passed it. Maintaining the same pace, Prentice kept his eyes fixed on the distant staircase where a pile of army packs lay huddled near the lowest tread. The next cabin door was also open, wide open. Smoke drifted into the companionway as the vessel heeled violently and Ford had to grab at the rail to save his balance. Prentice briefly slowed his pace while the sergeant caught up. That had been lucky – if it had happened opposite the open cabin door, Ford, dressed in British civilian clothes, would have been completely exposed to view. Prentice's mind was coldly alert as they came close to the doorway. From inside he could hear more animation, the sound of raucous laughter as a voice ended in a shout. Someone telling a story, he guessed. One Alpenkorps soldier, his fair hair cut to a stubble, lounged inside with his shoulder resting on the door frame and his back turned towards the companionway. Prentice kept walking forward and as he began to walk past the doorway another burst of laughter echoed inside the cabin. An NCO stood in the middle of the room, half-turned away from the doorway, waving his hands as he pantomimed something. An energetic attempt to keep up morale, Prentice was thinking, something to take the minds of the men off that destroyer outside in the night. But he thought the laughter was a little forced and short-lived. The main thing was it concentrated attention inside the cabin as they walked past it. Only one more cabin to pass, and the door was closed.

Then they were walking past the door and within a few paces of the staircase. At the foot of the steps Ford glanced down, saw inside a German army pack which had its flap drawn back. With his interest in explosives he paused involuntarily as he saw the demolition charge and the timing mechanisms. By his side Prentice sensed the pause and grasped his arm, urging him upwards without a word. The lieutenant was mounting the steps when the bows of the *Hydra* plunged downwards, elevating the staircase in his face so suddenly that he nearly fell over backwards, tightening his grip on the rail just in time. Half-way up, he looked quickly back along the companionway as he continued climbing. It was still deserted.

When he pushed open the door at the top it was almost torn from his grasp by the force of the wind. He waited until Ford was safely on deck, then used both hands to close it without a slamming noise. With the howl of the wind and the heavy slap of heaving water it seemed a needless precaution, but the thud of a door closing is a special sound and that guard might be somewhere on deck. The water-washed deck gleamed in the moonlight and beyond the funnel to port a burst of spray exploded near the rail. With Ford motionless at his side Prentice scanned the deck which seemed to be deserted. A moment later a gust of wind whipped the ill-fitting Alpenkorps cap from his head and blew it into the sea. He had lost the most distinctive part of his disguise. He looked to starboard and was staggered to see how close the destroyer was steaming, frowning when he saw the signal lamp flashing. Was she calling on the *Hydra* to heave-to? With a very slight turn of his head he looked towards the stern and saw the raft waiting for them, its canvas cover drawn back, and by the light of the moon he could see the rescue loops hanging from its sides and bobbing with the *Hydra*'s motion.

The raft had been covered with the canvas when he had last seen it and he hadn't recognized what the cover concealed. If it really carried distress lights they might just make it, might attract the destroyer's attention and be picked up. Not that he was too enthusiastic about the prospect of being aboard that tiny craft in seas like these. The whole surface of the Aegean was heaving up in a series of mountainous crests which raced towards the ferry with an insidious gliding movement as though intent on overwhelming it. He was about to make his way towards the raft, waiting for a moment when the ferry was pulling itself out of one of the great rolling dips, when he caught a brief twitch of a shadow to starboard beyond the funnel. The shadow of a huge man wearing a soft hat and standing close to a swaying lifeboat. Putting a warning hand on Ford's sleeve, Prentice kept perfectly still. It was the big German who had come aboard as a passenger at Istanbul. From the way he was standing he appeared to be talking to someone who was out of sight under the wall of the bridge. Go away, Prentice prayed. Get lost! The German began to move, to turn in his direction.

'Italian mines have been sown in the Gulf of Zervos.' This latest signal from the destroyer should have reassured Burckhardt but it sent a chill through him.

It should have reassured him because the destroyer's commander had sent the captain of the *Hydra* a friendly warning, but instead he was appalled. The passage from the narrow entrance to Katyra, at the head of the gulf, was a distance of twenty miles, and the prospect of sailing twenty miles at night through mine-strewn waters was not an experience he contemplated with great enthusiasm. Mechanically, he ordered Nopagos to signal a message of thanks to the destroyer while inwardly he cursed his allies. In the interests of security the Italian High Command had been given no warning of the Zervos operation, but it was the most fiendish luck that on this night of all nights they should suddenly decide to sow mines from the air in the vital gulf. This, he told himself grimly, is going to be a voyage to remember.

'Go down and have the British prisoners escorted to my cabin.'

He gave the instruction to the soldier not preoccupied with guarding Nopagos, his eyes still on the warship as the soldier left the bridge. There might be something in what that damnably arrogant Abwehr man had hinted at . . . His thought broke off as Nopagos completed signalling and stood waiting with a resigned look on his face as the destroyer sent a short series of flashes in reply. Yes, Burckhardt decided, it was a good idea to have the British prisoners questioned again, but this time he would let his second-in-command, Major Eberhay, undertake the interrogation. Like Lieutenant Hahnemann, Eberhay also spoke English.

'They wish us *bon voyage*!' Schnell was unable to keep the relief and exultation out of his voice.

Burckhardt could hardly believe it, but the feeling of salvation which flooded over him did not affect his judgement. He issued the warning swiftly to Schnell. 'Be sure to maintain exactly the same course and speed – it may be a trick to test our reaction.' He switched to speaking in Greek. 'Captain Nopagos, kindly stay exactly where you are until I give you further orders.' From the destroyer they would easily be able to see the *Hydra*'s bridge, Burckhardt was thinking as he remained in the shadows, and if the British commander were shrewd his glasses would at this moment be focused on the ferry's bridge. He watched the destroyer's course without too much hope and inside his coat pocket his hands were clenched tight. Had they really got away with it?

'She's still on course.' It was Schnell who had spoken and the note of anxiety had crept back into his voice. With an expressionless face Burckhardt continued to stare at the warship as more steam emerged from her funnel and she began to change course for the north-west. Incredibly, they had got away with it. Speaking a word of congratulation to Schnell, he left the bridge and went down the staircase in time to meet Major Eberhay who was at the foot of the steps. Behind him strolled Dietrich and behind the Abwehr man Hahnemann was running along the companionway towards them. Several Alpenkorps soldiers were moving away in the opposite direction. 'What's the matter?' he asked Eberhay.

'The British prisoners have escaped . . .'

'They were tied up!'

'We are searching now,' Eberhay explained crisply, his manner quite unruffled. 'Put two more men on the bridge,' he told Hahnemann, who issued an order, summoning two soldiers from the nearby cabin and then going up the staircase as they followed him. 'And I have met Herr Dietrich,' he went on as Burckhardt appeared to be on the verge of saying something, 'we have been discussing the British destroyer . . .'

'It's turning away . . .' Burckhardt began.

'You are sure?' Dietrich interjected.

Eberhay stared up curiously at the Abwehr man as Burckhardt stood on the bottom stair and glared at Dietrich with a look of thunder. More troops were filing out of the cabins under the orders of Sergeant Volber who was instructing several to search the engine-room, to mount a double guard on the wireless operator's quarters, but not to go out on the open deck yet. Volber would take a small section to the deck himself.

Dietrich was facing the colonel bleakly, not at all disconcerted by Burckhardt's attitude. 'I heard of a similar case,' he told them. 'One of our merchant ships off Norway raised the Argentinian flag as a British destroyer approached. The warship turned away as you say this one is doing now. But it made a complete circle and came up unexpectedly on the stern of the ship and boarded her before the sea-cocks could be opened. So the danger may only be starting.' Burckhardt stood quite still on the step, his feeling of relief ebbing away; he remembered the incident this damned Abwehr man had just recalled. Dietrich turned to Eberhay without waiting for a reply. 'So, if you don't mind, I'll come on deck with you and see what that ship is doing.'

Burckhardt said nothing as he walked past them, heading for his cabin while Dietrich followed the major up the staircase, turning up his coat collar when they reached the deck. A guard stationed permanently outside the door stood to attention as Eberhay went briskly to the bridge. Inside he noted that Hahnemann had stationed two more soldiers in the rear away from the light and stared with keen interest at the destroyer as Dietrich joined him.

'It will be an hour before we know whether they've really gone,' Dietrich commented as he looked at Eberhay. The contrast between the two men was startling. Whereas Dietrich was easily the largest man aboard the *Hydra*, Eberhay was small and lightly built, his face lean and alert as a fox's and his manner almost dandified. In his early thirties, he wore over his uniform a civilian raincoat belted close to his slim waist. The name sounded Hungarian in origin, Dietrich reflected, and there was certainly Balkan blood in his veins. Which probably accounted for the air of intelligence and sophistication which radiated from him.

'The escape of the prisoners is unfortunate,' Eberhay remarked, offering his cigarette case, 'but we shall soon find them.' Dietrich shook his head, noting that the contents were Turkish as he extracted his own case and took out a cigar. Eberhay lit the cigar for him as he stooped low to reach the match. 'I'm going on deck now to supervise the search.'

'It is the manner of their escape which is more than unfortunate – it could be catastrophic,' the Abwehr man observed.

Eberhay glanced sharply up at him and then, without replying, made his way onto the open deck followed by Dietrich. As they arrived in the open the *Hydra* plunged its bows into a massive wave and a torrent of spray drenched them. Dodging close to the starboard side of the funnel, Eberhay mopped his face with a silk handkerchief. Dietrich had also moved and now he was standing by a swaying lifeboat where he caught the full blast of the icy wind. He had to pull his hat down tight over his large head and on another man the compressed hat might have looked absurd, but on this man, Eberhay reflected, it only emphasized an air of physical menace which seemed to emanate from him.

'Your name suggests a Balkan heritage,' Dietrich rumbled, switching unexpectedly to an entirely different topic.

'My grandfather moved from Budapest to Munich last century,' Eberhay replied stiffly and a little uncomfortably. 'The family has been entirely German since then.' Something about Dietrich suggested to the sensitive Eberhay a whiff of the Gestapo, and he was reminding himself to mention this to Burckhardt when he saw two Alpenkorps soldiers slip past on the port side, their bodies crouched low as they made their way towards the stern. Dietrich had turned and was also looking towards the stern as though something had caught his attention, then he turned away again, and a moment later they heard one of the Alpenkorps call out.

Eberhay ran forward, saw two men standing near the raft as the Alpenkorps soldiers charged along the deck and within seconds a furious struggle had begun. Prentice found himself thrown back against the rail, temporarily winded. A clenched fist scraped his jaw as he jerked his head aside and lifted one knee. The soldier twisted to avoid the thrust, lost his balance and Prentice crashed down on top of him, his right hand reaching for the man's throat. But the German foresaw the attack again and buried his head in his chest to ward off the hand, trying to grab blindly for the lieutenant's hair. They fought ineffectually for a short time and then Prentice tore himself loose from the soldier's grasp and jumped up as though fleeing. The German came to his feet confidently, ran forward and received Prentice's aimed shoe on the point of his kneecap. He was doubling up as his opponent crashed into him and rammed him against the rail. Prentice had used the natural tilt of the vessel to port to give him added momentum and now the German was half-spreadeagled over the side as the vessel went on dropping to port, lifting the German over the rail. Scooping his arm under the German's crooked legs he hoisted and the soldier went over the side head first into the heaving sea. Eberhay had seen the danger and had run forward with his pistol held by the barrel to club Prentice. He himself had earlier given the order that under no circumstances must there be shots fired which might alert the destroyer which now presented its stern to the *Hydra*. Eberhay was close to the lieutenant when he slipped on a wet patch and sprawled headlong on the deck. In front of the funnel he saw running men as he lifted his head. 'Volber!' he shouted and then dropped his head just in time to escape Prentice's aimed shoe. Volber and two other men were struggling with Prentice while Ford still fought on the deck with the other Alpenkorps soldier as Eberhay looked quickly over the side. The seething waves had swallowed up the man who had gone overboard and there was no sign of him amid the churning crests.

In less than a minute both Prentice and Ford had been overpowered and were being taken along the deck with their arms pinioned behind them. Eberhay had warned Volber that they were wanted for questioning and that they must be looked after carefully, a necessary precaution after one of their comrades had been thrown overboard. Accidents could happen so easily and he didn't want Prentice tripped and thrown down the full length of the staircase. When he turned round, Dietrich was supporting his balance with a hand against a ventilator while he stared at the raft as though it might be alive.

'They almost got away,' were his first words.

'But they didn't . . .' Eberhay was unsure how to reply. The remark infuriated him since Dietrich seemed completely unconcerned that one of their men had just drowned.

'Three more minutes and they'd have been over the side,' the Abwehr man growled. He glared at Eberhay as though it were all his fault. 'And you wouldn't have dared open fire for fear you warned that destroyer.'

Eberhay rubbed his bruised hands with his silk handkerchief, almost lost balance again as the deck started to rise, then leant against the ventilator. The trend of Dietrich's remarks greatly disturbed him: he had heard that he Abwehr's chief, Canaris, had such a contempt for soldiers that he refused to allow any man who wore a military decoration to enter his office. It looked very much as though his aide shared his chief's views of the Wehrmacht. It had been a most unfortunate incident and the only officer present had been Eberhay himself. He tried flattery. 'You took a risk yourself coming out into the open like that.'

'So far as I could see they had no guns. I am not interested in displays of courage, Major Eberhay,' he went on bitingly. 'My usefulness to the Reich lies in staying alive as long as I can. Considering what has happened I must have a word with Colonel Burckhardt immediately.' He looked across the Aegean in a westerly direction. 'There are certain things which must be cleared up before we reach the entrance to the Gulf of Zervos. Have you ever made this trip before? No? It will be an experience for you – going into the gulf through that narrow entrance on such a night will be like entering the gates of hell.'

CHAPTER SIX

Sunday, 3 AM

At 2.50 AM the *Hydra* was steaming into the eye of the storm as seas of unimaginable violence began to take hold of her. The hull shuddered under the impact of the seventy-mile-an-hour wind, the bows of the vessel climbed a rolling wall of water, a Niagara of spray burst in the air and was flung against the window of the bridge with hammering force, blinding their view for several seconds. To stay upright, Burckhardt gripped the rail tightly as he watched the mighty waves swarming in endless succession towards the ship from Cape Zervos, waves which seethed and heaved with a dizzying motion, advancing relentlessly as though bent on the ship's destruction. Close to the colonel stood his shadow, Dietrich, his hat jammed low over his head and an unlit cigar between his lips. A few feet in front of Burckhardt the wheel was held by Schnell, standing with his legs apart and braced, the strain showing in his stooped shoulders, while to his right Nopagos, his face lined and drawn, held onto the rail as he gazed fixedly ahead. Turning, he spoke quickly to Burckhardt, his manner so harsh that for a moment it seemed the Greek had once more resumed command of his own ship.

'We must wait till morning – if you continue you will wreck us on the rocks.'

'For the sake of your crew you must see that does not happen.'

Burckhardt answered decisively but his outwardly determined attitude did not reflect his thoughts. The view from the bridge was quite terrifying; although the moon was fading there was still sufficient light to see what lay before them as a series of menacing shadows, and to the north-east the cliffs of the peninsula soared up into the night towards the three-thousand-foot summit of Mount Zervos. As the *Hydra* straddled the crest of another giant roller Burckhardt was able briefly to see the entrance to the gulf, a gap between the shadows so frighteningly narrow that from a distance it seemed as though the hull of the ship might well scrape both sides of the bottleneck. The bows plunged downwards into a fresh trough, the view was lost, and Burckhardt comforted himself with the thought that distance across water at night was doubly deceptive. So when they came closer the entrance must widen, even comfortably so, if that was a word which could be used under such turbulent conditions. Schnell, who didn't understand a word of Greek, asked the colonel what Nopagos had said.

'He wants us to wait until morning. I have said no.'

Dietrich noted that Schnell made no reply to this and he suspected that the German naval officer secretly agreed with Nopagos, who was acting as pilot. But Burckhardt would continue on course, he was sure of this, and his assumption was correct. The colonel was in an impossible dilemma: he was compelled to maintain the pre-arranged timetable, to land the expedition at Katyra by dawn. Under no circumstances could there be any possibility of turning back or waiting – his key force had a vital role to play in a far more gigantic operation and play it they must, whatever happened. Or perish in the attempt. And as Burckhardt stared from the bridge it seemed highly likely that they might indeed perish – his staff and the two hundred Alpenkorps troops huddled below decks.

The men on the bridge wore life-jackets – a precaution which Nopagos had insisted on – and the troops below were also similarly protected. But to Dietrich, as he surveyed the way ahead, the precaution seemed futile. If they struck the cliffs the *Hydra* would be pounded to pieces and no one could hope to survive in the boiling waters which surrounded them. As the vessel climbed again, breasting a further crest, he saw with appalling clarity – even through the foam-flecked window of the bridge – the mouth of the gulf, a rock-bound narrows which would require skilful seamanship in the calmest of seas in broad daylight, but at three in the morning, at the height of an Aegean storm, Schnell was going to have to take the ship on a course which most Greek sailors would have pronounced suicidal. And the weather was definitely deteriorating.

Eberhay stood a few feet away to the Abwehr man's left, and he stood so quietly and inconspicuously, almost like a wraith, that once Dietrich had looked to see if he were still there. He was watching the grim spectacle with interest and it might have been assumed he was nerveless, but in that earlier glance Dietrich had noticed a gleam of sweat across the small man's forehead. He made his remark to the major, knowing that Burckhardt was bound to hear him. 'If the vessel founders we mustn't forget that Greek tied up in the hold.'

'The guard has his instructions,' Eberhay replied. 'In the event of an emergency he will bring Grapos on deck. I gave the order myself.'

Burckhardt pretended not to have heard the exchange but the muscles across his stomach tightened a shade and he cursed the Abwehr man silently. 'If the vessel founders...' '...in the event of an emergency.' The phrases pointed up dramatically the desperate course of action he was committed to and he found the reminders unpleasant. Despite the hardening experiences of war Burckhardt was now frightened as he realized that the storm was growing worse. The deck rocked under his feet, the engines throbbed with the agonized vibration of machinery strained to the limit, and the howl of the gale was rising to a shriek. If they weren't careful the ferry was going to slip out of control. He could feel the tension reacting across his shoulder-blades from standing erect in one position, but he remained standing like a statue, determined to give an example of fortitude, compelling himself to watch the rise and fall of the sea which was going up and down like a lift. Yes, conditions were much worse, dangerously so. Beyond the bridge the world was a series of shifting shadows, shallow mountain peaks of sea which were now soaring and surging high above the *Hydra*'s masthead as the ship sank into another trough. It was weird and nerve-shattering – to see the waves jostling all around and high above them, dark, sliding slopes of water which might overwhelm them at any moment. He had a horrible feeling that exactly this could happen – the sea closing over them as the ferry capsized and plunged down to the floor of the Aegean. Then, once more, the ship seemed to gather itself to mount wearily and falteringly yet another glassy slope as it dragged itself up out of the depths. At the very moment when he least wanted it, he heard Dietrich speaking again.

'Nopagos could be right – we may end up as a wreck on the rocks.'

'That is a chance we must take. Personally, I am confident that Schnell will take us through.' Burckhardt paused, struggling to control his sudden rage. He had purposely left out that remark of Nopagos' when relaying what the Greek had said to Schnell, and it infuriated him that Dietrich should have repeated it for all to hear. But in spite of the immense pressure, the almost unbearable responsibility resting on his shoulders, Burckhardt's brain was still working and he had registered something he hadn't previously known.

'You understand Greek, then?' he asked abruptly.

'Perfectly. I speak it fluently – rather more fluently than yourself, incidentally.' Dietrich's tone of voice became scathing, a tone of voice which prickled the colonel's raw nerves. 'Why the devil do you think they chose me for this trip – one of the first qualifications, surely, is a mastery of Greek?'

'Any other languages?' It was just something to say and Burckhardt wasn't in the least interested in the reply.

'Yes, French. I don't anticipate being able to employ that particular talent on this voyage.' He spoke banteringly and his brief outburst seemed forgotten. This was another aspect of the Abwehr man's character which Burckhardt found so disconcerting: his moods changed with astonishing swiftness and kept you off-balance. He stiffened as Nopagos turned and spoke urgently, his eyes pleading.

'There is still time to change your mind – but you must decide now.'

'We are entering the gulf at the earliest possible moment. It is your duty to see that we make safe passage. For the sake of your crew, if for no other reason.'

Nopagos' manner altered. He stood up very straight and stared directly at the German with an authoritative expression. 'In that case we must change course. There is a dangerous cross-current from the east we must allow for if we are not to pile up on the rocks to the west. Tell your wheelsman...'

Burckhardt relayed the instructions automatically in German, instructions which he didn't understand completely and which he mistrusted. Nopagos had given the incredible order that they must steer straight for the cliffs of Zervos and the strangeness of the order raised an entirely fresh spectre in Burckhardt's already anxiety-laden mind. Quickly, he tried to resolve the fear before it was too late. Nopagos was undoubtedly a Greek patriot – his whole attitude had confirmed this to Burckhardt hours earlier – so to what lengths might he go to prevent the *Hydra* and its cargo of Alpenkorps troops ever reaching Katyra? Would he deliberately wreck his own vessel on those fearsome cliffs? He had a crew of his own countrymen aboard but would this prevent him from taking action which could only end in the death of every man aboard? Like Dietrich, Burckhardt was secretly under no illusion as to the chances of survival if the ship went down. If anything, they were less than they might have been ten minutes ago. It all depended on the inscrutable mind of one middle-aged Greek.

'There *is* a cross-current.' It was Dietrich who had spoken and now Burckhardt could feel the first signs of the ship heeling from starboard to port. The *Hydra*, its overstrained engines thumping heavily, began to move chaotically in the churning seas, like a gyroscope out of control. Sick with dread, Burckhardt watched Schnell struggling with the wheel to keep the vessel on the nightmarish course Nopagos had dictated, a course which seemed to have no direction at all as the ferry wallowed amid the inferno of near-tidal high waves rolling in all directions as the cross-current grew stronger. Soon the ship was being driven two ways – forward by the labouring engines and sideways by the powerful current from the east. Then for several minutes they suffered the illusion that they were making no progress – until the illusion was shattered in a particularly terrifying manner. Burckhardt had been under the impression that great bursts of spray in the near-distance were the product of huge waves colliding with each other and disintegrating, but as the spray settled briefly he saw an immense shadow rising in the night and knew that he was staring at the almost vertical rock face of the towering cliffs which barred their way. The surf was exploding at the base of the cliffs as the waves destroyed themselves against the barrier. Horror-struck, he heard Dietrich's voice close to his ear, a low rumble like a knell of doom. 'I estimate we are six hundred metres from them...' The *Hydra* reached the crest of a wave and now they were near enough to see huge billows shattering against the awful monolith of rock, sending up blurred spray which rose a good hundred feet above the gyrating crests of the Aegean far below. Burckhardt felt a constriction of the throat as he gazed with fascination at the spectacle – the rock face rearing upwards, the spurs at its base momentarily exposed as the sea receded, the lift of the *Hydra*'s bows, so close now that with their next fall it seemed they must ram down on that immovable rock base. And from the heaving bridge they could hear a new, sinister sound – the boom of the sea as it drove against the massive bastion of the headland. For the first time Burckhardt felt compelled to speak, to voice a navigational question. He had to lift his voice so that Schnell, still crouched over the wheel, could hear him above the shrieking wind and the steady roar of sea breaking against the cliff face.

'What's gone wrong? We're nearly on top of Cape Zervos!'

Schnell made no reply, didn't even turn round as Burck-hardt took a step forward, grabbing Nopagos tightly by the arm as he spoke harshly in Greek, trying to trap the man into an admission by the suddenness of his approach. 'We're too close, aren't we? You've done it deliberately...'

Nopagos stood perfectly still, his body frozen rigid under the German's grip. As he turned to gaze directly at the colonel, Hahnemann arrived on the bridge, slamming the door shut behind him and then waiting. Nopagos spoke with dignity. 'You think I would destroy my own men? Because you are a soldier you think you are the only one with responsibilities?' He looked down at the gloved hand which held his fore-arm. 'You are hurting me, Colonel. This is no moment to panic. You must leave it to Schnell – or hand over the wheel to me.' Burckhardt relaxed his grip, let go, his eyes still on the Greek's face. No hint of triumph, no suggestion of treachery in those steady eyes; only a touch of resignation. Burckhardt was unmoved by the suggestion that his nerve was going – it was immaterial to him at this moment what Nopagos thought so

100

long as he got the truth out of the man. And he believed him. The tilt of the deck almost threw him clear across the bridge as the *Hydra* heeled over again, but the soldier who was guarding Nogagos saved him. Holding firmly onto the rail Burckhardt listened while Hahnemann reported that all was well below but more than half the unit was sea-sick. As Hahnemann spoke Burckhardt was waiting for the first grind and shudder as the ferry struck. The lieutenant completed his report, saluted, and left the bridge. He closed the door as water surged over the port side, enveloping him when the wave broke against the bridge, and for a moment Burckhardt thought he had gone, but when the flood subsided Hahnemann was still clinging to the rail and he took advantage of the respite to dash below.

The not unexpected news he had brought depressed Burckhardt: within three hours the unit had to go ashore and the landing might be opposed. For such an operation the troops should be in the peak of condition and already half their energy must have drained away under the impact of their experiences so far – and the voyage was not yet accomplished. In fact, the worst probably lay ahead. Suppressing a sigh, he turned to face the cliffs and saw only spray. A second later every man on the bridge was petrified and their expressions of hypnotized fear were etched on Burckhardt's mind – a long drawn-out grinding noise was heard and the ship shuddered. *She had struck!* The message flashed through his brain and then the engines, which had missed a beat, started up reluctantly, and he knew that it was this which had caused the diabolical sound and tremor. He caught Dietrich's eye and the Abwehr man nodded, as much as to say, yes, this is gruelling. Burckhardt turned to look ahead as the vessel climbed, the spray faded and the entrance to the gulf appeared again. Within minutes their position had changed radically and they were now lying close to the narrows and well clear of the Zervos cliffs. But within a matter of only a few more minutes an even graver crisis faced them.

The enormously powerful cross-current which had carried them clear of the cliffs now threatened to carry the *Hydra* to a

101

new and equally total destruction. From the bridge Burckhardt could now see why Nopagos had advised the apparently suicidal course of steaming directly for the notorious cape – it was an attempt to take them close enough to the narrows to pass through the bottleneck before the cross-current swept them sideways beyond it. The Greek mainland to the west lay several miles away, but from its distant coast a chain of rocks stretched out across the gulf entrance, a chain which ended close enough to the cliffs of the Zervos peninsula to compress the entrance dangerously narrow. And the only navigable channel, Schnell had explained earlier, lay through the bottle-neck, guarded by the last rock in the chain. Burckhardt was staring grimly at that rock as the ferry ploughed its way forward towards the entrance, half its engine-power neutralized by the insidious sideslip motion of the cross-current which, only a few minutes before their saviour, was fast becoming their most deadly enemy.

In size the rock was more like a small island, a pointed island which rose straight out of the sea to its peak, a saw-toothed giant against which a warship might well destroy itself at the first impact, whereas the ferry they were aboard was a little more fragile than a steel-plated cruiser. Mountainous waves were surging half-way up the rock's face and the bursting spray smothered its peak. It had the appearance of waiting for them.

'It is fortunate that we did not plan to scale the so-called cliff path,' Eberhay commented. He had said the first thing which came into his head to break the tension permeating the bridge like a disease. 'I hardly imagine it would have been a great success,' he went on lightly. 'There might have been some difficulty in disembarking the troops at the base of the cliff.'

'I don't believe there is a path,' Burckhardt replied. When the operation had been planned one of the experts had mentioned this path which he said climbed the apparently sheer face in a series of zigzag walks leading eventually to the summit close to the monastery. Superficially, it had seemed an attractive idea – Burckhardt could have taken his main objective soon after landing instead of going to the head of the gulf and then marching twenty miles back down the peninsula. From the monastery he could have sent out patrols to the north to occupy the peninsula from the heights – the operation would, in fact, have taken place in precisely the reverse direction from the one now contemplated. The operation had been revised to its present form when the planners had realized that the Greek ferry reached the cape in the early hours of the morning; the prospect of scaling the cliffs at night had been considered impracticable and the ferry had to complete its run to preserve the appearance of normality up to the last moment.

'Yes, there is a track,' Dietrich informed the colonel. 'It links up the anchorite dwellings built into the cliff face. The anchorites are hermit monks who spend all their lives in isolation from their fellows – hence the extraordinary places they live in.' He chuckled throatily. 'I have always thought it must be similar to solitary confinement during a lifetime in prison.'

'How do you know this?' Burckhardt was twisted round one hand still gripping the rail as the bridge swayed alarmingly.

'Because I paid a visit to Zervos five years ago.' Dietrich regarded the colonel ironically. 'Which is simply another of my qualifications for being here. I travelled all over the peninsula.'

'You went to the monastery?' Burckhardt put the question casually but the information interested him intensely. He had only one man among the two hundred aboard who knew Zervos personally – Lieutenant Hahnemann – and he had worried over this ever since the expedition had been planned. Perhaps, after all, the Abwehr officer was going to prove extremely useful during the dangerous hours ahead.

'Yes, I visited the monastery. Why?'

'I simply wondered how widespread your travels had been. I understand there is no landing place along the peninsula coast between the cape and Katyra at the head of the gulf.'

'There is Molos – twenty kilometres south of Katyra.'

'Yes, I know. It is a small fishing village – but has it access to the interior?'

'It depends what you call access.' Dietrich was still holding the cigar unlit in his mouth and he didn't bother to remove it to reply to the colonel. 'There is a footpath which goes up into the mountains but often it is washed away during the winter.'

'I see.' Burckhardt replied as though this were news, but he had heard this at the planning stage and it confirmed that Dietrich did know the geography of the peninsula. 'There is a road south from Katyra, of course?'

'You know perfectly well there is, or I presume you would not be on board this ship. It is little more than a track and winds its way among the hills. You should have brought mules with you,' he told Burckhardt bluntly.

'We considered them – but it was hardly practicable to transfer animals from the *Rupescu* to this ferry.' Satisfied with Dietrich's replies he turned away, but the Abwehr man had the last word.

'All this is assuming that we ever penetrate that gulf. You see what is happening, don't you?'

Burckhardt, who had let his attention slip for the shortest period of time, looked ahead and stiffened. During the very brief interval while he had conversed with Dietrich, the *Hydra*, caught up in the main force of the cross-current, had been swept three-quarters of the way across the entrance and now he heard a fresh sound, a sound more muted than the breaking of the sea against the cape but no less sinister – the dull boom of the swaying Aegean against the base of the saw-tooth. They were very close to the narrows – close enough to see that there the water was quieter, although still it heaved and bubbled like a tidal race, but they were equally close to the saw-tooth. He looked away to starboard where the big rollers were rounding Cape Zervos and hurtling towards the ferry, a piling-up of the sea which had more than once shaken the vessel as though she were a toy ship. It was these mountainous rollers which posed Burckhardt's second nightmare. If a big one came just at the wrong moment as they were passing the saw-tooth... He noticed Schnell again turning his head to look to port, and Schnell's frequent glances in that direction worried him. The naval officer was clearly aware that they were engaged in a lethal race – to pass through the narrows before they piled-up against the rock. There was no longer anything they could do except to hope. Everything seemed to conspire to screw up their tense nerves to an unbearable pitch –

the engines were beating foggily as though on the verge of breaking down altogether; the vessel's movements were becoming laboured and had a discouraging, waterlogged feel; the cross-current seemed to be carrying them sideways faster than the bows of the ship moved forward. He heard Eberhay clear his throat and the sound alerted him, made him look again to port. They were about to enter the narrows but the saw-tooth was less than thirty metres from the hull. A wave broke on the rock's side and spray reached the apexed summit. Out of the corner of his eye Burckhardt caught a slight movement – Nopagos was staring in the opposite direction towards the cape as though transfixed.

Following his gaze, the colonel clenched his teeth and felt coldness like an affliction chill his spine. Another roller was coming, a roller more mountainous than any Burckhardt had seen. There must have been some accumulation of the waters, even an overtaking and merging of three giant waves to form the foam-crested colossus bearing down on them like an upheaval from the deep. All heads were turned in that direction now, even Schnell's before he dragged his gaze to for'ard by some supreme effort of will. The crest of the monster was well above funnel height. Hands gripped the rails tightly, bodies stood rigid with fright. Even Burckhardt took several steps back as Dietrich moved aside for him to brace his back against the rear wall. With the wood pressed against his shoulder-blades he stared incredulously at the appalling spectacle. The wave seemed to be climbing higher and higher, swallowing up more of the sea to swell itself to mammoth proportions. We'll be overwhelmed, Burckhardt thought, we'll never emerge from this: we'll plunge down to the floor of the gulf like a submarine out of control. God, had there been some frightful underwater upheaval, some shift in the earth's surface on the Aegean floor? The wave was within ten metres now. Half the wave's height would be clear over them ... His hands locked on the rail, felt the greasy sweat inside his gloves, and then the *Hydra* tried to climb, to carry itself up the side of the monstrous wave – and instead was swept sideways. Lifted like a paper boat, it seemed no longer to move forward at all as the screw churned frantically inside the pounding sea. Eberhay lost his grip and was hurled bodily across the bridge where he collided with the Alpenkorps soldier. Bracing himself afresh, determined not to follow Eberhay, the colonel looked to port again. For a moment he saw nothing except the wave travelling westward, a shifting wobble of sea which shimmered his vision, then a window appeared in the water and his jaw muscles tautened. Just beyond the ship, it appeared, the sawtooth was rushing towards them like the wall of a building toppling over on the port deck. He waited for the shuddering crash of hull disintegrating against immovable rock, the sinking sensation as the *Hydra* foundered.

Spray blinded the view. Unexpectedly he realized that the ferry was listing to starboard, was over the crest. Ahead lay the smoother water where the gulf was protected from the fury of the storm by the wall of the cape. He looked back through the window at the rear of the bridge in time to see the saw-tooth submerging under the surge of the sea, the spray bursting high above the summit as the whole rock was temporarily drowned under the immense fall of water. Then the rock began to re-appear as water drained down its sides and Burckhardt's mind functioned again. *The rock was behind them.* They had moved inside the Gulf of Zervos.

Three minutes later he was about to leave the bridge, his mind concentrated on the peril of the Italian sea-mines, when Hahnemann reported that the unit's wireless set had been sabotaged.

'The Gestapo? Dietrich a member of the Gestapo? What the devil put that crazy idea into your head, Eberhay?'

Burckhardt stared grimly across the table at his second-in-command. It was a suggestion he could have done without at this stage of the operation as the *Hydra* proceeded steadily up the gulf through the darkness. All its lights were ablaze to preserve the appearance of normality and from the bridge a powerful searchlight was beamed ahead as Schnell and Nopagos strained their eyes for the first sight of the dreaded mines. Inside the colonel's cabin Eberhay crossed his slim legs and smiled faintly. The two men were alone and it had seemed an ideal moment to voice his doubts. 'It is just a feeling I had,' he explained, 'when I was talking to him on deck some time ago.'

'Just a feeling!' Burckhardt was more annoyed than ever. 'No evidence – just a feeling. And why should Berlin secretly put a Gestapo official on board this ship?' His voice became more biting. 'You have a theory on that, I'm sure.'

'Yes, I have.' The little major, accustomed to the colonel's moods, was unruffled. 'Since there appears to be a traitor on board it could be someone the Gestapo has previously suspected. We know someone helped the Englanders to escape, and if the unit has been infiltrated this would account for Dietrich's presence – he is trying to locate the spy. Naturally, if he is Gestapo, he doesn't take us into his complete confidence. They never do. And the sabotage of the wireless set proves that someone is trying to hinder the expedition...'

'I agree,' Dietrich spoke the words from the door he had opened silently and Burckhardt's manner became icier as the Abwehr man came inside and joined them at the table after carefully closing the door. The sentry outside the cabin should have stopped him, of course, and the colonel reminded himself to deal with that later. But it was an interesting example of how the Abwehr man's powerful personality was dominating almost everyone on board. A short while earlier Burckhardt had overheard an Alpenkorps soldier explaining to his cabin mates that the Abwehr officer had been sent personally by the Führer to watch over the operation, a suggestion which had not endeared him to the huge German who now sat at one end of the table holding his cigar while he spoke.

'Major Eberhay is, of course, correct. Someone aboard this Greek ferry is trying to prevent you from ever reaching your objective. And he has the freedom of action to sabotage your wireless set. That I personally find most inconvenient – I wished to send a message to Berlin via your GHQ in Bulgaria at the earliest possible moment. When would you have been able to break radio silence?'

'Not while we are on board,' Burckhardt replied evasively. 'But you may still be able to send your message later.'

Dietrich looked relieved, nodding as he lit his cigar. 'That is certain?'

'I cannot be sure yet when that will be.' He paused, conscious of a feeling that he was being too close-mouthed with this Abwehr officer. For all he knew he could be Admiral Canaris' right-hand man. 'We have a second wireless set in perfect condition,' he said briskly. 'Military signals will, of course, have priority, but you will be able to communicate with Bulgaria at a certain time after we have gone ashore.'

'The other set is permanently out of action?'

'Possibly not. Someone smashed the tuning coil but the wireless op may be able to repair it in time.'

'It had been left unguarded?'

'No, not originally. But the man who was guarding it became sick and went to the lavatory. He was there for some time and because of his condition he didn't check the set immediately when he returned.'

'How can you smash up a tuning coil?'

Eberhay, who had seen the damaged set, explained this. 'Anything heavy would do the job – a pistol butt, or a rifle's – anything. It could be done in less than a minute.'

'Why did Schnell keep to his cabin during the early part of the voyage?' asked Dietrich. The sudden switch in topic surprised both German officers and again it was Eberhay who replied. 'He made the same trip aboard the *Hydra* a fortnight ago to study the vessel and its route. Although he was disguised on that earlier trip we wanted to eliminate any risk that one of the crew might recognize him this time.'

'And he carried the weapons for use in taking over the vessel inside that cabin trunk which caused so much comment?'

'Yes!' It was Burckhardt who answered now, disliking the final qualification in Dietrich's question. 'Both wireless sets, incidentally, are now under heavy guard. And the seizure of this vessel went exactly according to plan.'

'I agree that that part of the operation was well organized,' Dietrich said blandly with the underlying implication that the later stages had been little better than a dog's breakfast. Withdrawing suddenly from the conversation, he sat back in his chair and regarded both men through his cigar smoke. The German officers had taken off their outer civilian coats and wore field-grey Alpenkorps uniform: a tunic buttoned up to the neck, trousers ankle-wrapped with puttees, and heavily nailed boots. The footgear, Dietrich thought, was an improvement on the normal Wehrmacht jackboot he so disliked. Round his waist each man wore a wide leather belt with a hip holster slung on the left side and the Luger pistol set butt forward. He remained motionless while someone hammered urgently on the outside of the door and a moment later the knocking was repeated. Burckhardt called out for them to come in and Lieutenant Hahnemann appeared.

'What is it?' Burckhardt asked quietly.

'One of the ten-kilogram demolition charges is missing – and a time fuse.'

Dietrich came to life suddenly, was standing up as he fired the question, his great body overshadowing Hahnemann. 'That sounds like a large bomb?'

In his agitation Hahnemann replied immediately before the colonel could say a word, addressing Dietrich directly. 'If it is placed in the right position it could destroy the entire ship.'

'Something's upset their apple cart, all right.' Ford spoke quietly as he stood alongside Prentice by the porthole. Their cabin was being methodically searched by Alpenkorps soldiers who prodded the bedding gingerly with short-bladed bayonets, opened cupboard doors as though expecting something to fall out, and peered cautiously under chair seats without moving them.

'They're nervy, too.' Prentice watched the searching process curiously and he thought he sensed a desperate urgency in their efforts, like men working against a clock. Near the door Sergeant Volber stood directing operations, although his main task, under orders from Eberhay, was to protect the prisoners. During the search more than one man glanced murderously at Prentice who was responsible for the death of one of their comrades, and Volber was present to exercise strict discipline. A moment later the sergeant spoke in German, and when Prentice failed to understand, he waved his Luger to indicate they must move to one side. A soldier who pointedly did not look at them opened the porthole, peered outside, then rubbed a hand round the outer rim as though seeking something which might be suspended there. Satisfied with his search, he closed the porthole and Volber motioned them to take up their former position.

'What the hell's going on?' Ford whispered.

'Don't know – but they're as jumpy as hens with a fox in the yard.' Prentice was glad of Volber's presence: all the Germans carried carbines,* as the technically minded Ford insisted on calling them, and it had been known for a weapon to go off accidentally when aimed at a lethal spot. From the look on the faces of some of these hard-bitten youngsters a carbine could have discharged quite easily in his direction if Volber had omitted to attend the ceremony. Ford continued gazing out of the porthole where he could see on the mainland side of the gulf a chain of pinpoint lights crawling up the coast road to the north. He pressed his hand lightly on the lieutenant's arm.

'Look – must be our chaps across there.'

'I know, I've seen 'em.' Prentice hadn't relaxed his own gaze from the interior of the cabin. He could feel the deep animosity radiating from the dozen men who went on turning the cabin inside out. One soldier walking past him chanced to let go of his carbine and Prentice had to move quickly. The metal-sheathed butt of the weapon thudded heavily on the cabin floor where a moment before his right foot had stood. If that butt had contacted, it could have crippled him. Volber called out sharply in German and was still barking vehemently when the soldier left the cabin.

'Sounds as though he's going on a charge. With any luck,' Ford added. 'You know, sir, I don't think they really like us.'

'Just be ready to do a quick tap-dance if the occasion arises,' Prentice told him and continued to stare at any man who caught his eye. Yes, Ford had been right: it was a damned queer situation. On board the *Hydra* there must be at least a company of well-trained German troops and some of them expected to operate at high altitudes – he had seen several pairs of skis inside one cabin when they had been taken along earlier for interrogation by that slip of a German officer who spoke English. And behind them, a few miles across the gulf through that porthole, they could see the hooded lights of traffic moving through the night along that vital mainland road

* Ford was referring to the Gewehr 98 K bolt-action carbine.

110

to the north. Prentice had no doubt that those were the lights of Allied convoys driving up to the Alkiamon Line, completely ignorant of the fact that the ship whose lights they could see across the water was carrying a German spearhead aimed at Zervos. For by now Prentice had little doubt of the Alpenkorps objective – the Germans on board were on their way to seize that vital monastery observation post overlooking the road Ford was watching through the porthole.

'A whole load of them on the way,' Ford went on, 'I can see lights right up the coast.'

'What the blazes can this lot be looking for?' Prentice wondered out loud. 'And it bothers them. They're sweating.'

'They can melt away for all I care. What I can't make out is why they're still wearing their Mae Wests. It's as calm as the Serpentine outside now.' Ford's description of the gulf had an element of exaggeration because the *Hydra* was still steaming through a moderate swell, but contrasted with the seas off Cape Zervos it could indeed have been the Serpentine. The Aegean, one of the most unpredictable seas in the world, had subsided again.

'I told you, they were nervy,' Prentice replied. Inwardly, he assumed the wearing of Mae Wests was just another example of Teutonic discipline, but it was the object of the search which was nagging at his tired brain. Come to think of it, these boys didn't look as though they'd just got up in the morning. Which was a thought that gave him a certain amount of satisfaction: if they went on prowling round the ship like this they'd be exhausted before they ever got ashore. The soldiers were trooping out of the cabin when he went up to Volber. 'Speak with German who speaks Englische ...' he began. It took him a pantomime of gestures to convey that he wished to talk to the little officer who had interviewed them earlier, and when Volber returned he came back with Lieutenant Hahnemann instead.

'What is it?' Hahnemann rapped out. There was tension here, too – tension and irritability in the manner and expression with which he regarded the two prisoners.

'What are you looking for? We might be able to help,' Prentice told him blithely.

111

The reaction was unexpectedly violent. Hahnemann took a step forward and his right hand rested close to his hip holster. It had been a mistake, Prentice realized at once. The Jerries were more at their nerve-ends than he had realized. He spoke quickly and tersely, letting a little indignation creep into his tone. 'I meant what I said. Why wouldn't I? If I could tell you where it was – whatever you are looking for – it would have saved us having the bedding bayoneted to bits.'

'You will stay here and not send for me again.' He turned away and then looked back. 'Why are you not wearing the life-jackets?'

'Because there isn't a storm any more.'

'You put them on now and they stay on. That is an order. For your safety,' he ended abruptly. They were left alone with the guard while they tied on their Mae Wests again. Prentice was relieved to see that it was the same guard, a thirty-year-old who sat some distance from them with his machine-pistol always aimed in their general direction. A sturdy-faced character, he had shown no exceptional signs of hostility although he was careful never to let them come within ten feet of where he sat.

'I'd still like to know what they were after,' said Ford as he sat down on a pile of massacred bedding. He looked up at Prentice. 'How much longer?'

'About an hour, if they're keeping to the ferry's schedule.' Prentice's watch registered 4.30 AM and the *Hydra* had been due to dock at Katyra at 5.30 AM, a little before dawn. To keep awake he went over to the porthole again for another look at those tantalizing hooded lights of the convoy moving along the coast road. Another hour. Nothing much could happen in that time.

The ten-kilogram composite demolition charge stood on the table. It was enclosed inside a black-painted zinc container about the size and shape of a deep attaché case and there was a web carrying-handle at the top. Inset into the top face were two standard igniter sockets.

'Like that?' queried Dietrich innocently. He gave the impression that this was the first time in his life he had seen a ten-kilogram demolition charge.

'Its twin is hidden somewhere aboard this ship – with the difference that the clockwork time fuse has undoubtedly been attached and set in motion. Show him the fuse, Hahnemann.'

While Burckhardt waited, the engines of the ferry ticked over steadily, unpleasantly suggestive of the ticking of a time bomb. They were alone in the colonel's cabin with the exception of the temporary presence of Hahnemann who had brought in the demolition charge at the Abwehr man's request. As Dietrich had so unfortunately put it, he wanted to see what was going to blow him to kingdom come.

'The fuse,' said Hahnemann.

It was roughly shaped like an outsized egg-cup. Measuring a little over two inches across the top in diameter and six inches in overall depth, the casing was chocolate-brown bakelite, and when Dietrich picked up the device Hahnemann showed him how it worked. The top was a hinged glass lid which had to be lifted to set the clock. Still holding the time fuse, he looked up at the lieutenant.

'And one of these is definitely missing with the charge?'

'Yes. They were in a rucksack at the bottom of the companionway stairs.'

'Not guarded?' Dietrich was looking down at the mechanism.

Hahnemann glanced at the colonel, who nodded. 'There was a mix-up of rucksacks. I'm sure it would never have happened if half the men hadn't been sea-sick. Corporal Schultz thought he had the rucksack with the charges inside with him in a cabin. It was only discovered later that he had someone else's while his own rucksack had been left outside.'

Dietrich ignored the explanation. 'Corporal Schultz is waiting in the passage? Good, I'd like to see him.'

Hahnemann went to the door and let inside a slim man in his late twenties who was clearly not at ease, and his embarrassment increased when he slipped on the polished floor. He glanced at the colonel as he saluted and Burckhardt merely told him to answer questions. He had already had a word with the negligent NCO.

'These fuses are totally reliable?' enquired Dietrich. The pink-faced corporal glanced at Hahnemann who told him briskly to answer the question. Schultz was uncertain how much to say and the colonel barked at him to get on with it.

'No, sir, not always,' Schultz began. And having begun he gained confidence and spoke rapidly. 'They have a habit when set of stopping for no reason at all. Then they can start up again of their own accord – again for no particular reason. We do know that they can be affected by jolting or vibrations. They're weird – I heard of one case where a fuse was set to detonate the charge in two days. It was put under a bridge during training and then the man who had put it there died in a motor crash. Everyone forgot about it.' He paused, his eyes on Dietrich who was staring at him fixedly. 'Two years later the bridge blew up. Yes, sir – two *years* later.'

'Thank you.' Dietrich returned the time fuse to Hahnemann who picked up the charge by the handle and left the cabin with Corporal Schultz.

'And where does that get us?' asked Burckhardt.

'It gets us into a worse state of nerves than we were before, I should have thought. You heard what he said?'

'Of course! Which point were you referring to?'

Dietrich clubbed one large fist and began drumming it slowly on the table. It took Burckhardt a moment to grasp that he was drumming in time with the beat of the *Hydra*'s engines. He pursed his lips uncomfortably as Dietrich rammed the point home verbally. 'Affected by jolting or vibrations,' he said.

'We shall not be on board much longer.' He hesitated. It must by now be patently obvious when they were going ashore to anyone who knew the *Hydra*'s timetable. 'Barely an hour. In the meantime the search continues and they may find it.'

'Colonel Burckhardt.' Dietrich was standing up now, his hat in his hand. 'This is likely to be the longest hour of your life. I think I'll go and help them try to find it. You never know – they say heaven protects the innocent.'

As he went along the companionway, hands thrust deep inside his coat pockets, he heard the frenzied clump of nailed boots everywhere. The boots rarely stayed still for more than a short time, as though their occupants were finding it impossible to keep in one place while they continued their frantic search for the missing demolition charge. Inside one cabin he found men with moist faces pushing aside a pile of dark brown hickory skis which could not possibly have concealed the charge. A soldier who didn't look a day over nineteen was peering behind a fire-extinguisher, another impossible hiding-place. There had been tension aboard the *Hydra* ever since the Alpenkorps had arrived, tension initially through the knowledge that at any minute they might be stopped by a British warship, tension because they were aboard the vessel of a country which Germany still officially treated as a neutral in the war. But the earlier tension brought on by the secrecy, by the storm, by the sabotage of a wireless set and the death of one of their men overboard – this tension had been serenity compared with the stark, livid tension which now gripped the *Hydra*'s illegal passengers.

It manifested itself in little ways. The lift of a rifle as Dietrich came round a corner. The kicking over of a bucket of sand by an Alpenkorps soldier hurrying past. The disorganized clump of those nailed boots on the ceiling when he was walking along the companionway of the lower deck. The sentry who guarded Grapos was still at his post, his back to the port-holed steel door leading down to the hold where the Greek was imprisoned. Farther along the companionway Dietrich looked inside the half-open door which led down to the engine-room. He had one foot on the iron platform when a rifle muzzle was thrust in his face, reminding him of the muzzle which Volber had thrust at him as he opened his cabin door when they had taken over the ship. But this time he withdrew swiftly – the muzzle had wobbled slightly. In that brief glimpse he had seen below at least half-a-dozen field grey figures searching among the machinery while another man mounted guard over the chief engineer. The fear was a living mounting thing which he saw in men's faces as he climbed back to the top deck, faces damp, baggy-eyed and drawn with strain as they went on searching amid the ferry's complexities for something no larger than an attaché case. This is a formula for driving men mad, he was thinking as he went on climbing, for slowly shredding their nerves to pieces.

On the open deck it was quieter because there were fewer searchers: Burckhardt had given strict instructions that despite the gravity of the emergency only those men who could cover their uniforms with civilian coats were to be sent up here. Even now he was not prepared to risk a British motor-torpedo boat suddenly appearing and flashing its searchlight over the deck to illuminate men in German uniform. So far as Dietrich could see there were no more than a dozen, hatless men flitting in the shadows. But here again he heard the disjointed hurrying clump of those heavily nailed boots pounding the wooden deck. It was quite dark now, the impenetrable pitchblackness of the night before dawn, and a cold wind was blowing along the gulf. He leant against the ventilator amidships to light his cigar and a soldier came round the side and cannoned into him. When he saw the silhouette of the hat against the match-flare he apologized and hurried away. Dietrich sighed. Again he had seen the lift of the rifle prior to recognition. He went to the stern and looked over the rail where the screw churned the sea a dirty white colour, stumbled over a piled loop of rope, and went back along the deck to the illuminated safety of the bridge. It was 4.45 AM.

The ten-kilogram composite demolition charge swayed at the end of the rope. The vibrations of the ship's engines shuddered it in mid-sway and the rock of the ship's movements reproduced themselves in the sway itself. The charge thudded regularly against the metalwork as it continued its endless pendulum motion, but the sound of the thuds was camouflaged by the same engine beats which shook it. A man standing close by might not have heard those warning thuds as the charge dangled and swayed and shuddered. The clock was set and the mechanism was ticking, but the most vital sound – the ticking – was muffled by the larger noises. Occasionally the vessel plunged its bows a little deeper into the waters of the gulf and then the charge would strike the metal heavily, its rhythmic sway temporarily upset by the unexpected jolt. For a minute or more it would sway erratically, its pendulum balance disturbed, then it would recover its poise and resume the same even swing backwards and forwards with the regularity of a metronome. It was suspended a long way down the shaft, suspended from an Alpenkorps scabbard which still held its bayonet, a scabbard which had been jammed inside the shaft at an angle which might hold it there indefinitely. And as it went on swaying none of the hatless men who thumped along the open deck in growing desperation had, as yet, carefully examined the ventilator shaft amidships.

CHAPTER SEVEN

Sunday, Dawn

'The Greek has escaped – I have instituted an immediate and intensive search of the ship.' Hahnemann reported the news to Burckhardt whom he had found on the bridge standing next to Dietrich. He waited nervously for the colonel's reaction, but Burckhardt, holding a pair of field-glasses, simply looked at him as he asked the question.

'How did it happen, Hahnemann? He was tied up in the hold and Private Kutzel was standing guard over him.'

'He must have freed himself in some way.' Hahnemann hesitated: the next item of news was bound to provoke an explosion. 'Kutzel is dead – I found him on the floor of the hold with his neck broken.'

'And his rifle?'

Dietrich smiled grimly to himself as he heard the question and he gave the colonel top marks for competence under stress. The weapon, of course, was vital, could make all the difference to the degree of menace posed by the escaped Greek.

'I found that on the floor close to his body . . .'

'Good. He shouldn't be difficult to round up. You said an "intensive" search, Hahnemann. How intensive? How many men?'

'Fifty, sir.' Hahnemann at least felt confident that he had organized the hunt for Grapos on a sufficiently massive scale, even though there was something else which he dreaded mentioning. He wished to heaven that the Abwehr man wasn't standing there with his hands behind his back, his great shoulders hunched forward as he took in every word the lieutenant was saying. The colonel's reaction gave him an unpleasant shock.

'Fifty? You mean you have taken fifty men off the search for the missing demolition charge?' Burckhardt was facing the unfortunate Hahnemann now, his hands on his hips as he went on bitingly. 'When will you get your priorities right? An explosive with a time fuse has been planted somewhere aboard this vessel, an explosive powerful enough to sink us in the middle of the gulf before we ever go ashore. That, since it appears you don't realize it, is a far greater risk than one unarmed Greek civilian who is probably gibbering with fright in some cupboard. You will tell off no more than twenty men to look for him – the other thirty must immediately resume the search for that demolition charge.'

'He is armed, sir – with a rifle . . .'

'You said you had found Kutzel's rifle.'

'That is correct, sir.' Hahnemann's rigid stance reflected the extent of his unhappiness as he went on stolidly. 'I think the Greek must have surprised Private Wasserman also when he was asleep in a cabin on the lower deck . . .'

'Asleep!' Burckhardt changed the direction of his attack: what a soldier had been doing asleep during these vital hours was something he could inquire into later. Doubtless Wasserman had sneaked off into the cabin hoping no one would find him there. 'What has happened to Wasserman?'

'He's dead – strangled as far as we can tell. And his rifle and ammunition belt are missing so the Greek must have them.'

Burckhardt paused only briefly while he wished to God that the Abwehr man wasn't listening to all this, but he was still perfectly clear as to what must be done. 'You will still use only twenty men to hunt for the Greek. Issue a general warning that he's armed.'

'I have done that already, sir.'

'Then issue a special warning to those on the open deck – we don't want them starting to loose off at each other.' As Hahnemann hurried away he thought no, that would be the final disaster – to incur further casualties with the men shooting one another. Taking up a firmer stance, he stared ahead to where the searchlight beam shone down the gulf. It was 5.15 AM. A quarter of an hour to disembarkation. Coldly, he catalogued in his mind the risks and setbacks which had bedevilled the expedition since he had come aboard the *Hydra*.

A boatload of troops which had been very nearly capsized during the transfer from the *Rupescu*; one soldier sent into the sea by the Englishman, Prentice; one wireless set sabotaged by smashing the tuning-coil; the encounter with the destroyer which had almost proved fatal; a demolition charge of great explosive power planted somewhere in the bowels of the vessel; the escape of the armed Greek; and the death of two more Alpenkorps men during that escape. So three men out of two hundred were dead even before they set foot in Greece. Surely nothing more could happen during the remaining quarter of an hour? Actually, it was likely to be twenty-five or thirty minutes – they were behind schedule with this infernal ferry having to move more slowly because of the danger of mines – and Italian mines of all things. Schnell had insisted on the further reduction in speed to ensure that they sighted them in time. The irony of it was they hadn't seen a single mine since entering the gulf.

'I think I'll go and have a word with Major Eberhay – if I can find him.' Dietrich was already moving away and leaving the bridge to Burckhardt's relief – the large German seemed to dominate wherever he went, to hang over the ship like a prophet of disasters to come. Barely a minute later Sergeant Volber came onto the bridge and the colonel only had to take one look at his face to know it was not good news.

'What is it, Volber?' he rapped out sharply.

'We think Private Diehl may be missing, sir'.

Burckhardt instantly thought of the Greek who was prowling about somewhere with a loaded rifle. 'You *think*? Either Diehl is missing or he isn't?' Which is it?'

'We don't know, sir.' Volber lacked Lieutenant Hahnemann's capacity for telling a complete account quickly, forestalling his commanding officer's questions so far as he could, and the sergeant's habit of replying without explaining was a foible Burckhardt found intensely irritating. He felt the blood going to his head as he forced himself to reply coldly.

'What the devil does that mean?'

'He hasn't been seen for a long time – I've asked several of the men and they all thought he was somewhere else. They're very scattered . . .'

'You've allowed your section to become scattered?'

'We're on the open deck and it takes time to check everyone in the dark . . .'

'Report to me as soon as you can whether he's definitely missing. Definitely, I said, Volber.'

The strain was telling everywhere, Burckhardt thought as the sergeant hurried away. Schnell was being over-cautious, the NCOs were getting rattled, and the men were being steadily drained of their aggressive energies as they plodded round the ship searching for time-bombs and armed Greeks. And soon they would have to fight a campaign. Armed Greeks? The thought reminded him of a few vital questions he had to put to the captain. He took a step forward which placed him at Nopagos' elbow.

'The man called Grapos has escaped,' he said harshly. 'He has taken a rifle and ammunition – can he use them? Before you reply, remember that he is a civilian with no rights in war and I shall hold you responsible for the death of any of my men if you withhold information.'

Nopagos turned and stared at the German. His skin was lined and pouched with fatigue but he still held himself erect; what little responsibility he still held for his own vessel as its pilot would only cease when they docked at Katyra. He was tempted to tell Burckhardt to go to hell but he sensed something of the tremendous pressure the colonel was undergoing and it seemed senseless to take a risk when they had almost landed. 'He has been able to use a rifle since he was a boy,' he replied.

'But he has something to do with the monastery.' Burckhardt did not understand this at all and his mouth tightened as he held the Greek's eyes.

'He was a novice monk who had no vocation. When he left the monastery it was agreed that he should do odd jobs for them – like going to Istanbul on this ferry to bring back supplies of books and things like that. He has shot birds on the peninsula from an early age. Yes, he can use a rifle.'

'Well?'

'A marksman.' Nopagos gave this reply with a certain relish.

'His limp kept him out of the army?'

'It was his greatest regret. He would be an asset to any army in the world. Has he caused any trouble yet?'

'He has killed two of my men.'

'You see what I mean, then?' For a moment Nopagos thought he had gone too far. Burckhardt stiffened and a hint of fury came into his eyes and then faded as he regained control. He was careful to keep strict control as he put his next question.

'He knows this ship well?'

'Well enough to hide until we have reached Katyra as you have not found him now.' And with this last thrust Nopagos turned away and attended to his duties once more. But he was not able to resist asking a question which he carefully put in a polite tone. 'Have they found the time-bomb yet?'

'No.'

'So, there is still time.'

This simple comment stung Burckhardt more than anything Nopagos had said previously. He had given Eberhay orders to leave assembly for disembarkation until the last possible moment so they could keep on looking for that missing demolition charge – Burckhardt's greatest fear was that it would detonate just before they landed. He was thinking about this when Schnell, almost exhausted from his long hours over the wheel, straightened up as a soldier ran along outside the bridge and came in breathless. Burckhardt recognized him as one of the two men posted as lookouts as soon as they had passed through the narrows. In his anxiety to speak the man had trouble in getting out his message.

'Mines sighted, sir ... on the port bow.'

The explosion came at 5.45 AM as the *Hydra*, listing to port, her engines beating uncertainly, began the ninety-degree turn which would take her inshore to the distant light of the Katyra landing-stage. They were almost there, Burckhardt reflected as he stood on the bridge behind Nopagos, but the last mile was likely to be the longest of the voyage. The dangers surrounding the expedition were now so overwhelming that his mind had reached the point where it could hardly take in any more – those damnable Italian mines were growing more numerous with every quarter-mile they glided forward; an armed Greek was loose somewhere on board, and a marksman at that; and they had still failed to locate the demolition charge which might detonate at any moment. Lifting his field-glasses to focus on the circle of mines ringing the vessel, he ignored the newcomers arriving on the already overcrowded bridge. Because of the risk of imminent disaster he had ordered the British prisoners to be brought up from their cabin.

'Are we abandoning ship?' Prentice asked quietly.

'No!' Hahnemann's reply was savagely emphatic as his hand guided the lieutenant by the elbow to the rear of the bridge. 'We shall be landing shortly.'

'Through that lot!' Ford sounded incredulous as he gazed over the colonel's shoulder along the searchlight beam which cut across the darkness. To port and starboard of the illuminated avenue at least four mines floated, metallic spheres which gleamed palely, their surfaces speckled with small shadows – the dreaded nozzles which caused instant detonation on contact. Burckhardt spoke briefly over his shoulder, instructing Hahnemann to tell them about the missing demolition charge; after all, they were soldiers, so they might as well know the position. With waning enthusiasm, Prentice and Ford listened to Hahnemann and were then pushed to the rear of the bridge, squeezed in between a press of uniformed Alpenkorps troops. Looking to his right, Prentice found he was huddled next to the large German civilian who had come aboard at Istanbul. On their way up from the cabin they had seen him in the distance climbing a staircase and Prentice had enquired who he was.

'Herr Dietrich is with the Abwehr,' Hahnemann had replied with a hint of respect in his voice. Prentice looked up curiously at the huge figure who stared back at him as he lit a fresh cigar with one elbow rested on the shoulder of the corporal next to him. A rum cove, this Dietrich, was Prentice's reaction as he turned to listen to Ford who was keeping his voice down.

'How big did he say that demolition charge was? I couldn't catch all he said in this crush.'

123

'Ten kilograms. Is that bad?'

'It's not good, I can tell you that straight off. And if it's been dumped near the boilers and they go, too ...'

He broke off as Burckhardt issued a stream of orders to Eberhay who had appeared at the door to the bridge and then hurried away when the colonel had finished speaking. They were close to the moment of disembarkation, which required disciplined control, and the little major was facing something like near-panic as the troops filed up the staircases. It was then that Prentice saw the Alpenkorps equipment which confirmed his worst fears: he had a glimpse of men with skis of hickory wood passing beyond the bridge. The skis were carried on their backs which also supported rucksacks – which could only mean they expected to be operating in the deep snows on Mount Zervos at the far end of the peninsula. The Alpenkorps' main objective was the natural observation post of the monastery which overlooked the mainland road carrying Allied supplies northward.

'Funny that bomb hasn't gone off already,' he remarked lightly to Ford. He would have liked to feel that he was praying for the charge to detonate, but the truth was that he was sick with apprehension. 'Perhaps the chap who fixed it didn't know what he was doing,' he suggested.

'That's possible, sir. But their time fuses aren't all that reliable – a Jerry we had in the bag told me that. The damned things have a habit of conking out at the wrong moment.'

'You mean they become harmless?' Prentice tried to keep the hope out of his voice.

'Now I didn't say that, did I? Apparently they sometimes stop and then start up again. Vibrations can get them going again as easy as winking. The ship's engines are ideal for the purpose.'

'That's right, cheer us all up.' Prentice did not feel particularly reassured. Ford was an ammunition examiner who spent too much of his life fiddling with things which might go bang in his face at any second – including enemy explosives and equipment on which he was also something of an expert. But here on this German-held vessel he was displaying distinct signs of nervousness as he pulled at the lobe of one ear and kept looking round the bridge as though he expected it to disappear without warning.

'Fasten those straps at once!' Hahnemann had returned briefly to the bridge and had noticed that Ford's life-jacket was loose. Every man on the bridge wore his life-jacket and these cumbersome objects took up more space and further impeded movement. Prentice had the feeling that he would soon be lifted clear off the floor if anyone else crowded in on the bridge. He jerked his head round again to look through the rear window which gave a view along the deck towards the stern, a deck which was almost deserted since the order for uniformed troops to keep out of sight was still in force. Almost deserted, but not quite. Prentice's eyes narrowed as he watched sea mist drift past a lamp near the starboard rail: by its light he saw a short, heavily built man on the wrong side of the rail, a man who carried a rifle over his back. Something about the shape and the movement reminded him of the Greek civilian who had also come aboard at Istanbul. Grapos, the captain had called him. Mist blurred the view and when it cleared the poised figure was gone. He had dived over the side.

'Seen a ghost, sir?' Ford inquired.

'I've got a crick in my neck if you're referring to my expression of almost unendurable agony.' Prentice felt sure that at the last minute Dietrich had also glanced through that window, but by then the mist would have blotted out the lonely figure. He was greatly relieved when the German said nothing and continued quietly smoking the cigar which was now adding to the growing foetid atmosphere inside the packed bridge. So Grapos had made a dive for it and was heading for the shore fast. Some people are lucky, he thought, and then he remembered the mine-strewn waters the Greek was swimming through at that very moment and he suppressed a shudder. Despite the number of men compressed inside the confined space it was very silent on the bridge in the intervals between Burckhardt giving sharp orders as officers and NCOs appeared at the door, a silence of suppressed dread which hung over their still heads like a pall as the engines slowly beat out their mechanical rhythm and the *Hydra* continued to turn eastwards.

The bows of the vessel were now moving through drifts of white mist which were fogging visibility, yet a further source of anxiety to Burckhardt, who had now left off his civilian raincoat and was dressed in full uniform with the Alpenkorps broad-brimmed cap set firmly on his head. Nopagos stood like a man of wax, his eyes trying to bore through the mist-curtain at the earliest possible moment. Schnell was crouched in a permanent stoop over the wheel, glancing frequently to starboard where the nearest mine bobbed gently less than fifty metres from the hull. At least, he hoped that was the nearest mine. From his all-round view at the rear, Prentice was looking from face to face, noting the gleam of sweat on tightly drawn skin, the nervous twitch of an eyelid, the hands which gripped rifles and machine-pistols so tensely that the knuckles were whitened. These men, all over the ship, were under the maximum possible pressure. They were going into action by dawn. They knew that the sea ahead was alive with mines, and that somewhere, perhaps under their feet, the time fuse was ticking down to zero. If someone had determined to bring well-night unbearable pressure on their morale they could scarcely have planned it better than this. He looked to his right again. Dietrich, outwardly the most composed man on the bridge, was still calmly smoking his cigar and looking down at Prentice as though assessing his character and qualities in an emergency.

'Not more than half an hour at the most.' Ford's voice was little more than a whisper, a whisper motivated more by a dislike of breaking the doom-like silence than by a wish not to be overheard.

'Less than that, I imagine. If we ever get there.' Prentice looked again at the landing-stage light which was visible and closer now the mist had temporarily cleared. And there seemed to be light in the east on the far side of the peninsula. Hoisting his wrist upwards, he looked at his watch. Exactly 5.45 AM. Schnell was turning the wheel to straighten course as Burckhardt transmitted an instruction he had received from Nopagos; Dietrich was studying the end of his cigar rather dubiously; a soldier was wiping moisture from his forehead; and

Ford was looking round the bridge with quick darting glances when the explosion came.

The silence on the bridge was ruptured by a shattering roar. The *Hydra* shuddered from bows to stern as though struck by a mammoth blow and then wobbled. A wave was carried away from the ferry and swept towards the shore as it gathered up more water in its headlong flight from the vessel. For a few brief seconds it had been as light as day to starboard where a brilliant flash temporarily blinded those who had been looking in that direction. From beyond the open door of the bridge came a babble of panic-stricken voices and the sound of nailed boots scattering across the decks. Stark gibbering panic had seized the ship and on the packed bridge the hysterical murmuring was only silenced by Burckhardt thundering for quiet. He pushed aside Nopagos who had been leaning out of the window to starboard and leaned out himself. The sea appeared to have gone mad as it heaved and bubbled frothily. For a second Burckhardt thought that they had been struck by a torpedo and that a submarine was surfacing. Then the water began to settle. Schnell still held the ship on course, heading for the landing-stage which was coming closer and closer in the darkness, and he spoke without looking at the colonel. 'The mine was very close when it detonated.'

'It was a mine, just a mine, we have not been hit...' Hahnemann shouted out the news in German and then in English to stem the signs of panic.

'Well, if that doesn't start it ticking, nothing will,' Ford remarked grimly.

'It?' Prentice was still a little dazed with relief as well as shock.

'The demolition charge,' said Ford, whose mind was never far from explosives. 'If the time fuse mechanism had stopped only temporarily that thump was quite enough to get it moving again, believe you me.'

'I was under the impression that we had hit a mine,' Prentice told him icily. 'That's enough to be going on with, I should have thought.'

'Well, obviously we didn't – we're still steaming on course

at the same speed. The mine just went off on its own accord rather too close for comfort.' He was having to lift his voice for Prentice to hear him above the shouts on deck as Burckhardt thrust his way roughly off the bridge and went out on deck himself.

'You mean they can be defective, too?'

'Frequently. They can go off without rhyme or reason. On the other hand something else may have bumped into it – although I can't imagine what.'

Prentice began to feel slightly ill. He could imagine what else might have bumped into that mine in its frantic efforts to reach the shore. He had a picture in his mind of Grapos diving overboard with that protruding rifle attached to his back, of him swimming among the mines and so easily forgetting the barrel projecting beyond his body. There would be nothing left of the poor devil now. Prentice didn't like to think of what explosive which could take out a ship's bottom might do to a single human being as it detonated within a few feet of the swimming body.

'I think that little bang has rattled them,' Ford remarked.

'It rattled me,' Prentice replied with feeling. He looked back through the rear window where there was a state of confusion on the deck below. Alpenkorps men in full uniform who had been huddled close to the rail were being sent under cover by Volber who was waving his arms like a man shepherding sheep back to the fold. Within a minute the deck was clear and the babble of voices beyond the open door had ceased when Burckhardt came back to take up his post behind Nopagos. But the damage had been done. Another heavy blow had been dealt at the morale of troops who, on land would have taken the explosion in their stride, but cooped up on the unfamiliar sea the experience was having an entirely different effect. Prentice thought he could see in the faces in front of him a little extra strain, a trace more tension as the cold light from the east died in the false dawn and the landing-stage light at Katyra drew steadily closer.

Schnell was showing great skill as he steered the *Hydra* on the last stage of her perilous course, threading his way between a scatter of mines which floated in the path of the searchlight beam. An oppressive silence had fallen on the limping vessel as she moved through the dark water which was impenetrable beyond the beam, water supporting perhaps a hundred more mines for all Burckhardt could tell. The men on the decks below were waiting – waiting for the final collision with a mine, waiting for the still-hidden demolition charge to detonate under them, waiting for the tension-fraught moment of the landing – although which of these hazards was uppermost in their strained minds it was impossible to guess. The engines ticked over monotonously as the ferry slipped towards a blurred shadow which was the coast.

Plagued by a dozen anxieties, Burckhardt maintained his outward appearance of calm confidence while inwardly he fretted at the damnably crawling progress of the vessel. He was already nearly thirty minutes behind his timetable and he was praying that the news of the general offensive launched at 5.45 AM was not yet on the air. It was unlikely – an hour or two should pass before the world read the reports of the German onslaught on Greece and Yugoslavia spearheaded by the Panzers and reinforced with airborne troops – and the peninsula was still devoid of Allied troops and wide open to his attack. The whole key to the operation was a swift dash back along the peninsula and the capture of the monastery before the Allies had time to recover their balance. Just so long as there really was nothing standing in his way – and that they were able to land safely. He felt the chill of the early morning air filtering through his uniform and braced himself to control a shiver as Dietrich appeared at his elbow.

'The inhabitants of Katyra are bound to have heard the mine explode,' the Abwehr man remarked.

'I realize that,' Burckhardt replied non-committally.

'So there is a serious risk that someone may have phoned through to Salonika.'

'We have attended to that, so once again you can put your mind at rest,' Burckhardt began ironically. Then he paused: they were so close to going ashore that really he was free to speak more openly. 'There is only a single telephone line out of the peninsula, Herr Dietrich, and that was cut several hours ago.'

'Good. But Salonika may wonder why the line has gone dead.'

'Last night's storm will account for that. In a way it was lucky – it has provided an explanation.'

'And you have transport waiting for you as well?' Dietrich inquired genially.

'There are mules on the peninsula. It was impossible to bring them with us but we shall find mules available. The planning has taken into account every possible contingency. As to transport, other arrangements have also been made...' Burckhardt trailed off vaguely and lifted his glasses, focusing on a mine which floated, so it seemed, only a few metres off the port bow. The vessel was already changing course to avoid the menace.

'And you expect no opposition?' Despite the atmosphere of suspense on the bridge Dietrich's manner was almost pleasant as he bowed his head to listen to the colonel's reply.

'None at all. There is no one to oppose us – except a handful of fishermen.'

'There are two policemen on the peninsula – or there were when I was last here.' Dietrich was very close to becoming jocular and good-humoured, a mood he shared with no one else on the silent bridge.

Burckhardt made a great effort to respond. 'I think we can manage if they appear. You come ashore with me, of course.'

'I had assumed that!' Dietrich stared round slowly as though he found it instructive to see the reactions of a company of soldiers about to go ashore into the unknown as dawn broke. He met stolid eyes, tightly shut mouths, and once he caught Prentice's gaze as the lieutenant stared back at him curiously. 'I have my Luger,' he told Burckhardt amiably, 'just in case of trouble.'

'There is to be no shooting!' Burckhardt spoke sharply and for the first time he turned and looked directly at Dietrich. 'My men have strict orders to go ashore quietly. It will increase the element of surprise and their first task is to set up a road-block at the northern end of the village. The first troops ashore will see to that.'

'And when do you expect to take the monastery?'

'Who said we were interested in monasteries, Herr Dietrich? This is a war we are fighting, not a religious campaign.' And having delivered this rebuke the colonel turned away and devoted his whole attention to the lamp which was now so close that they could see it perched at the end of a stone jetty. Under the lamp stood two men, woken up doubtless by the explosion of the mine and anxious to hear what had happened. They're in for a surprise, Burckhardt was thinking as he saw the Abwehr man easing his way towards the door. I suppose he's checking up on our arrangements for the landing so he can put that in his report to Canaris. Still, with his knowledge of the peninsula he might come in useful yet. Burckhardt looked up as Hahnemann appeared in the doorway when Dietrich went outside.

'Start withdrawing men from the search for the Greek and assemble them for disembarkation,' Burckhardt told him.

'What about the demolition charge?'

'No sign of it, sir. We are still searching...'

'Withdraw all men from the search except for those in the engine-room. Any news of the Greek?'

'He hasn't been seen, sir.'

Burckhardt removed the glove he had been wearing from his pistol hand and nodded. 'The Greek doesn't matter any more. Later the search can be continued by the men left to guard the ship.' It was only a minor element in the meticulous plan – guarding the ship to make sure no one tried to take her across the gulf to warn the British. Burckhardt checked his watch. 5.55 AM. Yes, they were thirty minutes late. It would be dawn just about the time they landed; already he could see faintly a low ridge silhouetted against a streak of cold grey light. The countryside in this part of the peninsula was hilly, with a single road to the south which wound its way between the hills until it reached the plateau. From there on the terrain became steadily worse, culminating in the grim wilderness of precipices and sheer ascents of the heights of Zervos.

'You will be responsible for the security of the British prisoners,' he told Sergeant Volber who had just entered the bridge to report that his section was ready for disembarkation. He had already decided that they would be taken half-way

131

along the peninsula and then left there under guard. This obviated any possibility of their being captured and released by a Greek unit which might be sent to the peninsula from Salonika. The information they possessed as to the unit's strength was a little too valuable to share with the enemy. He glanced back at the two men who stared at him with expressionless faces.

'Looks as though they're going to make it,' Ford whispered, 'although I wouldn't bet a brass farthing on the outcome yet.'

'Looks as though *we* might make it,' Prentice corrected him drily. 'And frankly, I wish you hadn't said that – it's asking for that demolition thing to trip its whatnot.'

'There's time yet, sir,' Ford assured him.

Schnell was now having to conduct an awkward manoeuvre to evade a single mine floating dead ahead. He had to steer the vessel round the mine and then alter course afresh to bring the ship up against the side of the jetty. Burckhardt could see that the glowing lamp was a lantern fixed to the top of a low mast and underneath it a small group of figures was huddled. He sent several men off the bridge, ordered the rest to keep in the shadows and joined them. This last mine was causing further delay and he felt the impatience surging up: he wanted to be off this damned Greek ferry, to get ashore and get on with it. And it was not only the timetable which made him curse that so inconveniently placed mine – that object so thoughtfully dropped by his allies was providing more time for the hidden demolition charge to detonate. He prayed to God that it wouldn't happen at the last moment, but a streak of pessimism in his nature made him fear the worst. In war, the chance happenings, the coincidences, were always bad ones. He had learned that in Finland where he had experienced the Winter War as assistant to the German military attaché in Helsinki when the Finns had fought the Russians to a ferocious standstill, in Norway where he had commanded ... He spoke quickly in Greek as Nopagos moved to the starboard window. 'Stay by the wheel!'

'If they see me they will be reassured.' Nopagos still stood by the window as he looked over his shoulder. His face was despondent and he looked as though he could hardly stand up:

tnis was probably the last voyage of the *Hydra* and he was bringing home the most terrible cargo he had ever carried. 'I don't want any harm to come to them – if they start to run away . . .'

'My men have orders not to shoot.' Burckhardt hesitated. The fight had gone out of the captain and it gave a greater appearance of normality if he could be seen clearly on the bridge. 'You can stay there,' he said, 'but you are not to call out to them.'

Dawn was beginning to spread over the peninsula as Schnell edged his way round the solitary mine, and the bleak light showed a landscape still in the grip of winter. The olive trees on the scrub-covered hills were naked silhouettes and along the jetty a coating of frost glittered with the colour of *crème de menthe* over stones green with age. The little group under the lamp which glowed eerily in the half-light stood hunched up with their hands in their pockets and one man was stamping his feet on the stones. An appearance of absolute normality. Another ferry trip ending its voyage quietly as a matter of seagoing routine. Which was very satisfactory, Burckhardt was thinking. Near the end of the jetty, a simple mole which projected straight out into the gulf, the beach was visible, a beach of rocks and stones. And behind the beach a high sea-wall stretched away into the distance. The intelligence people had warned him about that unscalable sea-wall – had emphasized that the only entrance to the village was a gap in the wall at the end of the jetty where a causeway linked the mole with the road into Katyra. Burckhardt was looking beyond the wall now to the short line of two-storeyed houses which were shuttered and still like abandoned villas. The whole place had the look of a resort which is only open during the summer months. It was all going according to plan. They would land without any fuss, occupy the village, set up the road-block to the north, and within an hour the main body of the troops would be moving south into the heart of the peninsula. An officer Prentice had not seen before came on to the bridge to report and the colonel motioned him back into the shadows.

'Major Eberhay reports everything ready for disembarkation, sir.'

'Good. The wireless set is being guarded by two men, I take it, Brandt?'

'Yes, sir. The major saw to it himself.'

'Tell him those civilians on the jetty are not to be brought on board because of the demolition charge. He can keep them on the beach and they can be escorted back into the village later.'

As Brandt left the bridge Burckhardt thought about the wireless set. Until the sabotaged set was repaired it was their only means of communication with GHQ to confirm that the reinforcements could be flown in. It was, in fact, one of the most vital pieces of equipment in the expedition. Without that he would be on his own and there could be the most appalling muddle when they arrived at the plateau. The vessel had almost circumnavigated the pestilential mine and was creeping in towards the jetty where the little group had shifted position. Prentice had moved closer to the window and Burckhardt warned a guard that he mustn't get any closer. When he looked to starboard again the jetty was almost under the ship's hull.

The lower slopes of the hills were still in darkness as the gangway clattered onto the jetty. Major Eberhay was the first man ashore and a moment later Nopagos joined him, followed by a dozen Alpenkorps soldiers. These troops were unarmed, their collars nearly buttoned to the neck, and one man carried a plaque struck to commemorate the commencement of collaboration between Greek and German peoples. Only the space for the date was left blank. Drawn up in files of threes, they marched steadily along the jetty top in the direction of the causeway which led to Katyra. The plaque was for presentation to the mayor of Katyra. Outwardly, for the first few minutes, the disembarkation had the appearance of an arranged visit as the Alpenkorps paraded away into the distance. Only a band was absent to mark the occasion.*

'No resistance, please! We are overwhelmed!' It was

* The same technique was practised in Norway where the first unit of invading Germans ashore at Oslo was a brass band which played and marched through the capital to simulate a peaceful visit.

134

Nopagos who delivered the urgent message to the group of four men who stood stunned under the lamp as the troops passed them. It was not quite the message which Burckhardt had instructed him to deliver but it served the same effect. One man, larger and burlier than the others, took a step backwards as though to move away, but he was restrained by the leading soldier in the next section of troops leaving the ship. The German put a firm hand on the civilian's arm and ushered him back to the group which stared at the ferry as though hardly able to believe their eyes. The third file of men pouring off the vessel were heavily armed, their rucksacks on their backs, their rifles looped over their shoulders, and short bayonets sheathed in leather scabbards by their sides.

From the bridge Burckhardt watched the landing operation with approval and relief. It was all going according to plan. The leading section had already disappeared through the gap in the sea-wall and within minutes would reach their first objective – the mayor's house. It was light enough now to see the Greek flag fluttering in a breeze from a tower behind the wall. He checked his watch again as the file of armed troops began to cross the causeway. Half-way along the jetty the group of four Greeks was being hustled towards the beach while more troops marched past them. Yes, everything was going according to plan. A moment later the firing started.

The firing, which commenced immediately the Greek civilians were clear of the jetty, came at the worst possible moment for Burckhardt. The entire mole from gangway to causeway was dense with disembarking troops and the ski sections were just filing off the ship. It was one of these men, encumbered with the skis over his back, who fell as the first shot rang out. Instantly, what had been an orderly disembarkation became a scene of chaos as the falling soldier crashed into his comrades and caused several to stumble. A second shot rang out and a second man on the jetty fell close to the first casualty. There was a danger of an imminent pile-up of men as the mole seethed with field-grey figures. Burckhardt swore and leaned over the bridge to look down at the open deck below where Hahnemann was issuing quick instructions, shouting to the men to clear the jetty and move inland. A third shot was fired and four men close together half-way along the jetty paused, then began to run towards the causeway, but as they ran one of their number sprawled lifelessly on the jetty floor. Burckhardt left the bridge and made for the open deck. At the top of the staircase Dietrich was staring across the peninsula and as Burckhardt ran past him he noted a trivial detail: for the first time, so far as he could remember, the Abwehr man was no longer smoking a cigar. He was running down the staircase when he heard a fusillade of shots – the Alpenkorps were returning the fire, although what the God they thought they were shooting at Burckhardt had no idea. From his commanding position on the bridge he had been quite unable to locate the source of the attack.

At the bottom of the steps he noted a less trivial detail – the battalion wireless, the last set still in serviceable condition, was stowed against the wall with the flap opened back. An Alpenkorps soldier stood close by guarding the precious equipment. As soon as they had taken Katyra Burckhardt had to send the vital signal, *Phase One completed*. Despite the air of total confusion which now pervaded the vessel where men crouched low behind the rails or ran down the gangway urged on by Hahnemann, the colonel was still thinking clearly and a disturbing idea had entered his mind. Three shots, three casualties. That was the work of a marksman. It was quickly apparent that Hahnemann was disembarking the troops with all speed so Burckhardt, still concerned with his simple calculation, went swiftly back to the bridge where he could see what was happening. He arrived there in time to see more men hurrying along the jetty too close together as the firing continued. A man near the edge stopped as though struck by an invisible blow, tried to stagger forward a few steps, then plunged over the edge. He hit the water with a splash and when the body surfaced it floated motionlessly.

The fusillade continued for several minutes while the Alpenkorps constantly disembarked and ran the gauntlet of the exposed jetty. During the firing Burckhardt ordered the two remaining guards on the bridge to take Prentice and Ford below ready for going ashore. Schnell had left earlier so now he was alone on the bridge as the fusillade ceased suddenly.

He waited, turning his eyes now to the lower hill slopes still in the fading shadow of night. Hahnemann had carried out his order to cease fire abruptly and then hold fire for five minutes. Earlier, the colonel had assumed that those shots were coming from behind one of the shuttered windows, but so far he had seen nothing to confirm this. Half-a-dozen men were risking the jetty run again, their bodies crouched low as they ran past the huddled shapes lying on the stones. A single shot split the silence only broken by the thud of nailed boots on paved stone. One man fell. The others ran on, disappearing through the gap in the wall. On the bridge Burckhardt twisted his mouth grimly. He had seen it this time – the muzzle-flash in the hills to the south of the village. The marksman was indeed firing long-distance, and now he felt sure it was the work of one man. He left the bridge and Hahnemann met him at the foot of the staircase with news of the disaster.

'The second set is out of commission...'

'What!' Burckhardt was thunderstruck. He felt the blood rush to his head and paused before going on. 'How did it happen?'

'A bullet hit it – all the valves are smashed.'

A soldier was crouched over the set and he kept his head lowered as though afraid to face the colonel. Bending close to him, Burckhardt spoke very quietly. 'You were supposed to be guarding it, Dorff.'

'He could hardly have done anything,' Hahnemann interjected. 'He was by the rail firing off a few shots himself when it happened. He was never very far away from the set. It is just the most appalling bad luck, sir.'

'Bad luck, Hahnemann?' The colonel straightened up and stared at him. 'We have had one set sabotaged earlier in the voyage. Someone planted a demolition charge inside the vessel. And someone, at the beginning, set free the British prisoners. Haven't you grasped it yet that some unknown person is making sure that bad luck does come our way?' He turned as Dietrich walked round a corner and stopped to look down at the wrecked set.

'More?' he asked bluntly.

'A bullet has smashed all the valves. The set is quite useless.' Burckhardt studied the Abwehr man for a moment. 'Herr Dietrich, I believe you possess a Luger. Would you mind showing it to me?'

Without a word Dietrich extracted the pistol from his pocket and handed it to the colonel. While Burckhardt was examining the weapon he stood with his hands deep inside his pockets as he gazed along the jetty where the last troops were hurrying towards the village. It was almost daylight now and the buildings beyond the sea-wall showed up clearly in the pale sunshine. They had a decrepit, unpainted look and several tiles were missing from the shallow roofs which were a dull red colour. Once their walls had been brightly colour-washed but that had been a long time ago; now that the place could be seen properly in the dawn light it had shrunk from a shadowed village of some size to a tiny fishing hamlet of a few hundred people. Burckhardt had checked the gun, had found it fully loaded with seven rounds. He sniffed briefly at the barrel and then returned it. 'Thank you.' He looked at Hahnemann. 'We will go ashore. Tell Volber to bring the prisoners.'

Straightening his tunic, Burckhardt led the way onto Greek soil. Because of the *Hydra*'s list to port, the gangway was inclined at a steep angle, a detail he had overlooked, and he had to run down it onto the almost deserted jetty. Here again, he led the way, walking briskly but without undue haste, pausing to exchange a few words with two medical orderlies who were attending the casualties. One of them looked up and shook his head. Burckhardt resumed his even pace, knowing that men still aboard were watching him from the rails. Behind him came the Abwehr man, hands still inside his pockets, looking towards the south as he trailed the colonel, and behind him followed Prentice and Ford escorted- by Volber and a private. At the end of the mole the colonel stopped and called down to Nopagos who was waiting with the other civilians on the beach. 'That Greek, Grapos, what other qualifications had he that you didn't tell me about?'

'He speaks English.'

Nopagos hadn't understood what the colonel was driving at and he saw the German stiffen. Burckhardt's reactions piled on top of one another. Was he being insolent? The question going through the colonel's head had been whether at some time Grapos might have undergone military service, perhaps before he contracted his limp. Grapos spoke English? As he walked on to the causeway Burckhardt tried to recall the sequence of events aboard the *Hydra*. Could Grapos have freed Prentice and Ford? He had been imprisoned in the hold at the time. Had he sabotaged both wireless sets? Was he still on board? Then who was that marksman in the hills... Firmly, he pushed the riddle out of his thoughts as he went through the gap in the wall where a sentry had been posted. He saluted as the man jumped to attention.

Behind him Dietrich was taking his time about walking towards Katyra, dragging his feet until Volber and the prisoners caught up with him. He even stood quite still for a moment while he looked down at Nopagos, and when he continued along the causeway the prisoners and their escorts had passed and were a few paces in front of him. He appeared to be taking a great interest in the view to the south next, staring fixedly at the hills, and then he switched his attention to the sentry by the wall, noting the hand-grenade which hung from the soldier's belt. Finally, he looked back along the jetty to see if anyone else was close at hand. The gangplank was empty and there was no sign of more troops coming ashore. He turned round and called out.

'Volber! I think you're wanted back at the ship.'

The sergeant gestured to the prisoners to halt. They had just passed through the gap and beyond a dusty track wound out of sight past a stone building into the main part of Katyra. Burckhardt had almost reached the bend and Dietrich's words had not been spoken loudly enough to reach him. The sentry looked puzzled and stared at the *Hydra* where a tall figure could be seen at the head of the gangway with its back turned.

'What is it, sir?' Volber took a few paces towards the Abwehr man and his expression was uncertain. In the distance, over his shoulder, the colonel disappeared round the curve in the road which was now empty. Prentice was standing with his hands on his hips while Ford stared pointedly at the soldier who stood a few paces away with his rifle at the ready.

139

'I think you're wanted back at the ship,' Dietrich repeated. 'I saw Hahnemann beckoning.'

Volber was in a quandary. He had received explicit orders from the colonel to escort the prisoners personally into the village and he had no inclination to vary from Burckhardt's command by so much as a centimetre. But Lieutenant Hahnemann was the officer who could, and did, make life arduous for him. So he compromised briefly, waiting to see whether the beckoning was repeated from the gangway. Dietrich remained where he was, apparently absorbed in the panorama across the gulf. If one ignored the huddled group on the jetty and overlooked the signs of military invasion, it was an extraordinarily peaceful scene. By early daylight the Aegean was an intense, deep cobalt with a backdrop of misty mountains on the mainland which seemed almost unreal. At the head of the lonely gulf, where the sun caught the water at a certain angle, the sea glittered like mercury, and on the nearby beach small waves, rippled by the breeze, slid gently forward and collapsed.

Volber stirred restlessly. 'I can't wait any longer, sir,' he ventured, and Dietrich nodded as though he understood. He followed the sergeant through the gap and stopped suddenly when he saw, to his right, that two Alpenkorps soldiers stationed behind the wall had been concealed from his view. As he appeared they were looking at the hills to the south, but now they lowered their field-glasses, hoisted their machine-pistols more firmly over their shoulders, and walked back to the gap to take one last look at the vessel which had brought them all the way from Istanbul. Volber paused to have a word with them, making some joking reference to pleasure cruises, but Dietrich noticed that he was staring along the jetty in case Hahnemann appeared and started gesturing. Sighing out aloud, Prentice crossed onto the grass verge and sat down with his back to the wall where Ford joined him. Volber, standing in the middle of the gap with the other three soldiers, was about to reprimand him, when hell opened up on the gulf.

The reverberations of the detonation crashed round the hillsides, roared out across the gulf like a cannonade, and sent a shock wave like a bombardment through the gap in the wall. The demolition charge had reached zero. Dietrich, half-protected by the wall, was thrown sprawling onto the grass, and he thought he heard two explosions close together – the charge first, then the boilers going up. The full force of the wave had struck the four Alpenkorps soldiers like a giant hammer and they lay in the road like trampled rag dolls. Only two men were moving feebly and one of them fell limp almost immediately as he lost consciousness. The sentry was bunched up against the outside of the wall in a strangely twisted position. As Dietrich lay on the grass, temporarily deafened by the road, there was a stench of burning oil in his nostrils and Prentice and Ford, whose ears had not been affected, heard debris clattering on the village rooftops like spent shrapnel from ack-ack guns.

For both of them the immensely strong sea-wall had muffled the blast. But Dietrich was recovering quickly. As he staggered to his feet Prentice began to move up behind him with a rock in his fist. The Abwehr man, unaware of what was happening behind him, fished the Luger out of his pocket, looked quickly up the road and along the jetty, and moved towards the soldier who was climbing to his feet in the centre of the road. Prentice, moving soundlessly on the grass, followed Dietrich as he lurched towards the soldier who had now brought himself to his knees and was shaking his head like a dog emerging from a river. He looked up as Dietrich brought the Luger barrel crashing down on his head. He was slumping to the ground when Dietrich tugged the loop of the machine-pistol free. Prentice stared in astonishment, the rock still poised in his hand, but when he saw the machine-pistol he moved forward again. The Abwehr man turned, knocked the unsteady fist aside and thrust the weapon into Prentice's hands. 'This will be more useful – if you can handle the damned thing.'

He had spoken in English and without waiting for Prentice's reaction he hauled another machine-pistol loose from an inert German, tossed it across to Ford, and then extracted spare magazines from the pockets of the two men on the ground. When he stood up he noticed that it was Ford who was familiar with the machine-pistol and shoved the magazines at him. 'Here – it looks as though they'd be more use to you.

141

Now, we've got to get moving pdq. We go that way – along the wall to the south.'

'Who the devil are you?' Prentice demanded.

'Dietrich of the Abwehr.'

The reply was given ironically as the large man stared briefly along the jetty wall. The *Hydra* looked like a refugee from an Atlantic convoy. The funnel was bent at a surrealist angle and her bows were already settling in the shallow water. Around the hull men swam in the sea distractedly as a huge column of black smoke ascended into the clear sky like a gigantic signal which would be seen clear across the bay to the mainland. As he gazed at the wreckage a tongue of red flame flared up at the base of the distorted funnel. Soon the whole superstructure would be ablaze and would go on burning until the hulk was reduced to its waterline and the *Hydra* was a blackened shell. All Burckhardt's efforts at preserving an appearance of normality had gone up with the demolition charge. 'I thought she'd never blow,' he said half to himself, and then he saw Nopagos clambering up onto the jetty. The shock wave must have blown straight over the heads of the group on the beach. He looked back towards the town and the road was still empty. 'They'll be coming soon,' he warned, 'so let's get to hell out of here.'

'Which way? The village is crawling with them . . .'

'Along this wall – five years ago I walked all over this place. We've got to head up the peninsula . . .'

'But who the devil are you?' Prentice repeated, and when the reply came the Scots burr was even more pronounced.

'I'm Ian Macomber.' He grabbed at the lieutenant's arm. 'Now, if you don't want to get shot, follow me and run like hell!'

CHAPTER EIGHT

Sunday, 10 AM

By ten o'clock in the morning they had marched almost non-stop through punishing hill country which had caused them either to climb or descend most of the way, and they had still seen no trace of Grapos. It was Macomber who had urged them on mercilessly, insisting that they put as much ground as possible between themselves and the oncoming Germans before they rested. Several times Prentice had tried to talk and ask questions, but on each occasion the Scot had brusquely told him to save his breath for the march. They followed a footpath which twisted and turned as its surface changed, sometimes sand, sometimes rock and often merely beaten earth. A path which led them past olive groves, over hilltops ringed with boulders, and down into scrub-infested valleys where the streams raced with swelling waters. But now they had reached a hilltop where Macomber consented to pause briefly because it gave a clear view back to the north where the road from Katyra came towards them in a series of bends and drops down the near sides of hills dense with undergrowth.

'We can see them coming from here,' Macomber announced as he perched on a rounded boulder. 'And water is going to be our problem. There isn't much of it on the plateau.'

'This might help,' Ford suggested as he undid his coat and showed a pear-shaped water-bottle attached to his belt. 'I filched that off one of those dead Jerries while you two pulled yourselves together.'

'Ford gets his priorities right,' Prentice remarked, and then stared hard at Macomber. 'Mind if I hear a little more about you now?'

Macomber took a swig from the water-bottle, handed it on to Prentice and grinned faintly. 'I've spent the last fifteen months in the Balkans. Do you think that sounds cushy?'

'Depends what you were doing,' Prentice replied cautiously. 'What were you doing?'

'I'll tell you, then. I'm like Winston Churchill as far as ancestry goes – half-British and half-American. My mother was a New Yorker and my father came from Aberdeen. I spent a third of my early years in the States, another third in Scotland, and the rest of the time travelling round Europe with my parents. My father was a linguistics expert and I inherited his gift for languages.' There was no modesty in Macomber's tone but neither was he boasting; he was simply stating a fact. 'And that's where the trouble started,' he went on. 'Principally my languages are German, Greek and French – which comes in useful when you're in Rumania. I had lung trouble before the war . . .'

'Lung trouble!' Prentice looked sceptical, remembering the tremendous pace the Scot had set up while they were making their dash up and down those endless hills.

'It's cured now – at least so a quack in Budapest assured me. He said it was the pure clean air from Siberia which blows across Hungary in winter that had done the trick. But that lung kept me out of the Forces in 1939, so the Ministry of Economic Warfare asked me to do a job for them. Get your head out of the way, Ford, I can't see that road.'

'What sort of a job?' Prentice asked casually. Without appearing to do so he was trying to check the Scot's story.

'Buying up strategic war materials the Jerries wanted. You'd never believe the funds I had at my disposal. I bought up everything I could lay my hands on and had it shipped out of the Balkans. I had an idea the bright boys foresaw the German *Drach nach Osten* and wanted to denude the place before Hitler arrived.'

'Sounds interesting,' was Prentice's only comment.

'You think so? Just sitting behind a desk and making out orders in quadruplicate for a few thousand gallons of oil or the odd few tons of copper – is that how you see it?'

'I didn't say so.'

'No, but you looked so!' He took out one of his remaining cigars. 'What I don't think you've quite grasped is that I had competitors, Jerry competitors, and they can play very rough, very rough indeed. When I'd survived two attempts to kill me – one in Györ and one in Budapest – I decided my luck was running out and the time had come to go underground, so I acquired some false papers and set up as a German.' He looked quizzically at Prentice over his cigar, put it back in his mouth and went on talking. 'Don't look so damned unbelieving – false papers can be obtained almost anywhere if you have the money, and I had a small fortune to play with.'

'You set up as Dietrich, then?'

'No, he came later. I called myself Hermann Wolff, and, you know, necessity really did turn out to be the mother of invention. I found myself mixing openly with the German community in Budapest, which in the beginning was simply excellent camouflage, but later when I ran out of stuff to buy up it gave our Ministry brains another idea, a diabolical idea.' He turned again to look over his shoulder at the hill behind, in the opposite direction from where the Germans must come, and this was a gesture he had repeated several times.

'Isn't that the wrong direction to fret over?' Prentice inquired. 'Or could they have got ahead of us on the road while we were doing our cross-country route march?'

'Old habits . . .' Dietrich spread a large hand. 'I've spent so many months looking over my shoulder – because the danger always comes from where you least expect it.' He shrugged and stared at Ford for a moment. 'When it comes, it comes.'

'A diabolical job, you were saying,' Prentice reminded him. As he listened he scanned the deserted countryside to the north where a dark smoke column from the burning *Hydra* was still climbing into the brilliant morning sky. They'd see that smoke as far away as Salonika, almost, if the weather visibility was as good across Macedonia. It seemed incredible that a whole German expedition was mustering itself somewhere beyond those hills for a forced march south to Mount Zervos.

'Yes, truly diabolical,' Macomber repeated. 'There were hardly any more strategic supplies I could lay my hands on, but there was a mass of stuff the Germans had bought up which still hadn't been shipped back to the Reich. It was lying around in warehouses and railway sidings, so the Ministry brainboxes said would I have a go at it? Very obliging they were, too – sent out an explosives man to teach me a trick or two about things that go bang in the night...' He paused again, detecting a sudden freshening of interest from Ford, but when the ammunition examiner said nothing he continued. 'The trouble again was I was made to order for these sabotage jobs. I picked up information from the German community I was mixing with about what was where – and by then I was accepted in Budapest. We even used German explosives – like ten-kilogram demolition charges.'

'Why not British equipment?' queried Ford.

'Because I was operating in neutral territory and the Hungarian government might not have taken too kindly to British time-bombs being planted inside their goods wagons. Those bombs don't always function according to the book and sometimes they don't function at all. Even when they do, the experts can often piece together a few vital bits and tell the type of bomb that was used and where it was made.' He glanced over his shoulder and grinned again. 'And don't ask me how we got hold of German explosives because that's a state secret.'

'You were pretty successful in passing yourself off as a German even in Hungary then?' Prentice suggested idly. He felt close to exhaustion but his mind was still sufficiently alert to go on checking Macomber's identity so far as he could.

'I knew the Reich well by the time war broke out. In peacetime I'd been a shipping broker – some of my business was with the Reich and I spent a lot of time in Germany before 1939 and sometimes, even then, it was convenient to pass for one of the *Herrenvolk*. The trick is to learn to think like them, to feel you are one of them – and that's something I had to work overtime at while we were on the *Hydra*. I may tell you that was the longest voyage of my life, and it took just twenty-four hours.'

'How did you fool the colonel? That must have taken some doing.'

'The ability to bluff big – nothing else. I took a leaf out of the dear Führer's book there: if you want to believe a lie, be sure it's a whopper. If I'd tried to pass myself off simply as a

German civilian, I think they'd have restricted my movements, but the dreaded Abwehr was something quite different. I knew quite a lot about the Abwehr when I went aboard the *Hydra* at Istanbul – in fact, I thought they had somebody on my tail ready to do an assassination act before I could get home . . .'

'You weren't put on that ship deliberately then?' Prentice found it difficult to keep the surprise out of his voice. Ford was emptying the machine-pistol while he tested the mechanism and then re-loaded.

'No, I'd finished with the Balkans and I was on my way to Athens to get a berth to Egypt. The Germans had occupied the whole area and it wasn't possible to operate any more with the key points swarming with their security chaps. I was coming on the direct Istanbul–Athens ferry, but that was cancelled at the last moment. When Burckhardt's lot took over the ship I wasn't completely surprised – the presence of several Germans on the passenger list was something I'd been thinking about ever since I got on board.'

'But why pretend you were the Abwehr?'

'Because I knew how they operated – months ago they'd sent men to Budapest to investigate the sabotage. But mainly because it's the only organization inside Germany today which the armed forces get nervous about. Burckhardt was convinced I'd been put on the ship to check up on how he handled things – which gave me a psychological stranglehold over him from the outset.'

'You make it sound so damned easy.' There was a hint of admiration in Prentice's manner as he sat with his back propped against a boulder and waited.

'Oh, very easy – as easy as moving round inside Hungary and Rumania with top Abwehr agents on your tail. As easy as making frequent trips to wayside railway stations to collect suitcases left by someone you never see – suitcases containing demolition charges. As easy as lugging them across railway lines at two in the morning with engines shunting all over the place and guards with dogs looking for you.' Macomber's voice had risen to a low growl as he glared at Prentice with an intensity of rage which was alarming. 'As easy as going back to your flat late in the evening and noticing that the lock has been tampered with – so you know that inside that darkened flat someone is waiting for you with a knife or a gun or whatever particular weapon they've decided will do the job quickly and quietly. Yes, Prentice, and it was easy on that ship we've just left, too – easy putting those wireless sets out of action with two hundred troops all around you, easy coming into your cabin to cut your ropes to give you a chance to get clear and warn that destroyer . . .'

'I'm sorry,' Prentice said quietly, realizing for the first time the tremendous pressure this man must have lived under for months, catching a glimpse of what it must have been like to go on living alone in the alien Balkans surrounded by enemies while he went on with his deadly work. He supposed that the outburst was the climax of God knew how much pent-up anxiety and living on the nerves endlessly, until it had seemed it must go on for ever. Macomber made no attempt to apologize for the outburst but he smiled wintrily as he smoked his cigar and started talking again.

'Planting the demolition charge was simpler than you might imagine. I just saw it lying with the fuses in a half-open rucksack and grabbed it. There was a little trouble in the dark on deck when I ran into a soldier, but a knowledge of unarmed combat can come in useful. Afterwards, I pitched him over the side like you did your chap. The vital moment was when we'd just come ashore – I'd always foreseen that.'

'Why then?' asked Prentice.

'Several reasons. Burckhardt's whole attention was taken up with the landing and capturing Katyra quickly. Later, he'd have more time to think, which is just what I didn't want him to have. Then there was the problem of the other wireless set – I'd messed up the tuning coil with the butt of my Luger but I gathered they might be able to repair the thing. The moment they could wireless for confirmation of my identity I was finished. And you can thank whatever lucky star you were born under that the bomb didn't go off earlier – it must have stopped and then started again.'

'What time had you set it for?' Prentice was taking a great interest in the answer to this question and now he saw Ford looking over his shoulder towards the hill behind them. Macomber's fears were contagious.

'I set it to detonate at 3.30 AM while we were still well down the gulf.'

'Good God!'

A trace of the nervous reaction still smouldered inside Macomber and he didn't bother to put it too tactfully. 'I'm sure, Prentice, that by now you know there's a war on. There were two hundred German troops aboard who may yet do untold damage to the Allied cause – if I could sink them I was going to do it. And I still will, although how I haven't the slightest idea. You know they're heading for the monastery on Mount Zervos to set up an observation post, I take it?'

'I had an idea that was the objective. I agree we've got to get there first, if we can, but I can't quite see us forming the monks into a defensive battalion to hold off the Jerries. Is there any means of communication there we could use to get in touch with the mainland?'

'Not so far as I know apart from the telephone line to Salonika and that's been cut.' Macomber dropped the half-smoked cigar into the sand and carefully heeled it out of sight. 'But there's always something that can be done as long as you're there – that's something I've learned.' His expression became ferocious as he growled out the words. 'Whatever happens the Germans have got to be stopped from taking Zervos. Hell! If there's nothing else we'll have to set fire to the place to attract attention. There are British troops driving up that coast only a few miles across the gulf. Setting fire to the monastery may be the only solution!'

Prentice stared at the huge figure stooped forward over the boulder and realized that he meant what he said. Previously he had regarded Macomber as an enterprising civilian, with the accent on 'civilian', but now he began to wonder whether the war he had fought in the Western Desert compared with the shadowy, no-quarter struggle the Scot had waged inside the peace-time Balkans. He blinked to keep his eyes open as Macomber clasped both hands tightly and stared again at the road from Katyra with a dubious expression. It was over twenty-four hours since any of them had slept and the strain showed in their whiskered haggard faces; the brain was beginning to slow down, the reflexes to react sluggishly, and these were danger signals. He was about to speak when Macomber made the suggestion himself. 'I think three-quarters of an hour's sleep would work wonders. We may need every ounce of strength we can muster before the day is out but someone must keep watch.' He grinned. 'So, if you two are sufficiently convinced of my bona-fides, I'll act as lookout while you get some kip.'

'No, I'll stand watch while you and Ford sleep,' Prentice said promptly. 'You've been through more than us, anyway.'

'Suit yourself,' was Macomber's terse reply. Dropping down off the boulder, he lay on the sand after casting one final look back at the hill behind. The hill looked dangerous was his last thought before he fell asleep.

Macomber was a man who, when he woke up, became instantly alert, all his faculties keyed up for immediate action. The trait had been sharpened during his experience in the Balkans and on waking he had developed another facility – the habit of never opening his eyes until he had listened for a few seconds. Lying on the sand with his back against the rock, he listened carefully to the sounds with his eyes still closed. The scrape of a boot over stone, which told him someone was moving nearby. The quick dull click of metal on metal, which was the movement of a rifle bolt. A coldness down his back was the physical reaction of his brain warning him of danger. Then a voice spoke. Prentice's.

'Don't move, Ford, for God's sake!'

Macomber's prone body was still relaxed and lifeless as he half-opened his eyes. Ford was sitting up on the sand, his suit crumpled, his right hand withdrawing from the machine-pistol which lay close by his side. He had a drugged look and had obviously just woken up. Macomber couldn't see Prentice but the thought flashed through his mind that the lieutenant must have dozed off and during those unguarded minutes a German patrol had arrived. Lying on his side, Macomber's hand was tucked inside his coat pocket where it had rested when he had fallen asleep, and now his fingers curled round the butt of the

Luger. The problem was going to be to get in an upright position quickly enough. From the direction of Ford's startled gaze he calculated that the newcomers were stationed behind the boulder he was leant against. But how many of them? The boot scraped again and the shadow of a man fell across the sand in front of where he lay, the shadow of a man and a gun.

'Wait! For God's sake wait!' A note of desperation in Prentice's voice chilled Macomber. 'We can explain – don't shoot!'

The silhouette of the rifle barrel angled lower and Macomber guessed that it was now tilted downwards and aimed at him point-blank. He sensed that the slightest movement of his body would activate the shadow's trigger finger, and while he compelled himself to stay relaxed he felt the stickiness of his palm clutching the pistol butt. A strange tingling sensation sang along his nerves and his brain hung in a horrible state of prolonged suspension as every tiny detail seemed weirdly clear. The appalled expression on Ford's face, the mouth half-open, held as though in a condition of rictus. The wobble of the unknown man's silhouette as he shifted balance to the other foot to take the shock of the rifle's recoil. The flitting motion of some tiny insect hopping over the sand in the shade of the silhouette. Macomber's throat had gone so dry that he felt the most terrible compulsion to cough as a tickle crawled in his throat.

'Do you understand any English at all?' Prentice again, his voice throaty with tension. 'We're on your . . .'

'Yes, I speak English.' A deep-chested voice with a rumbling timbre which sounded familiar. 'Why are you with the German?'

'Look, Grapos,' Prentice pleaded quickly, 'he's not a German. He's British. If you let him wake up and speak he'll talk to you in English as much as you want . . .'

'There are Germans who speak English.' Grapos' tone was unimpressed and savagely obstinate. 'I speak English but I am Greek. He has made you think he is English? We have very little time. He must be killed, now!' The gun silhouette moved again as though the Greek was taking fresh aim and

Macomber waited for the thud of the bullet, the last thing he would ever feel. And there was an urgency in Grapos' voice as well as in his words which filled the Scot with foreboding. There was some other danger coming very close, he felt sure of it, a danger the Greek was only too well aware of. Prentice was talking again and this time he was adopting an entirely different tactic, abandoning pleading as he spoke crisply as though he were giving a command.

'Look, I'm telling you, mate. His name is Macomber. Ian Macomber. He's a Scot – that's from the topside of my country – and he's the one who planted that bomb which nearly blew up all those Germans, only it didn't go off in time. He speaks fluent German – a damned sight more fluent German than you speak English. To help us get away he half-killed a Jerry – a German – in front of me. He grabbed a couple of German machine-pistols and gave them to us. Since then he's led the way to where we are now because he knows the country and we don't. And if that isn't enough for you, you can go and dive in the sea again. So stop aiming that gun at him and let him wake up and speak for himself.'

'You are sure of these things?' Grapos sounded anything but sure of what he had been listening to and the rifle was still pointed down at the inert figure below.

'I'm perfectly sure! Don't you think I can tell when I'm talking to one of my own countrymen? Wouldn't you know when you were talking to a Greek even if you'd heard that same man speaking good German earlier?' Prentice deliberately lost his temper a little, and seeing the look of doubt on Grapos' face he followed up quickly while he had the Greek off-balance. 'And now, for Pete's sake, can he get up and speak for himself? He must be awake now.'

'Yes ... I ... am ... awake.' Macomber spoke slowly and very clearly, resuming his normal manner of speech only when he saw the shadow of the gun move away. 'So can I get up and let you have another good look at me?'

'Yes, you may get up.' Grapos' boots scraped again as he spoke and when Macomber climbed to his feet the villainous-looking civilian was standing several paces beyond him with his weapon still held so that it could cover Macomber with only a fraction of movement. A German carbine, the Scot noted. The one he had gone overboard with. The one he had used to shoot down the Alpenkorps men on the jetty. Macomber's hands hung loosely by his sides and he gazed at Grapos without friendship as he asked the question with a single word.

'Well?'

'You look like a German.'

'And you look like a bandit.'

The Greek's eyes flashed. The gun muzzle lifted and was then lowered. He stared back grimly but with a certain respect as he slapped his rifle butt once and then turned to Prentice, ignoring Macomber as he spoke rapidly. 'There is trouble. German soldiers are coming up that hill on the other side . . .' He indicated the hill which had worried Macomber, the hill he had glanced back at so many times. 'When they come to the top they will see you here. We must go quickly.'

'Which way?' asked Prentice.

'That way.' He pointed towards the hill crest over which he had just warned them the Germans were advancing. Prentice took a step forward, stooped to pick up his machine-pistol, which he looped over his shoulder, and then shook his head uncomprehendingly.

'Grapos, you've just said the Germans are coming over that hill, so we'd better push off in some other direction.'

'No. They come this way – so we go this way. You will see. Come! We must hurry.'

'Half a minute!' Prentice was not convinced and his naturally sceptical mind was now wondering whether he could trust Grapos. 'We haven't seen any Germans come along the road down there and they'd have to do that to get over there . . .'

Macomber broke in quickly, relieved to see that Ford's common sense had automatically made him turn round and watch the empty hill crest while the others argued it out. 'Prentice, the Germans were confident they could get hold of mules in Katyra – not enough for all their men, I'm sure, but probably enough to send ahead an advance party. If Burckhardt acted quickly and sent out a patrol on mules in time, they could have passed along that road while we were moving across country. In which case some of them would be ahead of

153

us – that was why I kept looking over my shoulder earlier.'

'Theophilous would supply them with mules,' said Grapos. He spat on the ground. 'Theophilous is at Katyra. He has German mother and Greek father, but he loves Germans. It is known for a long time. And Theophilous has mules...'

'And undoubtedly would know where to lay his hands on others,' Macomber interjected. 'All right, assuming they're coming up that hill from the far side, where do we go?'

'We go down here and wait.'

'Wait...?' Prentice still couldn't understand the Greek's plan but Grapos, without attempting to explain further, led the way down the flank of the hill which was fully exposed to anyone coming over the distant hill crest. From the summit of the hill where they had rested the view into the valley below had been obscured by an outcrop of rock, but as they descended through thick scrub which almost closed over the path they were able to see more clearly. A broad stream on its way to the sea ran along the narrow valley floor and at one point it was crossed by a series of stepping-stones which were barely above the water's surface. On the far bank, perhaps a hundred yards to the right of the primitive crossing point, Prentice caught a glimpse of the dusty track winding its way round the base of the hill towards Zervos. The hill crest, which reared above them now as a hard outline against the cloudless sky, was still deserted. What the devil was the Greek up to? He ran down the path and began talking as soon as he was within a few paces of Grapos who hurried downhill without looking back. 'Where are we going? I want to know.'

'To the pipe.' Grapos spoke over his shoulder without pausing, although he had begun to take a keen interest in the hill crest, staring frequently in that direction as he trotted downwards unevenly because of his limp.

'What pipe? What are you talking about?'

'The pipe takes the floods from the hill to the stream. It was built many years since to stop the waters rushing over the road. We go down the pipe. The Germans will not find us there.'

'How big is it, for heaven's sake?'

'It is big. I went down it when I was a boy.'

'You were smaller, then,' Prentice pointed out urgently. 'And they'll see us as soon as they come over that ridge.'

'That is why we hide. We are there.'

They were less than half-way down the hill when Grapos plunged into a deep gulley. The sides were lined with protruding rocks and it was deep enough to hide them from view completely. Prentice looked back as Ford and Macomber dropped into the ravine and then turned ahead to see Grapos on his hands and knees while he pulled at a clump of scrub with his bare hands. When Prentice reached him he had exposed the entrance to a large drain-pipe of crumbling concrete. The hole was at least three feet in diameter, a dark decrepit opening but large enough to crawl inside on hands and knees. Crouching beside Grapos, Prentice saw that it sloped down at an angle of about twenty degrees, so it should be navigable. Macomber and Ford were also bunched round the forbidding hole which was damp and smelled of decaying fungus, and the fact that there was no light at the end of the tunnel, no visible end at all, did nothing to increase their enthusiasm for the Greek's proposed escape route.

'Where does it come out?' demanded Macomber.

'By the stream. We cross by the stones.'

'And how long is it?'

'Not long.'

'How long is a piece of string?' Prentice muttered under his breath. 'Look, Grapos, we can't even be sure the Germans are coming in this direction. They could easily have changed their minds and be waiting for us farther along that road.'

'They were coming up the hill. You will see. We can see from here.' Grapos climbed out of the end of the gulley and stood behind a dense grove of undergrowth which was taller than a man's height. In places there were gaps in the vegetation which formed natural windows and when the others joined him they found they had a clear view of the hill beyond. Without much expectation of seeing anything, Prentice stared through a tracery of bare twigs, and it came as a shock when he saw figures against the skyline. There were six of them, well spread out, and they started to descend the slope in a semi-circle with the two in the middle maintaining a higher altitude than those on the flanks. Which was correct procedure, Prentice was thinking – the two men in the centre had better observation and could give covering fire to the men below if necessary. He recognized at once the field-grey uniforms and the distinctive caps of the Alpenkorps.

'Why should they choose this area for their patrol?' Macomber wondered out loud.

'Because Theophilous will have told them about the path,' Grapos informed him promptly. 'There are two main ways from Katyra to Zervos – the road and the path. They have come over the road by mule and when they do not find you they turn back – to trap you on the path.' He stared blankly at the Scot while he pulled at a tip of his straggled moustache and his continuing distrust of Macomber was only too obvious.

'They could seal us off inside that pipe with only one man at each end,' Macomber persisted.

'When they reach the stream and cross it, we go into the pipe. They come up this hill and we pass under them.'

'Sounds feasible,' the Scot commented. 'If it works.' Turning round, he renewed his observation of the patrol which was descending the hill slope rapidly; already they had covered more ground than he would have expected and he reminded himself that these six oncoming Germans were highly-trained Alpenkorps troops, men whose natural habitat was wild, untracked countryside, and who were now operating under ideal conditions. A disturbing thought struck him and he asked Grapos a question quickly. 'I suppose there's no risk that this chap, Theophilous, might have told them about the pipe, too?'

The Greek snorted contemptuously. 'He is not a man who ever walks or hunts – he would be frightened that he gets lost. We wait. When they cross the stream we go into the pipe.'

Macomber moved close to Prentice as he gazed through the dense thicket and he was frowning as though there were something he didn't understand. For a few minutes he watched the patrol, clambering over rocks, sometimes disappearing up to waist-height in undergrowth, but always maintaining their careful formation as they came closer to the stream, then he voiced his doubt. 'I don't like it – Burckhardt is using his men too wastefully.'

'What are you getting at?' snapped Prentice. Still without sleep, he could feel the strain telling and he knew he was trigger-tempered.

'Burckhardt has two hundred men at his disposal to take and hold Zervos. At least he had two hundred when he left the *Rupescu*, he told me. He lost four while on board the *Hydra...*'

'Four?'

'Yes, four. There was the man you threw overboard. Grapos killed two more while escaping, and I put one over the side when I was carrying that demolition charge up on deck. His bayonet and scabbard came in useful, by the way – I used them to support the charge inside the ventilator shaft. That's two per cent of his force without adding in those who died on the jetty and when the ship blew up. Yet he feels he can spare another six men to look for us. Does it suggest something to you, Prentice? Something alarming?'

'It suggests he feels he still has enough left to take care of a few monks.' Prentice was having trouble thinking straight. What on earth was the persistent Scot driving at now?

'It suggests to me that he expects heavy reinforcements in the very near future, which isn't a happy thought.'

'You mean by sea? Another boatload in broad daylight?'

'I doubt that. They may use some entirely different method this time.' Macomber found himself looking upwards. The sky was clear blue as far as the eye could see, its only occupants a flock of seagulls sailing high up in the sunlight as they flew away in the direction of Katyra. 'He wouldn't expend a patrol of six men just looking for us unless he was confident more help was on the way.'

'Just what we need at the moment, a Job's comforter,' Prentice muttered irritably. The Alpenkorps were half-way down the hill and they had begun to converge inwards towards the stepping-stones, although as a target they were still spread out over a considerable distance. Keeping his voice down, Macomber had now turned to question Grapos.

'You know the monastery well?'

'I lived there for two years.'

'Is there any other means of communication whatsoever

157

apart from the telephone which has been cut?'

'When they want things, they phone to Katyra. Sometimes they phone Salonika.'

'There is, of course, no wireless transmitter for emergencies?'

'No, nothing like that.'

Grapos was staring through the thicket as he replied without looking in Macomber's direction, and his replies were grudging, but the Scot appeared not to notice his reticence as he pressed on interrogating the Greek. 'You mean there is no other way ... are you listening to me? Good.' Grapos looked at Macomber directly and the brown eyes which looked back were compelling him to concentrate, to remember. 'Is there no other way at all whereby the Abbot can send a message if the phone breaks down?'

'Only the pigeons.'

'Pigeons?' Macomber's voice was sharp. 'You mean he keeps carrier pigeons? Where do they go to when released?'

'To Livai on the other side of the gulf.'

'On the mainland, you mean?'

'Yes. Livai is near Olympus and there are more monks there.'

Macomber nodded and said nothing more while the German patrol continued its descent to the edge of the stream. Even when they crossed they displayed good military caution, only one man moving over the stones at a time until they had all reached the bank below where Grapos and his group waited. As the last man landed on the near-side bank the Greek grunted and moved towards the mouth of the hole. Macomber had earlier noticed that they were standing in a natural water catchment area; above where they stood three small ravines converged into the gulley and he guessed that during bad weather a minor flood must pour into the pipe. A drift of heavy cloud had appeared in the sky and it was coming their way as he followed Grapos. Once again the unpredictable Aegean weather was changing and he prayed there wouldn't be a cloudburst while they were inside that unsavoury-looking pipe. The Greek was on all fours, about to enter the mouth, when he fumbled under his coat, extracted a knife from his jacket pocket, flicked it to eject the blade, then held it upright. The five-inch blade retracted of its own accord. He was putting it into his coat pocket for easier access when Ford rapped out his question. 'Where did you get that?'

Grapos looked over his shoulder and glared at the sergeant. For a moment it seemed as though he wasn't going to reply and then he answered resentfully. 'It is just a knife. My knife.' Ford glanced at Macomber who had immediately detected the note of suspicion in the sergeant's voice and told Grapos to wait a minute. 'It's a German knife,' Ford explained. 'A parachutist's gravity knife. What the hell is he doing with a thing like that?'

'We have to go into the tunnel,' Grapos reminded them sullenly.

'We have to know about that knife, first,' Macomber replied briskly. 'Where did you get it? Come on – I want to know.'

The German patrol must already have started advancing up the hill towards them but the possession of this strange weapon bothered Macomber and he was determined to get an explanation before they followed the Greek inside the pipe. For precious seconds it seemed like deadlock as the three men stared down at the Greek who gazed back at them with a hostile expression. Then he shrugged his broad shoulders, adjusted the rifle he had previously looped diagonally across his back and addressed Macomber. 'I took it from the German I shot.'

'You were miles away in the hills when you fired on the jetty,' Macomber pointed out. 'Just a minute, do you mean one of those Jerries on the boat?'

'No. The man I shot over there.' He made a gesture forwards to the hill the Alpenkorps patrol had just descended. 'There were seven men when I saw them. I shot the man who was to the right and he fell from a rock into the bushes. They did not find him and when they had gone I took the knife.'

'You mean you've alerted this lot! They know someone is close because you've already shot one of the patrol?' Macomber was appalled. He had accepted the Greek's stratagem for evading the Alpenkorps because he had been confident they were only searching hopefully. Now those six highly trained men below *knew* they were stalking someone who couldn't be far away, which meant they would be in a state of total alert.

'Yes,' Grapos confirmed, 'one is shot. When we go through the pipe they will not know we are on the other side . . .'

'So that's it!' Macomber stepped forward and gripped the Greek by the shoulder. 'You want us to go through the pipe and then open fire on them from the other side?'

'We have to kill Germans,' Grapos replied simply. 'When I go to join the army they say I am no good because of my limp. When I have killed many Germans I go to Athens and tell them – then I join the army.'

'Grapos!' Macomber spoke with low intensity. 'We have to get to the monastery before the Germans – in the hope that we can send a message to the mainland in time, or do something to upset them. If the Germans do take the monastery half a division won't shift them – maybe not even a division. Our job is to reach the monastery – to keep out of the way of any Germans we meet on the way, not to fight them.'

'Not fight!' Grapos was outraged. He looked up at Prentice. 'You are a British officer. I was told that when they wanted to know if I knew you. You agree with what this man is saying – this man who pretended he was a German?'

'Macomber's right,' Prentice said quietly. 'We want to get there and the only way we can do that is to dodge them – there are too many to fight. We may achieve a lot more by keeping out of their way.'

'Because it is you who say this.' Grapos glared in Macomber's direction and started crawling down the pipe which left less than a foot's clearance above his arched back. Dropping to his knees, the Scot followed the Greek into the insalubrious hole and the clearance above his back was barely six inches. Prentice, who had decided to bring up the rear, sent Ford down next, took one last look at the gulley to make sure the surface hadn't retained traces of footprints, then went inside himself with his machine-pistol over his back and a fervent hope that the Greek wouldn't start quarrelling with the Scot in this situation. Farther along the pipe Macomber was already finding his great bulk a distinct handicap as he crawled behind Grapos. He had only to lift himself a few inches and he found his back scraping the curved concrete; his contracted elbows grazed the sides of the pipe and his knees were slithering on a film of slime at the base of the pipe as he accelerated his awkward movements to keep up with the Greek's phenomenal rate of progress. The downward slope of the pipe helped him to keep up a certain speed, but he was beginning to dislike the feeling of being shut in as he went on shuffling forward through the total darkness beyond the mouth of the pipe.

Within two minutes he found himself taking great heaving breaths and this was no place for deep beathing – as he penetrated deeper inside the buried pipe the damp smell changed to an oppressive airlessness and the place seemed bereft of oxygen. How the broad-bodied Grapos managed to keep up such a killing pace he couldn't imagine and gradually the sensation of being entombed grew. He had expected his eyes to become accustomed to the darkness but it was still pitch-black and the only sound was the noise of scuffling feet and knees some distance behind him, a sound which reminded him of rats he had once heard scuttering inside a derelict warehouse. He plodded on, hands stretching out into the unknown, followed by the haul of his knees over the scum-like surface of the pipe which he now realized had been embedded in the ground for God knew how long; his hands told him this because frequently the surface of the pipe wall flaked off at his touch and more than once a large piece came away and clattered grittily on the floor. It was badly in need of running repairs but he imagined that when something was built on Zervos it was hopefully expected to last for ever. Nightmare possibilities began to invade his mind – supposing the far end was blocked? The only similar culvert pipe he could remember had been barred at the exit end by an iron grille to prevent small boys swimming in the river from investigating its interior. Grapos had been this way before years ago, but there was no reason why such a grille should not have been fixed more recently. At a rough guess the pipe must be a quarter of a mile long – so what would be the position if the exit were closed? He could never hope to turn round in this confined space and their only hope would be a slow, endless crawl backwards and uphill, a prospect he contemplated with no great relish.

As they went on and the angle of the pipe dipped more steeply, Macomber remembered that the hill slope dropped sharply when it approached the stream. He began to have a horrible feeling that they had taken the wrong decision – that they should never have entered this Stygian cylinder which might be their grave. For a brief second he paused to wipe the gathering sweat off his forehead and then ploughed on, his wrists aching under the weight they had to bear, the palms of his hands sore and tender with groping over the gritty concrete, the pain increasing across his back and down his thighs. When the hell were they going to get out of this blasted tunnel Grapos had led them into so confidently? There had to be a bend soon because only a bend would explain why there was still no light ahead. Unless the tunnel exit was completely blocked: that certainly would account for the continuing state of darkness they were crawling down through. It might also account for the worsening difficulty in breathing.

Macomber was having great trouble in regulating the intake of air now as he shuffled downwards blindly and automatically. But if the exit were stopped up they would be descending into a region of foul and foetid air where breathing might become well-nigh impossible. His great fear now was that they would discover the grim truth too late – that by the time they knew there was no way out they would have degenerated into such a weakened state that they would never be able to summon up the strength needed for the return trip. Years later when they excavated the pipe they would find... He suppressed the macabre thought and concentrated on keeping going, hands first, then that dreadful, wearying haul forward of the knees which it was becoming an agony to move. His head was vibrating gently and frequently he blinked as brief lights flashed in front of his eyes. He was aware of feeling warmer and he couldn't be sure whether this was an illusion or a symptom warning that something was going wrong with his system. He had moved forward mechanically for so long that his heart jumped with the shock when his outstretched hand touched something hard. The sole of Grapos' stationary boot. Was there a crisis? Had the Greek collapsed on the floor of the tunnel under the murderous physical strain? He called out. 'Grapos . . .' Because of the silence which had lasted so long he found he was unconsciously whispering as he called again. 'Something wrong, Grapos?'

The voice which came back out of the darkness was hoarse and breathless. 'We are at the bend. I can see the light at the bottom. When we arrive, you wait inside the pipe. You do not come out until I tell you.'

'All right. You're doing fine.'

Grapos grunted and began heaving himself forward again, on his stomach now because he found this an easier way to progress as the pipe angled downhill more precipitately. Macomber was about to follow when he felt a hand touch his own foot and he called back over his shoulder. 'Nearly there, Ford. We can see the end of the tunnel. Pass it on.' There was a considerable element of exaggeration in his statement but it seemed a reasonable moment to send back a cheerful message. As he rounded the bend, Macomber was able to appreciate the extent of his exaggerated optimism: the pipe was angled downwards at an increasingly nerve-wracking pitch and the blur of light in the distance was little larger than a sixpence. They were probably barely half-way down the hill slope. He was easing himself round the bend when his right knee contacted a particularly slippery patch and before he knew what was happening he lost balance and crashed heavily against the tunnel wall. He felt it crumble under his impact and a large piece of concrete slithered into his thigh followed by a shower of loosened earth. In places the damned thing was little thicker than paper. Calling back to warn the others, he crawled forward again with a sensation of moving down a chute. The brief pause had hindered rather than helped – his knees were wobbling badly and he expected at any moment to keel into the wall for a second time. When the accident happened it was so unexpected, so unforeseeable and bizarre, that it took away Macomber's breath. He had just caught up with Grapos and was within inches of his rearmost boot when the uncanny silence inside the tunnel was shattered by a ripping, cracking sound. Little more than a foot beyond Grapos' head the tunnel roof splintered, caved in and exposed a small hole – and thrust down through the hole was an Alpenkorps boot with a leg showing to the knee.

Macomber froze as Grapos lay rigid, his face inches away from the point where one of the Alpenkorps patrol had trodden through the rotting roof of the ancient pipe. Sufficient light percolated through the small aperture for him to see the pattern of large nails on the sole of the boot. Scarcely daring to breathe, he watched the leg withdrawing. For a few seconds it was held fast by the smallness of the hole when the boot tried to free itself, then it disappeared upwards, leaving the small aperture with ragged concrete edges. Still on all fours, Macomber prayed that the others behind him would lie still, that they had realized something had happened, that they would understand the desperate need for preserving total silence.

Grapos was still lying motionless on the tunnel floor, unable to reach the rifle looped over his back and having the sense not to attempt that dangerous manoeuvre. With agonizing slowness the Scot eased his tender knees forward a few more inches, wondering whether the hole was large enough for the invisible German to peer down and see Grapos, but he doubted whether that was possible. The Greek should be just far enough from the hole to go undetected. But how bright would that Alpenkorps man be? Would it occur to him to investigate the pipe, to kick in a little more of the crumbling roof? Originally, the pipe must have been laid just under the earth's surface, but over the years the rain had probably washed away some of the protecting soil until only a thin layer had remained. He found it an uncanny feeling to be lying there cooped up inside the narrow space, buried just underneath the hill slope and knowing that not three feet above them there was probably a German standing, undecided what to do about this phenomenon. Or had he gone away and climbed farther up the hill over their heads, cursing the pipe and not giving it another thought? He would have his orders to maintain the line of the sweep and German discipline gave little scope for personal initiative. But these were Alpine troops, men very different in training and background from the average breed of

Wehrmacht footslogger. Their training taught them to use their heads, to think for themselves.

All these rattling thoughts passed through Macomber's brain as four men lay absolutely still inside the pipe while two of them – Prentice and Ford – had even less idea of what was happening because they had been farther back. All they knew was that the wriggling, advancing worm of feet and heads had unaccountably stopped after that weird breaking sound had travelled back up the tunnel. Instinct alone, or perhaps a telepathic sense of emergency, prevented them from calling out to ask what had gone wrong. Macomber felt the boots resting against his knuckles begin to wriggle and he understood the signal – Grapos wished to move back a little farther away from the hole. To avoid the risk of two men's movements, Macomber simply perched both hands a little higher up the tunnel wall and the legs wriggled back underneath his own hoisted body, then stopped moving. He had made no sound during his short passage backwards but Macomber wished to heaven that he knew what had caused the Greek to retract that short distance. Was it in anticipation of something? The next moment he had confirmation that he had guessed correctly – a heavy instrument was hammered against the ragged rim of the aperture. Fragments clattered on the floor of the pipe and then the steel-plated butt of a rifle came half-way inside the pipe as a piece collapsed unexpectedly. The German was enlarging the hole to get a better view.

Macomber felt Grapos' body tense and then relax almost immediately – he had been about to seize the rifle butt and jerk it downwards out of the unseen hand holding it. Had the Alpenkorps man been alone it would have been a worthwhile action, but Grapos had remembered in time that the German was not alone on the hill slope. Grimly, Macomber waited for the hammering to be resumed, for the hole to be enlarged to a point where they must be seen, but as the seconds passed the hammering was not resumed and there was an unnerving stillness beyond the aperture. Apparently the soldier was now satisfied that it was simply a deserted culvert and he had continued uphill with the sweep. Or was this too comforting an explanation of the lack of activity above that tell-tale hole?

165

Had he, in fact, seen Grapos? Probably not – Grapos had moved farther up the tunnel just in time. The complacent thought had hardly passed through Macomber's head when he realized how fatally he had been wrong, realized that the German was still standing there just above them and that this was a man who was going to make sure of the business with very little expenditure of effort. The expenditure of a single hand-grenade, in fact.

The stick-like object fell through the hole and landed on the floor of the pipe. Macomber knew at once that they were going to die, that the grenade would detonate under perfect conditions. Inside that confined space the blast would be enormous with only a fraction escaping through the aperture; the main part of the explosion would be concentrated and funnelled along the pipe in a searing wave of bursting gases which would tear them to pieces. Prentice at the rear might just survive – survive with ruptured ear-drums as the hellish noise roared over him. Macomber felt Grapos stir under him and knew what he was trying to do, but the Greek was sprawled along the floor in a near-helpless position and he would never manage it in time. The Scot's hand closed over the grenade as he pivoted, taking his whole weight on his left hand to give him hoisting room. Gripping the throwing-handle and knowing that he held death in his fist, he looked upwards, calculated in a split-second and then jerked his hand, praying that the missile wouldn't catch the rim of the hole and come bouncing down again. The grenade sailed up through the aperture's centre and vanished as Macomber instinctively huddled over Grapos who now lay perfectly still. The detonation echoed back to the prone men as a hard thump like the thud of a rubber hammer against an oak door. Macomber let out his breath and then nearly fell over as Grapos scrambled out from underneath him, half-stood up, pushed his head through the hole and heaved with his shoulders to force his way through the fractured rim.

What the devil was he up to now? The manoeuvre took Macomber completely by surprise. Was the Greek on the German side, was he taking this last chance to get out of the tunnel and reach his friends? Still standing in a half-crouched position with his head and shoulders only above the rim, Grapos was doing something frantically with his hands and arms. Below him Macomber held the Luger aimed at the lower part of his body while he tried to work out what Grapos was trying to do. He waited a whole minute and then the Greek lowered himself back inside the tunnel, pausing on his knees to reach up outside the hole while he hauled clumps of vegetation over the aperture. His hands were streaked with blood and when Macomber caught a glimpse of the prickly undergrowth he understood – he had been clawing and arranging a screen of vegetation to conceal the hole from the rest of the Alpenkorps patrol. Grapos sagged into an awkward sitting position and wiped his streaked hands carefully underneath his coat while he took in great gasping breaths of air. When he could speak he looked at Macomber and his former mistrust had gone as he dragged out the words. 'The German is dead – the bomb must have landed at his feet. He is alone ... the others will come and will think the bomb went off by accident ... with luck. If they do not see the hole ...'

'You covered it completely?'

'I think so. If they search they will find it – but why should they do that if they think the bomb exploded by mistake? They will see it is not in his belt.'

'Thanks,' Macomber said simply. 'Think you can make it to the end of the tunnel? Good. And now you'd better be extra damned careful how you emerge.'

'I will manage.' Grapos wiped hair away from his face and stared at the Scot. 'And thank you – that bomb came within centimetres of my nose – if it exploded here I would have no head now ...'

'Get moving – those Germans will be here any minute.'

In spite of their cramped state the four men made speedier progress down the last stretch of the tunnel and then waited at the bottom until Grapos signalled that all was clear. Like the Alpenkorps, they crossed the stepping-stones singly, and in less than five minutes they came out from the undergrowth on to the deserted road to Zervos. Grapos grinned as he hoisted his rifle over his shoulder prior to leading the way. 'It will be good from now,' he informed them. 'We are in front of the Germans.'

'I wouldn't count on that,' Macomber replied sharply. 'I've got a nasty idea something very peculiar is going to happen between here and Zervos.'

CHAPTER NINE

Sunday, Noon

The advance guard of the Alpenkorps was in sight and since they were mounted on mules it could only be a matter of time before they overtook anyone moving on foot. Perched on the crag which hung over the road a hundred feet below, Macomber closed the Monokular glass which Prentice had returned to him and looked down at the roadside where Grapos waited for the oxen-carts coming from Zervos. It had been agreed that it would be better if he questioned the peasants riding on the carts alone and the three of them – Macomber, Prentice and Ford – had climbed up from the road to keep out of sight. For the Scot this had been a welcome opportunity to see a long distance back over the way they had come, although the view could have been more encouraging.

'I hope Grapos isn't going to take all day arguing the toss with those peasants,' Prentice said irritably. Lack of sleep was making it increasingly difficult to keep his eyes open and now it was only will-power which sustained his movements. The trouble was that he had missed even the short rest the others had enjoyed before Grapos had appeared on the hilltop.

'He may get some news from them – or at least find out where we can get some food,' Macomber pointed out.

'I couldn't eat a thing. And that lot following us hasn't put any edge on my appetite either.'

'It shouldn't take them too long to get here,' observed Ford. 'They'll drive those mules till they drop – and mules don't drop all that quickly.'

Macomber forced his sagging shoulders upright and began speaking rapidly. It was clear that Prentice was in such a low state that a few minutes of pessimistic conversation might be more than enough to sap his remaining resistance, so he deliberately instilled a rough vigour into his voice. 'We're standing on a good lookout point to check the geography of the area so you know what lies ahead of us. It's about ten miles from Katyra to the plateau, and the plateau itself is about six miles long. Then there's about another four miles from the far end of the plateau up to Zervos. That last four miles is pretty appalling – you climb up a winding road from the plateau which zigzags all over the place – so if we can conscript some mules for ourselves, we'd better do it. Grapos may manage to fix that up – I gather he knows just about everyone on the peninsula.'

'You mean we have another ten miles to do before we get to the monastery?' Prentice started to sit down on a rock and then remained standing; he had the feeling that if he relaxed he might never get up again. 'I don't see us getting there today,' he said firmly.

'Burckhardt will get there today – I'm sure that's the key to his whole timetable. And if you look over there I rather think you'll see Mount Zervos in a minute.'

From their elevated position at the top of the crag they had a panoramic view over the peninsula and to east and west the Aegean was in view, still a brilliant blue across the gulf where they could see the mountains on the mainland above the vital road the Allies were using. The surface of the water glittered in the sunlight and when Macomber scanned it with his glass he thought he could make out small dark specks amid the calm cobalt, the specks of Italian mines floating in the gulf. The mainland was still half-shrouded in mist but here and there the sunlight caught the tiny square of whiteness which must be the wall of a building. To the north a dark column of smoke still hung in the sky from the burning *Hydra*, but the plume was less well-defined now and less smoke drifted upwards to maintain its density. And it was in that same direction where a distant file of men on mules advanced towards the crag at a seemingly snail's pace, a file which was telescoping as the head of the file went down inside a dip in the white streak of road.

To the south a fleet of heavy clouds drifted low over the peninsula, but the clouds were thinning rapidly as they drifted out across the gulf beyond Cape Zervos and, as Macomber had predicted, the mountain slowly emerged from the clouds like a massive volcanic cone, a cone whose slopes were white with snow to the triangular-shaped summit. Prentice stood watching the mountain appear with a sense of awe – had they really a dog's chance in hell of scaling that giant and reaching the strategically vital monastery before the Germans took it? Borrowing Macomber's glass again, he focused and saw that the clouds had never really covered the peak; they had smothered the plateau and intervened between the mountain and the view from the north. So the met men had been right – Zervos was hardly ever obscured by the weather and once Burckhardt was established up there he would have a continuous view of the supply road. Prentice felt temporarily overwhelmed – overwhelmed by what was at stake and by the apparently insuperable problem of arriving on Zervos in time.

'It's not so good to the east, though,' Macomber warned them soberly. 'At this time of year the weather comes from that direction and I don't like the look of what's on the way.'

To the east the sea was still visible, a grey ruffled sea rapidly disappearing under a fresh formation of dense cloud banks which had a heavy swollen look. There was very little doubt that extremely dirty weather was coming, heading for the section of the peninsula they would have to cross. Prentice stared again southwards where the mountain was now fully exposed to its base, and when Macomber told him to focus on a certain spot he thought he saw a tiny rectangle of rock perched close to the sea. 'If you're looking at the right place,' the Scot told him, 'that's the monastery. It's pretty high up, as you'll see.'

'Pretty high. Well above the snow-line, in fact.'

Perhaps a mile farther on from the crag the last remnants of cloud were now clearing from the edge of the plateau which rose abruptly from the foothills like a wall. Again Macomber pointed out a certain spot and Prentice found the road which climbed up to the tableland. On the eastern side of the plateau a wisp of smoke eddied into the sky as it was caught by a strong wind and there appeared to be a huddle of buildings under the smoke. 'That's the village of Elatia,' Macomber explained in reply to Prentice's question. 'We shan't go near that – a spur track runs off the main road to reach it.'

'Main road? Some main road!' Prentice handed back the

glass and looked down to where the oxen-carts had stopped below while Grapos talked to several peasants who had gathered round him. At one moment Grapos gestured vigorously towards Katyra and Prentice guessed that he was warning them about the approaching Germans. Shortly afterwards something like panic gripped the gathering. Three of the four oxen-carts filled up with the peasants and began to leave the road to drive straight across the fields which stretched away from the base of the hill. One wagon got stuck as its wheels caught in the ditch and the shouts of the passengers urging the beasts to make greater efforts echoed up to the crag. The fourth cart, empty, remained standing in the road as Grapos stared up at the crag and waved both arms furiously to summon them down. As they started their descent Macomber took one last look northwards and saw the tail of the Alpenkorps column sliding out of view. When it emerged in sight again it would be that much closer to the crag and to Mount Zervos.

'The news is bad – very bad,' Grapos greeted them. 'The Germans attacked my country and Yugoslavia at 5.45 this morning. They say the forts at Rupel have held the first attack.'

'They said the Maginot Line would hold all attacks,' Prentice muttered under his breath. 'Why have they left this wagon?' he asked out aloud. Grapos had turned the cart round so that now it faced away from the Alpenkorps.

'For us! They are going into the fields to escape the Germans so that it did not matter that they knew you were here. With this we can save our strength and some of us can sleep. I know where we can get food and clothes.' He looked at Ford and Prentice. 'With those clothes you would freeze to death on Zervos.'

'Any other news, Grapos?' Macomber inquired quietly. 'And how do your friends know about the German offensive? The telephone line was going to be cut.'

'It has been cut since last night. They heard the news on the wireless.' Grapos' manner had become openly hostile as though he resented the question, and Prentice thought Oh,

172

Lord, those two are at it again! 'I tell you the truth,' the Greek added vehemently.

'Of course you do,' Macomber replied, completely unruffled. 'But I deal in fact and I like to know the details. Where can we get the food and the clothes?'

'At a house where the road climbs. We must go ...'

'Just a minute! You know this family well?'

'There is no family. There is one man and I have known him many years. He would be in the army fighting but he is old. And he has no German mother – if that would really worry you, Mr Macomber.'

'Then let's get moving. This will be a chance for you to get some rest, Prentice. Make the most of it. I have an idea it may be the last chance you'll get!'

The inside of the ox-cart was carpeted with straw and Prentice, who sprawled full-length after bunching up the straw into a makeshift palliasse, had fallen asleep almost as soon as the cumbersome vehicle started moving. Grapos held the long whip which signalled the animals that it was time to work again and they began lurching forward over the dusty road at a laboured pace across a small plain. The foothills continued on their right, hiding the gulf from them, but they became lower as the wall of the plateau crawled towards them with infinite slowness. It would have been at least as quick to march on foot but Macomber felt that Prentice must recuperate even though the Alpenkorps on mules must inevitably close the gap between them, and the cart provided a means of rest for all four men. Although convinced that it was crucial to conserve their energies for what might lie in front of them, the slow-motion pace of the cart irritated him almost beyond endurance. The wagon was drawn by two long-horned oxen which plodded along sedately as the ancient wagon creaked and groaned as though it might fall apart at any moment. They were coming close to the wall of the plateau when Ford asked Macomber his wry question. 'Anything worrying you – anything in particular, I mean?'

'Well, this ox-cart for one thing. It's not exactly the Orient Express.' He stared ahead as Grapos, who stood between them, glared in his direction. 'For another thing, I can't work out how we're going to communicate with the mainland forces in time to warn them of what is happening here. In time,' he repeated. 'Once Burckhardt has established himself on the heights no one will ever shift him – the place, the position, everything, makes it a natural fortress. But the thing which bothers me most of all is the size of his force – I'm absolutely certain that he's expecting massive reinforcements.'

'Hard to see how – unless they sneaked in by sea again. Could they land somewhere over there?' Ford pointed towards the eastern coastline which was still clear, although out over the Aegean the clouds were continuing to mass.

'There's no way inland. The cliffs go on until they reach the delta area in the north. But I can't see them risking a sea-going expedition twice – and this one in broad daylight. They can't be expecting to break through from Salonika in time or else they wouldn't have sent Burckhardt in the first place...' Macomber trailed off and stared ahead as he put himself in the colonel's position and tried to imagine his next move. Ford was standing with his back to the way they were going so he could watch the road behind but so far it stretched away emptily as far as he could see.

When they reached the base of the plateau wall Grapos took them inside a single-storey stone house concealed by a grove of cypresses and there the owner, a man in his seventies, divided among them the meal he had just prepared for himself. The food was strange and strong-tasting and consisted of balls of meat rolled inside the leaves of some unidentifiable vegetable. He offered to cook more but Macomber said they had no time and they ate with relish food they would normally have rejected as inedible.

Macomber was keeping watch by himself just beyond the cypresses while he drank *ouzo* from a large glass when he saw them coming. His Monokular brought them closer – Alpenkorps on mules, a file which extended back into the distance and which was a far more formidable force than he had imagined from his earlier sight of them. He ran back into the house to find Prentice and Ford trying on two ancient sheepskin coats the owner was providing and then exploded when the lieutenant started to write the man's name in a notebook so they could send him payment later. 'Prentice, you may have just signed that man's death warrant! If the Germans catch us and find that . . .'

'Of course! I must be half-asleep,' the lieutenant replied apologetically. He went to a stone sink and began setting fire to the page prior to washing away the embers. The room was stone-paved and stone-walled. A hideous place to spend seventy years of one's life.

'And we have about half a minute to clear out of here,' Macomber rapped out.

'I'm just burning a death warrant, as you so aptly pointed out.' Prentice had recovered his normal composure after the sleep in the cart and there was a faint smile on his face when he stared back at the large Scot. 'How close would you say?'

'Two miles. Maybe less.'

'Close enough, I agree. We'll have to hike it up to the top of that plateau. I hope you can walk faster than a mule, Ford.' He dropped the blackened paper into the sink and poured a stone jugful of water over the mess, pushing it down the drain with his finger. 'There's no way up except the road, I suppose?'

'No other way,' Grapos told him.

'Right! The road it is!' He turned to the old man. 'Tell him he has our grateful thanks for his hospitality. I rather fancy it would be a mistake to offer money for the food?'

'A mistake,' Grapos agreed abruptly. He was looking through the open doorway towards the road and hoisted his rifle higher as he moved towards it.

'Tell him also,' Macomber intervened, 'that when the Germans arrive and ask about us, he's to say he saw us get off the wagon we'd obviously stolen and run up the hill. If he tells them something they're more likely to leave him alone. Tell him also to wash up three of those plates and glasses and just leave his own dirty. They'll be looking for things like that. And don't forget the thanks.' He waited while Grapos poured out a stream of Greek and the old man kept shaking his head as though it were nothing, and he was relieved to see as they left that the old man was already starting to wash the dirty plates.

When Macomber looked back as they started to climb the

hill, the line of mounted troops was already appreciably closer and he knew that they must hide soon or be captured. With the Scot in the lead they ascended the winding road at a slow trot, but long before they reached the top they were slowing down badly. The gradient was steep and wound its way between huge boulders which seemed on the verge of toppling down the rugged incline. Groves of bare olive trees studded the hill slope and the frequent twists in the road soon hid them from the plain below, which had the advantage of hiding them from the Alpenkorps mule train, but had the disadvantage of preventing them seeing how close their pursuers were drawing. Cover was what they needed, Macomber was telling himself, and he was tempted to leave the road altogether and hide on the hill slope, but this would mean throwing in the sponge: the Alpenkorps would ride past and continue on to Zervos. I'm damned if I'm giving up as easily as that, he thought, after surviving that voyage from Istanbul.

'I'd say we have another thirty minutes left – at the outside,' Prentice called up to him.

'At the outside,' Macomber agreed. Thirty minutes before the leading Alpenkorps troops overhauled them. It was beginning to get a bit desperate and he was pinning all his hopes on seeing a chance to escape when they reached that plateau which stretched six miles to the base of the mountain. This was one area where he had very little idea of the topography because when he had travelled this way five years before it had been drenched in mist while they drove over the tableland. The stitch in his side was getting worse as he forced his legs to keep up the route-march pace and now each thud of his boots on the road pounded up his side like a sledgehammer. To counter the pain he stooped forward a little, cursing inwardly as Prentice caught up with him.

'Take it easy, Mac, you'll kill yourself. You're streaming with sweat.'

'Time is running out – we had a head start on them and we've lost it. We'll have to make a quick decision when we reach the top.' The effort of speaking was a major strain now but he was damned if he was going to give up. Keep moving, you'll work it off! Prentice was walking alongside him now and this gave him a pacemaker to keep up with. He forced himself to resist the impulse to look at the ground because this brought on greater fatigue. Straightening up, he stared at the ridge they were approaching. Was this the rim of the plateau at long last? He had thought so hopefully with three lower ridges and had been disappointed each time. In his state of extreme pained exertion the plateau above was now taking on the character of a promised land, a haven where there must be some salvation from the relentless Alpenkorps coming up behind.

He was hardly aware of the landscape they were passing as the pain grew worse and pulled at him like a steel wire contracting inside his body. Boulders, olive groves, clumps of shrubbery moved past in a blur as he fixed his eyes on the wobbling ridge moving down towards them as they turned another bend and then another. Despite his robot-like condition he was conscious that the air was cooler, that a breeze was growing stronger, and this gave him fresh hope that they were close to the head of the tortuous road which went on and on forever – another bend, another stretch of white dust, another bend...

'Must be nearly there – with this wind,' Prentice commented.

Macomber only grunted and stared upwards. Was he breaking the grip of the stitch? It seemed a little less agonizing, a little less inclined to screw up his muscles into complex knots. It left him quite suddenly and with the realization that he had conquered it he began to take long loping strides which Prentice could hardly keep up with. He wiped his face dry as he walked and then accelerated his pace, feeling a sense of triumph as he saw only sky beyond the lowering ridge. They were almost there! Revived by the small quantity of food and the wine he began moving faster still as the gradient of the road lessened, leaving Prentice behind in his anxiety to catch his first glimpse of the plateau. There must be no hesitation here – they must decide swiftly what they were going to do and do it. There might even be a convenient farm at the top. With a lot of luck there might even be bicycles – he had seen men cycling when he had visited Katyra before the war. A cycle should be a match for a mule. They needed some form of transport which would take them the six miles across the plateau, something which would put them well ahead of that blasted mule train of Burckhardt's. He put on a spurt, came over the top and the plateau lay before him.

The disappointment was so crushing that he stood quite still until Prentice reached him. A classic tableland spread out into the distance, an area of flatness devoid of any form of cover for several miles. In fact, he could hardly have imagined a region less suited for them to escape the Alpenkorps. The road was a surprise, too: a highway of recently laid tar which ran straight across to the mountain, the land greenish on one side and brownish on the other. They must have started the highway from the peninsula tip, a highway which in due course would be extended to Katyra.

'Not quite what we're in the market for,' Prentice remarked.

'It might as well be the sea for all the good it is to us.' Macomber glanced over his shoulder. 'How's the Greek?'

'Had a bit of trouble with his limp coming up. Ford stayed back to keep him company. What's exciting them now, I wonder?'

Ford and Grapos had appeared but they were standing together on an outcrop of rock a short distance from the road as they waved their hands with a beckoning motion. Prentice left Macomber gazing bleakly at the plateau and went back to the outcrop. The ground he scrambled up was dry and gritty, which confirmed that the storm of the night before must have blown itself out somewhere near Cape Zervos. And there was a trace of excitement in Ford's voice as he called down. 'Hurry up or you'll miss it.'

'Miss what?'

The sun which shone on the back of Prentice's neck as he hauled himself up on the rock had no warmth in it and the coldness of the light breeze was a reminder that they were approaching a zone of low temperature. Standing beside Grapos, he adjusted his sheepskin coat. It was too big and flopped off the shoulders; Ford, who was wearing another coat belonging to the same man, fitted far more comfortably inside his sheepskin. Had the Greek possessed a third coat? The thought had never struck Prentice during the flurry to get away from the house. Following the line of Ford's pointed arm he could see the top of the house now, its faded red tiles so levelled by the height that it looked flat-roofed. And only a few yards beyond the cypresses the head of the Alpenkorps column was approaching the foot of the hill road. 'There they come,' said Ford, 'the first of the many.'

'You're sure they are the first? There may be more of them already coming up the hill.'

'No, sir. You and Macomber were in such a perishing hurry to get up here I don't imagine you ever looked back – but we caught sight of them more than once and that's the head of the column.'

Prentice was surprised. Earlier he had been startled to find German troops in front of them when they came over the hilltop near the pipe, and now he was surprised at how long it had taken them to reach this point since he had glanced back when they rushed out of the house below. He waited for two or three men to turn aside and enter the house, but the column went straight past and vanished as it began to mount the hill road. The wagon had been left behind the cypresses, which also concealed the house, and the Alpenkorps were going to ride up the hill without ever realizing its existence. With a feeling of relief he jumped down from the platform and hurried back to where Macomber still stood, stood like a man of stone as he gazed upwards, his hands inside his coat pockets, the expression on his face so grim that it recalled his impersonation of Dietrich.

'What's the matter?' asked Prentice. He tilted his head. 'What's that – I can hear something?'

'The reinforcements – Burckhardt's reinforcements. By God, I expected something but I hadn't expected this. They must have half the Wehrmacht up there coming in.'

The sky to the north-east was still clear, more than clear enough for them to see the huge aerial armada which was descending on Zervos. The steady purr of their engines grew louder as they flew over the peninsula at a height of less than a thousand feet and they were close enough already for Macomber to see that they were three-engined machines with an iron cross on the fuselage and the swastika on the tail. 'Transport planes,' Ford said in his ear. 'They'll very likely have parachutists aboard.' In the distance, flying even lower, came more planes and these were towing other machines with different silhouettes. Macomber was focusing his glass on them as Prentice spoke.

'The Alpenkorps have just started to come up the hill behind us.'

'They'll take Zervos before nightfall. There's nothing to stop them,' said Macomber.

'Unless this airborne crowd is heading for the mainland,' Ford suggested without much conviction.

Macomber stared through the glass, holding his head tilted back as the planes flew in closer. The aircraft towing other machines were losing height rapidly while the transport planes circled above the plateau, their engines a muted roar. There were no Allied fighters to intercept them, of course, although a flight of Messerschmitts had now appeared: the bulk of the over-strained RAF was supporting the Greek war in Albania and even these formations were few and far between. With a feeling of appalled helplessness they watched the aerial fleet droning casually over the plateau like a flying circus putting on a show before an invited audience, although the only audience to watch this display of Luftwaffe air power was the group of four men on the plateau rim. There were probably between twenty and thirty planes, but it was the thought of what they might contain which frightened Prentice. 'Those machines they're towing are gliders,' said Ford. He saw Macomber nod in confirmation and now the shadows of the planes were flitting over the level surface of the plateau, a perfect landing ground for putting down an airborne force. A moment later a cluster of black dots sprayed from one of the transport machines and the dots became cones as the parachutists floated downwards. A machine detached itself from its powered carrier and the gliders started to come in to land.

The four men were retreating from the plateau towards the hillside above the road when Macomber called out. 'Wait a minute, Prentice! Something's going wrong with this one.' A glider detached from its powered transport was wobbling unstably as it headed for the earth and had the appearance of being out of control as it descended towards the rim of the plateau close to where Macomber waited. An ugly, ungainly beast, it was twin-tailed and the fuselage was squat, suggesting great carrying capacity.

Half a mile along the road more parachutists were floating down over the brownish ground which seemed to be the main landing area and the sunlight caught their tilting cones – white for parachutists and various colours for the 'chutes supporting supply containers. Only one transport plane had attempted a landing to the left of the road and his machine was propped at a dangerous angle with the nose well down and its tail angled in the air. On the other side of the road two transports had already touched down safely and a third was just coming in.

'That plane on the left will be in trouble,' Prentice said tersely. 'It's marshland on that side.'

'How do you know that?' Macomber asked quickly.

'Because I persuaded the pilot to make a detour and fly over here on our way to Istanbul. We'd been discussing Zervos before I left Athens and I wanted to see what the place looked like. He told me that the green area was marshy...'

'Those transport machines are JU 52/3s,' Ford interjected professionally. 'I've heard they can carry mountain guns...'

'This is hardly a good time to start cataloguing German equipment,' Prentice snapped. 'I say we'd better get out of here – and fast.'

'And this brute of a glider coming towards us is a Gotha unless I'm very much mistaken,' Ford continued, and then found he was alone as the others ran back towards the boulders and scrub at the top of the hill. As he followed them he could hear the whine of the wind rising and the steady beat-beat of more transports coming in. Ford, who had a fatalistic streak in his make-up had little doubt that this was the end of the line; they would spend the rest of the war in some German prison camp, unless they were shot in the process of being captured. He was close to the first boulders when the machine-pistol slipped off his shoulder and he had to turn back to pick it up.

The huge Gotha assault cargo glider was flying down at an

unpleasantly acute angle less than a hundred yards away. If it wasn't very lucky it was going to miss the rim of the plateau and go crashing down onto the plain below. Fascinated by the spectacle of the imminent disaster he stayed out in the open. Macomber seemed similarly affected, because now he came out from behind the rocks and stood close to Ford as the massive glider swooped down, tried to level out at the last moment, and then thudded into the soft earth a bare hundred feet away.

'For God's sake get under cover, you idiots!' Prentice shouted from behind them. Ford, the spell broken, turned to go, but Macomber still waited as he gazed at the machine. The shock of landing had righted the fuselage and now the whole of the nose of the aircraft was lifting back like an immense hood. A soldier stood near the entrance as the aperture yawned larger, exposing a vehicle like a large car which waited to emerge. The German was moving unsteadily as he climbed behind the driver's seat and he paused to wipe something which might have been blood from his forehead. The engine started up and the vehicle began to move slowly out of the nose with a rattling sound as the driver slumped over the wheel as though he could hardly hold himself up. There was little doubt that he had been badly knocked about by the crash-landing. Prentice, who had come out from cover with Grapos, spoke over the Scot's shoulder. 'If we could just grab that . . .'

'Exactly what I was thinking, but there are bound to be more men inside.'

Ford grabbed his arm and his voice reflected a rare excitement for the phlegmatic sergeant. 'It's a bloody half-track! Look!'

The clanking sound grew louder as the vehicle came out with painful slowness and the dazed driver remained still unaware of their proximity. Capless, he was wearing the uniform of the Alpenkorps, but it was the vehicle itself which Macomber was staring at as he put his hand inside his coat pocket and began to move forward purposefully over the grass. A long vehicle without any roof, its body was painted a drab olive-grey and at the front it was supported by two normal wheels, but there were no wheels at the rear; instead it was held up by two large caterpillar tracks. As Ford had said, a half-track – half-tank, half-car. The grinding of the tracks was muffled as they moved down onto the grass and now the driver lifted his head to see where he was going and saw Macomber standing a few feet away. The Scot spoke swiftly, rapping out the words in German.

'Brake! Colonel Burckhardt is here. He needs this vehicle at once!'

The driver reacted automatically to the command in German, braked, then stared hard at the man who had given the order. His eyes travelled over the Scot's shoulder to where Prentice and Ford were moving forward while Grapos watched the road behind. As he made a sudden movement to reach something Macomber pulled out the Luger and struck him across the temples. He had the door open and was hauling the soldier out before he had sagged to the floor while Prentice and Ford ran to either side of the open mouth of the glider. Heaving the driver out onto the grass with one hand while the other still retained the Luger, he looked up as another German soldier appeared at the open nose, his rifle at the ready. Two shots were fired within the fraction of a second. The first, fired by the soldier, struck Ford. The second, fired by Macomber, entered the German's body as Prentice ran round the back of the vehicle, arriving at the moment when the Alpenkorps man slumped down in the space between the rear of the tracks.

'Heads down!' it was Prentice who shouted as he snatched a grenade dangling from the fallen German's belt. The grenade sailed into the interior of the glider and detonated near the back. A moment earlier Macomber had caught a glimpse of movement from inside the plane, but when he raised his head after the thumping explosion there was no further sign of activity aboard the Gotha. Ford was holding onto the side of the tracks as he stooped forward on his knees, but he was trying to clamber up as Prentice and Macomber reached him. The passage of the bullet was marked by a neat tear on the right shoulder of his sheepskin coat. Prentice had an arm round his chest and was helping him to his feet as Macomber spoke.

'Get him aboard quick! I'll have to try and drive this

blasted thing – they'll be on to us in a minute.'

Ford was upright now, one arm clutching Prentice round the waist for support as he clambered inside a cut-out aperture which was the rear-door of the half-track. He spoke through his teeth to Macomber. 'Drives like a car ... any car ... the tracks move with the wheels.' Macomber was turning to go to the front when he saw the distinctive Alpenkorps cap on the head of the soldier slumped between the tracks. He scooped it off and rammed it down over his own head as Grapos arrived, running at a shuffling jog-trot with his rifle between his hands.

'The mules are here,' he gasped out. 'Coming over the hill quickly. I think the first man ...'

'Get in, for God's sake.'

Prentice had successfully manoeuvred Ford into one of the benches behind the two front seats and Macomber was behind the wheel as Grapos climbed aboard. Brake, clutch-pedal, gear-lever – it *looked* like an ordinary car. Ford told Prentice to shut up a minute and leaned forward. 'An ordinary car, Macomber, that's all it is – for driving, anyway.' He sagged back against the bench seat as Prentice grabbed at a first-aid kit attached to the rear of the driving-seat and then the vehicle began moving forward over the grass towards the road. The tracks clanked gently as they revolved over the field and the vehicle had a feeling of great stability.

Macomber was concentrating on three things at once – on getting to know how this queer monster worked, on keeping an eye on the hilltop over which the Alpenkorps might stream at any moment, and with what little attention he had left he cast quick glances to the south where the road ran past the landing zone. The sky was littered with a fresh wave of falling para-chutists and another transport plane had just come to a halt after a bumpy landing. Dammit, he said to himself and speeded up. The half-track reached the road at the moment when the leading Alpenkorps soldier crested the rise on his mule.

Hahnemann! Macomber felt certain it was the German lieutenant on that animal. He must have been hurled over-board into the sea when the *Hydra* blew up, must have been one of those men swimming in the water. The thought darted

184

through his brain as it all became a kaleidoscope and he reacted with pure instinct. Two more men on mules appeared
behind Hahnemann. Parachutists hitting the earth, their
'chutes landing and pulling sideways. A giant glider cruising
in to land on the brownish area. The steady throb of planes'
engines overhead mingling with the urgent shouts of the men
on the mules. Still feeling like a man towing a caravan, he
turned the wheel and the half-track climbed onto the road. As
its great metal tracks ground their teeth into the hard tar they
set up a jarring vibration sound and the unexpected barrage
of noise panicked the mules. There was more shouting, frantic now, as the animals headed across the hilltop, threading
their way nimbly among the boulders and away from the
strange machine. Macomber completed his turn, hunched his
shoulders, pressed his foot down, and the half-track began to
build up speed as the wheels spun and the tracks churned
round faster and faster, half-deafening its passengers with the
pounding beat of metal on tar.

'How fast can it go?' shouted the Scot.

'Twenty ... thirty ... forty. Fifty would be pushing it.'
Ford had his arm out of the sleeve now and was taking off the
right side of his jacket as he replied. There were three rows of
bench seats across the vehicle behind the front seats and
Grapos occupied the rear position. He had aimed his rifle at
Hahnemann but the half-track had lurched at the wrong
moment, almost throwing him off, and he hadn't fired a shot.
Now there was no target – the mules and their riders were lost
somewhere inside the tangle of boulders. He swore colourfully
in Greek when Macomber shouted over his shoulder for him to
get down on the floor out of sight – Grapos was rather too
distinctive a figure for his liking at the moment.

Ahead more transport planes were droning in the sky as they
waited their moment to come down, and already the plateau to
the right of the road had the look of a disorganized military
tattoo. So far there were no troops close to the road but a few
hundred yards away parachutists were grappling with the
supply containers and a number of men were already armed
with machine-pistols. Several looked up as the half-track
roared past and their uniform was very different from that of

the Alpenkorps, so different that they might have belonged to another army. They wore pot-shaped helmets not dissimilar to diving helmets, smocks camouflaged with mottled dark green and brown, and overall trousers which gave them a deceptively clumsy appearance, but there was nothing clumsy about their movements as they began to form up in sections. Macomber, having got the feel of the vehicle, was now sitting very erect so his Alpenkorps cap was prominently on view and frequently he drove with one hand while he waved with the other to the men assembling in the field, a performance which Prentice witnessed with some trepidation. It was typical of Macomber, he was thinking, to carry the bluff to its utmost limit.

'Look out!'

Prentice shrieked out the warning. Like Macomber, all his attention had been fixed on the airborne force's landing area and it was only by chance that he glanced to the left. A Gotha assault glider released from its tow-rope was coming in to land from the east. It was already flying very low, perhaps twenty feet above the ground, flying on a course which would take it directly across the road just ahead of the speeding half-track. Prentice guessed that the pilot was desperately trying to maintain flight long enough to take his machine beyond the marshland area and it was horribly clear that the two very different forms of transport were headed on a collision course. Macomber had time to slow down but nearby a drawn-up section of parachutists was marching steadily towards the road. If he slowed, stopped, they'd get a damn good look at who was inside the vehicle and they had machine-pistols looped over their shoulders. Without hesitation he accelerated and it became a race towards destruction.

His shoulders hunched again, he watched road and oncoming glider. It was an uncomfortably fine calculation – known speed of half-track against estimated speed of glider, with the added element of the plane's angle of descent. The half-track was now thundering down the road, which had begun to slope, at a pace which alarmed Prentice, the tracks rotating madly under increasing tension as the moving metal smashed its way forward with a rattling cannonade of sound.

Across the green field the glider grew larger as it maintained its course unerringly and lost more height. He must be mad, Prentice was thinking. Macomber's going to try and beat the bloody thing, to sneak past ahead of it! The glider was so close now that he wanted to close his eyes, to look away, but he felt a terrible compulsion to stare at the oncoming machine which now seemed enormous.

'We won't make it,' said Ford who had now become aware of what was happening, and Ford was good at this sort of hair's breadth calculation. Prentice would have felt even less happy had he known that exactly the same thought was pressing down on Macomber, and now it was too late to think of reducing speed. The converging projectiles were so close that he would probably smash into the tail of the glider as it passed. The only answer was a little more speed.

The downward gradient of the road was increasing as he pressed his foot harder and prayed – prayed against two catastrophes. He had heard somewhere that if you drive a tracked vehicle too fast a caterpillar could break loose, freeing itself from the small wheels over which it revolved and leave the vehicle altogether. If that happened at the speed they were moving at now there would be very little hope of survival. Grimly, he kept his foot down, his mind totally concentrated on the straight road ahead, the tortured gyrations of the over-strained tracks, and that huge drifting shape about to move across his bows. Prentice had one arm steadying Ford while the other hand gripped the side of the vehicle as the glider lost more height and cruised forward barely six feet above the plateau and less than fifty yards from the road. Grapos, lying resentfully on the floor with his feet under a bench and his back against the rear of the vehicle, had the shock of his life when he looked up and saw the bulk of the Gotha loom up. The half-track raced forward, Grapos involuntarily ducked, and the wing of the Gotha passed over the rear of the vehicle, landing a short distance beyond the road.

Prentice sagged against the back of the bench and stared at the back of the huge Scot, his lips moving soundlessly. Macomber was already slowing down to a safer speed, expecting some uncomplimentary comment from his passengers, but the occupants of the bench were stunned, so he was saved an argument. In the distance a transport plane was stationary close to the road and Macomber whistled under his breath when he saw something which looked like a part of a field-gun coming down a ramp through a large opening in the fuselage. 'How is Ford?' he called out over his shoulder.

'Ford is surviving,' Ford replied.

'The bullet grazed him,' amplified Prentice who was now fixing a bandage to his final satisfaction. 'He's lost a bit of blood and he looks like Banquo's ghost but the fresh air will probably tone him up a treat.'

'There's a plane ahead with something coming out – better try and identify it so we know what we're up against.'

'We can see what we're up against,' Prentice told him bluntly. 'The cream of the Wehrmacht. And I suppose you've seen there are more half-tracks over to the right? One's just nosed its way out of that Gotha which just missed us.'

'Do you think we're nearly clear of them?' asked Ford and there was a note of anxiety in his voice.

'Not much ahead as far as I can see. Why?' Macomber had detected the anxious note and was wondering what had struck the technically minded Ford.

'Because we've been lucky so far – it's wireless communication that worries me. If the Alpenkorps who came over the hill can send a message ahead we may have a reception committee waiting for us.'

It was a point which had worried Prentice but he hadn't seen any point in raising new problems at this particular juncture. So far they had got away with their audacious dash along the fringe of the assembly area, and this didn't entirely surprise him: the Germans had just landed on enemy territory and were taken up with carrying out a certain vital routine – collection of weapons from the supply containers, the unloading of heavy equipment from the gliders and transport planes, and the assembling of the men into their units. They had no reason, when their attention was so divided, to see anything strange in one of their own recently landed half-tracks speeding along the road to Zervos. But wireless communication was a different matter.

188

'We may be lucky,' said Macomber. 'I made a mess of both of Burckhardt's wireless sets and if he hasn't got that tuning coil fixed he'll have to wait until he finds one with this airborne mob. Now, watch it, Ford.'

He had been travelling at little more than twenty miles an hour to give the tracks a rest but now he began to build up speed again as they approached the transport plane which had landed little more than a hundred yards from the road. Men were scurrying round the machine and he saw beyond it another plane which had been hidden from view. Close to the aircraft stood a complete field-piece. Ford twisted sideways on the bench as they roared past and this time, to Prentice's relief, the Scot did not attempt his cheerful waving act. The planes were receding behind them when Ford spoke.

'They're 75-mm mountain guns – just what they need where they're going. And I saw several 8-cm mortars. This lot is really going places.'

'Some of the half-tracks will haul the mountain guns?' Prentice inquired.

'Yes, that's it. And they'll carry troops aboard as well. They've landed a beautiful heavy-nosed spearhead for the job.'

'Why send Burckhardt's expedition at all?' Macomber asked.

'That's very necessary,' Prentice explained, 'for a variety of reasons. First, if they hadn't had this patch of clear weather the airborne force could never have landed at all and then Burckhardt would have had to do the whole job himself. Second, I can see now that it was vital for them to land men at Katyra to seal off the peninsula . . .'

'And third,' interjected Ford, 'there's a limit to how much a glider or transport can carry. You can have heavy stuff – the mountain guns, the half-tracks – or you can have men, but you can't have both. So it's my bet Burckhardt's expedition is bringing in a sizable portion of the manpower while the airborne fleet brings in the heavy stuff. Together, it makes up a beautifully balanced force.'

'That's the second time you've used the word "beautiful",' Prentice complained. 'Frankly, I can't see one damned thing that's beautiful in what's coming to us.'

'Just a professional observation, sir,' Ford explained blandly.

'I think we've left them behind,' Macomber called out. 'It looks as though those two planes landed closest to Zervos.'

The road stretched away across the plateau and still ran straight as a Roman road, a perfect highway for the advance of the German invaders. They were much closer to the mountain now but it no longer rose from its base with majestic symmetry; a heavy cloud bank from the east was drifting across the lower slopes and the peak had a lop-sided look. The disturbed Aegean was no longer visible from the plateau and another formation of low cloud was gradually obliterating the tableland itself. The road was sloping upwards as it climbed towards the mountain wall and Macomber could feel a distinct drop in temperature as the wind grew stronger. The worsening of the weather was a development he viewed with some disenchantment; his photographic memory for places vividly recalled that murderous stretch of road farther on which zigzagged up the flank of the mountain, a road twisting and turning over precipitous drops as it ascended into the wilderness.

At least Burckhardt's tracked spearhead wouldn't be able to do a Le Mans over that course, but the trouble was he had to take the half-track up the same road. The gradient was increasing more steeply as Prentice called out to him.

'How are we off for petrol?'

'We had a hundred litres – a full tank – when we started, so that's the least of our problems.'

'The pilot of the glider would insist on a full tank before he took off,' Ford pointed out helpfully. 'That minimizes the risk of something going wrong during the flight – an explosion, even.'

Prentice groaned half-audibly. 'And talking about trouble, I don't much like the look of that dirty weather blowing up from the east.'

'Is the Greek still on the floor?' Macomber asked. 'He can get up now if he is and give us his opinion – a Met forecast, in fact.'

Prentice glanced round and lifted his eyes to heaven. Grapos was sprawled on his side with the rifle cuddled in his

190

arms and he was fast asleep. The coil of Alpenkorps climbing rope, which earlier he had pulled from under a bench and examined with interest, lay with a German army satchel at his feet. How anyone could kip down on top of those vibrating tracks passed Prentice's comprehension. 'The Greek,' he announced in a loud voice, 'is in dreamland.'

'Well, wake him up,' Macomber commanded brutally.

Disturbed from his slumber, Grapos sat on the bench behind Prentice who put the question about the coming weather to him. He stared across the plateau, pulling absently at one corner of his moustache and then feeling the stubble on his chin. Then he stared ahead to where the mountain was fast losing itself behind the vaporous pall which was drifting across the plateau in front of them. As he watched, the mountain disappeared. 'It is bad,' he said. 'It is very bad. The worst. There will be much snow within the hour.'

'Exactly what makes you predict that?' Macomber called back to him sharply.

'It is from the east. The clouds are low. They are like a cow with calf – swollen with snow...'

'First time I've heard of cows with snow inside them,' Prentice commented in an effort to lighten the pall Grapos himself was spreading over them. But the Greek was not to be put off by unseemly levity.

'The sea has gone from the plateau – that is another sign. The top of the mountain has gone – another sign. As we climb it will get worse and worse. It will be very cold and there will be a big fall of snow.'

'Thank you,' said Prentice, 'you're fired! We'll get another met forecaster from the BBC.'

'You ask me – I tell you. There may be landslides on the mountain. There will be ice on the road...'

'And the sea shall rise up and encompass us, so we'd better find a Noah's Ark,' said Prentice in a kind of frenzy. 'For Pete's sake, man, we asked you for a weather forecast – not a gipsy's warning of doom. Now can it!' And he looks a bit like a gipsy, the old brigand, he thought as Grapos glared at him resentfully and then gazed stolidly ahead as though drawing their attention to the appalling prospect which lay before

191

them. 'That answer your question, Mac?' he called out.

'I think so. Further outlook unsettled.'

It was the reference to ice on the road which most disturbed the Scot. He would have to take this cumbersome half-track up a route which, five years before, a car had found difficulty in negotiating in good weather, because during that trip only the plateau had been blotted out by low cloud. It would make it equally hazardous for Burckhardt, of course, so it really depended on which way you looked at the problem, but Macomber was going to be in front with the Germans coming up behind. He changed gear as the gradient increased again and they were moving at little more than twenty miles an hour when Prentice asked if he could borrow the Monokular glass. He kept it for only a short time and then handed it back as he spoke.

'You were right, the outlook is unsettled – behind us. A half-track is coming after us like a bat out of hell. It could be Hahnemann aboard, but I'm only guessing, of course.'

'How many men?' Macomber was already trying to coax a fraction more speed out of the vehicle.

'Three or four. I couldn't be sure. He's on the flat at the moment so he'll have to slow down when he starts coming up.' Ford and Grapos twisted round on their benches and saw in the distance the half-track coming towards them at speed. Macomber was watching what appeared to be the crest of the hill they were climbing and beyond it the cloud hid the base of the mountain which must be very close. He would have to out-drive Hahnemann up that devilish road: the snag was he would soon be slowed down by the mist while the German could drive full-tilt up to this point, thus narrowing the gap between them to almost zero. The weather was certainly not their friend at the moment. He drove up steadily, reached the crest, and immediately the road turned and dropped into a dip between dry-stone walls where it turned again. The oxen were massed at the bend.

There were three Greek peasants with the animals which had accumulated at this point, and they were shouting their heads off and flailing the beasts with birches made of slim stems. So far as Macomber could see as he drove down towards them their efforts were only adding to the confusion and the road was well and truly blocked. With the thought of that other half-track tearing towards them, he pulled up his own vehicle inches from the chaos of animals and drovers. 'Sort them out, Grapos! Get them moving and damned quickly! They can shove them on to that bit of grass by the next bend till we get past. Then tell them to block the road again.' He waited while Grapos got out of the vehicle and began shouting at the drovers, who, at first, simply shouted back. An ox rested its horned head on the side of the half-track and stared at Ford with interest. Grapos continued his shouting and gesticulating match with the drovers and Prentice felt his temper going. A minute later the animals were still milling round the vehicle and Grapos was still conducting his verbal war with his countrymen. Something snapped inside Macomber. He stood up, pulled out his Luger and fired it over the heads of men and beasts. The animals panicked and began to trot off down the road, followed by the drovers who penned them into the grassy area while the half-track grumbled past them.

'You told them to block the road again?' Macomber shouted back to Grapos who had resumed his seat on the bench.

'I told them the Germans were coming and they must make them wait.'

Macomber swore violently to himself: mention of the Germans coming would undoubtedly frighten the drovers so much they'd keep their animals penned up off the road until the second half-track had passed. They had closed the road to him but he felt sure they would open it to the Germans. Something pretty drastic had to be done to widen the gap between the two vehicles. The road was straightening out once more as it went down a hill between high earthen banks, so he accelerated. The half-track built up speed rapidly under the pressure of his foot and he felt a coldness on his face as the road flew away under him. The mist was floating aimlessly and as it drifted to and fro he caught glimpses of the mountain wall rising up like an immense fortress bastion. Here and there pinnacles of rock spurred upwards and then vanished as the mist closed in again. Glancing at the speedometer, he saw that they were moving at the equivalent of fifty miles an hour and he was well aware that only the weight and stability of the racing tracks were holding them on the road. When the mist parted again momentarily he saw a stone bridge at the bottom and the old route came back to him: beyond the bridge the road veered to the right and then started its fierce climb up the mountain. Within a minute or two he would be reduced to crawling pace as he attempted the first acute bend and the realization of this fact made him exert a trifle more foot pressure.

. Behind him Ford was white-faced with the aftermath of his wound, but Prentice was white-faced at the speed they were travelling as he clung tightly to the arm of the bench seat which was shuddering so violently that he was scared the screws attaching it to the floor might soon shake loose. Grapos had wedged himself in against the side of the vehicle, and when Prentice glanced back he thought he saw for the first time a flicker of uncertainty in the Greek's narrowed eyes. Ford's reaction was brief but significant: he leaned forward, stared at the speedometer, then braced his back against the bench. In his determination to out-distance the following half-track Macomber seemed to be going far beyond the bounds of a calculated risk as he drove steadily downwards, the high earthen banks sliding past them in a blur, the sound of the pounding tracks confined inside the sunken road like the noise from a stamping mill, and now the revolving metal was developing a disconnected rhythm which brought Prentice's raw nerves to screaming point. Was the Scot intent on killing every man aboard?

The mist had rolled like a grey fog over the gulley below, temporarily blotting out the narrowing distance between the rushing half-track and the bridge, and it was only when the greyness dispersed briefly that Macomber grasped his mistake, understood that he had overestimated his margin of safety badly, saw the bridge – with the right-angled turn beyond – soaring up towards him, alarmingly close. He began to lose speed knowing that he was too late, that the half-track must still be moving too fast when the moment came to swing the wheel, to turn to the left sharply over the bridge and then turn to the right even more sharply once he was across it. He lost more speed, lost it dangerously quickly, and behind him his

three passengers – Grapos now on his feet, grasping the rear of
the bench which seated Prentice and Ford – were like frozen
men, men who had lost all ability to move even as they stared
petrified at what lay ahead of them, knowing that they were
going straight through the bridge wall into the river below.

CHAPTER TEN

Sunday, 2 PM

Too late to brake, too late to reduce speed – by orthodox methods. Macomber veered to the left suddenly, immediately veered back to the right, straightened up again. At the speed they were moving the huge tracks at the rear responded a fraction later, as he had intended, and the left-hand caterpillar cracked into the earthen bank with shattering impact, jerking Prentice's bones almost out of their sockets as the caterpillar partially acted as a brake. The vehicle bounced smartly off the bank and a flurry of earth minced up by the revolving track showered over them as the other bank rushed towards them. Macomber had veered to the right now, then to the left, straightened up again, but this time the collision was far more violent and the wheel nearly leapt out of his hands, which would have brought on final disaster, but somehow he maintained his grip as the vehicle shuddered wildly, wobbled uncertainly, still holding its equilibrium as more earth burst in the air and rained down over them. The trouble was he had overdone it this time.

The right-hand caterpillar was acting superbly as an improvised braking system, had lost him a great deal of lethal speed, but the track rammed against the bank had become trapped and now it was rotating furiously inside the earth as it desperately tried to break free. Macomber was holding the wheel with a ferocious grip which signified more than an attempt to regain control – it also signified his fear that the track would come loose, break away altogether from the vehicle. Above the roar of the engine a new sound screamed out, a sound of churning metal rasping over rocks embedded inside the bank, a hellish sound which went on and on as the track revolved frantically and clouds of earth and loose stones soared above them. Then it freed itself and the half-track leapt forward down the natural gradient while Macomber wrestled to keep control, to lose more speed without tipping them over as the right-angled bridge rushed up to meet them. He hit the ice patch at the moment when he felt he might just make it.

The ice patch, starting at a point where part of the earth bank had collapsed into a ditch, was several inches thick, so instead of breaking under the enormous weight of the vehicle it propelled the half-track forward like a sledge sweeping over a skating-rink. Macomber turned the wheels, felt them take on a life of their own, as they hurtled down on the leftward turn over the bridge. He swung the wheels farther to the left, praying for the massive tracks to act as a sheet-anchor, then they were half-way round the bend with the tracks continuing the sweep behind them and Macomber had the feeling some irresistible power had taken hold of their tail as the momentum of track weight carried them farther and farther sideways. The wheels were half-way up the bridge when the right-hand track smashed into the stone wall, a dry-stone edifice of boulders unsealed with mortar. The impact of steel against stone was mind-shattering: Prentice was hurled along the bench, stopped by the side of the vehicle as Ford cannoned into him, and only Grapos, still upright, held his position by the tightness of his grip on the rear of the bench. A few feet beyond them, Macomber took less of the shock, but the impact sound was deafening as the track battered the wall open, tumbled huge boulders into the river below, and then they were suspended over the brink, half the right-hand track in the air over the drop. Prentice shook his head to fight down the stunned sensation, peered over the side and saw he was looking down into the river thirty feet below, a foaming torrent which carried along half-submerged floats of greenish ice. He felt the half-track tremble, begin to tip backwards gently. They were going over . . .

At the last moment Macomber had braked. A swift glance over his shoulder showed him the appalling danger – the jagged gap between the boulders, the greenish swirl, a third of the vehicle in mid-air, so probably at least half the equilibrium, then he, too, felt the tremble, the insidious lifting motion beginning. He released the brake, depressed his foot.

The engine throbbed, built up power; something bumped gently in front. Christ, the wheels had left the ground, had just returned to the road surface! Something had locked on-to the vehicle, holding it fast. He felt the floor rising under him again as they started to tip backwards again, the wheels clear of the ground. They were going to somersault over, the track weight no longer a sheet-anchor as it performed the function of a fulcrum to see-saw the half-track down into the roaring torrent. Mist like smoke drifted over the bridge, obscuring the view like a London fog, the clammy moisture settling on Macomber's sweat-stained forehead. His instinct – of self-preservation – urged him to leave the wheel, to jump for it onto the road still beside him – but for once he ignored the instinct, knowing that the others would go over the edge with the vehicle. He remained rigid behind the wheel, pressing his foot down still farther as the caterpillars revolved furiously among the scattered boulders, metal clashing so savagely with stone that Prentice saw flint-sparks fly in the mist. It lasted perhaps twenty seconds – the final skid, the smash into the wall, the first lift of the vehicle, the brief return to firm ground, the second more nerve-rasping tilt. It was the left-hand cater-pillar Macomber was counting on, the track less thrust out over the drop, the track whose treads still clawed at firm ground, and now the gamble began to work as the caterpillar shifted the mess of boulders and grated its way forward inch by inch – dragging the other track with it until that also gained a firmer grip and did its part in heaving the vehicle farther on to the bridge, farther away from the yawning gap. Macomber felt it coming, felt the wheels hit the road again, released some foot pressure just in time as the vehicle surged free, and in freeing itself the right-hand track let go of a section of wall which had leaned outwards under the shock of the initial impact. Above the growl of the engine they heard a muffled splash as a whole fresh section of wall dived into the river and Macomber steered the half-track over the bridge and started to take the right-hand turn, then braked. He looked back, his engine still running.

'Jesus ... I thought that was it ...' Prentice wiped his damp face while Ford licked his lips and held his wounded shoulder where it had cannoned into the lieutenant. Grapos, recovering more quickly than the others, had his rifle gripped in his hands as he stared backwards the way they had come, the way the pursuing half-track would come. 'Not much point in hanging about here, is there? Let's get moving,' Prentice demanded irritably.

'There might be – a point in waiting here for them.' Macomber stared back at the wrecked wall. The vanished section was perhaps twenty feet wide and he was seeing it as the Germans would see it when they reached the bridge, his mind racing while he tried to estimate their likely reaction when they reached the bottom of the hill. The mist, which had thinned but still swirled over the bridge, made the devastation look even worse, like the aftermath of a battlefield. He looked forward again to where the road turned to go up the mountain: the road turned right sharply, but to the left, where the bridge ended, a rock slope continued up from the road and disappeared behind a clump of trees only half-seen in the greyness. A gentle slope which looked firm enough, firm enough to take up the half-track. 'I want you all to get out and take up position for when they arrive. We'll fight it out here,' he said abruptly.'

'What the hell for?' Prentice was vehement. 'If we go on we should keep ahead of them with a bit of luck...'

'Up that mountain road?' Macomber was twisted round in his seat again where he could face Prentice and his expression was grim. 'Look, I've been up that road once before – it's just about wide enough to take this thing, it zigzags backwards and forwards up the mountain with a sheer wall on one side, a sheer drop on the other, and higher up it may be covered with shot ice. There's even ice in the river behind us. We'll be crawling up that mountain like a man going up on his belly ...'

'We'll still be in front,' Prentice persisted obstinately, 'and if we have to, we may discover a better spot to ambush them ...'

'Not as good as this.' The Scot was eyeing the left-hand slope speculatively. 'And we're more likely to get the element of surprise here – they'll think we went over with that wall.'

'Not when they look over and see nothing there, they won't . . .'

'So, we'll have to make sure that by the time they discover their mistake it's too late.'

'You'll have to hide the half-track,' Ford pointed out soberly. 'It would give the whole game away if they can see . . .'

'That's the guts of the thing.' Macomber extracted one of his three remaining cigars, lit it quickly. 'They won't spot it until it's too late if I can work this the way I see it.' He took several puffs and then pointed up the slope. 'I'll be up there inside those trees and I don't want anyone opening fire too soon. They'll come down that road, maybe a bit more slowly than we came down it, and they'll see the ice patch, which will slow them down even more, give them time to spot that smashed-up wall. But they won't stop on the ice – they'll keep on coming and pull up on the bridge to have a look. That's when I come down out of those trees. Then you can shoot as long as your ammunition lasts out.'

'You're going up that slope?' There was an incredulous note in Prentice's voice. 'You'll never make it – you must be bonkers even to attempt it . . .'

'What are you beefing about?' Macomber growled. 'You're not coming with me – and I'm just beginning to get the feel of this gadget. I could even get to like it. Now, for God's sake get moving – they'll be here any minute.'

Partly because he felt they had lost too much time to continue up the mountain, partly because he sensed the agreement of Ford and of Grapos, who had dropped into the road and was already looking for a good vantage point, Prentice reluctantly helped Ford out of the vehicle, and as soon as they were in the roadway Macomber let off the brake and began driving forward. The slope was a little steeper than he had anticipated but once the tracks gripped its surface he felt them steadily pushing the vehicle up the ascent. The mist was thickening again when he had climbed sixty feet above the bridge and he switched on his lights to see where he was going. The beams were blurred cones and the lights reflected off tiny particles of moisture as they penetrated the trees, showed up a massive slab of rock beyond. Tilted at an angle of perhaps thirty degrees, sagged back heavily against his seat, he steered the half-track cautiously between two tree-trunks, pulled it up with its nose inches from the slab, looked back and swore. The one essential of the ambush was a clear view of the bridge and the mist had closed over it, blotting it out completely. If it didn't shift before the German half-track arrived he was impotent, powerless to help, and the other three would have to fight it out alone. He took out the cigar, moistened his lips and waited with the engine ticking over. Another calculated risk – that the motor of the German vehicle combined with the mist would muffle the sound of his own engine. What the devil was keeping Jerry?

Waiting was an activity – if doing nothing can be termed activity – Macomber had some experience of. Waiting in the shadows of a warehouse on the Danube while he checked the supplies going aboard a barge; waiting beneath a manhole cover while a German soldier patrolled the street above; some of his most gruelling hours during the past fifteen months had been spent waiting. But at the moment waiting didn't suit him; it gave a chance for the fatigue to make itself felt, to settle in his weary limbs and his over-strained mind, and he wondered how much more he could take before his final reserves were drained. Even the slow-motion coils of mist which drifted below as he remained twisted round in his seat seemed to add to the appalling tiredness which was becoming his permanent condition. He blinked, thinking he saw a man creeping up through the mist, but it was only the vapour assuming strange shapes, and then, above the murmuring throb of his own motor, he heard the sound he had been waiting for.

The half-track proceeding cautiously down the hill echoed weirdly through the fogged silence, a distant engine sound combining with a more distinctive noise – the rattle and grind of the descending tracks. And still the bridge was lost, might be a dozen miles away for all he could see of it through the dense pall which smothered the slope so that now it might have been late evening or early morning. Had he known this was going to happen he could have stopped lower down, relying on the mist alone to conceal his presence, but it was far too

late to alter position, so all he could do was to wait and hope –
hope that damned mist would thin in time. The clanking
sound was closer now, the half-track still moving slowly, as he
had foreseen it would. His hand went towards the brake,
clutched it, and he had forgotten he was smoking as he stared
fixedly downwards, trying to make up his mind whether the
mist had thinned just a little. His eyes were feeling the strain
of staring in one direction and a dull ache was building up
behind his temples as the clanking noise grew louder, still a
muffled ratchetty sound, but definitely louder. They'd be at
the bottom any moment now, turning onto the bridge. It
wasn't going to work, there was going to be a tragedy down
there, Macomber felt it in his chilled bones, a chill brought on
by a feeling of almost unbearable frustration which twitched at
his nerves. I may be responsible for the death of three men, he
thought.

A breath of wind touched his face as he heard the engine
sound slow – they had reached the bottom, they were turning
the corner. He suddenly realized his lights were still on and
switched them off quickly. A blunder like that would have lost
him his life long ago. Pull yourself together, for Christ's sake,
this is going to be tricky enough as it is without going to sleep
on the job. A noise like gently falling water came from above
as the wind rustled the trees, then the mist began to retreat
rapidly, to dissolve back down the slope as the wind parted it
in melting eddies. He stiffened, his side rigid against the seat,
straining to see what was happening down there. Had a voice
drifted up from below? He was frowning ferociously, still trying to decide, when the mist cleared from the bridge and he
saw the German half-track turning the first corner as it lumbered up to the bridge and stopped, broadside on to the destroyed wall, stopped in the position Macomber had prayed it
would stop. Four men inside, and the man standing up by the
driver was Hahnemann. Too far away to see clearly, but
Macomber knew it was Hahnemann, knew it for a certainty
from the way he moved. Now!

He released the brake, accelerated, reversed down the slope
at gathering speed as the tracks churned and slithered their
way down, the revolutions increasing with every yard of the

descent. Had they reacted instantly, remained cool, taking deliberate aim before they fired, they might have killed the Scot, freed the half-track's steering so it would have careered in a different direction. But Macomber had counted on the element of surprise, on the element of terror which can freeze men's minds for vital seconds, on the view as seen from the bridge which a moment earlier had seemed so deserted, on the view seconds later as they heard the harsh grind and thunder of the descending tracks and saw the tank-like projectile coming out of the mist and roaring down on them. Still twisted round in his seat, both hands locked to the wheel, steering by feel alone, Macomber turned the direction of the onslaught a fraction, aiming the half-track square at the vehicle below. He saw Hahnemann react at last, saw him haul out his pistol from his holster, raise it, take deliberate aim, then collapse as Grapos, secreted behind a rock above the bridge, fired at the same moment as Prentice pressed the trigger of his machine-pistol. Hahnemann's three companions ducked, or fell, Macomber had no idea which, as the tracks bounded over a flat boulder and changed direction round the end of the bridge, smashing with enormous force into the side of the German vehicle parked by the gap. The collision was tremendous, a jarring shock which knocked Macomber backward into the wheel, and only his anticipation of what was coming prevented his being impaled on the steering column as he braked at the last moment, a split-second problem of timing since he needed all the force of the rushing descent to strike the half-track before he tried to escape following it to destruction. The battering-ram blow slammed the German vehicle half-way over the edge as one of the Alpenkorps men scrambled dazedly to his feet, acted intuitively and threw himself over the brink, only to be followed seconds later by the half-track which dropped sideways and buried him when it plunged into the river. A burst of water jumped up to bridge height, subsided, and Macomber, turning painfully round saw that his own vehicle was perched on the brink, but perched safely. He was lying forward over the wheel, taking in great gulps of mist-laden air when Prentice reached him. 'Are you all right, Mac?'

'I think so. Stand clear a minute.'

Afterwards he could never remember his automatic action of driving forward slowly and turning the half-track so it faced towards the mountain road before he braked, switched off the engine and staggered out onto the road where Prentice held him as his legs almost gave way. 'I'm not too bad ... I'll survive. I want to see ...' He stumbled over to a piece of the remaining wall and leant heavily against it while he looked over. The half-track, upside down, had been caught by two huge boulders thrust above the water, but as he looked down it lost its balance, tipped over sideways, wallowed briefly three-parts submerged and then sank. Bubbles coming up from it reached the surface and were then whipped away in the fast-flowing current, so he couldn't be sure whether his eyes had played him a trick. The sunken vehicle gave up one last memory, the uniformed body of an Alpenkorps man who came to the surface and then was swept away downriver, towards Molos, towards the Gulf of Zervos. 'Poor devil,' Macomber muttered, then he straightened up, still using the wall for support. 'There'll be others on the way, so we'd better get on – up the mountain.'

CHAPTER ELEVEN

Sunday, 2·30 PM

The ledge which supported the road was dangerously narrow – as Macomber had predicted they were hemmed in between a vertical wall of rock to their right, a wall which climbed high above them, while to their left the abyss fell away to unknown depths, unknown because the mist below prevented them from seeing how far down the drop continued. They were fifteen minutes' driving time from the wrecked bridge – no great distance considering he had been compelled to move up at a rate of only a few miles per hour – but in that time they had climbed steadily and Macomber calculated that soon they would have ascended a thousand feet, one thousand nerve-crushing feet. Before they had left the bridge Prentice had offered to take over the wheel, but the Scot refused the suggestion. 'I think I've a little experience of handling her now,' he had remarked drily, conferring a feminine status on the most unfeminine-looking object imaginable, 'you might even say I've had a crash course in coping with a half-track.'

'Crash is the word,' Prentice agreed humorously, 'and that's why I'm wondering whether you're in fit state to drive it up the mountain.'

'If I'm not, you should have time to nip off the back.'

Prentice was recalling this last optimistic remark as he stared over the side to where the world dropped away into nothingness. The tracks were grinding irritably over the shale-strewn road as he leaned forward to speak directly into Macomber's ear. 'You'll watch it, won't you, Mac? This isn't too good a place for nipping off anywhere.'

'You could slip over, too, even if you made it – you've seen what's coming up?'

Prentice stared ahead and was joined in his stare by Ford and Grapos who shared the same bench seat. Up to this moment the road had a dull, powdery look, but ahead it gleamed with a sinister sheen – a sheen of ice which coated the surface from wall to brink. 'That doesn't look too funny,' Ford remarked thoughtfully as he recalled vividly what had happened to the half-track when it hit the ice patch on their way down to the bridge. 'Think we can make it?' Prentice asked softly, subconsciously seeking reassurance.

'It may be all right,' Macomber replied non-commitally as he edged the vehicle forward. 'Nothing's ever as bad as you think it's going to be – once you try it.' But his confident reply, deliberately delivered in that form to keep up the morale of his passengers, hardly corresponded with his misgivings. Further evidence that they were climbing steadily was provided by the equally steady drop in temperature and already the mist drifting over his windscreen was lingering, settling to form streaks of blobbed ice. There was no wind worth speaking of at this height yet; just a relentless fall in temperature which caused the Scot to pull the scarf a little tighter round his neck, a purity of cold which inhibited speech and made a man want to sink into the stillness of the mountain. The tracks rumbled forward under them as the ice came closer and Macomber cursed their bad luck – this hazard had presented itself at the very moment when the ledge was narrowing so there was barely a foot of free space on either side of the lumbering vehicle.

He was finding it more difficult to handle in the confined space – no leeway for even the fraction of an error and the concentration required every second was beginning to sap his last reserves of energy, to dull the keenness of his nerves just when he needed every ounce of alertness he could summon up. The vehicle moved on, passing into the ice zone as Macomber sat up straighter, every fibre of his consciousness keyed up for the first sign of slipping, the first hint that the tracks were in trouble – because it was the tracks which would get them through if they survived this ordeal, their weight which would hold the vehicle on the ledge – and conversely it was their malfunction which could bring about the final disaster, the slither backwards which he might not be able to control, ending in their dropping over the precipice, hauled down by the weight which had earlier saved them. Above the slow clatter he heard a new sound, the chilling prickle as the tracks moved onto the ice, followed immediately by a crackle like breaking glass. He let out his breath: it was all right, the ice was breaking. He had to keep up this gradual pace and the tracks would anchor the vehicle while the wheels crossed the treacherous surface, then the tracks would fracture it to allow their own safe passage. Within a minute he was frowning, knowing he had miscalculated dangerously, that his remark that nothing was as bad as you expected was incorrect – things could be worse, infinitely worse. It was the *feel* of the half-track which warned him, something he was becoming familiar with, because now they felt to be moving over a permanent smoothness. The grip of the caterpillars into the road he had noted farther down was missing. They weren't gripping any more – they were moving upwards over a second more solid layer of ice beneath; only the surface had cracked. And he was coming to a bend. And he could see the first of the snow, white streaks garnishing the gleaming surface. Prentice leaned close to his shoulder, careful not to distract him, to keep his tone moderate and calm.

'Look, Mac, I think we have a problem. We're still moving over ice. The stuff must be inches thick.'

'I know. You'd better all move onto the rear bench – just in case.'

'I appreciate the suggestion...' Prentice was speaking with studious calm, a calm he was making a certain effort to assume, '... but I don't think that would help. If we start to go we'll go backwards, so I don't foresee any rush to leave by the rear exit.'

He was right, of course, Macomber thought pessimistically; they were totally boxed in – by the wall, the abyss, and by the danger of the vehicle starting to slide backwards. Their options were also critically limited in another direction which Prentice probably hadn't grasped yet: Macomber dare not risk braking – stopping on this glass-like surface – because once he stopped they would face the almost inevitable peril that when the half-track tried to move forward again the caterpillars would revolve uselessly over the ice, the first stage in the final slip-back. Boxed in, unable to stop, compelled to move up and up whatever faced them, Macomber began easing the vehicle round the shallow curve, his eyes switching constantly from one point to another – from the curving wall to the extension of the road ahead in case it narrowed even farther. He sat very still behind the wheel, his mind filled with the clanking sound of the turning metal, the curve of the sheer wall which went on and on, the sharp edge where the road ended and the blurred abyss began.

Behind him Prentice sat motionless on the bench in the position nearest to the drop, with Ford in the middle and Grapos seated close to the wall, a wall the Greek viewed with increasing disenchantment as it insidiously moved nearer to his right shoulder: the ledge was contracting. Perched above the brink, Prentice's gloved hand gripped the side of the vehicle as though attached to it and he felt the vibrations of engine and tracks passing up his arm, felt the freezing air numbing his cheeks, felt the tremble of the half-track when it wobbled as it passed over an ice-coated unevenness. The crackling sound, the thinly-iced layer crumbling under the weight, came to him above the engine's purr like the sputtering of a log fire, the symbol of warmth while he slowly froze into a state of immobility, and he couldn't take his eyes off the ribbon of ascending ledge which gradually unwound as the road climbed higher and higher. How much more of this could Mac stand? An audacious gamble – like the reversing of the half-track down the slope to hit the Germans on the bridge – he had grasped this side of the Scot's character; but this murderous, mind-killing creep up the ice-bound mountain, this was something else again, something which made him regard the Scot with far greater awe. And he must be nearly asleep over that wheel ... He pushed the thought out of his head quickly. It frightened him too much. Glancing at the others, he saw Ford's hands clasped rather tightly in his lap, his face wooden, whereas Grapos was leaning forward, watching the road intently as though expecting a fresh hazard any second. To take his mind off watching the road Prentice pulled out the looped rope from under the bench, saw that at one end a grappling hook was attached, and when he opened the Alpenkorps satchel he saw more climbing equipment – another rope, pitons, a hammer. As he shoved satchel and rope back under the bench something damp flaked his face, dropped into his lap. It had started snowing.

The snow started falling heavily as they navigated a fresh turn in the road and a rising wind met them, a bitter wind which blew the flakes into a turmoil so they danced above the ledge, driven this way and that in disconcerting flurries. For Macomber the coming of the snow was the final straw, the ultimate hazard. He had kept the half-track on the ledge, maintaining an even space on either side as it narrowed, as he found himself increasingly compressed between wall and brink; maintaining an even speed as it balanced itself delicately on the solid ice, but he had accomplished this gruelling task with a reasonable visibility. Now this only asset was taken away from him as blinding snow fogged his vision, pasted itself over the windscreen, blurred wall and precipice edge to mere silhouettes whose exact location he could no longer rely on. He switched on the lights and they sent out short-lived swathes penetrating only a few yards inside the frenzy of the snowstorm which was growing rapidly more violent as the wind rose to a moaning howl and the men on the bench seat behind him bowed their heads to shield themselves against the onslaught of the elements. Grapos, his chin dug into his chest, was peering warily to his right where the rock face seemed to be closing in; if they collided with that at the wrong moment it could veer the vehicle outwards and over the drop, and Macomber, seated on the other side of the half-track was less able to judge their distance from the wall than from the brink. In the faint hope that he might be able to issue a warning in time, the Greek lifted his head, ignored the whipping snow-flakes which stung his skin and stared ahead through half-closed eyes. No doubt about it – they were appreciably closer to the wall.

This slight change of position was not a mistake on the Scot's part as Grapos feared; it was a deliberate act to try and reduce a little the overwhelming danger they now faced. Unsure from moment to moment of the precise position of the abyss edge he had turned in nearer to the mountain, knowing that if they struck the rock face he at least had a chance to recover, and knowing that if the tracks tipped over the edge there would be no chance of survival at all. Macomber had seriously considered halting, but they were still passing over solid ice and they were still moving up a steepish incline, so if he could keep going until the storm died away the hazards were probably a fraction less dangerous than the hazards of stopping – to say nothing of the fact that somewhere not too far behind them Burckhardt's force must already be making its own way up the mountain road. And the possibility of finding himself stationary on the ice-bound ledge as armed men, more than likely men equipped with mortars, came round a corner in his rear was not a contingency which appealed to him. He turned his head slightly, shouted to make himself heard above the howling wind. 'Any idea how much farther, Grapos?'

'One kilometre beyond the big bend.'

'How far to this ruddy bend?'

'Soon – very soon now.'

'How do you know in this stuff?' Macomber bawled out sceptically.

'Because of the gash.'

Gash? The Scot glanced quickly to his right and saw for the first time a break in the endless mountain wall, a fissure scarcely wider than the breadth of a man, and beyond the gyrating snow he had a glimpse of a narrow tumble of water which fell almost vertically and which was frozen solid in mid-air. Then it was gone. Jesus, the temperature must be low up here. As he looked ahead again the road began to turn round the mountain, and it went on turning, which forced him to keep the wheel swung over permanently to the right, but at least this was an improvement on the zigzags he had encountered lower down, hairpin bends he doubted he could even have attempted if the snow had come then. He drove on, up and up, following the continuing curve of the wall, peering from underneath his Alpenkorps cap brim as his gaze switched from brink to wall and back again to brink, and so great was his concentration that it was a few minutes before he realized there had been a change in the weather. It was still snowing but the wind had dropped, fading away to a chilling stillness as the curtain of snow floated down almost vertically in the windless atmosphere. For the hundredth time he brushed his hand over the windscreen to clear the snow: the wipers had packed up some time ago and his hand was equally effective for removing some of the freezing snow which was steadily adhering to the glass at either end of the screen. And now the headlights penetrated farther, giving him a safer view of what was coming up – and they were only about one kilometre from safety according to Grapos. The thought had barely passed through his head when he stiffened, felt his hands grip the wheel more tightly. A short distance ahead a boulder rested against the inner wall, a boulder rounded and partly covered with snow, and as the headlights moved nearer he saw its massive size, that it was only partly protruding from a ravine similar to the one they had recently passed, that it must have tumbled down the ravine and then become jammed in the exit immovably just before it crossed the ledge and swept down into the abyss. The dream of safety receded as every turn of the tracks took them closer to the emergency. Macomber weighed up the chances quickly – the boulder appeared firmly jammed inside the ravine, they were within a kilometre of easier going, there appearing to be just sufficient room for them to squeeze past, but it would take them to the edge of the precipice.

'You'll never make it, Mac...' It was Prentice's strained voice which spoke, but the Scot maintained the same even pace as he called back to them.

'Prentice, get to the back and watch the tracks – the outside one. If I'm going over, signal Ford by waving your hand. Ford! You warn me by clapping a hand on my left shoulder – damned quickly, too!' He heard feet moving back along the floorboards. Someone slipped in the snow and swore as they saved themselves. On his own initiative Grapos went back to watch the inner track which had to pass the boulder. Macomber reduced speed to a point where he feared the engine might stop altogether and the snow-covered obstacle crept closer and seemed to magnify itself hugely as he steered away from the mountain wall to give himself maximum clearance, which involved placing the left-hand track on the very edge of the precipice.

The half-track crept forward through the deepening gloom, because now the snow drifting down had made it seem almost like night, and his headlights reflected weirdly off the ice covering which had formed over the mountain wall. It was like living through a bad dream, Macomber thought wearily – the drifting snow which he no longer brushed away from the windscreen, from his weighted coat; the uncanny silence, the muffled throb of the engine, the creak of the turning tracks, the blurred cones of the headlights, and now that frozen gleam off the rock wall. Inside his gloves his hands had hardly any feeling left, his feet were losing contact with the rest of his body, the dull ache in his forehead was fogging his mind, and he had the strange sensation that he was disembodied, that his limbs belonged to someone else, that he was reacting like an automaton. Perhaps his judgement had gone, he was attempting the impossible, and they would end up plunging into that abyss which could easily go down for a couple of thousand feet. He blinked, bit his lip, pushed the defeatist thoughts out of his mind and glared ferociously ahead as the trapped boulder moved closer and closer and the outer track revolved along the rim of the ledge. They were within yards of the obstacle now, would attempt to slide past it within seconds.

At the rear of the vehicle Prentice was leant half over the side as he followed the progress of the caterpillar which was starting to inch out over the precipice as they began to pass the boulder. It was a frightening sight – a portion of the moving belt suspended over the drop – and he was on the verge of signalling to Ford when he decided to wait a few seconds longer, to see whether the position deteriorated. On the far side, mid-way along the half-track, Grapos was gazing down at the boulder with equal intensity while the inner track churned slowly forward, drew alongside it and shaved snow from its encrusted surface. Glancing over his shoulder towards Prentice he frowned at the lieutenant's precariously poised position and then looked down at the boulder again. The main section of track was beginning to slide past it. Prentice, leaning over the outer edge, was supporting himself with one hand only to give himself the best possible view of what was happening, and the fact that his head was almost upside down probably brought on the attack. He was in the same position, staring intently as an inch of track revolved in mid-air, when the dizziness swept over him and he knew he was going to faint. Muddled, disorientated, he felt the quick movement of his right foot slipping over a patch of snow at the same moment as he heard the first grind of the vehicle against the boulder. His balance went completely, both feet sliding under him as Grapos lurched across the half-track, grasped his right arm and jerked him backwards. Prentice fell heavily, caught the back of his head on the bench and sprawled on the floorboards.

Macomber was concentrating on the precipice brink, his hands gripping the wheel, his foot ready to apply a little pressure, when he heard the scraping sound of the inner track contacting the boulder. He waited, his nerves strung up to fever pitch, waited for the hand to descend on his shoulder warning him to brake, and when nothing happened – confident that Prentice was still checking the outer caterpillar – he continued forward. The vehicle was shuddering unpleasantly as the scraping developed into a grinding sound and he suppressed the urge to glance back. His job was driving, not observation, but again he was obsessed with the mounting fear of what would happen if the caterpillar disengaged from the vehicle, leaving it with only two wheels and a single track, which must cause a state of fatal disequilibrium within seconds. The half-track shuddered again and the vibrations travelled up the steering column while he resisted the temptation to steer the front wheels, which were now well past the boulder, in towards the mountain wall. Then the shuddering and grinding noise ceased at the same moment. He drove a few yards farther forward and turned the wheel, taking the half-track away from the edge. Within minutes the road was fanning out, becoming wider as the weather began to clear and the snow drifted down more slowly, soon to stop altogether. To his right the mountain wall moved away from him, the road followed it at a distance, and on his left the precipice faded away where the ground sloped more gradually. He increased speed, experiencing a sense of exhilaration.

'Soon we shall see the monastery.' It was Grapos who spoke with hoarse confidence as he stood behind the Scot and stared over the windshield. 'We go down, pass a big rock, and there it is.'

'How are the others?'

'Prentice fell down and struck his head, but he is conscious again and Ford is helping him.'

Macomber glanced over his shoulder and saw Prentice seated on the rear bench with his head between his hands and Ford beside him. The lieutenant looked up, caught the Scot's frowning expression and waved back encouragingly. 'I'll be OK in a minute – how much farther before we see something?'

'Not far. Take it easy while you can.' Macomber looked up at Grapos. 'That rock you mentioned – I seem to remember it hangs out over the road, doesn't it?'

'Yes. We pass it – we see the monastery.'

They were travelling downhill but the view to the south was obscured by a snowbound slope as they lost altitude rapidly, descending into a bowl with wintry hills sweeping down on all sides. Along the ridges the wind whipped up the snow in flurries which eddied briefly and then vanished, but the sky above was a clear cold blue and the sun shone palely and without warmth. Macomber thought he had never seen such a bleak landscape, a wilderness where savage rocks reared up in strange shapes which reminded him of the wastelands of Arizona. They were close to one of these weird rock formations – the only one which towered above the road – when Grapos' hand gripped his shoulder tightly. 'There is someone up there – up on the crag.' Macomber looked up a second too late and they were already moving into the faint shadow the rock cast across the road. He slowed down, braked under the lee of the rock, and followed Grapos out of the half-track, flexing his stiffened fingers which had become almost locked to the wheel.

They had climbed only a few feet when the Greek pulled the Scot close to the rock and whispered. 'I go up this side – you take the other and wait. If he hears me coming he will go down your side – you wait and he meets you.' Macomber nodded, scrambled stiffly back down through knee-deep snow to the road, gestured to the other two men to stay where they were, and made his way under the looming rock. The far side was a steep slope covered with harder snow where the east wind had blown over it, and he had climbed less than fifty feet before he came up behind a large boulder which provided a perfect ambush point. With his Luger in his hand he settled down to wait, and while he waited he stared out at the panoramic view.

The monastery was in sight. Mount Zervos, remote above the vagaries of the weather was fully exposed to view. Crouched behind his boulder, Macomber saw that it was as he remembered it – the huge bluff shouldered out from the mountain, hanging over the sea on one side while on the other it plunged hundreds of feet to the lake below. The walls of the monastery rose vertically from the summit of the bluff; four windowed slabs like giant watch-towers linked together by battlemented walls. They seemed to grow up out of the rocky bluff as they sheered upwards and were silhouetted against the sea with the mainland beyond, the most remote and ascetic hermitage in all Europe – and the ultimate objective of Colonel Burckhardt.

The sea was grey and choppy but comparatively calm as the last of the snowstorm crossed the gulf. Macomber doubted whether the snow had even reached the bluff this time, so once again the monastery had retained its unimpaired view across the sea to the mainland supply road. Below where he waited. the ground receded away to the lake, a stretch of water at least half a mile wide, a lake frozen solid. The road went down to the eastern shore, turned along the northern edge of the ice-sheet, and then vanished before reappearing at the far end, close to the sea at the point where it began its unseen ascent to the bluff. A good half mile of the road was lost, blocked completely by an immense mass of snow heaped up against the slope below Macomber. This was drift snow, probably anything up to thirty feet deep, snow blown there recently by the high wind and which would strangle any type of powered vehicle attempting to drive through it. He stared down at the frozen lake, a sheet of water which must have frozen steadily thicker throughout the long winter. Was it solid enough to support half-tracks and mountain guns? A rattle of disturbed stones beyond the boulder warned him that someone was coming.

'Do not shoot! Please!'

Grapos' voice. Macomber lowered his Luger, stood up and saw the Greek leaning against the rock face with his rifle hoisted harmlessly over his shoulder. 'What's wrong?' he asked sharply.

'He is dead. Come, you must see.'

'Who's dead?'

But the Greek had turned back and was scrambling up again through the snow, using one hand to lever his limping foot more rapidly up past the rock. Macomber swore at his ambiguousness and went up after him. When he arrived at the top, receiving the full blast of the wind in his face, Grapos was staring down at a flattened projection just below which spurred out over the road, and Macomber found he could see down past the spur into the half-track where Ford still sat on the rear bench while Prentice stood in the road gazing up at them with his machine-pistol at the ready.

The uniformed figure on the spur lay sprawled over a machine gun. His attitude was that of a soldier watching the road from the north, the road they had just driven down in the half-track, but despite the presence of the two men above him he remained in his life-like posture until Grapos reached down and prodded him with his rifle tip. The uniformed figure went over sideways and ended up on his back with his face staring at the sky, a face with a rigid look and an unnatural bluish tinge. The poor devil had frozen to death at his post. Macomber gazed down at the Alpenkorps uniform, the stiffened Alpenkorps cap which still clutched the head, the weapon which still stood mounted in position, the barrel encased in ice and frozen snow so that it had the appearance of a glass gun. The Germans were already on Zervos, had already penetrated the monastery.

CHAPTER TWELVE

Sunday, Zero Hour

The attack on the monastery was planned, agreed in detail, and each man knew the part he had to play. The plan was Macomber's, a plan which relied on audacity, on an eruptive breakthrough into the heart of the sanctuary, and it was based on the unproven assumption that only a small number of Germans had taken over the place in preparation for the arrival of Burckhardt's army. It was also based on Grapos' intimate knowledge of the interior of the monastery, knowledge which Prentice had transferred to his notebook as a series of ground-plans which showed the layout. It was the basic assumption which still worried Prentice as he closed the book and tucked it inside his pocket.

'If there are more men up there than we think, we haven't a hope,' he warned.

'I agree,' Macomber replied briskly, 'but it's logical. They must have arrived as civilians – the only safe way they could travel before war was declared – and in that case a large party would arouse suspicion. They only faced the monks, so a few of them could do the job.' He checked his watch. 'And we've spent twenty-one minutes working this out, so we'd better get moving before Burckhardt lands on our tail. God knows there's enough to do in the time . . .'

He had kept the engine ticking over during their discussion; now he released the brake and the half-track began moving down towards the lake. Behind him the others were seated on the floor of the vehicle, their backs against its sides and their heads crouched forward, so from a distance it appeared that only Macomber, still wearing his Alpenkorps cap, occupied the vehicle. As they rumbled downhill at a steady pace the caterpillars whipped up the soft snow and cast it into the ditches on either side, and within a few minutes they had driven past the point where the road entered the massive snowdrift, had crossed a stretch of uneven ground and were pulling up at the eastern end of the lake to give Macomber a chance to study the ice. He would have liked to conduct a reconnaissance, to attempt walking out over the ice, but time was short. He had little faith in the Germans being held up for long by that boulder on the mountain ledge: with their man-power and the equipment they carried they would soon shift it higher up the ravine, and since he had negotiated the formid-able road the weather had improved. German luck again. The wind, bitter and penetrating, whined eerily across the frozen sheet and he could see snow powder blowing over the dulled surface, but was Grapos right – right in his conviction that the prolonged winter had solidified the ice to a depth which would support the enormous weight of a half-track? He turned in his seat as though looking back up the road and saw Prentice's anxious face staring up at him. 'You think we might make it?' the lieutenant inquired.

'Only one way to find out.'

'I have told you,' Grapos repeated hoarsely. 'In winter the monks take their ox-wagons over the lake when the road is blocked.'

'As late in the year as this?' Macomber asked critically.

The Greek hesitated and Ford, disliking the hesitation, looked at him quickly. Grapos cleared his throat before speak-ing again, but his voice was confident. 'It is not usual – but five years since we also have the bad winter and then they take the wagons across in April. That was also the time of the great landslide – the avalanche. Much snow had fallen all through the winter and when the spring comes the mountain comes alive . . .'

Macomber lit his last but one cigar, then interrupted the Greek's flow of words. 'Let's hope it's as thick as it was five years ago, then. And now I'd appreciate it if the League of Nations debate could be adjourned – this is going to take a little concentration.' He released the brake, exerted a little foot pressure and they were moving out over the ice.

He kept his speed down to a crawl, to less than ten miles an hour as the tracks rumbled hollowly over the ice sheet and their treads ground into the surface with a brittle sound which tingled his nerves. It was almost spring, the time of the year when the ice would imperceptibly begin to thin, to lose that extra inch of solidity which might make all the difference to whether they crossed safely or plunged through shattered ice into the depths below. And the depths were something which didn't repay thinking about. During their discussion the Scot had asked Grapos about the depth of the lake and his answer had not exactly raised anyone's morale. 'Fifty metres. More deep in places,' had been the answer. Fifty metres. More than one hundred and fifty feet of sub-zero water below the frozen floor they were crossing. The right-hand track wobbled gently as it mounted an area of unevenness in the ice and then there was an unpleasant crushing sound as the track squashed the tiny ridge. Inside the vehicle Prentice, with his back against the right-hand side, felt the slight incline, followed by the trembling fall. His heart leapt, his hands locked round his machine-pistol and his eyes met Ford's. The staff-sergeant had an opaque look but Prentice saw the flicker of fear as Ford observed the brief contraction of the lieutenant's eyebrows. Then the half-track was rumbling forward smoothly again while Prentice flexed his fingers and let out his breath, breath expelled like a small puff of steam in the chilled temperature inside the vehicle.

The ordeal was probably more mind-wracking for the men concealed on the floor than for Macomber, because hidden away inside the half-track they couldn't see where they were going or how far they had come, and they experienced everything by feel alone, leaving their imaginations free to conjure up the most frightful possibilities. At least Macomber had a task to accomplish, a vehicle to steer; but for him the pressure built up in other ways. He had intended keeping close to the shore, driving past the immense snowdrift as he followed the line of the invisible road, but shortly after moving onto the lake he had taken an irrevocable decision, plagued by the desperate shortage of time. So he had changed his mind and was now heading on a course which would take them along the diameter of the circle – straight over the centre of the lake.

The half-track was rumbling smoothly on, wobbling only

occasionally, a wobble which was probably only the natural sway of the unwieldy vehicle, although for Macomber it had an unpleasant similarity to the bowing of weakened ice under a great weight, when he noticed the paler colour of a huge area of ice towards the centre of the lake. His lips tightened – he was on course to cross directly over this strangely discoloured section. In early winter, when ice had formed, it must have formed first at the fringes along the shore before creeping inwards until eventually it had encompassed the entire lake. So the ice in the centre was the freshest, the youngest, probably the thinnest. The wheels were close to this distinctive section when he changed direction, steering a curve which would take him beyond this possibly treacherous zone. He only hoped to God he had turned in time, that he wasn't already moving over ice only a fraction of the thickness of what they had already crossed. With an effort he resisted the urge to reduce speed – the advantage now might lie in crossing this area as swiftly as possible – but he also resisted the succeeding temptation to increase his speed over ten miles an hour, since faster movement might intensify the danger.

The distant shoreline crawled nearer with agonizing slowness. The huge snow-covered bluff to their left where the rock rose vertically from the lake slid behind them as they drew level with the rampart walls of the monastery. And now Macomber saw that there was someone at the summit of the lofty tower which overlooked lake and sea, a tiny, faceless figure too minute to be identified as monk or German soldier, and the Scot blessed his foresight in arranging for the others to conceal themselves on the floor. The sun was low, casting the interior of the half-track in deep shadow, so even a lookout with field-glasses would see only a German half-track driven by one man, a man in a nondescript coat with an Alpenkorps cap rammed down over his head. You see what you want to see, Macomber told himself, so with luck a German lookout would see one of his own vehicles sent ahead to test the stability of the ice. He sucked in a deep breath of chilled mountain air to revive his flagging reserves. God he was tired, he was so damned tired! Within the next few seconds he was stirred into petrified alertness.

He was within two hundred yards of safety, coming closer to the shoreline where the road emerged from the snowdrift, when he felt the vehicle begin to tremble, saw the ice sheet ahead of him tilt and quiver prior to the moment of fracturing fatally, realized that the huge weight under him was beginning to drop ... His hands tightened on the wheel, his foot pressed down on the accelerator – reflex actions he was unaware of – and the sagging motion of the half-track quickened. He was speeding forward over the ice when he grasped what was happening – happening to him rather than to the vehicle: he was suffering a violent attack of giddiness. He leaned back hard against the seat, sucked in quick gulps of the pure air, felt his lungs expanding, his head clearing, and then he was closing the gap between lake and road, keeping his foot pressed down regardless and with only one idea in his mind – to get clear of this bloody lake come hell or high water. The wheels bumped over rock-hard ruts, the half-track drove forward through frosted grasses which broke off and scattered like pine needles as it moved onto the road, and it was soon ascending until it was lost from the view of the monastery under the leaning overhang of the bluff towering above them. Macomber pulled up, left the engine running and rested on the wheel. His eyes were still open when Prentice scrambled to his feet and laid a hand on his snow-covered shoulder.

'You've made it! Are you all right, Mac?'

'Give me a minute ... Look down there ...'

The words came out in gasps and while he struggled to get a grip on himself Prentice extracted the Monokular from his coat pocket and focused it out over the gulf. In the distance to the south a lean grey vessel was approaching with smoke streaming from its stack and a clear wake to stern. A British destroyer was heading for the peninsula. Her deck was crammed with troops and Prentice fancied he recognized the individualistic hats the Australians wore – Australians and some New Zealanders probably, steaming directly for Cape Zervos where the tortuous track led up the cliff face.

'It's packed with troops,' Prentice said quickly. 'Aussies and Kiwis. God, if only they'd get here in time.'

'They won't!' Macomber was recovering and he clambered

unsteadily out of the vehicle to stand by the lieutenant. 'Burckhardt should make it within the hour and . . .' He looked back at Grapos who was seated on a bench beside Ford. 'How long do you reckon it would take a man to come up that cliff track?'

'Three or four hours. It would depend on the man. Mules find it difficult.'

'There you are,' Macomber said grimly. 'And they haven't even landed yet – won't for a while. That's always assuming they're heading for the cape – they could easily be bound for Katyra.'

'Lord, no!' Prentice was appalled. 'If only we had a Verey pistol – or even a mirror.' He turned to the others. 'It would be just too damned convenient if anyone had a mirror, I suppose?'

It was too damned convenient; no one possessed a mirror. Macomber brushed snow off his leather coat and began walking stiffly downhill the way they had come, and every step jarred his cramped body, cramped with sitting behind the wheel, cramped with the tension of crossing the lake. Feeling as though at any moment he might keel over and fall in the snow, he reached the point where the road turned under the bluff to continue along the shore, and with Ford at his heels he came round the corner. He stopped abruptly, holding back the sergeant with his hand. 'There you are – that shows how much time we've got. Sweet Fanny Adams.' The bluff loomed above them, and above that rose the sheer climb of the monastery wall, terminating in the high tower which reared like a pinnacle in the sunlight. But it was across the lake where Macomber was staring, his face bleak as his lips chewed briefly. Round the flank of the snow-covered slope on the distant shore a small dark bug-like object was crawling forward. The first half-track had arrived already.

'You were right,' Prentice said tersely as he peered over their shoulders. 'Those chaps on the destroyer will never make it.'

Macomber turned round, talking as he started back towards the half-track, his weary feet scuffling through the snow. 'We'll go ahead with the plan exactly as we arranged. We've got to find some way of warning that destroyer – if they land men and start them up that track with Jerries in position at the top of it there'll be a massacre.'

'Burckhardt will know he can cross that ice when he sees our track marks,' Prentice called out, panting up behind him. The Scot had temporarily recovered his vitality, spurred on by the sight of Burckhardt's arrival, and he was moving uphill with rapid strides as he shouted over his shoulder. 'He'll see nothing. The wind has practically obliterated the marks we made, so he'll have to make his own recce. Which gives us extra time. Not bloody much of it, though.'

Taking a last quick look at the oncoming destroyer, he climbed back into the half-track, glanced to his rear to make sure they were all on board, and then began driving uphill. For a short distance the road fell away steeply to the west – to their right – where the mountain slope sheered down towards the wind-ruffled Aegean far below, while on their left the toppling wall of the bluff leaned over them. The road was deep with snow, soft snow from the recent fall, and streaks of whiteness smeared the bluff's wall. Across the gulf Macomber could see the ship-wrecking chain of rocks extending towards him from the mainland, ending in the saw-tooth which had so nearly destroyed the *Hydra*, and beyond the rocks he could see the mainland itself where Allied troops would be moving up the vital supply road. Then another rock wall closed off the view and they were ascending a narrow, twisting canyon on the last lap of their long journey to the monastery.

He had ascended perhaps two hundred feet, confined between the narrowing walls of the canyon which climbed vertically above them, when he saw a trail of cloud creeping over the road ahead, blotting out what lay beyond. Switching on his headlights, he reduced speed as they slipped inside the vaporous mist; ice-cold drizzle chilled his face and there was a sudden drop in temperature as he crawled round a bend and went up a steep incline. The headlights penetrated the cloud just sufficiently for him to see what was happening, to see where the road turned yet another bend as it spiralled up towards the summit of the bluff, and now water was starting to run down the snow-packed road and the snow itself was melting to slush.

He drove on up through the drifting cloud, feeling his clothes grow heavier as the damp clung to him, feeling the tracks slither once and then recover stability as they ground patiently upwards while he grew cold and miserable and sodden and it seemed as though the elements were flinging one final ordeal in his path almost within sight of their objective. Behind him the others had taken up position. Grapos stood at the rear of the vehicle, the Alpenkorps rope looped over his shoulder, while Prentice and Ford huddled on a bench close to him, their weapons gripped between their hands as they watched the Greek who stood facing the way they were going. Macomber turned another bend, saw the road levelling out, switched off his headlights, and heard the hammering of Grapos' rifle butt. The signal to halt.

He braked, left the engine running, and the tang of salt air was strong in his nostrils as the cloud began to thin and pale sunlight percolated through the haze. Grapos dropped off at the rear between the tracks and was followed by Prentice and Ford who went after him and vanished in the cloud. Behind the wheel, Macomber was wiping moisture off his watch-face while he timed five minutes exactly. The mistiness, which would have masked his onslaught until the last moment, was receding rapidly as the cloud left the peninsula and floated out over the gulf. He grimaced, saw ahead the final rise in the road which hid him from the monastery, checked his watch again. At four minutes and thirty seconds the cloud had dispersed completely, but again that would have been too damned convenient. Now for the break-in, the final effort – with everything staked on one vicious surprise attack.

With the cloud gone he was bathed in the cold bright sunlight of winter and he could see the Aegean to his right, but rising ground shielded the destroyer from view; he could see the stark triangle of Mount Zervos, a peak of whiteness where the light caught the snow crystals, but the monastery was still invisible; and he could see the deep, trench-like gulley along which Grapos had led the other two men, but they had disappeared. He checked his watch: ten seconds to go. Reaching inside his pocket he dragged out the Luger from the sodden

224

folds and laid it on the seat beside him. Five seconds left. His hand clutched the brake, waited, released it. He was off.

He accelerated rapidly, mounted the rise, crested it. The road ran straight to the monastery which rose up less than two hundred yards away. He took in the impression in a flash. The towers and the wall linking them were lower on this side. The greenish shell of a dome, which he remembered was the church, showed beyond the wall-top. The ancient gatehouse, a tumble-down wooden structure which appeared to lean back against the stone for support, was in the centre of the wall. Three or four storeys up wooden box-like structures were attached to the stonework, protruding from the wall like giant dovecotes, each structure faced with tall shutters which led out to a small balcony. The ground between the crest and the monastery was bare and level with huge boulders strewn close to the left-hand section of the monastery. Mid-way to the gatehouse he swerved off the road, crossing open ground in a sweeping half-circle, which brought him back on the road again with the half-track's rear presented to the monastery. So far he had seen no sign of life and the place had a derelict look. He changed gear, began reversing towards the closed gate which barred his way, twisting round in his seat as he kept one eye on the road, another on the gateway rushing towards him as he built up speed and the monastery came closer and closer.

He saw out of the corner of his eye movement on the roofed-in, railed walk which spanned the first floor of the gatehouse, the movement of a field-grey figure steadying himself as he took aim, and he knew something had gone fatally wrong. The Alpenkorps cap was not enough to make the German pause, or had he spotted one of the others at the last moment – Macomber had no idea which – but he knew that within seconds the German would open fire, that he must ignore the threat of almost certain death, that the rifle would be discharged at point-blank range if the man had the sense to wait only a few seconds longer when he couldn't possibly miss, firing down from his elevated position at a target moving rapidly closer under his gunsight.

During the final rush up to the closed gates Macomber became aware of everything around him – the snow-covered ground where rocks poked up through the whiteness, the shabbiness of the small balconies where decrepit paint exposed the mellow woodwork, the open-necked collar of the Alpenkorps soldier on the gatehouse who was steadying himself against the wall as he aimed his rifle, the rotting timbers of the large double gates, the mildewed-looking dome of the church vanishing from view as the wall rose up and screened it, the high-powered throb of the engine, the metallic grind of the whirling tracks . . .

He heard the report of the rifle above these sounds, a sharp crack, the first shot fired in the coming encounter – the shot fired by Grapos from behind a large boulder. The German on the balcony was stood immediately over the roadway and he staggered forward as the bullet penetrated, reached out a hand to steady himself on the frail balcony rail, sagged forward with his full weight, which was too much for the support, and he fell through it at the moment the half-track smashed through the gates, tearing both loose from the upper hinges so they toppled inwards and the vehicle stormed over them and continued reversing under the archway and into the vast courtyard beyond. Macomber blinked with relief, heard something thud down behind him, glanced back swiftly and saw the dead German folded over the second bench. The half-track roared on inside a stone-paved square which was larger than he remembered it, a square with a plane tree in the centre, the church to the right, an ancient stone well beyond the tree – a square large enough to accommodate a small army, overlooked on all sides by windows and arcaded walks which ran round the inner walls at each floor level. The vehicle was charging towards the tree when he reduced speed, changed gear, went forward and began thundering round the square, turning the wheel erratically as though the half-track had gone berserk. His Alpenkorps cap was prominently on view, as was the German soldier behind him, a soldier impossible to identify from his crumpled position. Macomber completed one circuit, heard the sound of shots, described a wild S-bend tour round the church and reappeared suddenly from the other side as he headed into the square again and accelerated afresh. For anyone inside the monastery the speeding half-track had become a hypnotic focal point – a focal point to divert their attention for vital seconds from what might be happening elsewhere.

When Grapos jumped from the stationary half-track as the cloud dispersed from the bluff he plunged straight into the gulley leading away from the road and towards the monastery, a ravine seven feet deep which hid the hurrying men from any possible observation from the monastery walls. He ran forward in a crouch, his rifle between his hands, the rope looped from his shoulder. He was heading for one of the towers which protruded out from the wall, so that the side farthest from the gatehouse formed a right-angled corner which couldn't be seen from that direction. Behind him came Prentice with Ford close at his heels. The staff-sergeant's shoulder still throbbed with a dull ache but he could use the lower part of his arm and, more important still, he could use his machine-pistol if he held it awkwardly.

Close to the wall, Grapos paused and lifted himself half-out of the gulley at a point where a large boulder hid him from the gatehouse. This was the position he must take up to cover Macomber when he had arranged the ascent of his companions. Dropping back into the gulley, he ran forward again and clambered out where the ravine ended at the base of the wall. They were now hemmed in by the corner, invisible from the farther extension of the wall unless someone came out onto a balcony. Ford took up a position where he could observe the receding wall while the lieutenant gazed upwards, his machine-pistol hoisted. It took Grapos less than a minute to prepare the rope for throwing, a rope weighted at the tip by the metal hook, and when he hurled it upwards and inwards the hook trapped itself on the floor of the projecting side-balcony twenty feet above them. Taking a long breath, Grapos jumped up the rope, held on, swayed briefly like a pendulum as he tested its resistance, then dropped to the ground again and glared at Prentice.

'It is good – but you must be quick. You remember the way?'

'Perfectly!' Prentice glanced at his watch, looped the machine-pistol over his shoulder, began to climb the rope hand over hand, his legs stiffened, his boots pressed against the roughened stonework as he half-hauled, half-walked himself up towards the balcony. The shaky structure trembled a little under his progress, but he ignored the warning of its instability, climbing faster as he got the hang of the ascent. If the bloody thing came down, it came down. Neck or nothing now. His face eased up to balcony level and he saw the hook firmly embedded between the open floor-boards. One final heave and he was clutching the shaky rail, hauling himself over the top, standing on the floor with the closed shutters behind him. He propped the machine-pistol against a post where he could reach it easily, looked over, saw that Ford had already tied the rope round his body and under his armpits. As he started to haul up the sergeant Grapos was slipping back inside the gulley and running along it to take up position behind the boulder.

Hauling up Ford proved strenuous: the sergeant tried to help by splaying his feet against the wall, but he was unable to lift himself by his hands which were concentrated on gripping the rope, so the lieutenant had to haul up his full weight length by length, the rope taut over the balcony rail which was shuddering under the pressure, the floor quivering under his feet as Grapos' warning flashed through his mind. 'The balcony has not been used for many years because it is dangerous...' Sweating profusely, his arms almost strained from their sockets, his legs trembling with the arduous exertion, Prentice saw a tangle of dark hair appear, a hand grasp the floor edge, and then the railing gave way, collapsed inwards like broken matchwood. He jerked in more rope, his back pressed hard into the shutters, his feet driving into the floor as he heaved desperately and Ford was half-dragged, half-scrambled his way through the smashed rail and ended up on his knees on the balcony. The sergeant was still recovering his breath, blood was still oozing from his left hand where the wood had gashed it, while Prentice untied the rope, released him from it, and then dropped the rope end down to the ground for Grapos to use later. 'All right, Ford?' he croaked, leaning against the shutters as he reached out for the machine-pistol.

'Just like the obstacle course at Chester, sir.' He stood up

228

cautiously and unlooped his own weapon. 'But maybe I need a refresher course. We'd better get inside – I can hear Mac coming.'

The clattering rattle of the approaching half-track was in their ears as Prentice dealt with the process of getting in. He used his machine-pistol butt to club the latch and the wood-work splintered swiftly under his third blow. Without realizing that the shutters opened outwards, he used his shoulder to go through them, head tucked well in as he rammed his body against and through the breaking shutters with such force that the impetus took him half-way across the room before he could pull up. He hardly saw the room: faded religious murals on the stone walls, a cloth-covered table, an ikon; then he reached the varnished door and opened it with great care. The musty odours of the unused room were in his nostrils as he peered both ways along a deserted corridor and from beyond the balcony he heard the grumble of the oncoming half-track. They'd cut the timing pretty fine. Beckoning to Ford, he ran down the passage to his left. It was like running through a cloister – wooden archways at intervals and large windows to his right which looked down on the square below – and the only sound in the monastic silence, now the walls had muffled the half-track's approach, was the sound of his clumping boots as he ran full tilt for the staircase at the end. He paused briefly when he arrived at the corner, looked to his right where another deserted corridor ran along the second side, glanced up the empty staircase and ran up it, turning at a landing before running up the second flight. On the second floor an identical view faced him – corridors stretching away from the corner in two directions. To his right, at the far end, Ford, who had just emerged from his own staircase, raised a thumb. Prentice returned the signal and went over to the nearest window, hid himself behind a section of the wall and waited.

In less than thirty seconds he saw the half-track coming backwards into the yard, but gave the vehicle only a brief glance as his eyes searched the windows across the square at different levels. His waiting time was very short – the half-track had entered the square, had reversed direction and started driving forwards round the square below them when a

229

window opposite opened and two German soldiers leaned out to stare down at the half-track's mad career round the square. Prentice raised his machine-pistol, thrust the muzzle sharply through the glass, and the shattering noise was lost in the long burst as he sprayed the window steadily, saw the Germans crumple and disappear as movement higher up caught his eye. Through an open window on the top floor another German was aiming his rifle downwards at Prentice when Ford's machine-pistol opened up with a murderous rattle, one much shorter burst, short but lethal. The German with the rifle lost his weapon and followed it down into the yard below as Macomber sped towards the church. A burst of answering fire from farther along the top floor hammered Prentice's shattered window as he jumped back behind the wall. He heard Ford's weapon replying as something moved behind him. He swung his gun round, knowing the magazine was almost empty, and the muzzle pointed at Grapos who froze at the top of the stairs. He must have come up the rope like a charge of electricity.

The explosion came as Prentice, inserting a fresh magazine, was grinning crookedly at Grapos. The grenade landed midway along the corridor between Ford and the lieutenant, but Grapos had seen it fly in through a window and was sheltered behind the staircase. 'Jesus, this is getting rough,' Prentice muttered half to himself. He knocked a shard of glass from his sleeve, staring down at the Greek who stood with his rifle and the rope looped afresh over his shoulder, and started to move round the corner into the next corridor. Ford, protected by a section of wall, was firing again across the yard as the German on the top floor opposite changed tactics. He must have assumed that there were men spread along the side corridor because suddenly a stream of bullets began shattering every window along the passage Prentice was about to move into. Glass was strewn over the floor, bullets scarred the inner wall while the lieutenant, safe behind the wall in the next corridor he shared with Ford, waited for the barrage to cease. The next grenade landed closer to Ford, sent a fresh shock wave in both directions, and for the first time Prentice grasped what was happening.

A German had entered the corridor below them. Knowing the enemy was on the floor above, he hadn't risked coming up a staircase: instead he was leaning out of a lower window while he tossed grenades upwards and inside the second-floor windows. It was only a matter of time before he chose the right aperture for his deadly missiles. Prentice hesitated, reviewing the situation. Macomber couldn't fire on the German while he was driving the half-track round the square at that pace, and the plan called for him to keep up this diversion whatever happened. The fusillade along the next corridor ceased briefly and Grapos called out, 'I will deal with him...' He gestured along the corridor and then downwards, took out his knife and ran down the passage before disappearing inside a room mid-way along the building.

The room which the Greek had entered also had a balcony, and it was towards this he ran after closing the door as a precaution against a grenade landing in the entrance. Thrusting open the shutters, he went into the sunlight and the firing in the square was muffled to a quiet rattle. It took him a matter of seconds to jam the hook down between the floorboards, to throw the rope over the edge, then he was slipping down the rope which dangled past the first-floor balcony below. His boots scraped the rail, felt their way inside it, and he slithered the last few feet on to the balcony. Inserting his knife blade between the ill-fitting shutters, he forced up the latch, fingered open the left-hand shutter gently and went inside the half-darkened room. The inner door was closed and he listened with his ear pressed against its panel for several seconds before gripping the handle with his left hand. The right hand held the knife ready for throwing as he eased the handle to the open position, stood to the opening side of the door and flung it back against the wall. When he went into the corridor he saw that the lone German had changed his position and was standing by the window below where Prentice was sheltering. The German had a grenade ready for throwing when he saw Grapos, changed his mind instantly, and hoisted it for a throw straight down the corridor. The knife left Grapos, sped along the passage, struck the soldier a second before he threw. He staggered, dropped the grenade, crashed into a window, one hand clutching his arm. The grenade detonated at his feet.

Macomber, hearing bullets ricocheting off a bench behind him, had driven the half-truck behind the church. His role as a diversion was over and it was time to give a hand with his Luger, so he drove out once more, pressed his foot down and headed for the ramp leading up into the arcaded walk on the eastern side of the square, the side where most of the Germans had appeared earlier. The half-track surged forward at an angle across the square and he was turning the wheel as he went up the ramp, swung round into the corridor, and realized too late it was a fraction narrow for the passage of the vehicle he had intended driving the full length of the arcade. The ground floor was enclosed from the square by a railing only and it was the left-hand caterpillar which encountered this railing, churning it to pieces as it rasped its way forward. The first stone pillar it met was the obstacle it refused to overcome; instead the track parted company with the vehicle, disengaged itself completely and whipped across the square as an intact ring. Macomber had braked at the moment of impact and he jumped over the windscreen, landing on the bonnet and sliding off on to the floor as the vehicle settled at a drunken angle. The engine sputtered and died. He wondered why there was no more shooting.

After waiting a minute, he hobbled slowly along the corridor and stopped at a short flight of steps leading down into the square at a point half-way along the arcade. Shattered windows everywhere, some starred with pieces still intact. And no sound of gunfire. The silence which had descended on the monastery seemed uncanny as he saw Ford peering out from the second floor, risking a quick look-round before withdrawing his head with equal abruptness. Macomber waited a little longer, but there was no sign of the enemy except for the crumpled figure in Alpenkorps uniform which had toppled from the fourth floor early in the battle. The German in the half-track had long ago been thrown to the floor by one of the Scot's wilder swerves. Still cautious, he made his way along the arcade, turned the corner at the bottom, and walked along the second side. Grapos met him at the foot of the staircase and nodded towards an impressive figure standing a few steps up. A man as tall as Macomber, a vigorous seventy-year-old, he was dressed in the long robes and the flat-topped hat of a dignitary of the Greek Orthodox Church. It was the Abbot of Zervos.

'I found him locked inside his room on the second floor,' Grapos whispered as Prentice appeared on the stairs behind the Abbot.

Macomber spoke in English, remembering from his visit five years earlier that the Abbot understood this language, and he wanted the lieutenant to hear what was said. 'We need information quickly, Father. How many Germans are there here?'

'There were ten men,' the Abbot began crisply. 'They arrived by car yesterday evening disguised as civilians, but they had their uniforms with them. There were three cars...'

'Just a moment, please.' Macomber held up his hand and looked at Prentice. 'Any idea how many you've accounted for yet?'

'Seven,' the lieutenant replied. 'I've been round the building with Ford and checked...'

'Eight then, including that frozen lookout – or nine with the man on the gatehouse...'

'*Seven*,' Prentice repeated firmly. 'I've included both those Jerries in my count...'

'There are three men on the north tower,' the Abbot intervened urgently, crossing himself. 'Captain Braun, who commands this unit, spends a lot of time up there with two other men. They have organized an observation post on the roof of the tower and I think they are watching the mainland road. They have a telescope, a wireless transmitter and a mortar gun...'

'A mortar!' Macomber looked up the staircase at Ford who had come round the corner with his machine-pistol tucked under his good shoulder. Despite his wound he looked the coolest man in the group as he stopped and listened to the Scot's question. 'Ford, could a mortar on that high tower cause the destroyer any trouble?'

233

'It depends. If it's an 8-cm job like the ones I saw on the plateau things could get pretty sticky. Mind you, the range would have to be right and the mortar man would have to be good – but being in the Wehrmacht he probably is. If he's damned lucky and drops a bomb down the stack into the boiler-room – well, you saw what happened to the *Hydra*...'

'We'd better get up there bloody quick,' Macomber snapped. He turned to Grapos. 'You know the way up, so get us up there ...'

The Abbot intervened again, fingering the crucifix suspended from his neck. 'This is a holy place and should never have become a battlefield, but the Germans have only themselves to blame and they have invaded my country. Captain Braun has taken over my bedroom on the fourth floor as his office – Grapos will show you the room I mean – so he may be inside there rather than on the tower.'

'I doubt it – after all this shooting.' Macomber frowned and thought for a moment. 'On the other hand none of you have been seen in the square since the firing stopped, so Braun may just have assumed we've all been wiped out.' He looked again at the Abbot and spoke quietly but firmly. 'And now I want you to go back to your room on the second floor and stay there, whatever happens.' He was following Grapos up to the first landing when he turned for a final word with the Abbot. 'What's happened to all the monks who live here?'

'They have been locked up inside the refectory – across there.' The Abbot pointed across the square towards the church. 'There is plenty of room for them ...'

'So it's best they stay there for the moment,' Macomber broke in briskly. 'Wait here until we've gone and then go to your room, please.' He turned to Grapos. 'There are only three of them but this could be the most dangerous job of the lot. Let's get going.'

They ascended to the third floor without incident and Macomber led the way with the Greek one step below him. The Scot was desperately worried about what might happen if the destroyer came within range before they reached the tower, but he still went up cautiously, pausing at each landing to listen carefully, climbing the stairs like the others on the soles of his boots, so they made very little sound as they approached the fourth floor. Macomber had reached the landing, was about to peer round the corner, when he heard footsteps coming along the top floor. Gesturing to the others below, he waited. The footsteps arrived at the top of the staircase, then faded. Macomber ran up the last flight, saw an empty corridor stretching away, a short passage to his left, an iron-studded door in the stone wall at the end of the passage, a door which must lead to the tower and which was open. He went silently down the short passage and listened at the open door, looking up a stone spiral which vanished round a corner in the gloom. He arrived just in time to hear someone hammering sharply on a wooden surface in a certain way, a signal which doubtless identified the new arrival. Metal scraped over metal as a bolt was withdrawn, nailed boots climbed the last few steps, a trap-door slammed shut and the bolt rasped home again.

'Who was it?' Grapos whispered in his ear while Prentice and Ford kept a watch on the corridors. Macomber waved a hand to make the Greek shut up and started up the spiral, feeling his way in the darkness with his hand on the roughened wall. The steps were dangerously narrow, fading into nothingness at the inner edge, and when his head touched something he knew he was at the top. He retreated down several steps and switched on his torch. The trap-door was a massive slab of wood, so close-fitting that no hint of daylight had shown through in the darkness. We'll never break through that, he thought, and went back down the spiral.

'We can't shoot our way up on to the roof,' Macomber informed them quietly, 'there's a trap-door like a piece of teak up there. Prentice, let's take a quick look at the Abbot's bedroom and see what drags the brave captain – if it is Braun – out into the open. Ford, you stay here while Grapos watches the lower stairs. If someone starts coming down this spiral, join Grapos, and we'll take care of ourselves.'

They approached the bedroom tentatively in case a guard had been left inside, but the room was empty. The windows looked out over the mountain and the only furniture was an austere bed, a wooden table and a chair. A wireless transmitter rested on the table with a pair of headphones laid neatly behind it close to the chair. 'So that's it,' Macomber commented. 'He's transmitting to Burckhardt from here now. He must have found the roof inconvenient. I'm damned sure he thinks we've all been killed – he hasn't even locked the door.'

'Couldn't,' Prentice pointed out laconically. 'There's no keyhole. Do you think he'll be back?' He was looking out of the window but the wall of the tower cut off any view down to the lake.

'I hope so. It's our only chance of getting up to that tower roof. I'd give anything now for a ten-kilogram demolition charge. Placed under that trap-door it would blow the whole roof into the lake. We'll have to work something simple out in case he does come down again. I expect he might – those headphones look as though he's expecting to use them again in the near future.'

This time Macomber let Prentice make arrangements for Braun's reception because he wanted to hold himself in reserve for what he proposed to attempt if Braun came down again. While Ford watched the staircase, Prentice and Grapos took up ambush station on either side of the doorway leading up to the spiral. Macomber waited at the end of the stone passage with his Luger ready for an emergency. It was a simple-seeming operation like this which could so easily go wrong. They waited and the minutes passed as Macomber wondered whether Braun was now permanently stationed on the roof, whether having radioed a warning of the attack on the monastery he was now going to sit tight until the first half-tracks poured into the square below. Or would he venture once more down the spiral to send a further message about the destroyer's progress? In the silence he heard his wrist-watch ticking and then he heard something else.

Something which thudded hollowly from the interior of the spiral. The trap-door had been opened very quietly this time, had then been closed with less sound than previously. Macomber stared down the passage to where Grapos waited pressed against the wall, his knife held by his side, to where Prentice waited on the other side of the doorway, his forehead moist although the temperature was low inside the stone passage. There was a long pause when they heard nothing and Prentice began to think it was a false alarm, but the Scot thought differently and could almost sense the presence of someone listening inside the spiral before he came out. Then a boot scraped over stone, the muzzle of a machine-pistol stabbed out of the doorway and a uniformed captain of the Alpenkorps came out behind it. Prentice grabbed with both hands as Grapos lunged with the knife, but the German swung round with a swift reaction which made Macomber take a step forward. The lieutenant had one hand pressed over his mouth, the other locked round his throat when the German swung so unexpectedly, tearing the hand free from his throat. Grapos had little better success when his knife hit the wrong target, was deflected along the barrel of the machine-pistol and skidded over the German's hand, which made him let go of the weapon but had no disabling effect. The German flung his whole weight on Prentice, catching the freed hand between himself and the bare wall, and the lieutenant thought his knuckles were broken as Grapos lunged a second time and the knife went home. Braun sagged, collapsed on the floor, and when Macomber checked his pulse he felt nothing. Captain Braun had become a permanent casualty.

'I'm going straight up,' Macomber said quickly. 'We're running out of time and they may think Braun's forgotten something if I go up now. Grapos, if I can get that trap opened, can get even half-way on to the roof, you follow...'

He was mid-way up the spiral when the pain caught him across the back, a sharp stabbing pain which locked him immovably for several seconds: he must have twisted something when he'd leapt out of the half-track. He suppressed a groan, felt Grapos bump into him, and forced himself up the last few steps. With the Luger in his right hand, his fingers felt the trap-door to check his whereabouts, then he rapped confidently on the underside of the lid in a certain way, the way Braun had rapped. There was a pause, long drawn-out moments when he thought the stratagem hadn't worked, followed by a rattling sound as the bolt was withdrawn.

It went wrong at once. The trap-door opened slowly and there was no one to shoot at as daylight flooded down into the spiral.

When the gap was wide enough he ran up the last few steps, aware of an unforeseen handicap – the trap was being opened from behind him by someone he couldn't see. He reached the stone-paved roof and half-turned round, only to find himself again temporarily immobilized in that position by the fierce pain which seared his back and cramped his movement, making it impossible for him to aim the Luger at the kneeling corporal who slammed down the trap and pushed the bolt home. The falling slab of wood had struck Grapos on the shoulder, leaving Macomber isolated on the roof with the two Germans. The corporal, still on his knees, was reaching for a pistol lying on the stones beside him when Macomber threw his Luger. The weapon smashed into the corporal's temple and he fell over sideways, his fingers still closed over the pistol as he lay still, facing the sky with his eyes open. The other soldier had been standing by the wall looking out over the gulf when Macomber came onto the roof, his body crouched as he pressed his eye to a powerful field-telescope mounted on a tripod, while close by a short, squat-barrelled mortar was set up on its own tripod near a pile of snub-nosed shells. Heavily built, the German's open collar exposed a thick neck, and he was only taken by surprise for a few seconds, then he dropped to his knees and began tugging furiously to free something caught under the canvas which cushioned the mortar bombs. It came free as Macomber wrenched himself into action and reached him.

The German, still on his knees, swung round with the machine-pistol and the Scot grabbed at the muzzle in midswing. Instead of pulling at the weapon, which the German expected, he pushed viciously and the soldier lost balance, letting go of the gun as he fell over backwards, but his elbows saved him from sprawling over the floor. Still in pain, Macomber made a mistake, thinking he had enough time to reverse the weapon and get a grip on it. He was still fumbling when the German came to his feet and went for his throat, and the momentum of his charge carried Macomber back against the waist-high tower wall. He couldn't even attempt to use the gun which was compressed between their bodies as they grappled fiercely and Macomber felt himself being pushed remorselessly backwards over the brink. The soldier was a few inches shorter but he was in prime condition and ten years younger, and the Scot was very close to the end of his physical resources. With the gun penned between them, the German had both hands locked tightly round Macomber's throat and now, as his back arched over the wall screamed with pain, he felt his air supply going. A momentary panic gripped him as he started to tip over the drop, the rim of the wall hard against the small of his back and acting as a fulcrum for the German to lever him down to the lake far below.

Knowing that he was winning, the soldier ignored the gun, squeezing his hands tighter and tighter as Macomber's face changed colour. The Scot's hands still held the machine-pistol and he managed to force it sideways, but he still couldn't use it. Had the German continued his pressure he would have sent Macomber over the edge within seconds, but he saw the gun come loose and released his right hand to grab at it, confident that the Scot was done for. And Macomber was almost done for – the German was holding his throat with only one hand but he had quickly inserted his thumb into the Scot's windpipe and his victim began to choke. Get rid of the gun! The message raced through Macomber's brain and he jerked feebly but with just sufficient force to snatch it out of the hand clutching the dangling strap. He let go and the machine-pistol disappeared over the edge.

As the thumb pressure increased reddish lights sputtered in front of his eyes and he felt his last remaining strength ebbing away. This was it. Nothing else left. His right hand fluttered, felt hair at the moment when the German's nailed boot ground down his instep. Pain shrieked up his leg like an electric shock and he was seized with a spasm of blind fury which sent fresh adrenalin through his veins. He grabbed a large handful of hair, clawed his hand, twisted it and dragged it sideways with all the energy he could muster, hauling at the hair as though to tear it out by the roots. The thumb pressure slackened, was released. Macomber sucked in a gasping lungful of cold mountain air, knowing that within seconds the brawny German would recover. Releasing the hair, he clawed his hand again and, as the soldier's face reappeared, he struck. The savagery of the onslaught unnerved the German and he propelled himself backwards away from the wall to save his face, catching the heel of his boot on an uplifted stone. He was fighting to restore his balance when Macomber's bull-like charge, head down, punched into his stomach, driving him headlong across the roof. The Scot was following him when his right foot tangled with a leg of the telescope's tripod and he crashed forward on his chest as the telescope toppled, broke away from its tripod and rolled over the roof. Macomber had hauled himself up on all fours, his chin sticky with blood where it had grazed the stones, when he saw that the wall had saved his opponent. The German had slapped his hands hard down on the wall-top to halt his momentum when Macomber, close to him, whipped a hand round his right ankle and lifted. The German made his second mistake. Acting by reflex, still off-balance, still groggy from the pile-driving blow in the stomach, he lifted his other foot to kick Macomber in the face. Elbow hard into the roof, the Scot hoisted as high as he could, no more than a few inches, but a fraction more of the German's weight was now poised over the brink than over the roof. The imprisoned foot jerked upwards out of Macomber's grasp of its own volition and the soldier was propelled outwards and downwards as the Scot climbed to his feet. The scream came up as a fading wail and he was just in time to see the minute spread-eagled figure strike the ice hundreds of feet below.

Using the wall for support, he made his way over to the trapdoor, kicking out of the way an opened notebook, the book they had used to record the passage of Allied supplies up the mainland road. Stooping painfully, be pulled back the bolt, but he let them open it, and when the lid lifted it was being raised by Grapos, with Ford below and Prentice bringing up the rear. It was the staff-sergeant who made the first comment. Seeing the crumpled corporal lying on his back he stared curiously at Macomber. 'We didn't think we'd see you alive again, but I thought there were two of them.'

'One went over the side ... you'd better look down here quick.' He was still holding on to the wall support and he looked haggard as he gently massaged his throat and stared down at the lake. 'Burckhardt's nearly here ...'

Burckhardt had moved with great speed: his force was already arrayed and moving far out onto the lake, so that as the Scot gazed down from the great height of the tower he had the sensation of watching a diorama in a war museum. Six half-tracks, spread out widely over the ice like toy models, led the advance, followed by Alpenkorps and parachutists on foot. Farther back more half-tracks crawled forward and each of the weird vehicles carried only its driver – to minimize casualties if the ice broke at any point Burckhardt had shrewdly emptied the half-tracks of all superfluous passengers. Several light ack-ack guns and 75-mm mountain howitzers, unlimbered from the half-tracks which had hauled them up the mountain road, were being drawn bodily over the ice, two men to a gun, and Macomber noticed that round all the vehicles and guns there were unoccupied areas of frozen lake – the men on foot were nervous of the weight this equipment was imposing on the lake's surface. The sense of looking down on a scale model was heightened by the heavy silence which had fallen over the mountain as the wind dropped, and no sound of the advancing army reached the watchers on the tower. Macomber looked at the staff-sergeant who was also gazing down at the threatening spectacle.

'Any hope at all, Ford – by using the mortar? It is an 8-cm, isn't it?'

'Yes. You mean break the ice under them? We can try, but I can't feed the mortar with this shoulder.' He looked across at Prentice who was nursing his swollen right hand. 'And neither can he. Grapos' shoulder is temporarily numbed from the blow it took from that trap-door.' He looked doubtfully at Macomber, who instinctively straightened up from the wall. 'Can you cope?'

'I'll have to. And we'd better get moving.'

Macomber looked back out to sea. The mounting crisis was of the worst possible magnitude. The destroyer had turned to come in closer, to steam directly for the cape, and within a matter of minutes it would have vanished under the lee of the peninsula prior to commencing landing operations. If Burck-hardt reached the monastery he would not only have achieved his objective – he would be in a position to slaughter those

241

troops as they wound their way up the cliff-face track. What on earth had warned Athens that something was wrong? He dismissed the question as academic and began a quick count of the snub-nosed shells lying half covered with canvas while they waited to service the mortar. Thirty bombs. It didn't seem many, not nearly enough. He rammed his last cigar into his mouth and chewed at it as Ford, the calmest man on the roof, stood by the parapet, turning his face sideways to gauge the strength of the fading breeze, screwing up his eyes against the sun as he estimated distances and trajectories. While they waited for the staff-sergeant to complete his calculations Macomber helped Prentice to fix his hand in a makeshift sling with the aid of his scarf, a hand which was swelling ominously, and he watched Burckhardt's progress tensely as he attended the injury. The half-tracks were crawling steadily forward like mechanical bugs – bugs which were now almost two-thirds of the distance across the lake as they approached the road up to the monastery. And even from the great height he looked down on them, Macomber could at last hear a faint purring sound travelling up through the cold mountain air, the purr of engines and caterpillar tracks grinding over the ice.

'That must be Burckhardt – in that car.' Prentice had looked up after testing the sling, and Macomber focused his glass quickly to where the lieutenant had pointed with his good hand. A compact open car, strangely shaped, was driving over the ice slowly as it reached a position mid-way between the distant shore and the leading half-tracks. Ford left the wall, lurching unsteadily towards the mortar as he made his comment.

'It will be a Kubelwagen. The car, I mean. Looks a bit like a squashed bucket close up – they'd bring that in by glider. Now, I need your help, Mac.'

First, they had to move the mortar, to drag it round away from the sea so that its muzzle aimed out over the lake, and then Ford, with considerable difficulty, cradled a bomb in his arms and showed Macomber what he must do. 'There are three basic things to remember – don't put a bomb down the barrel nose first, or else we can all say good-bye; slide it in – don't push; and keep your hands out of the way afterwards if you want to hang on to them. I'll try and give you a demonstration, and then you're on your own – I've got to be by the wall to see what's happening . . .'

'They're going up the mountain, too!' Prentice, who had again borrowed the Scot's Monokular, was focused on a point beyond the bluff as he shouted out. Colonel Burckhardt was proving himself an excellent tactician and was leaving nothing to chance: the greater portion of his force was assembled on the lake, but beyond the distant shore two straggled lines of dots were ascending the lower slope of Mount Zervos itself as ski troops made for the monastery by a different route. Seeing those two lines climbing higher, already disappearing behind the bluff, Macomber guessed the route they would follow. The southern shore of the lake was blocked by the bluff climbing vertically from the water's edge, but ski troops could ascend to a point above the bluff and then cross the mountain slope above it, until they reached a position where they could ski downwards over a slope which ended close to the monastery entrance. The snowbound mountain had an overloaded look above the bluff and Grapos, who also guessed at their route, spoke grimly.

'They will need care and luck up there.'

'Why?' demanded Macomber.

'The thaw is coming – the time for the mountain to move.'

'You mean an avalanche?'

'Yes.'

'We'll worry about them later.'

Ford completed his demonstration for the Scot's benefit. Replacing the bomb on the canvas, he then crouched down to make a careful adjustment to the angle of fire, went quickly back to the wall to check the target, and returned to the mortar to adjust it again. Macomber, in a rising fever of impatience to get the thing firing, also went briefly to the wall for a final appraisal. The Kubelwagen was moving closer to the front line, halting frequently for a few seconds, presumably while Burckhardt had a word with his troops. The six half-tracks in front were now three-quarters of the way across the lake and within minutes they would have reached firm ground. Feeling automatically for a match to light his cigar, he brought out his hand empty; this was going to be tricky enough as it was without smoke getting in his eyes. He went back to the mortar, checked to make sure that the blood on his hand was dried, wiped both hands briskly on his handkerchief, and then stooped to lift the first bomb as Ford took up position by the parapet and warned Prentice and Grapos to stay in their corners.

Prentice had the best view, squeezed into the north-east corner where he looked down on the entire lake. The first bomb went away seconds later, soaring out over the wall, diminishing rapidly in size as it described an arc and landed on the ice ahead of the leading half-tracks. Prentice's teeth were clenched with anxiety as he watched its fall. He saw a brief spurt of snow where the projectile hit. Then nothing happened. Nothing. His eyes met Ford's as the sergeant pressed his hands harder on the wall, his face expressionless.

'It didn't go off,' said Prentice bitterly.

'No. It must have been a dud. Let's hope the whole batch isn't. I hear there's a lot of sabotage in German factories.' He looked over his shoulder at Macomber who stood ready with a fresh bomb, gave a brief order. 'Fire!' The second bomb was away, vanishing to a pinhead. It landed close to the dud, followed by the sound of detonation, a burst of snow. Prentice swore out loud. The ice had remained intact. Was it too solid for penetration? The fear was in all their minds and Prentice's hopes hadn't been high from the beginning. 'Fire!' Ford had rushed to the mortar to make a fractional adjustment before returning to the wall and giving the order. The third bomb soared through its parabola, curved to its descent. It landed close to the leading half-tracks and the distant thump echoed back to the tower as snow flew in the air with the burst of the bomb. An area of black shadow fissured the lake as ice cracked and disintegrated and water opened up under three half-tracks. 'Fire!' The fourth bomb spread the fracturing process as the three half-tracks disappeared almost simultaneously. One moment they were there and then they were gone, swallowed up as a new lake spread, a lake of ice-cold water. Over fifty metres deep, Grapos had said. So the half-tracks were now settling one hundred and fifty feet below the lake's surface. 'Fire!' Ford had made a further minor adjustment before he rushed back to the wall, his head thrust forward as he scanned the whole lake and Macomber, already drenched in sweat, fed in a fresh bomb. At this stage even Prentice, who could see everything happening, had not grasped the magnitude of the plan the precise Ford had devised for the destruction of the entire German force.

The fifth bomb sped out over the wall, almost too fast for the eye to follow, descended, struck the lake in the middle of the three surviving half-tracks closest to Zervos. Another spray of snow flashed upwards, another thump reached the distant tower, and then a huge area of ice cracked. Prentice gazed in astonishment as a sheet of ice became a temporary island separated from the rest of the frozen lake, a sheet supporting the three half-tracks and a group of Alpenkorps gathered behind them. The island's existence was momentary. The sheet fissured in all directions, broke up and sank. With the Monokular screwed hard against his eye, Prentice saw one half-track at the outer edge of the ice go down, wheels first, the tracks tilting upwards into the air, and then the whole vehicle slid out of sight under the ink-dark water which had appeared. The chances of a single man surviving in those sub-zero waters was nil. 'Fire!' The next bomb landed farther to the right, just reaching the ragged rim of the still-intact ice, detonating while still above the water-line. Figures beyond the rim were thrown into confusion, some falling and some scattering in a hopeless search for safety. The whole ordered array on the lake was beginning to change, to falter, to break up into a vast disorganized chaos as Ford increased the rate of attack, frequently adjusting direction or angle or both as Macomber, the pain in his back now stabbing at him non-stop, his clothes sodden with sweat, his bruised body protesting with growing aches, worked away methodically stooping, grasping, lifting, feeding the barrel.

'Fire!' This bomb travelled much farther, the zenith of its parabola far higher above the lake, the descent point more distant. Prentice pressed the Monokular into his eye, focusing it on the Kubelwagen. He heard the thump and saw the snow dust at almost the same moment – dust which immediately rose behind Burckhardt's vehicle. The whiteness surrounding the car dissolved, became pitch-black water, and as the vehicle went straight down Prentice saw there were still four people inside. Burckhardt was drowning, surrounded by his own men. The fresh area of sinking ice stretched out towards the monastery road, tilting as men on top of it ran in all directions trying to escape. Prentice saw one man run straight off the edge into the water and as he took the glass away from his eye the ice sheet went under. A huge channel of dark water, perhaps a hundred yards wide, separated the frozen area of the lake from the road on the western shore leading up to the monastery.

'Fire!'

Ford had again made an adjustment and Prentice saw that the mortar's barrel was pointing at an extreme angle, saw also the bomb cradled in Macomber's arms nearly slip as the Scot forced his wearied body to further effort. The bomb coursed out over the lake, became a tiny dark speck against the whiteness below, and landed close to the distant eastern shore on the far side of the scattering troops. The thump was fainter. A fresh channel of water opened up, starting at the shoreline and spreading inwards towards the centre as three more bombs landed and black dots scurried over the diminishing white surface. Two mountain guns vanished. A half-track driving to the rear to escape the cannonade drove straight over the edge. More than a third of the attacking force on the frozen lake had disappeared and for the first time Prentice grasped the painstaking cleverness of Ford's plan. He had quartered the lake systematically in his mind and was destroying it section by section in such a way that he inflicted the maximum amount of damage, commencing with the vital section near the road up to the monastery, working backwards, and then over-leaping to destroy the ice near the far shore. His ultimate objective was to compress the surviving Wehrmacht force on a huge island of ice caught between water to east and west, the snow-drifted road to the north, and the sheer wall of the bluff to the south.

'Fire!' The bomb landed uselessly in clear water. 'Fire!' Prentice's glass was focused just beyond the most recent drop-

246

ping point and he saw two puffs of snow as the bomb bounced across the ice and detonated in the midst of a crowd of German troops fleeing towards the bluff. At this point some of the more quick-witted Alpenkorps were escaping. Using their climbing ropes, they had begun to scale the precipitous bluff face, realizing that only suspended in air would they be safe from the rain of missiles pouring down on them. Ford now turned his attention to the section of frozen lake which bordered the snow-drifted road. A large number of troops and a mountain gun were heading for the drift zone when the falling bombs began to shatter their escape route, driving them back on the huge remaining sheet of ice which covered perhaps a third of the lake. 'Fire!' Prentice removed the Monokular, dropped it into his pocket. The fatigue of staring through the glass made him rub his eyes and then dab them with his handkerchief, and all the time the bombardment was continuing as Ford concentrated on the huge island of ice covered with marooned Germans. 'Fire!' 'Fire!' 'Fire...!' Prentice lost count of the number of bombs Macomber slipped down the barrel, and the rate was increasing as Ford built up the barrage and Macomber, wiping his hands frequently on his trousers for fear of dropping a bomb, summoned up his last reserves of energy and went on feeding the mortar with fresh ammunition.

When Prentice looked out across the lake again he was astounded at the changed scene. The lake, which had so recently been a white plain, was now a dark sheet spattered with what, from that height, looked like slivers of snow, but which were really large spars of floating ice. The central island had almost disappeared and there was only a handful of men still marooned on a small patch of whiteness. Macomber fed in more bombs, surrounded the ice islet with five fountainheads of spurting water. Five misses. The next bomb landed dead centre on the remaining floe, fragmented it, tipped the survivors choking, drowning, sinking into the chill water. Perhaps a dozen Alpenkorps men still clung to the bluff which they were ascending slowly, but the invasion force on the lake had been annihilated.

'Like a target range,' Ford said. 'Unique.'

'Not quite,' Macomber reminded him. 'There was also

Austerlitz.'* In response to the shake of the sergeant's head, he replaced the bomb he was holding on the near-empty canvas and went stiffly over to the parapet. 'And now we've got to face that lot.'

There were three bombs left on the tower roof when Macomber made his grim remark and pointed out over the wall. Unlike the others, whose whole attention had been concentrated on the lake below, the Scot had been observing with increasing anxiety the ski troops' progress. They had now climbed the slope to an altitude well above the bluff and were coming forward in a line which curled over the flank of the mountain. The leading man was less than a quarter of a mile away as he sped closer towards the monastery. Grapos hobbled out from his corner and gripped Macomber's arm.

'You make avalanche,' Grapos said urgently. 'Where the dark hole is . . .'

'He means that hollow in shadow,' Prentice interjected. 'Why there?' Macomber had already gone back to the mortar, was helping Ford to shift the weapon's position, then waiting, cradling another bomb in his arms as the staff-sergeant checked the mountain slope and changed the angle of fire.

'Because,' Grapos explained, 'that is where the Austrian ski man started the avalanche. We had warned him not to go – but he laughed at us. I was standing on this roof watching him. He comes down over the hole and the avalanche begins. The mountain comes alive.'

'We'd better try it, Ford,' Macomber said quickly. 'It's a gamble, but it's the only one we've got. A hundred bombs could miss them all considering the speed they're moving at.'

He waited, still cradling the bomb, while Ford reconsidered the angle of fire and made a further adjustment. The reaction was setting in, his arms and legs felt like jelly, and he knew he might collapse on the roof at any moment. For God's sake stop fiddling with that mortar, man, and let's get on with it! Ford nodded – to indicate he was satisfied – and Macomber let the first one go. Because the mountain slope rose above the tower he was now able to see what was happening and he saw the

* At Austerlitz Napoleon destroyed a Russian army by firing at a frozen lake and drowning the enemy crossing the ice.

bomb hit the snow some distance above the hollow.

'Damn!' It was the first display of emotion Ford had shown since they had begun firing the mortar. The shot was wide and he knew it was his fault – not enough care taken over the initial preparation. And there were no bombs to waste this time on ranging shots. He adjusted the angle of fire as Macomber picked up the second bomb. The missile went away. Macomber saw this one land below the hollow, close enough to the Alpenkorps column to provoke a sudden swerve in the well-spread line – the section leader had not overlooked the lesson of what had happened on the lake – but no more than a swerve. Ford bit his lip as Macomber encouraged him. 'Third time lucky.' The staff-sergeant looked dubious – too high last time, too low this time. And only one more to go. But he kept his nerve: the first two shots had bracketed the target above and below, so now they must drop one mid-way between the two points. He took a deep breath, adjusted the barrel very carefully, then nodded to Macomber. The final bomb burst on the mountain a short way above the hollow.

It was very quiet on the tower and the four men stood perfectly still while they waited. Behind them the sea was empty, the destroyer had disappeared; below them the lake was still and lifeless; above them rose the peak of Zervos, crisp-edged against the palest of skies. The mortar barrel gaped upwards, as harmless now as a piece of old scrap iron, something they might as well tip over the wall so that at least the Alpenkorps would never use it. Probably it was imagination, but the Scot fancied he heard the swish of oncoming skis as he stood with his eyes fixed on Mount Zervos. He blinked and looked again, unsure whether his eyes had played him a trick. He had been watching the hollow but now he transferred his gaze higher up the mountain to a point near the summit where something had attracted his attention. Was there a gentle ripple of movement, so gentle that his eye might never have noticed it but for his fading hope? There seemed to be a trembling, a hazy wobble close to the peak. Slowly, like the rolling back of a sheet, the snow began to move in a long wave, the wave stretching the full width of the slope as it surged downwards, gathering height as it swallowed up more snow. And now Macomber heard something – a faint growl which gradually swelled and deepened to a sinister rumble as he saw fresh signs of something terrible happening. The slope was shifting downwards at increasing velocity, a moving slope at least a mile wide as the wave mounted higher, picked up momentum and thundered down on the Germans like a tidal wave. The mountain had come alive.

The slope seemed like a living thing as it seethed and rolled towards the lake far below, a whole mountain erupting sideways, the wave curling at the crest, the snow-slide roaring down, the rumble a tremendous sound in their dazed ears, a sound like the eruption of a major volcano, blowing its lava flow up from the interior of the earth. The Alpenkorps tried to scatter at the last moment – some ski-ing downhill, some whipping across the slope, all trying to race the wave which bore down on them and for a brief moment in time they were like a disturbed nest of ants scurrying away from catastrophe. Then the wave arrived, swept over the broken line, engulfing them, burying them, carrying them down the slope and over the bluff face where it cascaded down the precipice like a vast waterfall and washed away the men still ascending it before it plunged down into the depths of the lake. Prentice shouted his frantic warning as the wave reached the bluff's brink – the leading skier, not yet overwhelmed by the avalanche, had stopped, unlooped his rifle from his back, was taking aim at the roof of the tower. Macomber, his gaze fixed on the bluff, heard the shout too late. He was dropping to the floor when the bullet thudded into him and he was unconscious before he sprawled over the stones.

The Australian doctor had underestimated Macomber's vitality, so he came out of the drugged state at the wrong moment, the moment when they started to take him down the nose of Cape Zervos, strapped to a stretcher, powerless to move, but conscious enough to think, to remember, to experience to the full the unnerving ordeal of being transported in the prone position down a track a mule might jib at. The track, no more than a rather broad path, was the route from the cliff summit to the base of the cape where the Allied troops had landed. It was a fine morning, the sun was shining, there was not a trace of sea mist, so his downward view was unobscured as his life balanced in four hands – two holding the rear of the stretcher, two supporting the front. The stretcher tilted downwards at an angle of forty-five degrees as the two men carrying him found the way increasingly dangerous – ascending a precipitous zig-zag can be difficult, descending it may prove impossible. The Scot thought the unobscured view was impressive – a sheer drop seaward to the ruffled waters of the Aegean far below, a glimpse of a lower level of the zigzag, perched on another brink. And in his invalid state, Macomber had lost his head for heights.

He watched the uncertain gait of the man in front through half-closed eyes, half-closed because he was determined they shouldn't realize he had come awake – even a small surprise like that at the wrong moment could make a foot stumble, a hand lose its grip, could cause the stretcher to leave them and send him vertically down to his grave as the stretcher turned over and over in mid-air before it mercifully reached the sea and the waves closed over him. Cursing his over-vivid imag-ination, he tore his mesmerized gaze away from the trembling distant waters and tried to concentrate his mind on what had happened, on what Prentice had told him when he first re-covered consciousness. 'He got you in the shoulder ... the bullet's out now ... the quack says you'll be all right ... they'll be taking you to Athens.'

Macomber wasn't sure what day it was as he went on staring at the back of the man below him, but he remembered other things the lieutenant had told him. The Australians had come up this hellish track like demons. With the New Zealanders. They had dragged up dismantled twenty-five-pounder guns by brute strength, had reassembled them on the heights, were now in full command of Zervos. The blowing up of the *Hydra* had warned them something was seriously wrong; the great cloud of black smoke rising over Katyra had forced a quick decision – the sending of a destroyer laden with troops. I wish I had one of those bloody German cigars, Macomber thought as the man behind him tripped and the stretcher wobbled uneasily. They should have let Grapos take the rear. But at least the bearer had held on firmly, had regained his balance quickly. They went slowly down another section, then another, poised over sheer drops, the only sound a slithering of boots over the treacherous ground. Time stopped for the Scot, went into a state of suspension, so that it seemed to go on for ever. They were close to the half-ruined jetty at the base of Cape Zervos, but still a hundred feet above the sea, when the man in front stumbled over a hidden rock, fell sideways onto the track, saving himself by cannoning against a boulder and completely losing his grip on the stretcher. Macomber's legs hit the earth with a bump. He braced himself for the long spiralling fall.

The rear of the stretcher sagged a foot, then steadied and was held there by two hands only until the other man climbed to his feet, started to apologize, then stopped as he saw the look in the eyes of the man holding Macomber. He lifted the stretcher again and they went on down the track to where the launch moored by the jetty waited to transport the Scot to the destroyer anchored farther out. Macomber delayed his official awakening until he was rested on the jetty wall, then he twisted his head round to say thank you. Grapos' whiskered face stared down at him. 'I come with you,' he said simply. 'Now they take me in the Greek army. Yes?'

Colin Forbes
The Stone Leopard £3.99

'A real cracker ripping through Europe. The heart of the story is a plot which could destroy the Western world. The action is based on the threat to a President of France from a mysterious and vicious resistance leader from the past. Hard, bitter and compulsive; and the ending ... Wow!' DAILY MIRROR

Tramp in Armour £3.50

The time is that fateful spring of 1940 when the Panzers rolled across Northern France with nothing to stop them. Stranded behind the German lines, a solitary Matilda tank and its crew, led by the resourceful Sergeant Barnes, scheme, smash and manoeuvre their way towards Dunkirk.

'A caterpillar-tracked cliff-hanger' DAILY TELEGRAPH

Year of the Golden Ape £2.99

Racing at Concorde speed from the Middle East through Europe to California, a ruthless battle of wits reaches unparalleled tension as mercenaries hijack a giant British tanker, arm her with a plutonium bomb and sail into San Francisco harbour.

Jack Higgins
Solo £3.50

'A brilliant but psychotic concert pianist who murders for pleasure in his spare time makes the mistake of killing the teenage daughter of a tough Northern Ireland SAS soldier, a trained and vicious killer himself. As soldier stalks maestro for vengeance, the tale builds to a tense, shattering climax' SUNDAY EXPRESS

The Eagle Has Landed £3.99

The order: 'Bring me Churchill out of England' – Adolf Hitler 16 September 1943.

The plan: To kidnap the Prime Minister during a quiet weekend at a country house in Norfolk.

The people: Kurt Steiner and his handful of crack paratroopers, an embittered woman spy, an IRA gunman and a Free Corps traitor.

The date: 6 November 1943 – the most audacious mission ever conceived is poised to strike . . .

Storm Warning £3.50

Across 5,000 miles of wild Atlantic dominated by Allied navies – twenty-two men and five nuns aboard the barquentine *Deutschland* battling home to Kiel . . .

A U-boat ace captured in a desperate raid on Falmouth . . . an American girl doctor caught in the nightmare of the Flying Bombs . . . a gunboat commander who's fought from the Solomons to the Channel . . . a rear admiral who itches to get back into action . . . all drawn inexorably into the eye of the storm . . .

'Stunning . . . the work of a superb storyteller' DAILY MAIL

Gavin Lyall
The Wrong Side of the Sky £2.99

A chance encounter in an Athens bar with a war-time flying buddy
sets Jack Clay on the trail of a missing fortune.

Clay didn't want to grow old and obsolete together with the
dilapidated Dakota in which he flew everything anywhere on a wing
and a prayer and a bottle of Scotch. This might be his last chance.

But there were others whose needs were as great as Clay's. People
prepared to lie, cheat, murder and maim to get to the diamonds
first . . .

All Pan books are available at your local bookshop or newsagent, or can be ordered direct from the publisher. Indicate the number of copies required and fill in the form below.

Send to: **CS Department, Pan Books Ltd., P.O. Box 40, Basingstoke, Hants.   RG21 2YT.**

or phone: 0256 469551 (Ansaphone), quoting title, author and Credit Card number.

Please enclose a remittance* to the value of the cover price plus: 60p for the first book plus 30p per copy for each additional book ordered to a maximum charge of £2.40 to cover postage and packing.

*Payment may be made in sterling by UK personal cheque, postal order, sterling draft or international money order, made payable to Pan Books Ltd.

Alternatively by Barclaycard/Access:

Card No.

Signature:

Applicable only in the UK and Republic of Ireland.

While every effort is made to keep prices low, it is sometimes necessary to increase prices at short notice. Pan Books reserve the right to show on covers and charge new retail prices which may differ from those advertised in the text or elsewhere.

NAME AND ADDRESS IN BLOCK LETTERS PLEASE:

....

Name ⎯⎯⎯⎯⎯⎯⎯⎯⎯⎯⎯⎯⎯⎯⎯⎯⎯⎯⎯⎯⎯⎯⎯⎯⎯⎯⎯

Address ⎯⎯⎯⎯⎯⎯⎯⎯⎯⎯⎯⎯⎯⎯⎯⎯⎯⎯⎯⎯⎯⎯⎯⎯⎯

⎯⎯⎯⎯⎯⎯⎯⎯⎯⎯⎯⎯⎯⎯⎯⎯⎯⎯⎯⎯⎯⎯⎯⎯⎯⎯⎯⎯⎯

⎯⎯⎯⎯⎯⎯⎯⎯⎯⎯⎯⎯⎯⎯⎯⎯⎯⎯⎯⎯⎯⎯⎯⎯⎯⎯⎯⎯⎯

⎯⎯⎯⎯⎯⎯⎯⎯⎯⎯⎯⎯⎯⎯⎯⎯⎯⎯⎯⎯⎯⎯⎯⎯⎯⎯⎯⎯⎯

3/87